A Man of Honor

Loree Lough brings *A Man of Honor* to her readers, and she delivers a woman of honor, as well. Although Grace and Dusty have endured and survived much in the past, both struggle to provide the care they know others in their lives deserve. Readers will experience friendship, tragedy, love, and the uplifting power of faith as they live the story right along with the characters. Loree has crafted yet another book that kept me turning pages all night long.
—ROBIN BAYNE, author of ten novels/novellas, including Carol Award winner *The Artist's Granddaughter*

As always, Loree Lough takes her fans on a deeply emotional journey in *A Man of Honor*. With her dynamic storytelling style, Lough has masterfully crafted scenes that are sure to leave readers breathless and knowing there's hope, even after the most tragic events anyone can imagine.
—DEBBY MAYNE, author of *Sweet Baklava* and the upcoming Class Reunion series.

Be prepared for one of Loree Lough's most moving tales yet. The challenges Grace and Dusty face in *A Man of Honor* will plunge readers into moments of shattered innocence and tragic loss, in a search for truth, love, and healing, not only for themselves but for all the people that surround them. Book 3 in the First Responders series reminds readers that " . . . the greatest of these is love."
—RITA GERLACH, author of *Surrender the Wind* and other reader favorites

Other Recent Books by Loree Lough

From Ashes to Honor, Book 1 of the First Responders series

Honor Redeemed, Book 2 of the First Responder series

Suddenly Daddy/Suddenly Mommy (two full-length contemporary romances)

Accidental Family (Book 3 in Accidental Blessings series)

The Lone Star Legends series: *Beautiful Bandit, Maverick Heart, Rio Grande Moon*

Love Finds You in Paradise, Pennsylvania

Love Finds You in North Pole, Alaska

Love Finds You in Folly Beach, South Carolina

Be Still . . . and Let Your Nail Polish Dry (devotional with Andrea Boeshaar, Sandra D. Bricker, and Debby Mayne)

His Grace Is Sufficient . . . but Decaf is NOT (devotional with Sandra D. Bricker, Trish Perry, and Cynthia Ruchti)

A MAN OF HONOR

Book 3 of the First Responders Series

Loree Lough

Abingdon Press fiction
a novel approach to faith

Nashville, Tennessee

A Man of Honor

ISBN-13: 978-1-4267-1462-7

Published by Abingdon Press, P.O. Box 801, Nashville, TN 37202

www.abingdonpress.com

Library of Congress Cataloging-in-Publication Data

Lough, Loree.
   A man of honor / Loree Lough.
      p. cm. — (First responders series bk. 3)
   ISBN 978-1-4267-1462-7 (book - pbk. / trade pbk. : alk. paper)   1. First responders—
Fiction.   I. Title.
   PS3562.08147M36 2012
   813'.54—dc23

                                                                        2012015940

Scripture on page 7 is from the Common English Bible.
© Copyright 2011 by the Common English Bible. All rights
reserved. Used by permission. (www.CommonEnglishBible.com)

Prayer on pages 331-332 is taken from www.allaboutprayer.com
published by AllAboutGOD.com ministries, M. Houdmann,
P. Matthews-Rose, R. Niles, editors, 2002–2011.
Used by permission.

Printed in the United States of America

1 2 3 4 5 6 7 8 9 10 / 17 16 15 14 13 12

*To my beloved mom (who joined the Father
while I was writing this book).
Her love of books and talent for storytelling
put me on the road to writing.*

*And to my dedicated readers . . .
without all of you, none of this would be possible!*

Acknowledgments

My sincere thanks to Susannah Charleson, whose outstanding book, *Scent of the Missing,* inspired me to feature rescue dogs and the dedicated people who train them in two of the First Responders series novels.

Heartfelt gratitude to the Reverend Robert Crutchfield, who not only wrote the first responders prayer but also graciously allowed me to share it in all of the First Responders series novels.

Thanks, too, to the spirit-led people at *All About God,* for granting permission to use the moving prayer found in this story. (To learn more, visit http://www.allaboutgod.com)

Last, but certainly not least, thanks to God . . . for gracing me with this story idea and delivering daily doses of energy and enthusiasm to bring it to a satisfying conclusion.

Dear Reader,

No matter your age, there's a good chance you're lugging around *some* emotional baggage. Broken hearts, broken homes, health issues, the death of a loved one, a runaway child, unemployment, fear of foreclosure . . . the list of stuff that our nightmares and bad memories are made of goes on and on!

Surviving each tragedy is the exercise that builds moral fiber and the strength of character required to steer clear of the potholes on life's rocky road . . . and to keep our eyes on the light at the end of the proverbial tunnel.

When a stranger's heartbreak brings Dusty and Grace together, they're instantly drawn to each other. But before they can realize their dreams of a bright future together, they must first leave the darkness of past hurts and disappointments behind them.

This is what I pray for you, dear reader . . . that you'll always have the strength to maneuver around any hurdles that are preventing you from realizing your own hopes and dreams!

Blessings to you and yours,
Loree

No one has greater love than to give up one's life
for one's friends.
—*John 15:13 CEB*

1

*D*usty stifled a yawn and deployed the Harley's kickstand. The handlebar clock said 5:15, and beside it, the temperature gauge registered seventy-two muggy degrees. He shook his head and hoped weatherman Marty Bass was wrong about thunderstorms in the forecast, because if he wasn't, more than this morning's search and rescue mission—SAR for short— was in jeopardy. It meant he'd have to put off fixing the roof. Again. And *that* meant new mattresses for the boys who called The Last Chance their home.

Grumbling under his breath, he stowed his helmet, and after squeezing rain from his ponytail, pulled up the hood of his sweatshirt, soaked clean through by the deluge that had chased him halfway around the Baltimore Beltway.

Dusty shouldered his way through the tunnel of waterlogged branches that canopied the footpath. If he'd stopped for a sack of burgers from the twenty-four-hour McDonald's on North Howard, his stomach wouldn't be groaning now. But then, he wouldn't have beaten the morning gridlock, either. Tradeoffs. Lately, they seemed to dominate every facet of his life.

A fat raindrop oozed from a leaf and landed on the tip of his nose, then slid to the blacktopped footpath where it gleamed like a new dime. Up ahead, the blue and red strobes of emergency vehicles sliced through the gray mist, and the *whoop* of sirens silenced the usual chirp of tree frogs and crickets. If that didn't lend gritty balance to the postcard-pretty sight, Dusty didn't know what did.

He passed two stern-faced cops, interviewing a guy in a baggy orange jogging suit. "Shadow is the best-behaved dog I've ever owned," he heard the guy say, "but he spotted something over there . . ." The man pointed to a break in the tree line, "and went completely off his nut."

Dusty took note of the German shepherd's stance—ears pricked forward and tail straight out—as it stared at the spot, some twenty yards away.

"Probably just a squirrel or something," the owner said, "but with the story of that young girl, I figured—"

"We appreciate the tip, sir," the tallest officer said. He tucked a tablet into his shirt pocket while his partner returned the guy's driver's license. "Don't worry, if we need anything more, we know how to get in touch." He gave the pocket flap a pat.

In other words, Dusty thought, *hit the road, dude, so we can get to work.* The jogger took the hint and led his dog across the parking lot as Dusty joined the small circle of SAR workers already assembled. Jones, this mission's Operation Leader, quickly brought them up to speed: Melissa Logan, age sixteen, hadn't been home since the night of her prom. Last seen a few miles west of the park, her disappearance had sparked an intensive dawn-to-dusk manhunt that left everyone scratching their heads. And when the jogger's shepherd started acting spooky, the dominos began to fall, starting with its owner's 9-1-1 call and ending with another search, here.

"It's been nearly a week since she went missing," Jones warned, "so prepare yourselves."

Meaning, dead or alive, Melissa Logan wouldn't look very pretty, even in her fancy prom gown.

They all knew the drill, but Jones went over it, anyway. "Let's try not to make too big a mess, stomping through the underbrush, shall we?"

Because the cops will need every scrap of evidence to catch the animal who did this.

Next, came the OL's reminder to double-check field packs for standard equipment: Compass, knife, matches and rope, sterile dressing and bandages, bottled water, space blanket, and metal mirror. Memory of the time he'd needed the snake-bite kit faded as the sound of surgical gloves, snapping into place, went around the circle.

The team field tested their radios and counted off, starting with Dusty and ending with Honor Mackenzie, the best rescue dog trainer he'd ever worked with. Today, she'd brought Rerun, instead of the more experienced Rowdy. His gut—and those dark circles under Honor's sad eyes—told him something bad had happened to the personable Golden Retriever that had earned awards, a fan page on Facebook, and the respect of every team member, two-legged and four. Maybe later he'd ask her about that. . . .

"You volunteers," Jones said, "pair up with somebody who's wearing a pack."

Technically, they were all volunteers, but SAR personnel had earned their certs by putting in long, grueling hours of training, while the rest—friends and family of the girl, mostly—had probably never done anything like this before.

"And you with packs," Jones continued, "double-check to make sure your partners are wearing gloves, too." He met Dusty's eyes. "Parker, you want to start us off with a prayer?"

As chaplain of the local fire department, he was expected to ask God's blessing on the mission, and Dusty had never let them down.

Until today.

Today? He couldn't think of a single thing to say, and he didn't have a clue *why*. Didn't need to open his eyes, either, to know that the team—even guys who weren't particularly religious—needed him to find the right words to fit this circumstance.

Two empty seconds ticked by: Zero.

Four seconds: Zip.

Six: Nothing.

And because they continued to stand there, waiting in the prickly silence, Dusty launched into a bland, one-size-fits-all-occasions petition. "Father," he began, "we ask your blessing on those assembled. Show us, Lord, the signs that will lead to Melissa. Let us find her alive, suffering only exhaustion and exposure. And if. . . ."

He paused, searching his mind for words that would help them cope when they found something more ominous, instead.

No one could read his thoughts, so why had he chosen if rather than when?

When the answer refused to materialize, Dusty lifted his head and exhaled a deep breath. "And now, if you'll join me in reciting the first responders' prayer. . . ."

"Father in Heaven," they said together, "please make me strong when others are weak, brave when others are afraid, and vigilant when others are distracted by chaos. Provide comfort and companionship to my family when I must be away. Serve beside me and protect me as I seek to protect others."

A dozen "Amens" echoed around the tight circle, followed by a few "Thank-yous" and "Good job, Dustys." Then, nodding and muttering, the crew marched forward, some poking at the ground with sticks, others employing a slow slide-kick method to keep from stepping on evidence that might lead to the missing girl.

A few minutes into the search, a soft voice near Dusty's elbow said, "Mind if I follow you?"

Young and wide-eyed, her expression told him she belonged with the "never did anything like this before" group. He had a notion to ask, "Why do *I* get stuck with all the newbies?" Instead, he said, "Does Jones have your contact info?"

"He does."

He gave her a quick once-over. Wasn't likely she'd keep up with him on legs that short, but even if she did, her to-the-point answer gave him hope that she wouldn't hammer him with inane chatter.

"Move slowly and steadily, and stay a yard behind me and to my right." *So I can keep an eye on you.* "And if you see anything, point it out to me and *do not touch it.*"

"Got it."

There was something in her trembly tone, in her worried eyes, that told him she had a link to the missing girl. He started to ask about the connection when the toe of his boot tapped against something. One hand up to stop her, he took a knee and parted the weeds . . .

. . . and revealed a glittery high-heeled shoe. Six inches to its left, he saw the mate, and a few yards ahead of that, the once-pretty young woman who'd worn them to her prom.

Rising slowly, he radioed his location, then backpedaled, taking care to match every footfall to the boot print he'd left in the damp grass. He'd almost forgotten his tiny, human shadow, until she stepped up beside him.

"Oh, God," came her shaky whisper. "Oh, no. . . ."

Jones's voice crackled through the radio. "Roger that, Parker. Keep a clean scene. I'll point the cops your way."

Dusty reholstered his handset, then inspected his temporary partner's face. "You okay?"

She swallowed, hard enough that he heard it, then croaked out, "I'm fine."

But she wasn't, as evidenced by her wavering voice and ashen complexion. He saw her knees buckle, and knew if he didn't do something fast, she'd fall, right where she stood. One hand gripping each of her upper arms, he held tight as she knelt in the wet grass, then sat back on her heels and combed rain-dampened fingers through her hair. Five seconds of silence ticked by before she whispered, "Her name is Missy Logan. Melissa. Melissa Logan." Eyes closed, she lifted her face to the grey clouds overhead. "She's one of my students. English. Art. And Art History, too."

She hardly looked old enough to *be* in high school, let alone teach in one. When she met his eyes, he knew she hadn't chosen the profession for monetary reasons. The pain glittering in the big brown orbs told him that Missy Logan had meant something to her. Maybe she'd mentored the girl. Dusty would have asked if that was the case, if Jones and half a dozen SAR members hadn't jogged up right then.

The OL groaned, wincing with deep pain when he saw the teenager's broken, bloody remains.

"Oh, man," echoed another, grimacing.

The teacher got to her feet as Dusty said, "This young lady says the girl is one of her students."

"*Was* her student, you mean," said a voice Dusty didn't recognize. He looked over his shoulder, intent on aiming the stink-eye at the rude bozo. When he turned face-forward again, she was gone, no doubt pulled aside by one of the investigators now swarming the scene.

Jones waved his team closer to hear his usual "how to handle stupid reporter questions" lecture. Then, one by one, SAR personnel were rounded up and questioned by the FBI agents assigned to the missing girl's case. Working in twos, the agents made fast work of taking statements, handing out business cards, and securing each team member's promise to call the Baltimore field office with details that might come to mind later. Halfway through his own interview, Dusty's stomach began to churn. He blamed it on lack of sleep. The midnight pizza, devoured while helping one of his boys study for finals. The disturbing sight of the girl who'd never go home again.

He'd been at this for years. Melissa Logan hadn't been his first "find." So why the jitters and sweaty palms? Dusty stuffed an agent's card into his pocket and promised to call if anything came to mind an hour or even a day from now. Then he walked away, stifling a frustrated groan as he slapped a palm to the back of his neck. Why didn't any of the mind-over-matter tricks that helped his pals cope with stuff like this ever work for him?

Leaning his backside against a tree, he pulled a bottle of water from his pack and unscrewed the cap. With any luck, it would settle his roiling gut. Staring through the rippled plastic as he gulped, the scene took on a hazy, surreal look. What he wouldn't give for the images to blur that way tonight, tomorrow, every night for weeks as the images flashed in his dreams.

"Idiot," he muttered. For one thing, a guy had to *sleep* in order to dream, and he couldn't remember the last time he'd slept more than an hour or two at a stretch.

He glanced at his watch. In half an hour, Mitch would load the Last Chance boys into the van and drive them to Our Daily Bread, where they'd spend the day stocking shelves, cleaning, peeling potatoes, and doing dishes. If Dusty left right now, he might just get ahead of the traffic snarl on 695, and catch a few Z's before joining them.

Stuffing the water bottle back into his pack, he jogged toward his Harley, and nearly collided with the two agents who'd interviewed him. They were with the pretty young teacher now. She clutched both blue surgical gloves in one hand as she stood, head down, nodding. He followed Agent One's line of vision; he, too, had noticed that she was trembling all the way down to her soaked sneakers. *Give the kid a break,* he wanted to say. Because if the morning had been this tough on him, how much more had it affected a first-timer?

As he got closer, Dusty overheard Agent Two ask about her teaching credentials while One pecked data from her driver's license into his iPhone. She'd earned a few points back there— for keeping up with him, for not asking inane questions, but mostly, for not falling apart when she got that first gruesome eyeful of the girl's battered body. He gave her a few more points now, for holding it together under the agents' onslaught: How long had she known Missy? Had she heard of any bad blood between Melissa and other students or teachers? Was she aware of boyfriend problems? As a chaperone at the prom, did she believe alcohol or drugs played a role in the girl's disappearance and death? Would she be willing to help them access school records, saving the time it would take them to get in touch with Missy's parents by other means?

"Yes, yes, of course," she said, "but you need to know that Missy is. . . ." She shook her head and pressed her fingertips into her temples. ". . . was an only child. And that her father died, just last spring."

Agent Number Two returned her license. "Is that right?"

She glanced toward the grassy hill where they'd found Melissa. "Well," she said, standing as tall as her five-foot-something frame would allow, "Mrs. Logan has barely had time to adjust to being a widow, and now. . . ." Those sad, dark eyes darted back to the knoll, where the narrow strip of yellow plastic flapped in the breeze.

And now this, he finished silently.

She cleared her throat. "I just thought you should know, so that you can take it into consideration. When you could break the news to Missy's mom, I mean."

Before he'd nearly stumbled over the body, her cheeks had glowed with vitality. Now, it reminded him of that delicate porcelain serving platter his mom dragged out when it was her turn to host bridge club. Dusty had a feeling that stubbornness, mostly, was the only thing keeping the poor kid conscious and upright. He stepped up beside her, thinking to catch her if she passed out.

Agent One said, "We're finished with your interview, sir."

It wasn't the first time he'd been branded by the hot glare of a cop, and he met it with one of his own. "I'm here for moral support."

The agents exchanged a "What's his problem?" expression, then shrugged.

"What did Mr. Logan die of?" Agent Two asked the teacher.

"Bone cancer. It was a very long and painful illness. I remember how hard Missy took it when his doctors were forced to put him into a drug-induced coma."

"Why did they have to put him in a coma?" asked One.

"Because the slightest movement, even the weight of his own body, shattered bones, and none of the drugs were powerful enough to ease his pain." She cringed, as if the memory hurt her, too. "Mrs. Logan is a librarian. I don't remember which branch, only that it's somewhere in Baltimore County. I ran into her in the hall at school, when she came to get some things from Missy's locker. She told me that she'd taken a leave of absence, and that she was waiting for a sorority sister to let her know if she could drive down from New York, to stay with her while . . . well, while . . . you know."

Now Dusty cringed, too. *While the cops looked for her little girl.*

She shook her head again and started over. "I'm not sure if her friend is still in town, but I do remember hearing at Mr. Logan's funeral that she doesn't have family nearby." On the heels of a deep breath, she took a step forward. "If you think it'll help, I'm happy to sit with her while . . . when. . . ."

When you tell her that her little girl was slaughtered?

Dusty ground his molars together. If he ever got his hands on the animal who—

"Will you go to her house? To break the bad news, I mean? Or will it be necessary to make her come to your office?"

Dusty didn't hear the agent's answer, because his cell phone rang. Mitch Carlisle, the caller ID block said. Turning, he took a few steps away to answer the call from his assistant pastor at the halfway house. "Think you'll be back before we leave," the younger man asked, "or should we head on over to the soup kitchen without you?"

Dusty glanced over his shoulder, thinking he'd offer to tag along with the teacher, wherever the agents decided to break the bad news to the girl's widowed mom, but she was gone. "Hold on a sec, Mitch," he said, taking the phone from his ear. "Where'd she go?" he asked Agent One.

"Home. To feed her cat, I think she said," he answered before turning back to his partner.

He could've kicked himself for not asking her name. It wasn't like he hadn't had time. *You're an arrogant idiot,* he chided. If he hadn't been so busy feeling put-upon for getting stuck with yet another newbie. . . .

Armed with that fact, alone, he could have pried more information about her from any one of a dozen officials on site.

"He who hesitates is lost" had been one of his Uncle Brock's favorite adages. Brock's second favorite, "Too little, too late," fit just as well.

"Sorry," he told Mitch, "I'm back."

"So did you guys find the missing girl?"

Dusty heard concern in Mitch's voice. "'Fraid so."

"Uh-oh. Dead?"

"Uh-huh."

"Exposure?"

The image of her battered body flashed in his mind. "I wish."

On the heels of a lengthy pause, Mitch asked, "Do the cops have any idea who killed her?"

"Not a clue. At least, not yet."

"I'll lead the boys in a prayer for her and her family, and everyone who was there when they found her."

When they found her. . . . Memory of the way it felt when the toe of his boot made contact with Missy's shoe caused an involuntary flinch. "Thanks." First thing Dusty intended to do when he got home was trash these ugly reminders of what he found next.

"And for the cops, too, so they'll find something, soon, that'll lead to her killer."

Butcher was more like it. "Say one for the girl's teacher, too. She was practically in my lap when I found the body."

"You got it."

And while you're at it, send one up for me.

Because though he couldn't explain it, and it went against every self-imposed rule he'd written about merging the personal and professional aspects of his life, Dusty needed to find her.

2

*G*race clenched her teeth and prayed for the self-control to keep a civil tongue in her head.

It was bad enough that the agents insisted on interviewing Mrs. Logan at their noisy, crowded office in Baltimore County, rather than the quiet comfort of her own home. Did they have to pummel the poor woman with questions that made *her* look like a prime suspect in her daughter's murder, too?

They'd closed the blinds in a half-hearted attempt at privacy, but the bent slats had been pried apart so many times that anyone passing by could peer into their workspace through any one of a dozen v-shaped gaps. One of those openings gave Grace a clear view of her SAR sidekick, standing on the other side of the glass, nodding. She took it to mean that he approved of her decision to remain at Mrs. Logan's side as the agents' pounded out question after question:

Had she talked with the other parents before granting permission for Melissa to attend the after-prom slumber party? Which parents had agreed to transport the girls from the school gym to the friend's home? And was she aware that, instead of going there, the youngsters had booked a room at a nearby hotel, where a keg of beer and half-empty bottles of tequila and whiskey had been found? Had she verified *any* aspect of her daughter's story before letting her leave home with a boy she'd never met before prom night? And why had she waited until mid-afternoon of the day *after* prom to wonder about her daughter's whereabouts?

Out there in the hall, Grace saw the SAR guy frown, then shake his head. "Sorry," he mouthed, hands extended in a gesture of pity.

Not as sorry as Mrs. Logan, I'll bet, she thought as the agents described—in gory detail—what Melissa had looked like when she was found. Would they pull out the shocking crime scene photos, and force her to look at those, too? Grace prayed they would not, because if *hearing* the cold, hard facts of the case could reduce Mrs. Logan to a weepy bundle of nerves, what would *viewing* full-color images of her little girl's mangled, bloodied body do to her?

"We'd like to have a look around Melissa's room," said Spencer.

His tone and stance made it clear he'd just issued an order, not a request. Grace bristled, but kept her silence; if Mrs. Logan hadn't exploded into a fit of hysteria when the agents told Grace to wait outside, she'd be out there in the hall, waiting alongside the stern-faced SAR guy. She plucked a tissue from the box on Spencer's desk and handed it to Mrs. Logan.

The woman blotted her eyes. "But . . . but you people have already gone through her room."

Timmons jutted out his big square chin and adjusted the Windsor knot of his navy tie. "We're just being thorough, ma'am." He poked his ballpoint back into the pencil cup beside the tissues, then made a move to help her up. "Now then, whatsay we pick up this conversation over at your house."

They'd referred to this meeting as an interrogation, an interview, a simple discussion, and now, a conversation. In

Grace's opinion, it was a bully session, plain and simple. And she was sick and tired of standing by quietly as they continued to browbeat the poor woman. "*I'll* drive her," Grace said when he pulled out his keys. "She's exhausted, and I'm sure she could use a bite to eat. We'll meet you at her house in a couple of hours."

Mrs. Logan gasped. "Oh, would you do that?" she said, clasping Grace's hands.

The agents exchanged a frown before Spencer pulled back his left shirt cuff and glanced at his watch. "I suppose that'll be all right."

"But let's meet up in an hour," his partner inserted.

And when Grace opened her mouth to object, he quickly added, "The sooner we get all the loose ends tied up, the sooner we can write our report and get out of her hair, once and for all."

"That would be fine," Grace began, "if we weren't a half hour's drive from her house. Surely you don't expect her to order a burger and fries at some drive-through window, then wolf it all down in just a few minutes. Not after all she's been through." She drilled his eyes with her own. "*Do you?*"

Timmons grinned a bit and leaned toward Spencer. "Now, if that isn't a living, breathing example of the old 'if looks could kill' maxim," he said from the corner of his mouth, "I don't know what is."

When Spencer nodded, Grace decided to lean on an adage of her own, and get while the getting was good. "I'm taking her somewhere quiet, for something that won't upset her stomach." She didn't wait for their approval. Instead, Grace helped Mrs. Logan to her feet and, as she led her to the door, wondered if her SAR partner would still be out there in the hall. Last time she'd seen him, he'd been leaning against the wall, arms folded and booted ankles crossed as he nonchalantly maneuvered a toothpick from one side of his mouth to the other. A quiet note of disappointment rang in her head when she rounded the corner and he wasn't there. All the way outside and across the parking lot, the reaction continued to surprise her. *Seriously, Grace, get a grip, and remember your decision. . . .* "So," she said, opening her Jeep's passenger door, "what are you in the mood for? Italian? Asian? Good old American?"

The woman moved as if dragging twenty-pound weights. "I really don't care," she said, sliding across the seat. "I'm not the least bit hungry." She gave Grace's hand a little squeeze. "Be a dear, will you, and do the choosing?"

"I know just the place."

She'd take Mrs. Logan to T-Bonz, where the friendly staff and fun menu would help her relax, at least enough to get a few bites of something healthy into her stomach. An hour later, after emptying a bowl of hot crab appetizer, the women polished off their sweet iced tea and started the short drive to Mrs. Logan's house. Grace suggested using her GPS to get them from the steakhouse to the quaint Ellicott City neighborhood, but Mrs. Logan waved the offer away. *Just as well*, Grace thought. Perhaps directing the lefts and rights would provide yet another diversion for her poor overwrought mind.

She drove five miles under the speed limit, hoping to delay their arrival as long as possible. The historic townhouse was the first and only home the Logans had ever owned. Missy had been born and raised there. If she'd lived, the girl would have slipped into her wedding gown in her bedroom, and it's where she and her husband and kids would've celebrated Thanksgiving and Christmas dinners, too.

All too soon, they made the final turn onto Oella Avenue. Grace's heart lurched when she spotted the ominous black SUV parked alongside the curb.

"Wonder how long *they've* been here," Grace grumbled.

"Lord only knows." On the heels of an exhausted sigh, Mrs. Logan said, "You can pull in behind my car if you like. It isn't like I'm going anywhere any time soon."

Nodding, Grace nosed her Jeep into the driveway. The agents were out of their vehicle and marching closer even before she slid the gearshift into park. *In a real hurry to pick up the bully session right where you left off, eh boys?*

Mrs. Logan's hands trembled as she dug through her purse in search of her keys. When she found them, she pressed them into Grace's palm. "I'll never get the front door open in the condition I'm in."

The condition deteriorated rapidly as she stood wringing her hands in the doorway of her daughter's room, watching the agents turn every pocket inside out and dig through every drawer. Not even the girl's diary was off limits. Mrs. Logan was nearly hysterical when she cried out, "If you'll just tell me what you're looking for, perhaps I can help you find it!"

"I know this is tough," Spencer said quietly, "but the truth is, we're not sure *what* we're looking for."

"We'll know when—*if*—we find it," Timmons agreed. He looked at Grace to add, "Maybe it would be best if you two waited downstairs. This won't take much longer."

For the first time since meeting the men, Grace agreed with them. She slid an arm around Mrs. Logan's shoulders. "I don't know about you," she said softly, "but I sure could use a cup of coffee. If you'll show me where you keep things, I'll make a pot, okay?"

At first, the woman resisted. "They're making a huge mess. Again," she complained as they headed downstairs. "It took a whole day to put things back in order last time they were up there. Why can't they just leave me in peace?"

Grace had no idea how to answer the question, so she didn't even try. Instead, she focused on making the grieving mother as comfortable as possible. Coffee, she soon learned, wasn't going to accomplish that.

"I don't have any decaf. Last thing I need," she said, extending a trembling hand, "is something that'll make me even shakier!"

What did comfort her, as it turned out, was talking about Missy. Mrs. Logan slid a photo album from the bookshelf, and for the next thirty minutes, told Grace the story of her daughter's life. Ballet recitals, solo performances with the school choir, Girl Scout outings, leisurely summer trips to Ocean City, birthday parties, and Christmas mornings, all captured in vivid color. "This was taken right before her father was diagnosed with cancer," she said, pointing at a picture of the smiling threesome, standing in the spray at Niagara Falls.

"You all look very happy," Grace told her.

She'd barely finished the sentence when the agents bounded down the stairs.

"We tried not to mess things up too much," Spencer said.

Mrs. Logan closed the album and returned it to its proper place on the shelf. "So you're finished at last, then?"

"Not quite." Timmons gestured toward the sofa, his not-so-subtle way of telling her they'd be a while. When Mrs. Logan stood her ground, he shrugged. "Why did you wait so long to report Melissa missing?"

The question hit her like a hard backhand to the jaw. Huge silvery tears spilled down her flushed cheeks as she sagged to the floor, like a marionette whose puppeteer had let go of the strings. If Grace hadn't reached out when she did, the woman would have a bruise on her temple to go with the one on her heart. Once she got her settled on the couch, Agent Timmons said, "She'll pass out for sure if you don't give her some space."

The only thing keeping Grace quiet now was her belief that impudence would only add to fuel to the agent's ire. She stared Timmons down and said through clenched teeth, "Are you quite finished?"

"Listen. Lady. We appreciate your willingness to help, but—"

Spencer silenced Timmons with a stern frown that softened to a smile when he faced Grace. "Think maybe you could find something cool for her to sip on?"

Good idea, she thought, because as much as Mrs. Logan needed something cool to sip on, Grace needed an excuse to leave the room. With her luck, she'd say or do something in the woman's defense that might get them both arrested. She was halfway to the door when Spencer said, "Miss Sinclair, would you do me a favor while you're in the kitchen?"

Grace stopped, but didn't turn around as he said, "Could you look for her personal phone book?"

Now she faced him. "I have no intention of snooping through her cupboards. You seem to have mastered that art. Why don't *you* look for it?"

Spencer raised a hand, traffic-cop style, then crossed the room to meet her. "Sometimes Timmons takes the 'good cop, bad cop' thing way too seriously," he said quietly. "He's like a pup with a bone once he smells a clue, so I'd rather not leave her alone with him." He took a step closer and lowered his voice still more. "I just want to see if the family doctor's name is in there. If it is, I'll give him a call, let him know what's been going on here." He shrugged. "Hopefully, he'll prescribe something to help her sleep."

She cut a glance at Mrs. Logan, who sat crying softly in the corner of the sofa. His suggestion made so much sense that Grace almost felt guilty about prejudging the agents as bad-mannered boors.

Almost.

"Of course I'll help in any way I can."

Smiling, he winked. "Thanks, Miss Sinclair. You're a bigger help than you realize."

Grace followed the hall until it emptied into the Logans' homey kitchen. The contrast between the bright atmosphere here and the somber mood in the living room was so staggering that it brought tears to her eyes, because there wasn't anything sunny about the situation. "Knock it off," she scolded, knuckling them away. Mrs. Logan needed her right now, strong and calm, holding it together.

She started her search in the most logical place: the narrow drawer beneath the wall phone. Grace found ballpoint pens, pencils, paperclips, twist ties, and rubber bands. "I thought *everyone* kept their phone books there," she muttered. The directory wasn't in any of the other drawers, either. Finally, she located it in an upper cabinet, mixed in with recipe cards and coupons. She credited God for leading her to it, because its bright pink paisley cover had been torn off, leaving only a tattered paper spine that was barely visible among computer-generated recipe cards. It seemed a very odd and out-of-the-way place in this perfectly organized kitchen, where the spices and canned goods had been stored in precise, alphabetically ordered rows.

She grabbed a bottle of cold water from the fridge, and on the way back to the living room, spotted an afghan that Mrs. Logan had draped over the desk chair in the adjacent home office. When she carried them into the living room, Grace found Agent Spencer near the window wall, talking on his cell phone and scribbling in a small notebook. Timmons, much to her surprise, was on the couch with Mrs. Logan, murmuring reassuring words as he patted her back.

Spencer put away his tablet and reached her in three long strides. "See, Timmons is a classic example of the guy who inspired the 'all bark, no bite' adage."

More surprisingly, Timmons's nurturing actually looked sincere. "I can see that."

Spencer relieved her of the book. "It appears you're quite the little investigator."

He wouldn't say that if he'd seen her rummaging through all the cupboards and drawers, trying to figure out where Mrs. Logan kept the nondescript little thing.

He turned the directory over, then over again. "What in the world do you reckon happened to it?"

It looked to Grace as though Mrs. Logan, or even Missy, had deliberately removed the cover to assure it would blend into the baked goods cabinet. Is that what a seasoned investigator would think? He'd already started thumbing through the pages, and she took it to mean he'd only been thinking out loud. Since a reply wasn't necessary, Grace stepped up to the couch.

"Here's your water, Mrs. Logan."

"Thanks," she said, accepting the plastic bottle. "But please, call me Molly." She unscrewed the cap and took a tiny sip. "You're just the sweetest, most caring little thing. No wonder my Missy thought so much of you."

It looked for a minute as though she might fall apart again, but she squared her shoulders and lifted her chin. "Would you like me to brew a pot of coffee? It won't take but a minute."

Timmons held up a hand. "None for me, thanks."

"Same here." Spencer smiled slightly. "Already had my quota for the day."

"There's root beer and ginger ale in the fridge, if you'd prefer something cold. My Missy just loves. . . ."

Memory of her daughter's favorite soda opened the flood-gates again, and as Timmons went back to murmuring and patting, Spencer gently grasped Grace's elbow and led her into the hall. "We offered to give her a lift to the ER to see if maybe they could prescribe something to calm her nerves." One shoulder lifted in a helpless shrug. "Turned us down flat."

"I'm sure she'd much rather see her regular doctor. You know. Under the circumstances?"

He tapped the phone directory. "My thoughts, exactly." He cast a furtive glance over his shoulder. "No point making her listen as I run through the reasons for the call, over and over, trying to figure out which of these guys is her GP. So would you mind keeping her out of the kitchen while I make the calls?"

Like his partner, Spencer looked as sincere as he sounded. "I'm more than happy to do it. You know, if it would free you up to . . . for other things."

"Nice of you to offer, but I'm afraid you wouldn't get very far, thanks to those ridiculous HIPPA regulations." He squeezed her shoulder. "You're far more useful right here."

He made a *psst* noise to get Timmons's attention, then aimed a forefinger toward the hall and mouthed "Kitchen."

His partner gave a nod, then went back to murmuring and patting as Spencer lumbered out of the room. Halfway down the hall, he stopped and faced Grace again. "You wouldn't hap-pen to know how I might get in touch with that rescue guy you were with this morning, would you?"

She could have described intense blue eyes and rain-slicked black curls that peeked out from the shadows of his hooded sweatshirt, or that his driver's license no doubt listed his height at six-two or more. She might have mentioned the calming effect of his quiet prayer, or the big powerful hands that gently steadied her when the sight of Melissa's body made her knees buckle.

"Sorry, but with everything that was going on, I didn't get his name." Grace didn't know which disappointed her more . . . that she hadn't thought to introduce herself, or that he hadn't, either.

"No problem. I'll get it from the agents who interviewed him. Just thought maybe you could save me a phone call."

"Why? Did they forget to ask him something?"

Frowning slightly, he waved the comment away. "Not really. Just a question that popped into my head. Happens, sometimes, in an investigation like this."

She was about to ask him what he meant by "an investigation like this" when he said, "You know where to find me if. . . ." He glanced at Mrs. Logan, who, though her sobs had subsided, held on to Timmons the way a drowning woman clings to a life preserver. ". . . if anybody needs me."

Strange, but standing in the middle of the Logans's well-appointed living room, she felt just as confused and lost as she had this morning. What was she supposed to do next? Take Timmons's place beside Mrs. Logan? Stand quietly until someone called her name?

One thing was certain, she wouldn't leave. As soon as Agent Spencer was finished with the phone book, Grace would make a few calls of her own, to find a sympathetic friend or relative who'd stay with Mrs. Logan until. . . . Grace cringed, realizing the poor woman wouldn't be allowed to make funeral arrangements until after the authorities concluded their investigation.

Easing onto the edge of an overstuffed chair, Grace helped herself to one of the magazines in the symmetrical fan-shaped stack on the coffee table. She opened to the table of contents, but didn't read it. Instead, her gaze traveled the room, absorb-

ing what these professional investigators would probably consider trivial facts, totally unrelated to their investigation. . . .

The bookshelves flanking the fireplace held hardback novels that stood alphabetized in color-coded groups. Every throw
pillow leaned against the cushions at carefully determined
angles; and she didn't see a single fingerprint, not so much as a
speck of dust on the mahogany tables; and the window panes
were so spotless they seemed invisible.

No doubt, the fear and worry of hearing that her only child
was missing had interrupted Mrs. Logan's sleep. Had she
attempted to distract herself from painful reality by throwing
herself into a cleaning frenzy?

Perhaps.

But something told Grace the perfection found throughout
the house couldn't have been achieved in the span of a week.
She pictured her own slightly untidy place, and wished she'd
been blessed with the woman's meticulous tendencies.

Spencer chose that moment to walk into the room and signal his partner, who joined him in the hall. After a moment
or two of mumbling, Spencer waved, inviting Grace into the
foyer. She put the magazine down, taking care to duplicate
its former angle on top of the stack. As she walked toward
the agents, Grace saw Mrs. Logan lean forward to adjust, then
readjust it, a mere fraction of an inch. On second thought,
maybe it best that she didn't have the woman's organizational
skills. *Because you'd drive yourself and everyone around you stark
raving mad!*

"Got hold of her doctor," Spencer said, "and he's calling in
a script. Nurse said the pharmacy will deliver it in an hour or
two. Can you stay long enough to sign for it, make sure she
gets the right dose?"

Before leaving for the park this morning, she'd added her
cereal bowl and coffee mug to the supper dishes, already

soaking in the sink. By now, the load of laundry she'd tossed into the dryer on her way out the door would have to be pressed. *Pressed? Who are* you *kidding!* First chance she got, Grace would rewash them. Anything to avoid the steam iron and spray starch. But what about the vacuuming and dusting still left unchecked on her To Do list? Wasn't the whole point of taking the day off to get ready for the party she'd planned for her senior students' graduation? There were a dozen valid reasons to say no. But the sight of Mrs. Logan, eyes squeezed tightly shut as she cupped her elbows made her say, "Of course I will," instead.

Timmons slid a business card from his pocket and scribbled something on the back. "My home and cell numbers," he said, handing it to her. "If she gets too hard to handle, don't be afraid to call."

She looked from the tiny white rectangle to his blue-green eyes. "Hard to handle?"

"Sometimes," Spencer explained, "once reality sets in, people go a little crazy."

Her heartbeat doubled as she glanced at Mrs. Logan, rocking to and fro on the sofa. "And you think she's one of those people?"

"No way to know for sure." Spencer opened the door, then handed her his card, too. "If you can't reach Bob, here, feel free to call me. Any time. Day or night."

She stacked the cards one atop the other until their corners lined up, perfectly. Was it possible that this oh-so-tidy place was rubbing off on her? "Thank you," she said. "But just between us? I'm going to pray like crazy that you won't be hearing from me."

Smiling, the men stepped onto the front porch. Spencer was half-in, half-out of the driver's seat of the boxy black SUV when he said, "Uh, by the way? Thought you ought to know that when I interviewed that SAR guy you were partnered up with today, he asked for your name and phone number."

When she'd stepped up and asked permission to tag along with him during the search, he hadn't exactly gone out of his way to hide his annoyance at having to partner with an untrained volunteer. And yet his no-nonsense instructions had been delivered with a gentle respect.

Spencer grinned. "Weird. I thought you people made a point of knowing who you were working with."

What's weird, she thought, *was that the agent had lumped her in with skilled rescuers. Weirder still, if he hadn't interviewed "that SAR guy," then how had Spencer known that the man asked about her?* She watched him slide behind the wheel, and shrugged it off. They'd all been stuck in that same small department at FBI headquarters . . . more than ample time for the guy to ask for routine information.

But *why* had he asked for it?

"Don't worry," Spencer said, answering her unasked question, "he won't bother you, because I didn't tell him anything. Agency policy, y'know?" She watched him buckle his seatbelt. With that, he slammed the car door.

As the agents drove away, Grace closed Mrs. Logan's front door and pictured "that SAR guy." She barely knew the man. It should come as a relief to know he couldn't get in touch with her. Then why, she wondered, throwing the deadbolt into place, did she feel regret, instead?

3

The days leading up to the search had been a whirlwind of trips, from Home Depot for supplies to repair the leaky roof, to Goodwill and the Presbyterian consignment shop for dressers and beds to replace furniture destroyed by the recent soaking rains, then to Value City for inexpensive mattresses and bedding. Not because his boys complained—they'd have slept in sleeping bags on the floor indefinitely if he'd let them.

But no way he'd let them.

On the day each boy walked through that creaking front door with nothing but bad memories and the clothes on his back, he'd promised to provide a proper home—preferably one with a roof that didn't leak. As things turned out, keeping the once-decrepit, old house running was providing more than a legitimate address, it was teaching them skills in carpentry, roofing, window and siding installation, and wiring. They were learning how to work as a team, too, figuring out how to jury-rig the inner workings of ancient, hand-me-down appliances and tools. If not for the loving generosity of his aunt and uncle, who welcomed him into their home and treated him like one of their own, Dusty knew he would have ended up just like them. And since God had seen fit to give him a shot at normal family life, he'd move mountains, if that's what it took, to give these boys the same chances.

Good intentions, regrettably, didn't guarantee success. In the five years he'd been pastor and administrator here, sixty-seven boys had been sent to him. Abandoned, neglected, or abused by parents whose crimes and drug addiction led them to the prison yard or the graveyard—this place was, literally, their last chance. Of the sixty-seven, one was killed in a drive-by shooting, one died of an overdose, and six went the way of their mothers and fathers. All the experts said those were great odds, considering what he had to work with. But Dusty didn't see it that way. He grieved every one like a death, saw each as a personal defeat, and blamed himself for failing them.

That is, until fresh-out-of-seminary Mitchell Carlisle knocked on that creaking front door and asked for a job.

There was a lot to like about the young pastor. Hard-working and insightful, the kids took to him from the get-go. He'd majored in classic literature and excelled in math and science, making him the go-to guy for help with tough home-work assignments. Like Dusty, Mitch could play just about any instrument he picked up, and in the year since he'd joined the Last Chance household, he'd given the boys nearly as many guitar and piano lessons as Dusty had. As if all that wasn't enough, Mitch could turn simple, inexpensive ingredients into hearty, healthy meals.

His talent for citing chapter and verse to solve just about any problem was the only source of strife between them. The bone of contention began when Dusty confessed his guilt at failing those eight boys . . . and Mitch accused him of being guilty, instead, of the sin of pride. It had taken every ounce of Dusty's self-control not to whack Mitch with his own ragtag old Bible. That feeling didn't last long, though; hard as it was to admit, the young pastor had hit the proverbial nail square on its head.

And they'd been like brothers ever since, sharing an unspoken understanding, one of the other.

Take last night, for example, when Dusty came home dog-tired and emotionally drained after his gruesome discovery in the field at Gunpowder State Park. Mitch, God love him, knew exactly what he'd needed, and provided it: Thick soup, crusty bread, and an evening of peace and privacy. While he and the boys attended a movie, Dusty emptied the stewpot and polished off the loaf, then hit the showers and headed for his tiny room on the second floor, where not even the sounds of sirens kept him from falling into a deep, dreamless sleep.

Then, at precisely 3 a.m., he found himself wide awake. Nothing unusual about that. Dusty rarely slept more than a few hours at a stretch. And rather than toss and turn, he did what he always did, and padded downstairs. He made himself a pot of coffee, and sipped it while balancing the Last Chance checkbook. Unless he'd made a critical error, things were looking up; nearly $200 left after paying the utilities and setting aside money for groceries. Relieved, he decided to listen to the CD the kids had made—with Mitch's help—while he worked on the speech he'd been asked to give at the next Rotary meeting. Feet propped on his footstool and pencil eraser tapping the legal pad on his lap, he tried to decide whether to start off with a corny joke or a Bible verse.

Somewhere between "A funny thing happened on the way to the club" and the doodles beneath it, he dozed off. A crick in his neck woke him.

Or so he thought.

"You gotta remember to lock up at night, dude . . ."

At times like these, Dusty was glad that his Marine training ran deep; though his heart was beating like a parade drum,

Hector Gonzales would never have the satisfaction of knowing he'd startled Dusty.

". . . else some real bad people could get in here."

Dusty made a show of yawning and stretching, then sat up and put his tablet and pencil onto the table beside his chair.

The gang leader chuckled. "What, you deaf *and* dumb?"

He ignored the sarcasm. "How 'bout joining me in the kitchen, Gonzo?"

"Is that your idea of a joke, man?"

On his feet now, Dusty crossed both arms over his chest. "Give me a minute to get my brain into gear. I was dead to the world when you came in." Poor choice of words? Dusty hoped not. He scratched his head. "Joke?"

"Not all Mexicans work in the kitchen, you know."

"Ah. *Now* I get it." He'd say one thing for the kid . . . in the few years he'd been in this country, only a trace of his native accent tinged his speech. He wanted to believe the misunderstanding was rooted in the remaining language barrier, but more than likely, Hector Gonzales was trying to pick a fight. It was his turn to chuckle. "I've got a fresh pot of coffee out there. Thought maybe you'd like a cup, is all." He didn't wait for a response. Instead, he grabbed his mug and headed down the hall, hoping with every step that Gonzo would follow quietly. Last thing he needed was for the boys to wake up and get into it with this guy.

Concentrating—so that his hand wouldn't shake noticeably as he refilled his mug—Dusty said, "I drink mine black. How 'bout you?"

Gonzo stood all of five-foot-seven, even in his high-heeled cowboy boots. He held up a forefinger. "One cream," he said. Then, the index finger popped up beside it. "Two sugars."

After putting both mugs on the table, Dusty pulled out a chair. "Take a load off, and tell me what brings you here at this ungodly hour."

As if he didn't already know. For months now, Gonzo had been pestering the Last Chance boys to join *Los Toros de Lidia*. How long, Dusty wondered, before one of them caved to the pressure and signed on with the Eutaw Street gang? Never, if he had anything to say about it.

Gonzo took a long, loud slurp.

"Sweet enough for you, Gonz?"

Nodding, the boy said, "It will do." Eyes narrowed, he added, "You should know that only my most trusted friends call me Gonzo."

So the gang leader planned to draw this out, did he? Well, two can play that game, Dusty thought. He leaned back and, after propping both feet on the seat of the nearest chair, casually linked his fingers behind his neck. And just for good measure, he yawned again. No point letting all those months of Special Ops training go to waste. "We've always been on good terms. Guess that means I can call you Gonzo, right?"

The coffee maker hissed and sputtered, and Gonzo lurched.

Dusty pretended he was too busy sipping from his own mug to notice. No point putting the kid on the defensive, either.

"Gonzo will do." He smirked. "For now." He took another gulp of coffee, then met Dusty's eyes. "So." He put the mug down hard enough to slosh coffee onto the back of his hand. "Let me tell you why I am here," he said, then licked it clean.

As a Marine, Dusty had faced opposing forces in half a dozen countries. Whether in the Middle East, Asia, Central or South America, the enemy shared one distinct trait with this young, tough thug: Cold, soulless eyes.

Gonzo aimed a thumb at the ceiling. "Those kids sleeping peacefully upstairs? They are the only ones in the neighborhood who are not with me." Linking his fingers on the table, he added, "And you know what they say. . . ."

If you're not with me, you're against me.

"Ah," he said with a nod of approval, "I will take your grim expression to mean that you do remember the adage."

How long before Gonzo tacked on a time limit, and threatened gun violence—maybe worse—as the price for Dusty's refusal to allow his boys to join the gang?

Not long, as it turned out.

Eyes glittering like black diamonds, Gonzo whispered, "It is long past the time for things to change."

Dusty felt the chill all the way to the soles of his feet. He needed to buy time. Time to figure out how to beat this bandit at his own game. And if he couldn't be beat, then time to find a new place to hang the Last Chance sign.

He matched the glare, blink for icy blink, then held up his mug, as if to offer a toast. "And if it doesn't?"

A slow, dangerous smirk tilted Gonzo's mustachioed mouth. "Then this, *friend,* will be our last cup of coffee."

4

*O*nly fifteen days of school left for Grace's seniors, twenty-one for everyone else. "That's a joke," she said to herself. She could count on both hands the number of kids who'd show up in her classrooms these last few weeks, and they fell into two groups: Those with no place else to go, and the ones with college in their futures. Grace would never admit it out loud, of course. Somebody had to play the Pollyanna role, and it might as well be her. So when the subject of low attendance came up, she blamed the rundown buildings, erected during the turbulent 40s, with no air conditioning and painted-shut windows for the low attendance.

The real enemy was apathy. Indifference to higher education started at the top, with politicians and government regulations, trickled down through the school administrators and teachers, and ended in a murky puddle in homes divided by divorce or poverty or both. The fact that a handful of kids made it to class at all was something to be thankful for, so she put the same effort into lesson plans as she had the rest of the school year.

A disheveled girl slouched into the art room and, as usual, avoided eye contact. Kylie Houghton, whose naturally blond hair was hidden beneath a rainbow of dull streaks that hid long-lashed gray eyes. One rainy morning, the dampness washed thick makeup from her cheeks, allowing Grace a glimpse at freckles that dotted her rosy cheeks. And a month or so ago, when a classmate's joke induced a faint smile, Grace found herself praying for a polite way to tell Kylie how lovely she'd be . . . with just a little attention to her appearance.

The girl never participated in lively discussions, not even when called upon, but she never missed a day of school or a homework assignment, either . . . at least not in Grace's English and art classrooms. In fact, Grace couldn't decide if Kylie's essays and poems were more thought-provoking and mature than her paintings and sketches, or the other way around.

Today, she'd worn raggedy jeans and a drab blue T-shirt that said STOP READING MY SHIRT and hid choppy, chin-length curls under a grubby baseball cap. School policy forbade hats and logoed clothing, and Kylie knew it as well as Grace.

"You look cute today, Kylie."

Elbows resting on the desk, she cupped her chin in her palms. "Y'think?"

Helping her to comply with regulations would require finesse. "How long have you been in my class, Kylie?"

"I dunno. Couple years, I guess."

Three, to be precise, Grace thought, nodding. "So you know me pretty well then, right?"

Kylie pursed her lips. "'Bout as well as any student knows a teacher, I s'pose."

"Then you know that *I* don't have a problem with T-shirts and hats with writing on them. . . ." She ignored the girl's bored sigh. ". . . but the school board feels differently. If you're caught wearing those things anywhere outside my classroom, you know what will happen, right?"

And there it was again—that "I don't give a hoot" look.

"Whatever."

The girl was smart. So smart that, when she transferred in from the DC suburbs, she'd been placed with kids five, six, and in some cases, seven years her senior. Kylie had breezed through the academics, but her brilliance came at a hefty price, and put her behind her older classmates, emotionally and socially. In a matter of days, she'd graduate. And then, what would become of her?

Grace had tried to gently coax the girl toward college, but in a house already overflowing with foster kids, the advice seemed to have fallen by the wayside. A pang of guilt echoed inside her, because between grading finals and keeping things afloat at Angel Acres, she hadn't checked to see if Kylie had talked with Gavin Martin about scholarships, or anything else related to furthering her education, for that matter.

Hopefully, it wasn't too late for the grizzled guidance counselor to pull a miracle out of his files. *Only one way to find out,* Grace told herself. She had a free period coming up, and God willing, Gavin would have a few minutes to discuss Kylie with her.

Meanwhile, there was the matter of Kylie's outfit to consider.

She'd violated the clothing restrictions rules before, so many times, in fact, that the principal had warned her what would happen if she broke them again. The automatic suspension wouldn't just destroy her perfect attendance record, it would keep her from graduating with her class, as well. If Kylie had been blessed with maturity in equal measure to her intelligence, she might have realized that, in years to come, she'd regret the decision.

But Grace understood it, and if she had anything to say about it, Kylie would graduate on stage—and walk away holding a perfect attendance certificate *and* a high school diploma.

She went to the cupboard behind her desk and plucked a denim shirt from its hanger. "There's some paint on the cuffs," she said, draping it over one arm as she walked toward Kylie's desk, "but it'll cover up the lettering on your shirt. And the pockets are enormous," she continued, laying the shirt beside the girl's raggedy purse. "More than big enough so that you could tuck the hat into one of them."

In the silence that followed, Grace expected Kylie to frown. Refuse the offer. Maybe even storm out of the classroom. But it was a chance she had to take, because she would be a sorry excuse for a teacher if she didn't at least *try* to give the girl some happy memories to carry into the future!

"But . . . but Miss Sinclair . . ."

Grace braced herself for rejection.

". . . it's Friday." She tapped a finger on the pocket's faux pearl snap. "I . . . I wouldn't be able to return it until Monday, at the earliest. Because . . . because I'd want to wash it." She met Grace's eyes. "Y'know?"

Well, that was the last thing Grace expected her to say!

Much as she would have liked to *give* the shirt to Kylie, Grace couldn't risk having her see it as charity. "No rush. Any time before. . . ." She bit her lower lip as an idea took shape in her mind.

"Before what?"

"Oh, my. You're going to think I'm crazy. Even worse, you'll think I'm cheap!"

A frown was the girl's answer.

"What if we called it a graduation gift?" Grace explained. "Then you wouldn't have to rush around, washing and drying it, so that you could return it before school's out."

"Well," she said, shrugging into the shirt, "you're sure right about one thing."

Laughing, Grace said, "Ack! I knew it! You *do* think I'm crazy, don't you?"

Kylie fingered the frayed, stained cuffs. "No," she said, her black-lipsticked mouth slanting with a grin, "but you're cheap, all right."

Grace would have hugged her . . . if she thought for a minute the girl would allow it. She laughed instead, because Kylie's little joke filled her with incredible hope.

Two boys and a girl sauntered into the classroom, chattering like magpies. "What's so funny?" the girl asked, plopping her books onto the desk beside Kylie's.

"Miss Sinclair was just asking where I get my hair done."

The girl looked from Kylie's multihued hair to Grace's mop of brown curls. "Wow," she said, giggling, "who knew . . . you're smart *and* funny!"

Grace read passages from *White Fang* and *Call of the Wild*, but not even stories of the wilderness and the untamed animals that called it home kept the kids from falling asleep on their desks. All except Kylie, that is.

The rest of the day seemed to grind by—each tick of the clock like off-key harmony to the grinding blades of the big, rusty fan near the door. Finally, the last bell rang, and once the last kid had bolted from the room, Grace grabbed her backpack. On the way to the guidance office, she checked her mail cubby. It was a long shot, but perhaps a concerned parent had questions about final exams or called to RSVP the graduation party she'd organized for her students. Disappointed—but not surprised—she found nothing in her box.

Grace's annoyance vanished the instant she saw Gavin finger-walking across the tabs of manila folders in a battered, sickly brown filing cabinet, his salt-and-pepper hair giving him an Albert Einstein look. He couldn't have been more than fifty, if his bio was accurate. So why did it seem that he worked so hard at looking and behaving like a much older man?

"Don't just stand there gawking, Sinclair," he said without looking up. "Get on in here and tell me which of your pet juvenile delinquents brings you to my humble burrow today."

"Nice to see you, too, Gavin."

Peering over wire-rimmed reading glasses, he matched her grin with one of his own. "Sorry, Gracie," he said, chuckling. Then he held up his hands, exposing every swollen, bloodied cuticle. "This secretarial work drives me mad. Only thing I hate more is trying to cram a thousand folders into a drawer intended for a hundred." He slammed the drawer, then pointed at the seat of a threadbare chair, piled high with newspapers, magazines, and books. "Just put that stuff. . . ." He looked around, and shoulders sagging, said, ". . . put it anywhere you can find a spot and make yourself at home."

Grace zipped her backpack. "Much as the cat would love a fuzzy little treat, I wouldn't want a mouse to crawl in there," she joked, dropping it to the floor.

"Ha. Like a mouse could survive in here. But just listen to you," he said, as Grace gathered an armload of paper, "*still* calling that poor animal 'cat.' How long have you had her?"

"Years." *Years and years,* she thought, remembering the day she'd helped Leslie's mom box up clothes, Hummels, a couple dozen wolf plaques and figurines, and pack them all into the back of a U-Haul van. If the woman hadn't spent hours sneezing and blowing her nose, she'd have taken the cat home, too.

"Are you *ever* gonna give her a proper name?"

Grace sat down and crossed her arms. "She doesn't seem to mind the moniker. Why should you?"

The counselor rolled up his shirtsleeves. "Well, you understood why I had to ask. What kind of counselor would I be if I didn't?" Then he sat down behind his desk. "So tell me, what can I do for you on this sweltering Baltimore afternoon?" he asked, unbuttoning his collar.

"Well, I have this student, see, and she shows a lot of potential."

"Gee. I'm shocked." He loosened the Windsor knot of his tie. One good tug, and it slipped off with a quiet *hiss*. "A kid with potential. Here." He pointed at the floor. "In the heart of Baltimore?" Eyes closed, he pressed a hand to his chest. "Be still my heart."

Grace only sighed, and when he opened his eyes, she said, "When the school board chooses a date for your award ceremony, be sure to let me know, will you? I want plenty of time to shop for a little black dress."

"Award ceremony . . . ?" Brow furrowed, Gavin tucked his chin into his collar. "So you can. . . . *Huh*?"

"Oh please. No need to feign modesty on my behalf." She snickered. "You know, the banquet where the commissioner will name you 'Baltimore's Most PR-Savvy Guidance Counselor.'"

"Ahh, *that* award." Laughing, he tossed the tie onto a chair, and watched it slither to the floor, where it coiled like a silky blue snake. "Oh," he said, propping his glasses on top of his head, "you're a hoot. But I don't know what my attitude toward the system has to do with this kid you're here to see me about, but. . . ." He held up a forefinger. "No. Wait. Don't tell me. Let me guess." Squinting one eye, he cupped his chin in a palm. "She can't decide whether to have an abortion now, or wait until after graduation. . . ."

"Good grief, Gavin. I can count on one hand the number of my girls who quit school because they were pregnant, and I'd have fingers left over." She clucked her tongue, as if to underscore the point. "Not *every* kid I come to talk with you about is in trouble." She pictured Kylie's baggy clothes and crazy-colored hair, the *I'm* so-o-o *bored with life* attitude. "At least, not *that* kind of trouble." Grace remembered the way Kylie shied away from boys, even the cute ones who blatantly flirted with her. No surprise there, considering the five-year age gap. "Kylie isn't going to have a baby. She's bright and articulate, one of my best students, in fact. Her problem, if she has one, is that her foster parents haven't helped her map out the future. *That's* why I'm here . . . I'm hoping you can point me toward a program, a therapist, a volunteer activity . . . something, *anything* that'll lend some direction, some purpose to her life, before it's too late."

On his feet now, Gavin walked back to the row of filing cabinets and slid open a drawer. "Kylie . . . Kylie. . . . That wouldn't be Kylie Houghton, would it?" he asked.

"Amazing."

"What," he said, returning to the wall of filing cabinets, "you're surprised that Mr. PR-Savvy actually *knows* the kids he counsels? Hmpf." He opened a drawer, plucked out a folder, and dropped it onto his curling, peeling desk blotter. "I take it you know her history, right?

"Some of it," Grace admitted. "But I'm sure you're privy to things I'm not. . . ."

Gavin leaned forward slightly. "I'm not supposed to reveal stuff like this," he whispered, "but I believe you might be on to something there." And shoving back from the desk, he propped both feet on the window sill behind him. "Houghton is her foster mother's last name. No idea where she's from, originally, or why she ran away in the first place." He put his glasses back on. "She has flat-out refused to talk about her past." He swiveled to face her again. "To anyone. Cops picked her up at the Greyhound station a couple-three winters ago, shivering, hungry, dirty as a gutter rat. After a couple weeks in a group home, they placed her with a foster family. She gave 'em a month, and ran away. And ran away from two more before some savvy social worker figured out that Kylie has 'male head of household' issues."

Kylie's skittishness around the older boys made even more sense, hearing that.

"They handed her off to Mrs. Houghton," Gavin continued.

"How long has she been there?"

Gavin shrugged. "Six months, give or take." He tapped the folder. "She was in here not two weeks ago, sitting right where you are now, asking about student loans and dormitories and all the rest of the go-to-college stuff."

Grace brightened. "Well, that's good news. Surprising, all things considered, but good."

"It would be . . . if she'd cough up some information about herself. Can't help her get a student loan without i.d."

"I guess a scared little girl doesn't think to grab her birth certificate as she's running out the door. . . ."

"True. But let me tell you a little secret. . . ." He leaned forward and waved Grace closer. When she scooted to the edge of her chair, he said, "Thanks to that kid, I owe favors all over town." He leaned back and sighed. "Pulled a few strings, and managed to get her an appointment with a pal of mine . . . admissions counselor at U of M."

"My alma mater!"

"Mine, too. She could do way worse than the University of Maryland."

"A whole lot worse."

"Fear the turtle!" they said together, then laughed.

"You know what?" Gavin said, sliding his Rolodex closer. "I think I know just the guy to help her. He's my cousin, but don't hold that against him," he said, grinning. "Mostly, he works with boys, but he's good with people. Straightened out more juvies than you could shake a stick at."

Grace pointed at Kylie's folder. "You know as well as I do that Kylie has never been in any trouble."

"I know, I know . . . never missed a day. Never late for class. Not one suspension. 3.8 GPA. College-bound. . . ." He plucked a card from behind the P tab and held it out to Grace. "Remind me again why we think a kid like that needs outside help."

"Because we know that with a little guidance, she could be so much more than she is." Grace took the card, then grabbed a pen from the tortoise-shaped pencil cup on his desk, and scribbled the name and number on the palm of her hand.

"Grace. Stop. What on earth—"

"It'd take half an hour to find my notepad in this thing," she said, shouldering her backpack.

Arms akimbo, he said, "You're surrounded by paper. Or haven't you noticed?"

Laughing, Grace returned the pen and the card and got to her feet. "Oh, trust me. I've noticed. I'm just afraid if I slide one sheet from a stack, I'll activate an avalanche. And it's Friday. We could very well stay buried until Monday!"

Gavin glanced around his cluttered little office. "Well, I'll say one thing for you," he said, grinning, "when you're right, you're right."

"Thanks, Gavin. I'll let you know how things work out with. . . ." She read the name penned on her palm. "And now I'd better get out of here, so you can get back to your, ah, *secretarial work*."

"You know," he said, on his feet now, "back in college, I was lead guitarist in a band." He slid an arm across her shoulders and walked with her toward the door. "Our percussionist handpainted some very wise words on his bass drum: 'Nobody likes a smart aleck,' it said." A mischievous glint sparkled in his eyes. "You should know that I cleaned that comment up, what with you being so young and naïve and all."

"And I appreciate it." She started to leave, then asked if he planned to attend the graduation party she'd organized.

"Have you ever known me to pass up a chance at free food?"

"Good point," she said, one hand on the doorknob.

"Can I bring anything?"

"Just your ornery self."

"See you later, kiddo."

"Not if I see you first," she teased. And despite the closed door, she heard his gravelly laughter, halfway down the hall.

5

*A*s she crossed the parking lot, Grace looked at the name and number scribbled on her hand. Would this guy be like Gavin—all bark, no bite, with a wild mop of hair and eyebrows that looked like steel wool? Or more like the reverend she'd grown up listening to every Sunday, whose tinny voice didn't fit his big-as-a-grizzly stature? Should she call and make an appointment, or just drive over there, and trust that he'd have a few minutes to talk with her about Kylie?

Distracted, Grace caught the heel of her sandal on a glob of tar near the curb, and nearly landed face-first on the sidewalk. The heat of a blush crept into her cheeks, though a quick glance around told her no one had seen her misstep. "Lord," she said, unlocking her tiny SUV, "remind me why I don't believe in omens, please."

But instead of the Bible verses she'd expected to come to mind, a third text message from Mrs. Logan popped onto her cell phone's screen. There must have been a hundred names in the woman's phone directory. "So why does she keep calling *me?*"

Maybe, she thought, typing the reverend's address into her GPS, *because the grieving mother had begged her to come along as she selected the coffin and "just the right words" for her daughter's tombstone . . . helped her decipher the quickly mounting charges, and arrange the memorial service, and decide which hymns the organist should play.*

At Mrs. Logan's insistence, Grace chose Missy's dress (though the condition she'd been in when they found her made an open casket impossible), and arranged transportation for the sorority sister, who'd stay with her until after the funeral. Finally, Grace had left a message for Agent Spencer, asking that he call Mrs. Logan as soon as possible to reassure her that the authorities still planned to release the body by the end of the week.

As she blended with traffic on I-95, Grace had a horrible thought: *Had he called back with bad news? And if he had, couldn't the sorority sister take care of things for a change?*

The image of Mrs. Logan's wan, teary face flashed in Grace's mind, and with it, the "Do Unto Others" proverb. Guilt would have made her turn around, put off the surprise visit to Reverend Parker . . . if traffic hadn't slowed to a crawl, effectively trapping her in the middle lane. . . .

Grace thumped the steering wheel and loosed a low growl. Until the guy in the car to her right said, "Ditto!"—she'd forgotten the windows were down. "How spoiled and pampered are *you*," Grace chided herself, "that a little gridlock can completely sour your mood!"

The cat had food and water enough to last a few hours. The traffic wouldn't make her late for an appointment, or put her on the receiving end of a "Where have *you* been?" glare from a babysitter. With traffic at a dead stop now, she couldn't get a ticket for talking on her cell phone while driving. *Might as well find out what the poor woman wanted,* she thought, dialing Mrs. Logan's number.

"Hi, Mrs. Logan. It's just me, Grace, returning your call. Feel free to call me at home when you get this message. . . ."

Nothing to do now but stick to her original plan, and see if the good reverend could suggest something that might help Kylie. A familiar tune wafted from the car's speakers, and she turned up the volume to harmonize with Blake Shelton. The song had barely ended when the GPS-recorded voice said, "Arriving at address. On left."

Sure enough, the house number she'd written on her palm mirrored the one on the big hand-painted sign hanging from the porch. Above it, a bigger sign that said LAST CHANCE. On the front lawn, a guy operating a circular saw seemed too engrossed in his project to notice that she'd parked beside the glossy black motorcycle in the driveway. Didn't hear her slam her car door or holler "Hello!"

On one sweat-glistened bicep, a tattooed cross. On the other, a skull, and on the handles of the crossed swords beneath it, the words *Semper Fi*. A diamond stud earring winked from behind dark, gleaming curls that escaped his Yankees baseball cap. And tucked into the back pocket of his snug jeans, a Harley Davidson bandanna.

But gawking wasn't getting Kylie the help she needed. Wasn't getting the man's attention, either. She'd call out, but what if that startled him? She'd never forgive herself if he lopped off a thumb or something.

Grace stepped off the sidewalk and waved both arms above her head.

The high-pitched whine of the saw stopped instantly.

Smiling, Grace made her way up the walk.

But he didn't look up. Didn't look in her direction, either. Instead, he jerked the plug free of the big gray metal outlet and began winding the cord around the tool's handle. Maybe he hadn't seen her, after all. She opened her mouth to say hello again when he looked up.

"Well, well, well," he said, "as I live and breathe."

Grace stifled a gasp. If this wasn't a "small world" example, she didn't know what was: There she stood, not two feet from the man who had found Missy's body. He'd pulled up his sweatshirt hood on that dismal, rainy morning; that explained why she hadn't noticed the tattoos or pierced ear. It didn't explain why he was *here*.

"I was told I'd find Reverend Parker at this address?"

"Really?" He thumbed the baseball cap to the back of his head. "Who told you that?"

She hadn't noticed the ponytail, either. "Gavin Martin."

"Gavin was right."

Grace caught herself staring into those intense blue eyes and forced herself to blink. She swallowed, too. "*You're* Reverend Parker?"

"'Fraid so." He thrust out his right hand. "And you're . . . ?"

"Grace," she said, putting hers into it, "Grace Sinclair."

"Nice meeting you," he said, releasing her. "So how do you know that old rascal?"

"I'm a teacher . . . at the high school where he works as a guidance counselor."

"Funny."

If curiosity killed the cat, she didn't want to find out what might happen if she asked *what* was funny.

"You don't look like the type who could handle herself in a rough, inner-city school."

She hitched her backpack higher on her shoulder, then crossed both arms over her chest, trying to figure out what to respond to first—his insinuation that she wasn't equipped to teach, or his crack about the quality of city schools. True, she'd encountered her share of unruly kids over the years, but even her friends who taught at private schools complained about the occasional bad apple mixed in with good students. "Exactly what would that type look like?"

"Bigger. Older. And way tougher looking than the likes of *you*. For starters."

"Gavin says you're the go-to guy when it comes to troubled teens," she said, ignoring his comment. He hadn't been the first guy to say a "you don't look your age" line, but he'd been the first to deliver the line in a silky baritone. She caught herself staring. Again. And reminded herself that she hadn't endured forty minutes of rush hour traffic to swap Hepburn-Tracy banter with Easy Rider, even if she *had* been hearing that rich DJ voice in her dreams, ever since that day in the park. "I'm hoping he's right."

"Sometimes," he said, brushing sawdust from the sheet of plywood he'd just cut, "Gavin talks too much."

Grace pictured Kylie, with her unkempt mottled hair and big sad eyes, struggling through life because no one had taken the time to show her that she had choices, that with a little effort on her part, the world was her oyster. She had no one but herself to blame for her wasted hour. Two, if she counted the trip back home. What did she expect, coming here, unannounced?

Nothing ventured, nothing gained, she told herself. Surely in that giant Rolodex wheel on Gavin's desk, there was at least one other name, someone who could—

"I, ah, I guess I owe you an apology."

"An apology?" she echoed. "For what?"

"For jumping to conclusions. From what you just said about this Kylie girl, well, I'd have to say you're handling yourself just fine."

She couldn't have said all that out loud.

Could she? She must have.

"What time is it?"

"Time?" Grace wavered between confusion and embarrassment.

Chuckling softly, he took hold of her wrist. "You know, ti—" One glance at the dial silenced him. He let go and whipped off his cap, slapping it against his thigh, "I was supposed to have supper on the table five minutes ago."

At first, she felt guilty that her impromptu visit had sidetracked him. But if she hadn't driven up when she did, he'd still be sawing away at that sheet of plywood.

Right?

"You any good in the kitchen?"

My, but he had an eye-catching smile. . . . "I can hold my own, I suppose." Guilty, flustered, confused, captivated, exasperated—how many things would end up on her "what I'm feeling" list before *normal* popped up?

"Tell you what. How 'bout if you help me get some food into my boys, and afterward, you can tell me all about your Kylie."

His boys? Funny. She didn't remember Gavin mentioning a wife and kids. But then, why would he, when *her Kylie* was the only reason she'd come here? Grace added *stupid* to her list, because what kind of ninny got all weak-kneed over a guy she'd just met, even if he *was* good looking enough to make the cover of a romance novel!

"Spaghetti's fast and easy," he said, "but last time I checked, there were fish sticks and chicken nuggets in the freezer. The boys would eat rocks if I let 'em."

Meaning, if she stayed, he expected her to choose?

Just say no, she thought. *Tell him the truth: You have to get home, feed Leslie's cat, throw some towels in the washer. . . .*

"Anybody you need to call first? Husband? Parents? Kids?"

"Just call me footloose and fancy-free, Reverend Parker."

Wrong answer, she thought, groaning inwardly, *because it implied that she was staying. And single. And happy about it.* Where *was* the proverbial hole in the floor that swallowed people up when they said dimwitted, embarrassing, absurd things?

He laughed. "If it's okay with you, I'll call you Grace." He stepped up onto the porch. "And I hope you'll call me Dusty."

Was it her imagination, or had he just sent an unspoken "remember that, for next time" message? But why would a married man—a father and pastor—*do* such a thing! "Dusty," she repeated. "Is that short for Dustin?"

"Nope." He held open the door. "It says Dusty Parker on my driver's license."

Like an obedient pup, she went inside, doing her best to ignore the question pinging in her head: If there *was* a little woman, why was the good reverend Dusty Parker in charge of supper? She'd started a new list—of occupations that required shift work—when he said, "Come on in the kitchen and meet my boys."

In the moment it took to be introduced them, Grace understood why Gavin hadn't mentioned a wife. None of the boys bore even the slightest resemblance to Dusty, and their ages—anywhere from twelve to sixteen—was as varied as their ethnicity. The sign out front made sense now, too, and so did Gavin's obvious respect for the man who'd "straightened out more juvies than you could shake a stick at." And, in that moment, Grace decided Dusty could be the poster boy, proving the folly of judging a book by its cover.

Perhaps later, she'd ask him how they'd come to share this big old house. And share it, they did, as evidenced by the warmth that connected them all. It was something to admire—

and something to envy—since she didn't believe a family was in God's plan for her.

Then Dusty aimed that amazing, heart-stopping smile at *her,* and she thought maybe, just maybe there *could* be . . . in a place called Last Chance.

6

*T*hat day in the park, she'd worn a bouncy ponytail, and today, shimmering curls spilled down her back and over her shoulders like a dark, silky cape. Something told Dusty he was in trouble, because he already knew that he'd hear her lyrical voice and see those big Bambi eyes in his dreams tonight.

Again.

The only other woman he'd invited to supper—a self-professed teen expert—had shocked him by cowering near the door, as if expecting one of the kids might gouge her eyes out with a fork. She hadn't pitched in to chop lettuce and tomatoes for the salad, didn't offer to help set the table, barely ate a bite of the rib-sticking meal Mitch had prepared. "I'm surprised the plates didn't fly out the door behind her, like in a Tom and Jerry cartoon," Axel had joked when she made her hasty getaway.

By contrast, Grace elbowed her way up to the stove, swapping one-liners with the boys as she shared her secret to lumpless gravy and smooth mashed potatoes. Supper had never been boring at Last Chance, but her presence turned an ordinary meal into a fun family feast.

It ended all too soon, though, as Tony reminded them that "just because there are only a few days left of school doesn't mean you can skip your homework."

Nick gave him a brotherly shove. "Who do you think you are, the homework sheriff?"

"Yeah," Jack agreed. "We've got dishes to do first, Tony Balonie."

"Towels to fold," Dom put in.

"And-and-and f-floors to m-mop, t-t-too," Guillermo added.

"Tell you what," Grace injected. "I'll clean up the kitchen, if Dusty keeps me company."

She looked at him, waiting for confirmation. "Sounds good to me."

The exchange was met with whoops and whistles and good-natured cackles. "Ooh-la-la," Montel singsonged, "the pretty lady wants you to keep her company, Du-ust-y-y."

Laughing, Grace finished with, "And as long as he'll just be sitting here, he might as well fold the towels." She locked those big brown eyes on him to add, "Those floors can wait until tomorrow, can't they?"

Between the boys' stunned expressions and her flirty grin, what could he say, except, "Why not?"

Snickering, the boys wasted no time thundering from the room. "Make tracks, dudes," Trevor teased, "before he changes his mind!"

Grace wasted no time, either, clearing the table and loading the dishwasher. She had the job mostly done by the time he returned from the basement with the basket of towels, and before he knew it, she was sitting across from him, helping with that chore, too. "You don't have to do this, you know."

"I know. But I'm here. So I might as well make myself useful." Her tiny hands blurred before his eyes as she snapped a hand towel, and folded it into a tidy square. "So who's this Mitch the kids were talking about all through supper?"

"Assistant pastor. Assistant administrator." Dusty picked up a towel, too, wondering why it hadn't made that efficient popping sound when he flapped it. "Though neither title seems fair," he admitted, "since just about anything that needs doing around here gets done by Mitch."

"I'm looking forward to meeting him."

Could he take it to mean she'd be back? *A guy can hope. . . .*

"He has the night off?"

"Not exactly." *Bad idea,* he cautioned, *mixing business with pleasure. . . .* He grabbed another towel. "He's representing us at a dinner with the mayor. If all goes well, we'll get the extra police protection the city has been promising us for months."

"Police protection! Why do you need *that*, for heaven's sake?"

Man, but she was gorgeous when she widened her eyes that way. "This used to be a great neighborhood," he said, stacking his towel atop the others, "until about a year ago. No crime—unless you count jaywalking—quiet and peaceful. And then *Los Toros de Lidia* moved in. Nothing's been the same since."

He told her about the gang leader's stealthy attempts to entice the boys into joining "The Fighting Bulls." And how lately, his invitations had been downright blatant; as an example, he added the story of Hector Gonzalez's late-night visit.

Her eyebrows rose slightly, and he could see that Grace was doing her best not to look at the door, at the windows. She had the most expressive, open face he'd ever seen, with the sole exception of his Aunt Anita's; if she *wasn't* wondering if Gonzo could get in here, right now, he'd eat his hat. And it made him feel like a heel, scaring her that way.

To her credit, she shook it off quickly, and eyes narrowed, she said, "Bullies are just . . . just *horrible*. I mean, as if those sweet kids haven't already been through enough, now they have to live under a threat like that?" She punctuated the question with a little growl. "That's just plain *wrong*." She took the towel he'd been fumbling around with and folded it as she added, "I'm going to start praying like crazy that the mayor *does* give you the police protection you need, and that he does it soon. And if he doesn't. . . ." She shuddered. "Well, I'll just have to start a letter-writing campaign. Or make a few calls to Channel 13, and see if Mary Bubala will do a story on the . . . what did you call them? The *Los Toros de Lidia?*" Another growl, then, "Because I don't even want to think about what could happen if that ruffian comes back!"

He'd called Gonzo a few things, but "ruffian" had not been one of them. He might have hugged her, because everything—from the glint in her dark eyes to the way she'd thrown back her shoulders—told him she felt protective of the kids. The reaction told him she was one of the few who actually *got* it, who understood that for these boys—victims of abuse, abandonment, and neglect—this really *was* their last chance. *So much for your 'separate business from pleasure' rule.*

But was it his fault that she had a knack for asking just the right questions in that sweet, non-threatening way of hers? Maybe she should have become an investigative reporter instead of a teacher, because once Dusty started talking, he couldn't seem to shut himself up.

He told her how every boy had come to Last Chance, and how each arrival reminded him of the way his aunt and uncle had taken him in when his parents were killed.

"How old were you?"

"Ten."

He could have hugged her at that moment, because big shiny tears filled her eyes as she sandwiched his hand between her own. "Something else we have in common," she said.

He was puzzling over the "something else" when she said, "I was sixteen when I lost my folks. Moved from New York to Baltimore to live with my mom's parents."

How they went from that to his admission that he'd wasted way too many years, tap dancing on the thin line between what was legal and what was not before joining the Marines, Dusty couldn't say. One minute, he was telling her his best memories were those Special Ops missions in the Persian Gulf. The next, he heard himself talking about the top-secret memo from the Secretary of Defense, delivered in June of 2001, warning U.S. troops and citizens abroad to be on alert, because an attack by bin Laden was more likely than not. "And you know what happened that following September," he finished.

Grace nodded slowly. "Yes," she whispered.

Dusty recognized the haunted look that crossed her face, because he'd seen it often enough in the mirror. It told him that Grace had a dark and direct link to 9/11, too. He might have asked what it was, if she hadn't said, "Will you look at the time!"

How could it be after ten already?

"I'd better get home before the cat decides to punish me for hours of neglect."

"What kind of cat?"

On her feet now, she said, "Tabby. Gray and white. With big green eyes."

"What's its name?"

Grace laughed quietly. "Llewellyn. But no one knows I call her that." And when he laughed, too, she added, "She isn't really mine."

It was a small thing, really, but the sharp edge to her musical voice told him she wasn't referring to the solitary and independent nature of the species. Rather, the cat had something to do with her 9/11 connection.

The screen door's rusty spring squealed when she stepped outside. *Should've taken care of that yesterday, while you had the oil can out. . . .*

"I don't mean to sound all vague and mysterious," Grace continued, crossing the porch. "It's just that I sort of inherited her, when my best friend . . . when she died."

So she'd lost her parents and a best friend, probably the grandparents she'd talked about, too, from the sound of things. Either she made a great first impression, or she really didn't feel sorry for herself. He liked that. Liked it a lot. Way too much, in fact, to be healthy for either of them.

Or was it?

Next thing Dusty knew, they were standing beside her car. The gentlemanly thing would be to open the door; would a gentleman consider asking her to go back inside for another glass of lemonade?

She answered by opening it herself, then slid behind the wheel and laughed. "I can't believe I drove over here to see if you could help me with Kylie," she said, flopping back against the headrest, "and I barely mentioned her name!" Groaning, she thumped her own forehead. "You must think I'm a total nitwit."

"Hey, it isn't your fault that I'm such a blabbermouth."

A moth flew into the front seat and darted around the dome light, and to her credit, Grace didn't even flinch. Maybe, staring up at him the way she was with those big doe eyes, she hadn't noticed. Dusty's ears grew hot and his palms went all clammy. He knew what he was *supposed* to do next: Close the door. Say goodbye. Tell her to drive safely, that he'd see her soon. Instead, he leaned in, thinking the least he could do after she'd cleaned the kitchen and folded the towels was grab the pesky thing, so it wouldn't buzz her face as she drove home. It put him an inch from her face, more than enough to kiss her . . . if he had a mind to. She licked her lips. Blinked. Swallowed hard enough that he heard it, and he took it all to mean that if he *did* have a mind to, she wouldn't stop him.

Just as his fist closed around the moth, he felt her warm breath on his cheek, and his resolve nearly fizzled. *Better watch it*, he thought, remembering his "never mix business with pleasure" rule. "Gotcha," he said, backing out of the car. And turning the moth loose, he said, "Why don't you and Kylie come join the boys and me on Flag Day? Fort McHenry does fireworks after dark, and if it isn't raining, we can see them from the roof. We could maybe do a cookout or something. That would give me more than enough time to size the kid up, see whether or not you're making mountains out of molehills."

Her left eyebrow went up, and so did one side of her mouth. "You're not the only one who's been around the block a time or two, Reverend Parker."

Now her mouth formed a perfect O . . . right before she hid it behind one hand. "Oh my goodness," she said. "Yikes. That came out *all* wrong. I didn't mean. . . ." On the heels of an exasperated sigh, Grace said, "What I *meant* to say was, Kylie has been my student for several years. I've already done an assessment of her. What I *don't* know is how to get her to see that her future is worth fighting for. And after seeing what you've done with those boys . . . well, it's a miracle, that's what it is, and I'd love to make something like that happen for her."

"They have as much to do with what's working in their lives as I do. More, even." He wouldn't tell her about the eight kids he'd failed. And remembering what Mitch had said about that, he bristled. *You really can't win 'em all, but you sure have to try.* "So what do you say?"

"About going with you guys on the fourteenth?" She nodded. "Sounds like fun. But. . . ."

Heart sinking, Dusty forced a grin. "Sorry. Can't take 'but' for an answer."

"No. Wait. I was just going to ask . . . would you mind if I asked Mrs. Logan to join us?"

Melissa's mom, Dusty remembered, who'd lost her husband and daughter in the same calendar year.

"Might be good for her to get out of the house, spend some time with young people, take her mind off . . . you know . . . everything."

It was the "young people" remark that sounded warning bells in Dusty's head. What if she got all weepy and weak-kneed, being surrounded by kids her daughter's age? The daughter who would never see fireworks—or anything else, for that matter—again?

If he sat the boys down, explained what the poor woman had been through, they'd be fine. Half of them had survived major losses in their lives, too, and he'd bet his Harley they'd treat her with kindness and understanding. "Sure, why not?" he said, closing her car door. "Buckle that seatbelt, you hear?"

"I will. . . ." She grinned up at him. " . . . *Dad*."

With that, she drove away, leaving him alone on the sidewalk, staring into the dark until her tail lights were nothing more than two tiny red dots, winking into the night.

How could he miss her already? And why was his brain trying to count down the hours until June 14th?

Head down and hands in his pockets, Dusty chuckled as he made his way back inside.

"Yeah, brother," he mumbled, taking care to lock and bolt the door, "you're in trouble, all right."

If he'd seen the shadowy figure watching him from beyond the hedgerow surrounding the front yard, Dusty would have had a whole lot more reason to believe he was in trouble.

Big trouble.

7

"Hey," Mitch said. "Ran into an old friend of yours last night."

"That's never good news," Dusty said. "This friend got a name?"

"Derek something-or-other."

"Whitman?" He pictured the tall freckle-faced guy he'd practically carried through boot camp.

"Yeah, that's him."

"You sure? Last I heard, he was KIA." Besides, if memory served, wasn't he from Rhode Island?

"Give me a minute to translate. KIA is 'Marine' for killed in action, right?"

Dusty nodded. "Yeah. Sorry. Old habits die hard."

"Here," Mitch said, flipping open his cell phone. "I figured you'd like a trip down memory lane, so I snapped his picture."

It was Derek, all right, and except for a receding hairline, he hadn't changed a bit. "Where'd you run into him?"

"Couple of us stopped at the Double T Diner for a bite to eat after the mayor's speech. And the waiter was wearing one of those crazy pins. You know. Like your skull and crossbones thing."

"Crossed swords," Dusty corrected, "not bones."

"Yeah, yeah, whatever. So anyway, I told him my boss had one just like it. And he goes, 'No kidding? What's his name?' And when I told him, I thought he'd keel over. All six-foot-ten of him." Mitch fished a small square napkin from his shirt pocket. "Says while he was doing his stint at Bethesda, his dad died of a stroke and his mom grieved herself to death. And since he liked the East coast weather, he didn't see any point in going back where he came from."

"Makes sense." Except for the part about Derek working at the Double T. He'd graduated from Yale with a law degree, and bored them all silly with talk of joining his dad's law firm, once the Marines released him.

"Spent some time in rehab, and swears he's been clean for going on seven years."

He'd been a major pothead back in the day. *Who are you to talk?* Dusty thought; the only difference between them was that *his* drug of choice had been scotch. It was only by the grace of God that he wasn't waiting tables, too.

"Said if you need a volunteer, or somebody to scare the boys with some straight talk, you should give him a call."

Not a chance. But rather than explain why, he decided to change the subject. "Still seeing that little redhead?"

Mitch frowned and blushed, ran a hand through his white-blond hair. "Nah. What's that term the lawyers use? 'Irreconcilable differences'? Yeah, that's it. Only thing we had in common is that we both thought she was gorgeous."

If he hoped his laugh masked his heartache, Mitch was sadly mistaken. And with his own dismal record in the romance department, Dusty had no idea how to comfort his friend. "There's some pie left from supper," he said. "Apple."

Mitch grabbed a plate and a fork, then slid the pie out of the microwave. "Aw, man, that hurts."

"I could say the same thing." Dusty feigned shock. "How long have you known about my hiding place?"

"'Bout as long as you've been stashing stuff in there," he said around a mouthful of crust. "But don't worry. Your secret's safe with me. And Montel, and Axel, and Guillermo, and—"

"Please. You're depressing me."

"Here," Mitch said, sliding the pie tin closer. "Dig in. Took the edge right off *my* self-pity." He speared an apple. "I've been meaning to ask . . . what did you do . . . go on a rampage last night?"

"No. Why?"

"Because last time I saw the kitchen this clean. . . ." He swallowed, then washed the pie down with a gulp of lemonade. "Y'know, I don't think it's *ever* been this clean." He used the fork as a pointer. "Okay, cough it up, dude. Who did what? And how'd you use it to make *this* happen?"

Dusty only sighed, remembering how cute Grace had looked with that dish towel tucked into her belt as she stuffed the dishwasher. "You staying the night?"

"Might as well." He crossed both arms over his chest. "So . . . you wanna talk about it?"

Dusty didn't know what 'it' was, and didn't much care to find out. "Thanks for dragging the trash cans to the road."

"Change the subject if you want," Mitch said, raising an eyebrow, "but those tricks you taught yourself during your party-all-night years ain't workin', bud."

"Everybody has a restless night now and then. No big deal."

"It is when you start looking like somebody who's on his way to a costume party . . . dressed up like a ghoul. . . ."

"You're like a puppy with a bone, you know that?"

"Yeah. So why not just spit it out, save yourself all the back and forth?"

He didn't know whether to blame his mood on the visit from Gonzo or his irrational reaction to Grace. Didn't know if he wanted to delve into all the memories Derek had roused, either. But before he knew it, Dusty heard himself yammering on and on about those last weeks in Iraq.

"Every soldier in the unit," he began, "knew exactly what to do if the enemy launched a rocket into camp or lobbed grenades over the barbed wire." Keeping the insurgents at bay—while protecting innocent Iraqi civilians—often came at enormous cost, but it was a price worth paying if it meant *America* remained untouched by battle. "Yet there we were, thousands of miles from home when the reports started trickling in: The United States. Under attack. New York. DC. A random field in Pennsylvania. . . ." For hours after the memos started arriving, Dusty remembered, his men sat glassy eyed and silent, because Uncle Sam hadn't included a section in the training manual to prepare them for *that*.

"We paced and cussed, and cussed and prayed, waiting for a turn at the phones and computers." Every soldier, he said, needed to hear their spouses, fiancés, parents, and siblings, to make sure they were safe. After two days of raw worry, Dusty connected with his aunt, but instead of the relief he'd expected to hear, he got the second worst news of his life: His uncle Brock, retired Marine-turned-investor had been in his office on the 95th floor of the World Trade Center when Flight 11 plowed into the building . . .

". . . and I couldn't get *home*."

It had taken weeks, Dusty explained, to arrange transport, ". . . and I spent every minute of it breaking just about every rule in the books." One gloomy afternoon, as he listened to chatter on the radio, he lost all control: territorial soldiers had gotten their hands on a bunch of AK-47s, and after burning a few of the locals alive, started firing into the school and hospital. "It was the last straw, I tell you," he ground out, pounding a fist onto the table. "I signed out a deuce-and-a-half and drove full tilt into them. I figured if I got shot up or blown up, well so be it. At least I was in control of *something* for a change."

His commander was waiting when he rolled that big sandy vehicle back into camp, looking more like Mr. Clean in uniform than a Marine officer. And he'd launched into an earsplitting harangue about the rules of engagement, the reasons for the military's pecking order, what could have happened if Dusty had injured a civilian during his tirade. "Three's the charm," he told the somber-faced Mitch. "I'd been warned twice. That time, instead of a warning, I got an ultimatum: sign the paperwork that put my discharge into action, or spend a couple of years in the brig."

"Well," Mitch said, "at least they weren't *dishonorable* discharge papers."

"No kidding." Ashamed as he was now, he knew it would have been a hundred times worse if he'd been forced to tell his newly widowed aunt she could write to him, in care of Leavenworth.

Suddenly, Dusty had had enough. On his feet, he said, "Much as I appreciate this, Father Confessor, I'm beat."

Mitch's pale eyes were sad, but he managed a grin. "You are forgiven, my son," he said, making a backwards sign of the Cross. "For your penance, you will say the Twenty-third Psalm. The Lord's Prayer. The Gettysburg Address, and the Preamble to the Constitution. And you will repeat these until you fall asleep."

"Beats counting sheep," Dusty said, grinning back. "Reminds me too much of the days when Mrs. Wilhelm used to make me fill her chalkboards with a thousand lines of 'I will not talk in class.'"

"Well, if your penance doesn't lull you to sleep, why not try scribbling a couple hundred 'Clear your mind and go to sleep' lines on the blackboard of your brain?"

Actually, that wasn't a half-bad idea. "I might just give that a shot, preacher."

The glowing blue digits of the alarm clock had read 11:37 when Dusty climbed into bed. It said 2:07 when the phone roused him from a deep, dreamless sleep. "This better be important," he grumbled into the mouthpiece.

And it was.

Bob Crutchfield, friend and 9-1-1 dispatcher explained how an arson fire took down three row homes in historic Pig Town. "Engine No. 8 boys worked for hours to get things under control, and it cost 'em. . . ."

Heart pounding with dread, he sat on the edge of the mattress and clenched his teeth. "How many?"

Crutchfield paused long enough to exhale a gravelly sigh. "Two gone, one critical over at Hopkins, couple more still coughin' up smoke back at the house."

"On my way," he said, and hung up.

It took all of five minutes to get dressed and look in on the boys, then he stopped in Mitch's room at the end of the hall. "Hey," he whispered, nudging the younger man's shoulder, "heads up . . . I'm heading over to the Number Ten."

Without opening his eyes, Mitch groaned. "How many?"

Dusty was halfway to the door when he said, "Two."

Levering himself up on one elbow. "Any names yet?"

"I'll stop at Hopkins on the way home from the station. Hopefully, to let you know the number's the same."

"Well," he said around a yawn, "don't worry."

"I won't. You're an old hand at holdin' down the fort." With that, Dusty closed Mitch's door and jogged down the stairs, praying with every step that Gonzo didn't have one of his goons out front, watching the place; last thing Mitch needed was a face-to-face confrontation with the gang leader. He was a lot of things, but diplomatic wasn't one of them, and the lack could literally get him or the boys hurt. Or worse.

He didn't turn on any lights. Why draw attention to the fact that he was leaving? And instead of firing up the Harley in the driveway as he would if the sun was up—and Gonzo hadn't paid him that little visit the other night—Dusty walked the bike to the end of the block. Only a few restaurants and shops down there, so no worries that some harried mom would pelt him with her bedroom slipper for waking her sleeping baby.

The ride between the shelter and the engine company took all of five minutes, and Dusty used every one to pray. He'd been with comrades who died in combat—a different kind of war, to be sure—and he understood the agony of loss. Still, that didn't mean he'd walk in there equipped with the words they needed to hear tonight.

The big door was up when he arrived, and the bright glow of the overhead lights silhouetted the guys out front, slouched in sagging, aluminum lawn chairs. Their still-damp hair was proof they'd tried to wash off the soot and stink, but the scent of smoke had worked its way into the gussets of their turnout gear, and clung to the boots and Nomex hoods, lined up along the far wall. He parked the bike and hung the helmet on the left handlebar as Max greeted him with a nod.

"Where are the rest of the guys?"

"In the head, or in bed," Max said. "Better question is, what brings you to this part of town?"

He shrugged. "Coffee pot's on the fritz. Thought maybe I could sneak a cup of Charlie's fancy imported brew."

"What!" Charlie grated. "Aw-right . . . which one of you good-for-nothin's told this long-haired, Harley-riding, tattooed hoodlum where I hide my special beans?"

Earl laughed. "Special beans," he echoed, drawing quote marks in the air. "Next thing, he'll announce he's dating Martha Stewart."

"I'm hurt, Earl. I told you that in the strictest confidence, and now you've gone and *spilled* the beans. I declare, you're a worse gossip than my grandma." Hands in the air, he sent Dusty a look that said, *See what I have to put up with!* Instead, he said, "You know where everything is. Help yourself."

Nodding, Dusty started inside as one of the guys hollered, "Tell 'em *Charlie* sent ya!"

Memory of the old Starkist Tuna commercial and the guys' laughter followed him into the kitchen, where he grabbed a mug from the bright-yellow pegboard above the sink. He could still hear them, hee-hawing as if everyone who'd climbed aboard the ladder truck had come back with it. Their tough, take-it-on-the-chin mentality was all part of the job, and they didn't much care for all the warm and fuzzy "share your feelings" stuff suggested by department trauma experts. Every man—to the last—was doing his level best to hold it together for the benefit of his brothers. At least, here at the station. Sooner or later, they'd get into their pickup trucks and SUVs and sports cars and go home, where there wouldn't be so many things and people to distract them from the agony of knowing they'd just lost two of their own.

It was up to Dusty, then, to listen for the right opening, because for all their bluster and blow, the ache of seeing their brothers die in the line of duty went deep. He'd let them know they could talk to him, whenever they were ready, because whether they wanted to admit it or not, the only way to ease the pain was to get the ugliness of this night out in the open.

If it took telling them what clamming up cost him, then he'd cluck like an old biddy until they got the point. And until they were ready, he'd pray with—and for—them.

When he went back outside, he carried his mug in one hand, the stainless carafe in the other. "Anybody up for a refill?"

"You can hit me again," said Aubrey.

Max held up his mug, and so did Charlie, but Earl shook his head. "So how'd you get wind of what happened over in Pig Town tonight?"

"Don't tell me," Charlie said as Dusty put the pot on a low table, "Bob called you."

Dusty shrugged. "Doesn't he always?"

"I know he means well," Aubrey said, "but sometimes, I wish he'd keep you out of stuff like this."

"Why?" He'd been through similar things with them before—not death, thank God—but enough that they should have expected he'd show up to offer support, lend an ear. . . . He took a sip from the mug. "You want to tell me about it," he began, staring at the silvery reflection of the fluorescent lights, rippling on the coffee's dark surface, "or should I start guessing?" He took another drink to give them time to mull that one over, and when no one spoke up, Dusty said, "How many spectators this time?"

"Just neighbors, mostly," Aubrey said. "Guys in PJs, and women in flowery robes." He frowned. "Not nearly as many as usual, and *that's* unusual."

"Anybody get any pictures of them?"

Max snorted. As the youngest—and the smallest in stature—Max felt he had to prove how rough and ready he was. "Seems Ansel Adams was busy with a shoot at the Inner Harbor. . . ."

"Pipe down, pipsqueak," Earl said. "You know what Parker's getting at. Besides, that guy's as dead as Keith and Tucker."

He didn't know which caused the alarm on their faces . . . hearing the men's names, or acknowledging that the arsonist might have stood between some beer-bellied guy in boxers and his curlers-in-her-hair missus, watching as the EMTs carried their fallen brothers into waiting ambos.

The story poured out like rain from a gully washer: from the start of the primary search, choking smoke all but blinded them. Its source? A turpentine-soaked pile of rags, burning on the attic floor. Hot water bottles, nailed to the rafters directly above it, each steadily dripping more of the accelerant through pinhole leaks. In one blink, they were on their feet, dealing with the low-rolling smoke swirling around their ankles. In the next, the flashover put them all on their backs. No time to wait for the pumper; those who could scrambled to their feet, shouting Rapid Intervention Crew instructions into their radios as Max grabbed Keith and Aubrey shouldered Tucker. Simon, dazed and badly burned, managed to stay with them until they hit fresh air, then collapsed in the street. Keith was pronounced DOS, but Simon fought like a champ all during the bumpy ambo ride to Hopkins, where the ER doc's quiet apology didn't make it easier to hear "DOA."

Was it West Virginia grit or firefighter determination that helped Aubrey get all that out without blubbering like a baby? Dusty knew this much: if he had possessed a sliver of the man's willpower back in Iraq, he might still be on active duty.

He'd been waiting for God to tell him what these good men needed to hear, and finally, he knew what to say. He drained his mug, then sat it on the table beside the carafe. "I, ah . . . would you guys mind doing me a favor?"

Charlie bent forward and leaned his elbows on his knees. Hands clasped in the space between, he grinned. "Spit it out, Easy Rider, and we'll let you know."

One hand up, traffic-cop style, he cleared his throat. "I read this poem a year or so ago. Don't know why, but I memorized it. So I—"

A round of grunts and groans circled the group. "Never would have figured you for the roses-are-red type," Max kidded.

"Yeah," Earl agreed. "I always wondered how you spent your time in that big house once those juvenile delinquents of yours are sawin' logs." A dry chuckle punctuated his comment. "Guess now we know."

Charlie aimed a forefinger, first at Max, then at Earl. "Knock it off you two, and let the man talk." Smirking, he added, "The sooner he gets this Wadsworth thing out of his system, the sooner we can hit the hay."

A chorus of snickers raised the man's eyebrows. "What?"

Earl said, "It's *Words*worth, you dunderhead."

And Aubrey wasted no time adding, "And they say West Virginians are uneducated!"

"Wordsworth, Wadsworth . . . potato, poe-tah-toe. The floor is yours, you hog-riding versifier."

It would have seemed inappropriate, reciting the poem on the heels of all that cheerfulness . . . if Dusty believed for a minute any of them meant a word of it. "Rumor has it this was written by the mother of a firefighter, but it said 'Author Unknown' at the bottom of it."

"You know what that means. . . ."

Dusty looked at Max, and waited for the explanation that was sure to follow.

"Whoever wrote it didn't know how to spell *anonymous*."

More grunts and groans, and then Dusty began:

> " 'He is the guy next door—a man's man with the
> memory of a little boy. He has never gotten over
> the excitement of engines and sirens and danger.

He is a guy like you and me with wants and
worries and unfulfilled dreams.
Yet he stands taller than most of us.
He is a fireman.
He puts it all on the line when the bell rings.
A fireman is at once the most fortunate and the
least fortunate of men.
He is a man who saves lives because he has seen
too much death.
He is a gentle man because he has seen the
awesome power of violence out of control.
He is responsive to a child's laughter because his
arms have held too many small bodies that will
never laugh again.
He is a man who appreciates the simple pleasures
of life—hot coffee held in numb, unbending
fingers—a warm bed for bone and muscle com-
pelled beyond feeling—the camaraderie of brave
men—the divine peace and selfless service of a job
well done in the name of all men.
He doesn't wear buttons or wave flags or shout
obscenities.
When he marches, it is to honor a fallen comrade.
He doesn't preach the brotherhood of man.
He lives it.'"

Somber silence shrouded the station house, and when Dusty got to his feet and clasped his hands, every head bowed. "Almighty God, bless these brave men with strength as they mourn the loss of their brothers." It took every bit of *Dusty's* strength not to ask the Almighty to help authorities find the less-than-human-being who'd caused destruction and misery and deliver an equally brutal punishment; what kind of shepherd would he be if he allowed the guys to witness the fury-born vengeance burning in his heart? "We ask that You watch over Simon, who still fights for his life. Heal him, Lord, and comfort his wife and children. Amen."

The men sat quietly, nodding and fighting tears. After a moment, Charlie cleared his throat. "I'd forgotten how good you are at that."

"But you're done now, right?" Earl wanted to know.

"Yeah, I'm done."

"Well amen to that!" Aubrey said. And then he blew his nose.

Dusty walked toward the Harley, and as he strapped on his helmet, Max stepped up beside him. "Next stop, Hopkins, right?"

"Right," he said, straddling the bike. "Anything you want me to tell Simon?"

A moment of somber silence shrouded the space, and Charlie filled it with "Yeah. Tell that lazy slob this won't get him off the hook."

Max hit the button to bring down the big door. "You got that right. It's still his turn to swab the head."

Whatever else they said as they stepped inside was drowned out by the Harley's engine.

And as he roared through the quiet streets, Dusty wondered what he'd say when he arrived at Johns Hopkins, and stood face to face with Simon's worried wife.

Except for the short list of ways he could dole out a honking dose of "eye for an eye" to the pig who'd started that fire, nothing came to mind. Maybe he wasn't cut out for this chaplain stuff, after all. Wasn't cut out to act as hospital liaison, either.

The hospital's iconic dome came into view, reminding Dusty that beneath it stood *Christus Consolidator,* the imposing eleven-foot Carrara marble statue of Jesus. A dozen times— maybe more—he'd seen visitors and patients, and even a white-coated doctor or two, rub the feet of Christ in much the same way as tourists buff the nose of the Bronze Boar in the hope it would bring them back to Florence one day.

Dusty didn't believe in luck. But he intended to stand at the feet of *Christus* and ask for help in reassuring Simon's family and, in the days to come, Keith and Tucker's loved ones, too. He'd pray that his boys would stand strong in the face of Gonzo's threats, and that whatever happened between him and Grace was in God's greater plan for both of them.

He had to laugh as he parked the bike, and he was still laughing when he got off the parking garage elevator, because only an idiot thinks he's in love after two—three hours at most—in a woman's company.

Well, nobody would ever confuse you for Einstein, he thought as the enormous revolving doors spit him into the main lobby. He stopped at the desk and asked where he could find them in the ICU, and after showing his I.D. to the guard, made his way to the dome.

If there was any truth to the report that God watches out for drunks and fools, he had a pretty good shot at catching the Big Guy's ear.

8

"Are you sure I can't help you get situated back there?" Grace asked as Gavin stretched his white-casted leg across her back seat.

"No, no, but thanks. This thing makes me slow and clumsy, but you're better off if I tuck myself in."

"*I'm* better off?"

"If I bang my bare-toed foot on something, you've got nothing to feel guilty about."

He wouldn't have to worry about banging his bare-toed foot, she thought, *if he'd let me do something to make him more comfortable.* But she knew better than to argue with the man.

When at last he'd buckled his seatbelt, she closed the rear door and slid into the driver's seat. "I don't know which was the bigger shock," she admitted, punching the address into her GPS, "hearing that you'd been in an accident—one serious enough to total your car—or finding out that your cousin was one of the firefighters who died in that horrible fire."

Gavin nodded. "Yeah, though it's unfair to call him cousin when the truth is, we were more like brothers." A shaky breath, and then, "It's sad, but now that Tuck's gone, there's no one to pass on the family name."

Until today, she'd only seen the upbeat, "there's a solution for every problem" Gavin. The hitch in his voice plucked a distant, almost forgotten chord in her own heart. The fact that he'd let down his guard and let her see and hear his grief told her that, although she really hadn't done anything to earn it, Gavin considered her someone who could be trusted with his very personal grief. Since his quiet admission, though, he'd grown quiet. Was he back there wondering what she might do with the information? He didn't know it yet, but he had no cause to worry. In time, she'd prove how well she could keep a secret. And until then, she'd simply be his friend.

The preprogrammed GPS voice, Stephanie, said, *"Please follow highlighted route."*

"Arrgh!" she said, giving it a flick. "I really need to dig out the instruction manual for that thing, because 'Australian Stephanie' drives me nuts. Especially when she mispronounces Baltimore. And Maryland. And just about every street I could name!"

When she heard his quiet chuckle, Grace felt it was safe to direct Gavin's thoughts back to something he'd said a moment ago. "I think you're forgetting someone."

"What?" He sat up a little straighter. "Who?"

"You, silly!"

"Grace. Give an old guy a break. I don't have a clue what you're talking about."

"When you said that with Tucker gone, there's no one left to carry on the Martin name." She paused. "Why can't *you* do it?"

That roused a chuckle. "Now *you're* being silly. With no kids or a wife—and none on the horizon—I'm afraid Tuck really was the end of the line."

She guessed Gavin to be in his early fifties. If Tony Randall and Anthony Quinn could father children in their seventies and eighties, why couldn't he? A broken heart? Guilt over one *he'd* broken? Some rare disorder that he didn't want to hand down to the next generation? "Didn't I read in his obituary," Grace said, "that he has two daughters?"

"Yeah. . . ."

She shrugged. "Maybe one of them will keep her maiden name when she marries. Maybe *both* of them will. There's no law, you know, requiring women to take their husbands' names when they say 'I do.'"

"Ah. So that's your plan is it? To keep your maiden name after *you* say 'I do'?"

"Now who's the silly one? I thought you knew . . . I'm never getting married."

"In point-four miles, turn right," Stephanie said, *"on Mary-land Ah-vin-you."*

"Never?"

"Nope."

"Pretty li'l thing like you? Besides, you know what the sages say. . . ."

When she didn't respond, Gavin said, "Never say never."

Grace fixed her attention on the GPS, and hoped that would help her sidestep his comment. She didn't much like admitting how much time she'd spent praying for the "white picket fence" life. She'd need a man of honor for that, and two broken hearts, a cousin and an uncle who seemed dedicated to stealing her blind left her with the belief that such a man didn't exist.

"Keep right. At ramp. . . ."

"So how are things over at Angel Acres these days?"

The man had an incredible knack for being able to read her mind. Grace wondered if he did it with everybody, or only with her. "I hate to admit it, but I'm so far behind that I can't decide if I lost my horse or found a rope."

Gavin slapped a palm over his eyes. "Aw, you can do better than that old saw, Gracie! It's old as the hills and twice as dusty!"

Dusty. Even that slight reminder of him sent a shiver down her spine. "Speaking of whom, tell me about him."

"Who?"

"Your cousin, Dusty. Youth counselor. Chaplain. Only God knows what other titles he holds. Well, God, and maybe you. . . ."

"His dad and mine were brothers, figuratively and literally. They were in the same band, see, and . . . and they died in the same bus crash."

Dusty had skimmed over that part of his history. Hearing even that small detail roused an ache inside her. Knowing her friend had suffered the same pain only intensified the feeling.

"You're probably too young to remember The Rangefinders," Gavin continued. "They'd been together for about five years when one of their singles—'Seasons'—went platinum. They were nominated for three Grammys that year. They were driving to the awards ceremony. It was dark. And raining. And the road to LA isn't exactly the straight and narrow."

He paused as Stephanie said, *"In three hundred feet, turn left."*

"A truck driver fell asleep at the wheel and swerved into their lane, and. . . ." He clapped his hands together. "And *bam!*"

It made Grace jump, dislodging the GPS. Stephanie was on the floor when she said, *"Arriving at address. On left."*

"I was nineteen, and Dusty had just turned ten. My mom wasn't in the band, like his was, so my life didn't change as much as his did."

"So sad," she whispered. "So very sad."

"His dad's brother took him in. Houseful of rowdy boys and dogs and cats, and if memory serves, a potbellied pig."

Gavin chuckled at the memory. "He was a tough kid. Adjusted pretty fast, and turned out well, all things considered, don't you think?"

"Yes, I do." Her heart ached for Gavin. For Dusty, too. Though she'd been older—nearly sixteen when her own parents died—she had a first-person understanding of what they'd gone through.

"Uncanny, isn't it?"

She parked alongside the curb at the church entrance. "What's uncanny?"

"How much the two of you have in common."

"There you go, being silly again." She held up a forefinger. "One similarity. *One,* Gavin. That's hardly ironic."

"*Uncanny* is the better word, by a long shot. Oh. And by the way, he'll be here today, probably with Mitch and the boys."

Now, why did hearing that Dusty might show up start her heart to pounding like a parade drum? Grace made a big deal of wrapping the cord around the GPS and stuffing it into the glove box. "Now then," she said, opening her car door, "stay put, okay, while I go inside and save us two seats near the door. I'll be right back."

He launched into his Humphrey Bogart imitation. "Yer a schweetheart," he said, winking. "Why, if I wasn't schuch an old fuddy-duddy, I'd marry you, myshelf."

"If you wait until I'm old and suffering from dementia," she said, winking back, "I might just say yes." And she closed the door before he had a chance to respond.

The instant her high-heeled shoes hit the blood-red carpet, she saw that Dusty and his boys had nearly filled the pew, second from the back. He was whispering something to Axel, who sat on his left, when Grace stepped up beside him. "You clean up well," she said.

"Hey, Grace," he said. "Didn't expect to see you here today."
He stood in the aisle. "You didn't get a chance to meet Mitch
the other night." Dusty invited the younger man to join them.

"I've heard a lot about you," she said when he extended a
hand.

Grinning, he countered with, "Not as much as I've heard
about *you,* I'll bet."

"All good things," Dusty interjected, hand raised in the Boy
Scout salute. Then he smiled, sending her heart into overdrive.
Again. *Get a grip,* she thought. "I'm here mostly as Gavin's
chauffeur. He had an accident. Totaled the convertible and
broke his leg."

"No way!" Dusty stood, looked past her toward the door.
"Where is he?"

"I came in to save two seats, so he wouldn't have to walk too
far. He's right outside."

"You parked in a handicap zone?" Mitch rolled his eyes.
"With a hundred cops milling around!"

"Only for a minute," she said, laughing. "Surely when they
see that gigantic cast. . . ."

Dusty took her elbow and eased her to the door. "No point
taking chances. While you're moving your car, I'll get him
situated."

Ten minutes later, her elbow was still buzzing from the
warmth of his gentle touch as she and Gavin sat side by side,
watching Dusty slide the strap of an acoustical guitar over his
shoulder. He tapped the microphone—*thump-thump*—then
announced that the wives of the fallen men had requested two
songs. He'd only sing one verse from each, he promised, to
leave enough time for friends and family who wanted to say a
few words. The strings went *plink* when he removed the pick
from under the tuning keys. "If you know the words, I'm sure
Tucker would want you to sing along."

And then he strummed, filling the church with mellow, melodious tones.

Gavin leaned in to whisper, "Did I tell you that he inherited his parents' musical abilities?"

No, she started to say, but Dusty's voice, soft and low, drifted all through the church, and made the words stick in her throat.

"Let us look beyond the grave," he sang, "for death is not the end. Death is but the door to God for our departed friends. Lord be with us who remain for our brief stay. Bless and comfort us who mourn, and wipe our tears away. . . ."

If she'd ever heard a more beautiful sound, Grace didn't know where. She rooted around in her purse in search of a tissue. By the time she found one, buried under her wallet and cell phone and a handful of ancient Hall's lozenges, he'd finished that hymn and started the next one.

It was a song she'd harmonized to, years ago, when she joined the youth choir at her grandmother's church. Written by Ray Dahrouge and Mickey Holiday, it had always been one of her favorites. But just because she was descended from angels didn't mean she could sing like one. The group leader *said* the right things: "I love your enthusiasm!" and "Your joy is contagious!" But he always made sure to put her as far from the microphone as possible.

Despite the bittersweet memory, Grace closed her eyes and hummed, and soon the music moved her so much that she was swaying and singing—quietly—but *singing!* "One day I was wondering, what's it all about? Life is full of heartbreak, restlessness, and doubt. Then a gentle Stranger whispered words of love; pointed me to heaven, and wrote my name above. Now I know where I'm goin', and who I'm gonna see; I have a friend named Jesus, waiting there for me."

When she opened her eyes, Dusty sent her such a sad smile that she could hardly keep from racing to the front of the church and wrap him in a comforting hug.

"I'll make a deal with you," Gavin said, breaking into her thoughts.

"A deal? What kind of deal?"

"I promise never to do another Bogart imitation if you promise never to sing that loudly again."

The comment struck her so funny that it was all she could do to prevent a giggle fit, just like the ones that attacked her and Leslie, right in the middle of Sunday services. It seemed the harder they tried to stifle their laughter, the longer it lasted. Oh, how she missed that sweet, big-hearted, crazy girl!

One after the other, firefighters and cops, EMTs, and SAR members told Tucker stories. And most of them, Grace knew, would be right back here tomorrow, to do it all again for Keith's funeral.

Next, family and friends shared personal memories. "What about you?" Grace asked Gavin. "Are you going to say a few words?"

He rapped quietly on his cast and shook his head. "Later," he said, "at the grave." A deep furrow formed between his eyebrows. "If I can hold it together long enough to choke out a couple of words. Maybe."

Nodding, she gave his hand an affectionate pat as Dusty returned to the pulpit, gave cursory directions to the memorial park, and turned off the mike.

If the time between service and cemetery seemed like a blur to Grace, who'd never even met Keith or Tucker, how much more surreal did it feel to their wives and children?

A gust of wind skittered across the green carpet and rippled the flag-draped coffin, blowing enough grit to *ping* the big brass bell that hung from an arched support near the pulpit.

If not for the diligence of Dusty's boys, Old Glory might have floated away. Standing every bit as tall as the color guard and looking older than their years, each tucked one hand behind his back, and rested the other protectively on the casket, determined to prevent a repeat of nature's folly. They remained in place as pipers played "Amazing Grace" and fellow firefighters, most wearing dress uniforms, filed slowly, reverently by.

"Any last words?" Dusty asked.

Gavin held up one hand. His voice trembled as looked at those gathered and said, "Tuck and I go way back, and I love him like a brother. . . ."

Head down, he paused. At a time like that, every second seems like a minute. Grace slid a half step closer, until shoulders touched, praying that the insignificant action would reassure him—he could lean on her if he wanted to.

He must have read her loud and clear, because he gave her hand a squeeze. "Love you, too, kiddo," he ground out. "Not like a brother, of course, 'cause, well look at you."

"Happy to!" said a deep voice from the back.

A quiet ripple of laughter filled the green tent, and when it faded, Gavin said, "Being that I'm ten years older than Tuck, we didn't have much in common—except for fishing. I guess we spent a couple hundred hours over the years, waiting for our rod tips to bend. And when we weren't complaining about sunburn and mosquitoes and the Orioles' lousy coaching staff, Tuck talked about becoming a firefighter. Never changed his mind, like some boys do. Not once. Even for a minute."

He used the tip of one crutch as a pointer, directing attention to the coffin, then cleared his throat. "This past Memorial Day, Tuck and I were out on the Chesapeake, and he caught the biggest, fattest rockfish either of us had ever seen. He threw it back. 'Are you nuts?' I asked. 'It's regulation . . . you can keep it!' And Tuck told me I didn't get it—that when a man already has the perfect life, he'd be a fool to rock the boat."

Gavin looked at Tate and the girls. "He was right. I *didn't* get it. But I get it now, and I'm jealous. Because unlike most of us here, Tuck was content with his life, thanks to you and those kids . . ." Now his eyes met those of the men who'd worked with him, day and night, "and firefighting." On the heels of a shaky sigh, he concluded with "I sure am gonna miss that guy."

Dusty broke the somber silence with, "Tuck once shared with me that when he couldn't sleep after a hard day, reciting the Twenty-third Psalm never failed to relax him and help him fall asleep." He opened his beat-up Bible and began reading the psalm. One by one, others joined in, until at the end, they all recited together, "Surely goodness and mercy will follow me all the days of my life; and I will dwell in the house of the LORD, forever. Amen."

The firefighters who'd served double duty as pallbearers and honor guard stood at attention and saluted. They removed the flag and carefully folded it, then presented it to Tate. Tuck's daughters hugged their mom—and the red, white, and blue triangle now clutched to her chest.

As the color guard snapped off a white-gloved salute, Charlie took a step forward, the crumpled sheet of paper he held fluttering in his trembling hands. "I'm not much of a talker, but—"

"Says the man who never shuts up!" came a voice from somewhere behind him.

Snickers, and a few whoops and whistles, made him smile. "Some of you would do well to remember that I don't need near as much sleep as you do. . . ."

An unidentified voice said, "Uh-oh, we're in for it now" while the first man said, "You're the stuff nightmares are made of, Murphy!"

. The wheeled bell platform was rolled into place, bringing the moment of much-needed merriment to a close.

"I'm not much of a public speaker," Charlie said again, "but I stayed up half the night, thinking about what I'd say to those of you who never attended a firefighter's funeral before, so that when you go home today, you'll go with a better understanding of *why* we do what we do."

With a wave of his hand, he brought attention to the men and women, standing at attention among the civilians in attendance. "They're all decked out in their Class A dress uniforms," he said, "as a show of respect for the brave man who gave his life so someone else could live. Most of you," he added, "put on *your* Sunday best today for the same reason. The pipers, the flag, the clothing, the Maltese cross, the choice of red for fire engines . . . all symbols of honor."

Max had volunteered to ring the bell, and he grasped the mallet as the honor guard stood and prepared to engage the mechanism that would take Tucker's casket on its slow descent into the grave. When all were ready, Charlie said, "But probably none is more moving than the tolling of the bell.

"A bell rings at the start of every shift, and when a fire breaks out somewhere, another summons us to duty. When the fire is out, a bell signals 'duty completed.' So now . . . three bells, the first to symbolize our brother's call to duty. . . ."

Max lifted his arm and brought the hammer down, and the bell rang the first haunting note.

Amid its echo, Charlie said, ". . . the second, to honor his sacrifice. . . ."

Another clang rang out as Charlie's voice dropped to a near whisper:

". . . and a third, to symbolize his final return to quarters."

The note hung in the air for a moment, then rolled across the manicured lawn, where, at the same moment as the coffin disappeared into the hole, it was silenced by the waiting treetops.

Gavin said, "Gone, but not forgotten."

And Dusty nodded. "He's gone home."

9

*F*or the first time that day, Tucker's wife let go of her teary-eyed daughters' hands. Together they stood, approached the grave, and plucked a rose from a vase beside it. "My coworkers and neighbors," Tate said, clutching the flower to her chest, "are back at the house, cooking and baking like fiends." She faltered, but only for a moment. "If you don't join us, the girls and I will be eating casseroles and Swedish meatballs for months!"

A year or so ago, a rosy-cheeked student named Tate sat front-row center in Grace's English classroom. Curiosity inspired a bit of research, which taught her the meaning of the girl's unusual name: *Cheerful.* A fitting name, as it turned out, and judging by the serene expression on her face, it fit Tucker's wife even better.

"I hate to impose after everything you've already done, but do you mind spending a few minutes over there?" Gavin asked. "We don't have to stay long. . . ."

"I don't mind a bit." And she didn't. "We'll stay as long as you like."

"Thanks, Grace. You're a good friend."

During the silent drive from the cemetery to Tucker and Tate's house, she wondered if Gavin was replaying the morning's events in his mind, too. Of all the funerals she'd attended, three were memorable: Her parents', her grandfather's, then her grandmother's. She'd never forget this one, either. And though it shamed her to admit it, Grace was thankful that she wouldn't be required to attend Keith's services tomorrow.

All this reminiscing brought her back to September 2001, when—

"What's going through that mind of yours?" Gavin wanted to know.

"Oh, nothing."

"Baloney. Which reminds me. I'm starving. What's that goofy GPS of yours say about how long before we're at Tucker's house?"

"Unless 'Stephanie' is mistaken, we'll be there in fifteen minutes."

"Good. Because I'm about to start gnawing on my crutches. Now spit it out, girl, before I poke you with one of them."

"That wouldn't be wise," she said, "considering you're wholly dependent on me today. And then there's the fact that I'm behind the wheel. On one of the most dangerous inter-states in the country."

"Good point. How about this for a threat, then: if you don't tell me what's on your mind, I'll tell Dusty that in a weak moment, you confessed to me that you're head over heels in love with him."

Grace gasped. "You wouldn't." *What would Gavin say if he knew how close he was to the truth?*

"I might, and then again. . . ."

She laughed, and waited for him to explain.

"Think of it this way . . . you'll either clear your mind of something that's obviously bugging you, big time, or I'll spare you the trouble of figuring out how to tell that motorcycle-riding preacher cousin of mine that you're crazy about him."

"I wish you'd told me that you suffered head trauma in that accident. . . ."

He leaned forward as far as the seatbelt would allow. "Bet you didn't know I'm like a nosy old woman, did you?"

"No, but I should have known. On the first day of Psych 101, my professor told the class two things. First, that crazy people marry crazy people, and they have crazy kids who grow up and marry crazy people."

"Astute. I'd like to meet that guy. I think. What was the second thing?"

"That you can define anyone involved with the psychiatric profession in two words: Nosy and nuts."

"Ha. You're a riot. But if you think that little trick distracted me, you have another think coming." He made a rolling motion with his hand. "You should know that I'm at least as persistent as I am nosy. . . ."

Grace sighed. She hadn't talked about Leslie—to anyone—ever. Maybe it would be therapeutic, sharing the story with Gavin.

"I was thinking about Leslie," she began, "my best friend in all the world."

"Before me, you mean."

Snickering, Grace said, "Yes. Before you. I met her in kindergarten."

She told him how they were together, nearly every day, right up until they were sixteen. "That's when my parents died," she said, "and I went to live with my grandparents."

"Ahh, the infamous angels, who made you the proprietress of Angel Acres. . . ."

Yes, she thought, *the generous act that turned every male in her family into greedy—*

"So anyway," she continued, "we managed to stay in touch, and Leslie spent the next two summers at Angel Acres. She liked it so well that when it was time to enroll in college, she chose the University of Maryland. We shared a room, and a car, and a boyfriend or two before graduation."

That's when Grace took a job teaching English and Art in a Howard County middle school, and Leslie's degree sent her to New York, where she spent her days, wheeling and dealing with the Wall Street crowd. "And then 9/11 happened. . . ."

More than a year had passed, she told him, since they'd seen one another. They hadn't even had time for a phone call in more than a month. "I'd taken that day off to nurse a stomach virus. While I was in the bathroom, my principal called and told me to turn on the TV. By then, both planes had hit the Towers, and the first person I thought of was Leslie. My hands were shaking so hard from trying to remember which floor she worked on that I misdialed her cell number three times before I got through to her."

Grace took the exit to Route 100, remembering how at first, she thought she'd dialed a fourth time. "I didn't recognize her voice. She was scared. And crying. Talking nonsense. Saying how sorry she was."

"For what?"

"I'd loaned her a black dress for her initial interview with the firm. She swore up and down it brought her luck. Couple of times, she made plans to visit, using the excuse that she needed to return it. But things came up, so she started promising to box it up and mail it to me. And that day . . . that day she was wearing the dress. 'I'm up for a promotion,' she told me; 'figured it couldn't hurt to wear my lucky dress.' That's when she apologized. For not returning the dress. Said she was wearing my red scarf, and that she was sorry she hadn't returned that, either."

"Gracie," Gavin said, "pull over. There," he pointed. "Long Gate Shopping Center. Right now. And I'm not kidding."

She did. And until the car stopped, she hadn't realized that she'd been crying.

He handed a starched white hanky over the seat. "I hope you weren't on the line with her when . . . at the end."

"No. No I wasn't."

"Well, thank God for *that*."

"Half a second after she apologized about the dress, we were disconnected. I tried and tried, but never got through to her again. And then . . . and then I sat on the floor in front of the TV. I don't even know how *long* I sat there. My stomach went crazy again, and when I got back from the bathroom that time, I saw her. The camera zeroed in on a window on one of the upper floors. There was black smoke. Flames shooting out. A woman, standing on a beam or something. She was wearing a black dress. And a red scarf."

"Leslie. . . ."

Grace nodded. "The wind picked up her bright red scarf and carried it away. Then she blessed herself, held out her arms, and jumped."

Gavin reached up and squeezed her shoulder, and she lay her hand on top of his.

"So," she said, "bet you're *really* ready to get into that buffet line now, aren't you?"

"I was wrong. When I said you and Dusty have one thing in common. Turns out, you have two things."

She used the hanky to blot her teary eyes, and when she saw that her mascara had smudged it, Grace said, "If this won't come out in the wash, I'll buy you a new one."

"Make that three things." He counted on his fingers. "You lost your parents in an accident, you're both resilient, and neither of you wants to feel beholden to anyone else."

While she was trying to think of a snappy comeback, he added, "I'm wrong. Four things. He's dedicated to kids, and so are you." He smacked his forehead. "*Five* things! He's nuts about you, and you feel the same way about him."

"I hope this doesn't sound ungrateful coming on the heels of exposing you to my blubberfest, but *you're* the nut. Dusty and I barely know one another!"

He sat back. "You seem fit to drive now. You may go."

Grace cranked up the engine, and, blending into traffic, said, "Thanks, Gavin, for letting me get all that off my chest. It might interest you to know that you're the first—and only—person I've ever shared that with." She'd left out the part about how, for months, she nursed a grudge against Leslie; if the girl hadn't been so all-fired determined to become a big name in finance and banking, she wouldn't have been in New York on that awful day. Or that for months after that, Grace asked herself how bad it was up there on the 95th floor that Leslie preferred leaping to her death to whatever was on the other side of that window.

"I'm honored."

"You're also the only person I'll *ever* share it with." Hopefully, he'd take the hint, and keep the long, sad story to himself.

"I have one thing to say, and then you have my word, I'll never mention it again."

Grace tensed. "No announcement worth hearing ever started like that. . . ."

He waved her comment away. "You'd be good for one another."

Dusty and me, you mean. . . .

"That's my opinion, anyway. And you know what they say about those."

She didn't, but Grace had a feeling Gavin was about to enlighten her.

"'Opinions are like armpits . . . everybody has a couple, and mostly they stink.'"

10

Grace," Dusty called from across the room, waving as she and Gavin walked in. "When you get that crippled cousin of mine settled," he said, "join us. There's someone I'd like you to meet."

"Cripple?" Gavin echoed. "Is your ponytail so tight that's it's affecting your thinking? Who says 'cripple' these days?"

But Dusty hadn't heard him, because he'd gone back to talking with the pretty redhead beside him. "You're taking notes, I hope," he said as Grace helped get him into the recliner.

"I'm not following. . . ."

"If that's his idea of an apology, he'll make a terrible husband."

A nervous giggle popped out. "Good grief. Let's not put the cart before the horse, shall we?" She leaned his crutches in the corner and glanced at the buffet table. "So what are you in the mood for? Fried chicken? Lasagna? Swedish meatballs? I think I even see roast beef over there."

"Yes," he said, smirking.

"Well I'd better round up a TV tray or something first, or I pity that chair. And the carpet under it."

"Hmpf. With your talent for knowing what a man needs, maybe you *could* make it work with that buffoon." He snickered. "I was just wondering if I'd leave here with more food in my belly . . . or in my lap."

She glanced around the room. "Good grief, Gavin . . . give it a rest, will you? What would Dusty think if he heard you say—"

"Heard him say what?"

Dusty. . . .

Heart thudding, her cheeks went hot and her palms grew clammy. How much *had* he heard? "Oh. Hi. I thought you were way over there. Didn't know you were right behind me." She was rambling, and knew it, and yet the words kept tumbling from her mouth. "Good thing I didn't back up. I'd have tromped all over your shiny shoes. Or turn around too fast, and elbow you in the stomach." *Shut up, Grace. Just. Shut. Up!*

"So what got to you? The tolling of the bells, or Tate and the girls, taking roses from the bouquet?"

"What . . . ?"

"You've been crying."

"Oh. That." Memory of her self-pity party flashed in her mind. *Should have kept your big mouth shut, Grace.* "It's allergies, mostly." The plan had been to get Gavin settled, then find a bathroom and do her best to repair the damage her self-pity party had done to her makeup. But then Dusty had called her name and completely distracted her. She smiled, and like her rapid-fire dialog, Grace had a feeling there was too much of *it*, too. "Soon as I get your crippled old cousin something to eat, I'll—"

"Hey," Gavin broke in. "I'm lame, not deaf."

Grace patted his hand. "Sorry. No offense intended."

"Aw, don't fall for his sensitive act. He's got a shell like a turtle." And before Gavin could respond, he said, "I'd like you to meet Honor Mackenzie, best search and rescue dog trainer this side of the Mississippi. She's here from New York."

A man Grace hadn't met joined the group. "She was up there training SAR personnel to work with rescue dogs," he said, kissing Honor's cheek. "Broke my heart when she left me to advance her already advanced career."

Was it Grace's imagination? Or did she hear a tinge of sarcasm in the man's statement?

Honor said, "But I came back. . . ."

"To *stay?*" Dusty asked.

"To stay."

"For good, I hope."

"For*ever*," they said together.

Even Grace, who'd never met them before, could see how in love they were. Had career aspirations really been the thing that put so many miles between them, or had other issues caused the separation?

"And this is Matt Phillips," Dusty said.

"He's a reporter," Gavin said, "for *The Baltimore Sun.*"

"Not the Pulitzer-winning—"

Smirking, Matt stuck out his hand. "You may kiss my ring."

"You aren't wearing a ring, you idiot." Gavin laughed. "And you're keeping Grace from fetching my food." He knocked on his cast. "I'd do it myself, but. . . ." He shrugged.

"I'll go with you," Honor said. "I promised to fix Mr. Pulitzer, here, a plate."

As they made their way down the table, Grace said, "Were you part of the search for Missy Logan a few weeks ago?"

Honor stopped loading Matt's plate. "I almost didn't recognize you without your sweatshirt and sneakers on. You're to be commended, girl, for keeping up with Daddy Longlegs over there." She grabbed a biscuit and broke it in half. "He doesn't make it easy on first-timers," she said, slathering it with butter, "and just between you and me, I think it's on purpose."

Grace remembered all too well how she'd almost had to run to keep up with him. She also remembered that he hadn't said a word about that day, since. . . . "Probably just his way of separating the wheat from the chaff," she said. "I don't suppose you guys would get much done if every Tom, Dick, and Harry was allowed to tag along on missions."

"I don't know about those three," Honor said, slathering gravy over Matt's roast beef and potatoes, "but *you* surely held your own."

Oh, right, Grace thought. Obviously, Honor hadn't been around when she nearly fainted dead away after her first glimpse of Missy's body. Even now, the image alone was enough to make her wince. "Did they ever find the guy who did that to her?"

"Not that I've heard."

Tucker's wife walked up, rested a hand on Honor's shoulder. "Sweetie," she said, bussing her cheek, "I'm so glad you could make it."

"Sorry I missed the service. My train got stalled on the tracks, someplace outside of New Jersey." She raised Matt's plate slightly. "I'd hug you, but you know me . . . I'd dribble gravy on your shoes or get mashed potatoes in your hair." Then she glanced at Grace. "Have you two met?"

Grace shook her head. "Not officially. It's a pleasure, though I wish it could have been under different circumstances."

Tate sighed. "Me, too. But I have the comfort of knowing Tuck is in Firefighter Heaven." She grinned. "Probably giving the angels fits . . . reminding them to change the batteries in their smoke alarms." Her smile faded a bit when she asked Honor if she planned to attend Keith's services in the morning.

"Absolutely. And you?"

"Yes. Hannah isn't handling Keith's death well. Not well at all, I'm afraid."

"Not every woman is cut out to be a firefighter's wife. I'd heard through the grapevine that she'd been nagging Keith to quit."

"I heard that, too." Tate shook her head. "Tucker came home one night last week, talking about how upset Keith was that she'd given him until the end of the month to resign . . . or find a good divorce attorney."

"Oh, wow. That's rough."

Because Keith's widow is probably wondering if her ultimatum had distracted him enough to play a role in his death.

Honor sighed. "Tuck was lucky to have you. Real lucky."

Tate's eyes shimmered with unshed tears, but she was smiling when she said, "No, I'm the lucky one." Then she winked. "Not every woman gets to sleep with a real live hero!" She squeezed Grace's hand. "But listen to us, chattering like a couple of chipmunks without including you. You must think we're horribly rude!"

"Not at all," Grace admitted. "It gave me time to load up Gavin's plate." She glanced in his direction. "Guess I'd better get over there before he sends someone else to do it, and he's stuck with two dinners."

"Oh, you don't have to worry about him," Tate said. "Under that cast is a hollow leg."

A child's voice rang out. "Mo-o-om. . . ."

"Uh-oh . . . I recognize that whine . . . it's one of my girls. Better see what's up. Will you be at Keith's services tomorrow, Grace?"

"No, I never had the pleasure of meeting him, so I wouldn't want to intrude."

"Well, if I don't see you again before you leave with Stumpy over there," she teased, using her chin to point toward Gavin, "it was nice meeting you. It's good to see Dusty so happy, so thank you for that. I hope you'll use your influence to get him over here a little more often!"

When she was out of earshot, Honor said, "I thought it was just me." She looked at Dusty. "You must be some kinda special, girl, 'cause Tate's right. I've never seen him look happier."

Grace looked at Dusty, too, and he *did* look happy. But what could she have possibly had to do with it?

"I can't remember *ever* seeing him look at a woman the way he looks at you." Honor laughed. "That's saying a mouthful, because back in the day, Dusty looked at a *lot* of women!"

Her face was probably glowing like Rudolph's nose. And she wondered if Honor could hear her heart, knocking against her ribs.

"Look, I know this isn't any of my business, but. . .." Honor glanced at Matt, " . . . but he's the best thing that ever happened to me, and I came *this* close to losing him. In fact, I'm not sure yet that I *haven't* lost him, after everything I put him through. But months of long distance therapy with Dusty helped me come to terms with the *real* reasons I ran away, and see that if I don't at least try to make things right with Matt, I'll spend the rest of my life regretting it." Now she looked at Grace. "Whatever demons you're struggling with, Grace, trust me—fight them off. He's worth it."

Grace looked at Dusty, who for some crazy reason, had assumed the Karate Kid's one-legged stance while two little boys, each toting a full plate, ran circles around him. One little guy crashed into the other, and they both fell into Dusty, who landed on his back. For a moment, it seemed that someone had hit a Pause button, because everyone froze as a hush fell over the room.

The guilty-faced young offenders darted into the kitchen as Grace unceremoniously handed Gavin his food. "Hey," he groused, "you expect me to eat with my *fingers?*"

"I'll be right back with your silverware," she said, kneeling beside Dusty. "O my goodness," she said, plucking salad bits from his hair and roast beef from his chest, "are you hurt?"

He levered himself onto one elbow and scraped a fingerful of mashed potatoes from his cheek. "Only my ego," he said, popping it into his mouth.

Grace peeled a slice of beef from his tie. "I hope it isn't ruined."

"If you find a fork down there," Gavin called from his chair, "I could sure use one. . . ."

Two of Dusty's boys stepped up. "Whoa, man," Montel said, "you look good enough to eat."

Laughter exploded around the room as Grace got to her feet. "You've got gravy on your knees," he said, then stood beside her. Dusty reached across the small space that separated them and ran his fingers through her hair. It wasn't until he held up a tomato seed that she realized the splash had hit her, too.

At the church earlier, a fit of giggles had threatened to disrupt the ceremony. Now, as he wiped it on his already-soiled shirt, she felt the same urge and did nothing to stifle it. Nervous laughter, induced by Honor's speech? Or relief at being so near him?

He gathered her close and collapsed onto a chair, bringing her with him, then pressed his palms to her cheeks and silenced her with those oh-so-blue eyes. Thankfully, everyone else had gone back to talking and laughing and eating, and weren't paying any attention to them. At least, Grace hoped that was the case, because unless she was mistaken, Dusty was about to kiss her. She closed her eyes, partly because she didn't want that biscuit crumb on his upper lip to start the giggling up again, and partly to spare herself some major disappointment . . . in case she was wrong.

She was not.

A moment later, when she opened her eyes, he was smiling at her.

"Montel was right," she said. "You *do* taste pretty good."

"Y'think?"

Instead of answering, she kissed him again.

11

*Y*ou're lucky she didn't slug you," said Trevor.

Jack, the youngest Last Chance kid, held his stomach. "I thought I was gonna puke."

Dom nodded. "Or go blind."

"Yeah. Like, *dude*, what were you *thinking*, layin' one on her like that? At a funeral dinner. With a hundred people in the room!"

Montel gave Nestor a playful shove. "Aw, man, you can say that again."

"It was a learning experience, I tell you," Axel put in.

"Learning experience," Tony echoed. "What did you learn, pipsqueak?"

Axel ran a hand over tight reddish-blond cornrows. "Well, for one thing, I learned that white girls turn red as Santa's suit when they get caught kissin'."

"What else did you learn?" Jack wanted to know.

Aiming a smirk at the rearview mirror, he said, "That white *boys* turn as red as Santa's suit when they get caught kissin', too."

The van's interior pulsed with youthful laughter.

Dusty took their ribbing in good-natured stride. He had no one but himself to blame, after all, because the honest answer to Nestor's question was, he *hadn't* been thinking. One minute, he'd been flat on his back under a blanket of food, and the next, she was in his lap, looking all cute and contrite, and before he knew it. . . .

Groaning inwardly, he steered the van into the narrow driveway beside the house, and it came to a creaking, jerking halt. If he thought it would do a bit of good, he'd pop for a lube job, an alignment, new tires. But few things annoyed him more than throwing good money down a rat hole, and that's exactly what he'd be doing if he invested another dime in the old clunker.

He wondered if Mitch had made any headway at today's meeting with Reverend Jackson and his budget committee. The Last Chance for Deliverance church parishioners had given the word *generous* a whole new meaning, and without their financial support, the Last Chance House for Homeless Boys would never have been possible. The elders had been pleased with what he'd accomplished with the kids, but thanks to Gonzo and his bunch, money was tight.

Was it coincidence that the gang leader knew to keep the price of replacing windows and removing graffiti lower than the insurance deductible? Dusty didn't believe in coincidence any more than he believed in luck.

"Look at him," Guillermo whispered into a cupped hand, "all lost in his thoughts. . . ." He elbowed Billy, who said, "What you daydreaming about, Dusty . . . your pretty little *girlfriend?*"

Dusty blew a stream of air through his teeth, and grinned as he shook his head. "You have a doctor's appointment first thing in the morning," he said to Axel.

"You think the cast will come off tomorrow?"

"I sure hope so." Jack pinched his nose. "Smells like toe cheese under there."

The kids headed straight for the kitchen, where they made sandwiches and poured lemonade to devour while watching *The Cowboys* for the umpteenth time. They'd memorized every line, trying their best to say "We're burnin' daylight!" or "Big mouth don't make a big man" half a tick in time before John Wayne's character said it. More often than not, it was Guillermo who won the contest . . . and paid for it with a hearty round of good-natured ribbing as they mocked his Spanish accent. When the movie ended, they were quick to carry their drink cups and paper plates into the kitchen, and in no time, the music of their youthful snores floated down the stairs.

Alone for the first time in days, Dusty's thoughts turned to Grace. He replayed that scene in Tate's living room half a dozen times, mostly because in the middle of thinking about that kiss, he didn't have to think about where he'd get the money for a new van, or how he'd protect the kids from Gonzo. *A man could go far with a woman like that in his corner. . . .*

But it was selfish and self-centered to even consider taking their friendship to the next level, because she deserved better than the likes of a has-been Marine whose only experience with commitment came by way of a broken-down old house filled with a passel of troubled teens.

Well, that wasn't entirely true. Back in his cop days, he'd had *one* longer-than-a-weekend relationship, but he and Randi had been way too messed up to define what they'd shared as a committed relationship.

If he had any decency left, he'd figure out how to put some distance between himself and Grace, instead of trying to find a good excuse to see her again.

And so it went, all through the night. When the alarm woke him at 5:30, he resisted the temptation to throw it across the room. He dragged himself to the kitchen, where he rummaged in the fridge. No eggs. No milk. No bread. "Looks like the kids will have to make do with instant oatmeal," he muttered, spreading bowls, napkins, and spoons onto the table with the dexterity of a Vegas dealer.

The boys grumped and groaned when they saw the assortment of brown envelopes on the table. "What, gruel? *Again?*" Tony complained. "I feel like Oliver Twist."

But he ate the stuff, and so did the other boys. Dusty had a feeling their compliance was born of bad memories, of too many mornings when swallowing wads of paper was the only way to quiet their growling bellies.

He started a list and left it on the table, along with a note asking Mitch to make the grocery store run. The assistant was the only other person who knew where he'd stored the jar of cash donations, delivered weekly from what little was gathered during the second collection of Sunday services. God willing, it would be enough to cover everything on the list.

He made another list, this one citing household and yard chores, and left Montel, the oldest Last Chance resident, in charge. "Ready?" he said to Axel.

"Ready as I'll ever be, I reckon."

No one knew much about young Axel, except that after his ironworker dad was sentenced to two life terms at West Virginia's Mount Olive Correctional Center for killing his wife and her lover, the boy didn't figure he had much of a future in Gauley Bridge. So he squeezed himself between the rolls of sod stacked six-high on a Baltimore-bound flatbed truck and never looked back. When the authorities found the scrawny, freckle-faced and red-haired boy, he and a mangy dog were wrestling over a half-eaten chicken thigh . . . and Axel still wore the scars of victory across the left side of his mostly freckled face.

He buckled his seatbelt, then abruptly slapped the seat. "Meant to grab me a sack, and I clean forgot."

Dusty turned the key in the ignition, wincing in anticipation of the backfire. "A sack," he echoed. "For what?"

"So's I can save this here hunk of plaster. Be a shame to chuck it, what with all my friends' names scribbled all over it."

Dusty reached over and tousled his hair. "I'm sure somebody at Dr. Milton's office has a bag of some kind."

Nodding, Axel stared through the windshield. "Sorry about yesterday, Dusty."

"Uh-oh. What sort of mischief have you gotten into this time?"

A lopsided grin exposed wide-spaced teeth. "I gave my word when I fell off the garage roof and busted my arm that I wouldn't be no more trouble to you, and I meant it. Why, I doubt there's a boy at Last Chance who's kept his nose as clean as I have."

"Then what's the apology all about?"

"All that teasing, about you kissin' the schoolteacher. Didn't feel right, getting involved in all that, but. . . ." He shrugged. ". . . reckon I was more troubled about what the guys would think if I *didn't*."

Not knowing how to respond to that, Dusty only nodded.

"She's right pretty, and to put it plain, I can't say I blame you for kissin' on her. Besides," he said, nose crinkling as he poked a finger under the cast, "you'd *better* do something about your marital status before you're too old to get down on one knee."

Laughing, Dusty said, "I don't remember seeing 'Cupid' written on your file."

"I guess I had that comin' for being part of that nonsense yesterday, but still and all. . . ."

He paused. Pointed at the sign at the entrance to the ortho-pedist's office. And Dusty would have sworn he was about to say they'd made good time. But he picked up right where he'd left off. ". . . but still and all, what I said is the truth. And if you had the sense God gave a turkey, you'd put a ring on her finger."

It surprised him a bit that a boy who'd witnessed infidel-ity at its worst still believed in marriage. What surprised him more was that *he* believed in it, too, enough that he came *this* close to saying "Gobble, gobble."

Inside, Axel and Dusty went straight to the counter. "The doctor had a cancellation this morning," the pretty, young receptionist said. "So you can go right back."

He heard the *ding* of the elevator, just down the hall, and it reminded him of the tolling of the bells. "You want me to go with you?" he asked, tensing slightly when the bell above the waiting room door rang.

"No. Thanks." Axel's reply was pleasant enough, but that "are you *trying* to humiliate me?" expression could have cur-dled milk.

When the girl opened the door leading to the exam rooms, Axel was right on her heels. Then he turned, walking back-wards and grinning like the Cheshire cat. He pointed at himself, then wiggled the fingers of his good hand. "Five years . . . " he mouthed, aiming a thumb over his shoulder, ". . . she's *mine*."

Chuckling, Dusty studied the selection of magazines in the rack beside the counter, as the door to the waiting room closed.

"That boy has good taste," said a voice from behind him.

"Gavin, hey. What're you doing here?" And nodding at the cast and crutches, he said, "Kind of soon to be getting out of that thing, isn't it?"

"The leg started aching yesterday at the cemetery." He tried—and failed—to wiggle his exposed toes. He knocked on the cast. "So Milton ordered X-rays, just as a precaution."

"How'd you get here?" He hoped Gavin would say *Grace*.

"Taxicab. Not even the gas tax excuses what those guys charge. Highway robbery, literally." He smirked. "The driver was none too happy when I hobbled up the steps without giving him a tip."

"Then I guess you'd let me drive you home."

"Because . . . ?"

"Because with your luck, the same guy will pick you up, and as payback for not getting a tip, he'll hit every pothole and bump between here and your place, that's why."

"Aren't you the voice of optimism today?" He patted the seat of the chair beside his. "How long did it take you to wash the gravy out of your ponytail?"

"About twice as long as it took you to change the subject just now."

Gavin leaned forward to get a better look at Dusty's face. "Maybe it's these harsh fluorescent lights, but you look a little peaked today, if you don't mind my saying."

He did mind, mostly because Gavin's remark inspired a yawn. "Didn't sleep very well last night," he said.

"Hmpf. Up all night, thinking about Gracie, I'll bet."

Dusty only shrugged. Gavin always could read him like a book, so what was the point of denying it?

"I feel sorry for her. Between work and trying to keep Angel Acres afloat, it's a wonder she can keep a civil tongue in her head."

"She doesn't seem the type to go in for pity, self or otherwise."

"True enough. But after the life she's lived?" Gavin whistled. "It's hard *not* to feel sorry for her."

"Doesn't seem the type who's all bogged down with baggage, either."

"If you asked her, she'd say the same thing."

In other words, she *was* all bogged down with baggage? Dusty didn't want to believe it. He'd rather go on thinking she was perfect in every way. That way, when he finally did the right thing, and put some time and space between them, he wouldn't miss her quite so much. Which was ridiculous, when he admitted that he'd only spent, what, a dozen hours—if that—with her?

The fax machine spewed pages into the paper tray as the beep of a call-on-hold kept annoyingly perfect rhythm with the click-clack of the secretary's fingers, flying across her computer's keyboard.

"Grace will never trust me again if she ever finds out that I told you this, so—"

Now Dusty was *sure* he didn't want to hear more. "What, you took a confidentiality oath or something?"

"No," he said, chuckling, "nothing as dramatic as that. It's just. . . . Well, when you get to know her better, you'll understand how much she hates talking about her past. So it isn't a big leap to assume she doesn't share many details about it."

Then how'd you *get the information?* he wanted to ask. "Then maybe you'd better keep your secret."

"No, I've given this a lot of thought. On a personal and professional level, I think it's best that you hear it, considering. . . ."

His heart beat once, twice before Gavin added, "I've seen the way you look at her. The way she looks at you." He held up a silencing hand. "No point denying it. If you could see yourself, you'd say the same thing."

Gavin had a point. A good one. Because if he looked at Grace with anywhere near the affection she looked at him. . . .

Gavin's raspy voice overrode the mechanical and human sounds of the busy medical office as he told Dusty about Grace's mini-breakdown on the way to Tucker's house. He told the whole sad Leslie story, too, right down to the red scarf that floated away just before the girl jumped to her death from the North Tower . . . while Grace watched it all on TV. Then he leaped back in time, to the night her parents were run off the road by a drunk driver, and how, at sixteen, she was sent to live with her grandparents. Skipped forward to her more recent hassles with her cousin and uncle, who—more from details Grace left out than from those she'd provided—were pressuring her to hand over some free acreage.

Dusty was still mulling it all over hours later, while the boys inspected the pink, shriveled skin of Axel's arm, and held their noses as he passed around the smelly, now-hollow cast. Long after they were sound asleep, he flicked on the TV. But how was he supposed to concentrate on the rapid-fire one-liners of his favorite sitcom when all he wanted to do was call Grace and make sure she was okay?

When the clock said midnight, he was still wide awake and prowling the semi-darkened house. He tried his aunt Anita's "tried and true" remedy for sleeplessness, but warm milk and honey didn't do the trick.

Then he did what he should have done in the first place, and grabbed his beat-up, old Bible. He cranked up the footrest on his La-Z-Boy and tilted the shade of the lamp beside the recliner. "Come to me all ye who are weary," he read, "and I will give you rest."

12

Half an hour later, his thumb bookmarking the page, Dusty dozed as images of the things Gavin had told him—Leslie, plummeting to her death; innocent young Grace, plucked from the only home she'd ever known and transplanted to a farm; luminous brown eyes boring into his as strips of lettuce and crusty bread crumbs sprinkled through her curls—and the memory of that warm and wonderful kiss swirled in his brain.

Shattering glass.

A wooden *thud*.

High-pitched howls and whoops of raucous laughter, drifting in from outside.

Then utter, complete stillness, followed by the sounds of bare feet, pounding down the stairs.

"What's going on down here?" Trevor demanded, knuckling one eye.

Dom, close on his heels, pointed at the narrow area rug that ran the length of the front hall. "What's *that?*" he grated, bending at the waist.

"No! Don't touch it!" Billy hollered.

Dom's outstretched fingers closed into a tight fist as he straightened. "Why not?"

"You'll get your fingerprints all over it, and—"

Dusty turned off all the lights and told the boys to be quiet, to stand still. Then he lifted a slat in the blinds and stared into the moonlit yard. The shadow of a bat darted under the streetlight, where moths floated like dust motes in a sunbeam. To the right, a yapping dog was silenced by a distant threat: "Shut up, you mangy mutt, or I'll feed you to the *Los Toros de Lidia!*" To the left, a wide-eyed cat disappeared into the hedgerow. And across the way, the silhouettes of young men—who were really just boys in do-rags trying hard to look like men—hunkered down behind a parked car.

"Hand me the phone," he whispered, one hand extended as he kept his eyes on the street.

Crouching, Axel slunk across the room, grabbed it, and slapped it into Dusty's palm.

He leaned slightly left, widening his view. Mitch wasn't scheduled to report in until morning, but thanks to his chronic case of insomnia, he could show up at midnight or any time after. What if he got it into his head to check in early tonight? Dusty couldn't let him walk unprepared into . . . only the good Lord knew what.

He'd call Mitch, and *then* 9-1-1, and hope he could catch him before he hit the road. Dusty thumbed the talk button and waited for the familiar buzz of the dial tone. Instead, he got nothing. Had the kids left it off the hook again, and drained the battery? He hoped that was the case, because only one other thing explained the dead, empty silence.

Uttering an oath under his breath, he tried to remember where he'd left his cell. In the kitchen, charging? In the pocket of the shirt he'd worn to Tucker's funeral?

The quick-witted Nestor put two and two together, and raced to the kitchen while Dusty turned back to the window. He was sweating, and his heart pounded as if he'd just run a marathon. His hands were shaking, too, he noticed as he parted the slats in the blinds. If *he* felt this frazzled—a guy who'd been on the front lines in battle, who'd wrestled armed killers and robbers into handcuffs—what must his boys be going through?

He took a deep breath and willed himself to calm down. He'd just exhaled when Nestor returned, cell phone in hand.

"Thanks, kiddo," he said. He looked over his shoulder to add, "Say a prayer, guys, that if I can get a signal for a change, AT&T won't drop the call."

Dusty slid the phone open and dialed 9-1-1, and when the dispatcher picked up, he blurted out his name and address so fast that he hoped she'd understood him. "Somebody just threw a brick through my front window," he told her, "and I think whoever it was is still outside."

She promised to send the nearest patrol car, and advised him to stay inside. If he lived alone, that's exactly what he would have done. But he'd accepted responsibility for eleven boys, and he aimed to keep them safe . . . or die trying.

He repeated the dispatcher's advice, and even in the dark, he could see that fear and dread had widened their eyes. Until moving here, none of them had known any kind of stability. Violence, whether verbal, emotional, or physical was as much a part of their days as sunshine and moonlight. None of them had come from stable backgrounds. Would this propel one— or God forbid more—of them into a tailspin?

"How long will it take them to get here?"

"No idea, Dom. Just sit tight."

"Oh. Right," he complained. "Sit tight. In the dark. With a giant hole in the window. While that—"

"Easy, Dom," Dusty said, squeezing the boy's shoulder. "Maybe we can read the message without touching the brick." He left his lookout post and got down onto one knee amid the shattered glass. It appeared to be an ordinary construction brick, emblazoned with choppy black letters, scrawled in what appeared to be a broad-tipped permanent marker.

Axel stepped up beside him. "What's it say?" he asked, resting both palms on his knees.

Dusty didn't know, but he would have bet his Harley that Gonzo had delivered it. Or, one of his minions.

"Well," Jack blurted, *what does it say?*"

Dusty didn't want to know. At least, not now with all the kids standing around, doing their best to hide the fact that from the oldest to the youngest, they were scared stiff. He hadn't told them about Gonzo's middle-of-the-night visit. *If he had, would they have been more prepared for this?* But the kids had formed a tight circle around him. *No point second-guessing himself now. No way out of this one,* he thought.

"One of you guys grab a pen off my desk, will ya?"

Since Montel was closest, he ducked into the living room. "What you gonna do, man, write an answer even before you read the note?"

His attempt to lighten the tense atmosphere worked, as evidenced by the quiet ripple of chuckles that swept around the circle.

Dusty stuck the pen into one of the holes on the side of the brick and slid it slightly, so that it rested in the shard of light spilling in through the broken window. "You know what you have to do," Jack read aloud. "What the—?"

It meant, Dusty answered silently, *that Gonzo hadn't been kidding the other night:* his vague deadline for gaining control of the boys had come and gone. And *that* meant he'd better arrange a meeting with the little criminal . . . before he took his threat to the next level.

The strobes of a squad car painted red and white stripes on the room's darkened walls. "Let me do the talking," Dusty said, opening the door, "unless one of the cops asks you a direct question."

"Why?"

"Because for one thing, you weren't in the room when that thing came through the window."

"What's the other thing?"

"Because I said so, that's why." Dusty flipped on the lights in time to see and hear Montel expel a bored sigh.

Two cops jogged up the steps and stood side by side on the porch. The taller one had one hand on his sidearm's grip as he looked up and down the street. His partner asked, "What seems to be the trouble, sir?"

Dusty glanced at his name plate. CARTER. Stepping aside to let them in, he pointed at the brick.

Carter took a knee, and, his voice a near whisper, read the inscription. Standing, he stamped his feet to shake glass chips from his trousers. "How long ago did you receive your, ah, special delivery?"

"Fifteen minutes, give or take."

Weise, the other cop, joined Carter in the foyer. "*Los Toros de Lidia*?" he asked, nodding toward the shadowy figures, lurking across the street.

Dusty nodded. " 'Fraid so."

"First time they've shown any aggression?" Weise asked.

Dusty considered taking the cop aside before telling him about Gonzo's visit. But his boys were safer, knowing the facts. "Just the usual stuff, until a few nights ago. I was up late, paying bills, when Gonzalez let himself in." He remembered the eerie feeling that came over him when he opened his eyes and looked into Gonzo's cold, black eyes.

"Let himself in?" Weise added Dusty's comment to his notebook, then looked up. "What? You have an open door policy around here?"

"Hardly. The kids don't even have keys."

"Tell me about it," Montel grumbled, elbowing Guillermo.

But Dusty continued as if he hadn't heard the discontent that ricocheted around the room. "He told me I had some hard decisions to make, regarding these guys."

"Lemme get this straight," Carter said, using his pen as a pointer. "You had a B and E, in the middle of the night, and you didn't call it in?"

Good thing you aren't as stupid as this guy thinks you are, Dusty told himself, *or you wouldn't know how to tie your shoes.* "Seemed the lesser of two evils to keep you guys out of it. No point antagonizing him, if you get my drift."

Arms crossed and feet planted shoulder width apart, the cops searched the boys' faces. "Has Gonz ever approached any of you?" the tall one asked.

Nopes and nuh-uhs went around the foyer, and the officers looked to Dusty for confirmation. "Far as I know, he's never talked with anyone but me." *So far.* He hadn't needed any help discerning Gonzo's implied threat: get the boys on board, or suffer the consequences.

The cops put their backs to Dusty and the boys, and, head to head, muttered for a minute or so. Dusty picked up an occasional word: Threats. Missing. Fires. . . .

"Mind if we sit," Weise asked, "while we get some routine info?"

Dusty invited them into the living room, where one cop sat on the couch and the other on the recliner. He offered them coffee or water, but they politely declined. It took all of ten minutes to fill half a dozen pages in their notebooks: Names and ages of each of the boys, Dusty's driver's license data, and even Mitch's contact info.

"When we write up our report," Carter said, standing, "we'll see about getting more patrol cars over here."

Weise stood, too, and as they pocketed their notebooks, Carter aimed a glare in Dusty's direction. "But in the meantime, don't try to be a hero. If that punk comes back—alone or with his soldiers—you call us, hear?"

As Dusty nodded, he found it interesting that while the older, supposedly more streetwise boys nodded right along with him—enthusiastically, respectfully even—the younger kids' brows faces showed something midway between suspicion and contempt. He shouldn't have been surprised, since they'd spent the least amount of time at Last Chance, but their postures and expressions made him more aware than ever how vulnerable they were to Gonzo's promise of *familia* and all the loyalty and neighborhood prominence that went with it.

The cops were halfway down the porch steps when Carter turned. "You got something to close up that hole with, right?"

"Matter of fact, I do." Good thing he hadn't let Mitch talk him into hauling the leftover roof repair plywood to the dump.

"Good. Wouldn't want moths and bats . . . or that bunch," he said, his thumb reminding Dusty of the menacing shadows, still hovering across the way, "getting in here."

No, Dusty thought, *we wouldn't want that.* By the time he and the boys got the plywood cut and screwed into place, the clock said 5:52.

"Why don't you guys go upstairs and turn off your alarms. By the time you've dressed and showered and made your beds, I'll have a good start on a rib-stickin' country breakfast."

For the first time since the crash in the front hall, smiles lit their faces.

"Pancakes?" Nick asked.

"Sure. Why not."

"Sausage or bacon?" Nestor wanted to know.

"Seems to me I saw both in the fridge."

Dom offered to make toast, and Billy volunteered to butter it, while Axel announced that he'd set the table.

"Last one downstairs has to wash the dishes!" Tony bellowed. He'd barely turned the corner into the hall when the rest of them joined him in a mad race up the steps.

Guillermo pushed past him, hollering "I get dibs on the shower!"

They'd adapted quickly to having clothes and shoes to call their own, and dresser drawers and closet space to stow it all. Would they ever get used to the idea that he'd spent a considerable amount of time—and a huge chunk of his renovations budget—turning the smallest bedroom into an eight-by-eight foot tiled space that boasted eight shower heads?

Soon, the kitchen light fixture rattled, but the playful roughhousing wasn't fooling him a bit. That brick through the window reminded every last one of them of the violence and turmoil that had been part of their everyday lives . . . lives that had taught them the only way to survive was to adopt a take-it-on-the-chin attitude. That attitude might fool the casual observer, but Dusty saw it for what it was. He slid two egg cartons from the fridge. It did his heart good to hear them, snickering and roughhousing. That didn't mean it hadn't rattled them. So he'd let them have their fun, because once they'd said the blessing and started filling their bellies, he intended to fill their heads with some much-needed information about Gonzo and his merry men, and follow it up with some well-disguised psychotherapy.

The plan brought to mind the first time he'd heard Jeremiah 29:11, as quoted by his cousin Flynn, eldest son of Uncle Brock and Aunt Anita. . . .

As boys, Dusty and Flynn had shared the attic bedroom. As men, they'd shared the graveyard shift at the 6ᵗʰ Precinct. It hadn't taken long to figure out that his birthday surprise from Flynn that year—tickets to a Yankees game—had an ulterior motive. "Dunno what sort of horrors you saw during the war," he'd said during the seventh-inning stretch, "but it's high time you quit your brooding and got some help. You've got Mom all tied up in knots, worrying about you."

He clattered a frying pan onto the front burner and scooped a dollop of butter into it. The flame, hissing, wasn't unlike the brotherly dressing-down that made him realize that, just as his behavior after 9/11 had ended his military career, his crazy behavior of late could just as easily ruin his career as a cop. It made him remember a buddy, too, who tried to re-up after recuperating from IED-inflicted injuries. "The Marines told me it'd be cheaper to train a new recruit," he'd said, "but the Army was happy to have me."

Firing up the double-burner griddle, Dusty grimaced, because memory of the day after his birthday was still raw, even after all these years. He'd gone to the recruiting office down on Battery Avenue, fully expecting to trade his blue uniform for green. Instead, he got an earful of why the Army couldn't use him, which turned him from a quiet brooder, who'd worried his aunt, into a brazen brawler. Nearly eighteen months had passed before Flynn got fed up with it all, and met him in the parking lot after a graveyard shift. He hadn't said hello. Hadn't asked how the night had gone. Hadn't even commented on the weather. Instead, he'd filled his fists with Dusty's navy blue shirt and folded him backward over the hood of his Jeep. "If you're trying to kill yourself," Flynn had snarled, "you're going about it the right way."

After cracking two dozen eggs into a big ceramic bowl, Dusty toweled egg white from his hands, much the way Flynn scrubbed both palms on his uniform trousers that night, as if trying to wipe off Dusty's taint. Then he'd screwed a fingertip into Dusty's shirt and said through clenched teeth "'I know the plans I have for you . . . plans to prosper you . . . to give you hope and a future.' You keep this up, cousin, you won't *have* a future."

He beat the eggs until they formed yellow froth and dumped them into the frying pan. The fork clattered against the bowl's bottom when he tossed them into the sink. The memory shouldn't have riled him. But it did. Big time. *Focus on the good that came from it,* he told himself. If not for that little set-to, he wouldn't be here, scraping scrambled eggs from the edges of one frying pan while poking at the bacon in another. . . .

It hadn't been so easy to turn in his badge and weapon that rainy morning after Flynn's no-nonsense speech. And it wasn't. It should have been scary, after all he'd been through to, enroll at City University and then the General Theological Seminary. Just thinking about it all was enough to make his hands shake as he flipped the pancakes, lined up in a tidy row on the griddle. He could've paid his tuition with funds that, thanks to his uncle's investment know-how, had turned his parents' life insurance policies into a tidy nest egg. But he hadn't. Because if he failed at that venture, too, he could not forgive himself for squandering the savings made available by their deaths.

Steady thumps and snickers overhead reminded him that he *hadn't* failed. The eleven boys up there depended on him for food and shelter, clothing, medical care, an education, and counseling of both the emotional *and* spiritual kind. With

Mitch's help, he was delivering all of that and more. Two degrees, earned by dint of hard work and dollars from his job as an executive security guard—and hundreds of volunteer hours at Baltimore's bustling Strawbridge School, which proved the need for smaller facilities that could provide more concentrated interactions with kids in need. Prayer led him to the dilapidated, old house behind the Last Chance Church, and the minute he saw it, Dusty knew how to invest his savings. Since then, the generosity of parishioners and Mitch's talent for drumming up donor monies kept the wolf from the door.

He was pouring the last of the orange juice when he realized that, after breakfast, they'd be out of bread and butter. Eggs, too. There was money enough in the checking account for this week's grocery store run. But what about next week, and the week after that? His last sit-down with the bank statement showed black and white proof that Gonzo's threat wasn't his only problem.

It occurred to him that Gonzo might know that, too; he wouldn't put it past the cold-hearted little gangster to have slipped into the house when no one was home to look for weaknesses in the foundation. . . .

"Somethin' smells good in here," Nick said. "Reminds me of weekends. When I was a kid. Before my mom got carted off to Jessup."

When he was *a kid?* It had only been a week since he'd blown out twelve candles on his birthday cake. "How about washing your hands and finishing setting the table?"

"You're kidding, right?" he said stepping up to the sink. "I just got out of the shower."

Smiling, Dusty said, "You can't be too clean."

Montel rounded the corner, beaded braids clacking and fingers snapping. "Can't. Be. Too. Clean," he chanted, rap style.

"Think I'll write a song. And when I get famous," he said, taking Nick's place at the sink, "I'll tell Dave Letterman how you inspired it, Dusty."

He returned the kid's playful smirk. "I'd rather see you on Letterman, talking about how your new surgical technique separated conjoined twins."

"Yeah. Right." Nick snickered. "Like he's gonna be a brain surgeon."

"You mean like what's his name?" Montel asked.

"Ben Carson," Dusty told them. "I read his bio. Believe me, if he can do it, so can you."

Nodding, Montel mulled that over. Nick, on the other hand, seemed content to distribute forks and butter knives . . . upside down.

Montel had spent the past five years at Last Chance. Nick had been nine when he moved in. If Dusty had anything to say about it, this is where they'd all be when they turned twenty-one, and state regs required them to move out. By then, God willing, they'd have some college under their belts, and aspirations that didn't involve rap music. He grinned. Or a talent for annoying flatware placement.

Like all of the boys who'd called Last Chance home, these two had come from tough situations. Most didn't know who their fathers were, and those who did would rather not admit they were descended from murderers, drug dealers, robbers, and rapists. Those who had mothers pretended they hadn't learned about addiction and prostitution at the feet of the women who'd consistently put drugs and men and booze ahead of their kids.

Thankfully, Dusty could pretend that pouring sausage gravy into a bowl without spilling a drop took all of his concentration, because of all the things *he'd* learned during his years of pastoring and counseling, hiding what he thought of their so-called parents wasn't on the list. Every time a kid's HIV tests came back negative, he saw the results for what they were: Nothing short of a miracle. If God could protect them from the deadly disease in environments like that, surely He could get them out of *here* with a few bucks in their pockets and a future to look forward to.

Nestor strutted into the room, smirking, chest puffed out to show off his Cowboys baseball cap and T-shirt.

"What in the . . . ? Of all the. . . ." Dusty bit off the rest of his simmering insult. "You know better than that," he growled. "Take 'em *off*."

"Hey, dude," he said, frowning, "I paid for these with my own money. You can't make me—"

Dusty took a step closer. "I can, and I will . . . if I have to."

By now, nine of the eleven boys were in the kitchen, some sitting, others milling around, all chattering happily as they sipped juice and munched buttered toast, waiting for Dusty to get breakfast on the table.

Nestor said, "So how come you get to wear Harley stuff?"

It was a good question. Just not one he chose to answer. At least, not right now. Nose to nose with the kid, he said, "You know as well as I do what message you're sending Gonzo and his goons, walking around in stuff like that."

The silence in the room was almost as startling as the boys' stunned expressions. Clearly, they understood that this set-to could end badly. And Dusty couldn't help but wonder which side they'd take if, God forbid, it came to that.

"Have some breakfast first," Dusty told Nestor. "Then find something else to wear. Something that won't get you killed."

Trevor and Cody, the only true blood brothers in the house, stood closer together as Billy said, "I read an article online, about some kid who got himself shot because he was wearing some posse's colors." He shook his head. "And the big dummy didn't even *know* it."

The others chimed in with stories they'd heard, about how team jerseys and brand name running shoes had long been identifiers of various gangs across the country.

"Aw, that's just crazy," Nestor said. "Same as sneakers on phone lines and graffiti is some kinda secret territory marker."

"That stuff is true," Dom said. "My dad said so, last time I visited him at Jessup."

But Nestor seemed adamant. "I ain't scared of those Bulls. I'll wear what I want, when I want, and *nobody*," he ground out, glaring at Dusty, "better try and tell me I can't."

The dare was as blatant as the hat on his head. With the exception of Jack, the youngest, every kid here had, at some point, pulled a similar stunt. Dusty knew better than to force the issue. Knew better than to ignore the challenge, too. With kids like these, who'd cut their teeth on brutality and rage, he had two choices . . . show them who was in charge, or let anarchy rein.

He slid an arm across Nestor's shoulders, and, grabbing the back of the boy's neck, exerted enough pressure to send the subtle message: *Even if I hadn't fought in two wars, I outweigh you by fifty pounds. . . .* Message received, as evidenced by the taut muscles under his hand. "Blue isn't your color anyway, kiddo," he said, turning the grip into a sideways hug. "Is it guys?"

A collective sigh of relief floated around the room. "Uh . . . no," Cody said. One pinky in the air, his voice raised an octave to add, "You'd look *so-o-o* much prettier in pink."

Now, laughter replaced the sighs as, one by one, the kids' good-natured shoves and taunts tamed Nestor's ire. Unfortunately, Dusty had one more thing to accomplish before *he* could breathe a sigh of relief. "Tell you what, Nestor. I'll pack up all my Harley stuff and donate it to Vietnam Veterans . . . if you'll do the same with this." He tapped the blue star on the boy's chest, then touched the one on his cap. Then, for good measure, he met each boy's gaze, one by one. "Same goes for the rest of you."

As before, the silence was palpable. Axel broke it with a hearty, "Deal!"

Mitch walked into the room just then, stretching. "What's all the whooping and hollering about?" he asked around a yawn.

Nestor smirked. "Oh, nothin' much," he said. "'Cept we figured out a way to make Dusty get rid of all his Harley Davidson junk." Laughing, he added, "You owe us five bucks, Mitch."

"Each," said Nick.

And Billy said, "Yeah. *Each*."

Dusty could only stare, dumbfounded, as he tried to figure out if Mitch looked more smug than guilty, or the other way around.

"Hey. What can I say?" The younger man shrugged. "Guy's gotta do what a guy's gotta do, y'know?"

"Fooled you, Dusty!" Montel sang as Guillermo fist-pumped the air, and Jack and Cody did a celebratory jig.

Trevor shook his head. "Oh, I dunno . . . he's pretty sly, himself." He thrust out his chin. "Admit it," he said with one eye narrowed. "You were in on it, right from the get-go, weren't you?"

It would have been dishonest to say that he was. But he couldn't very well admit that he'd been clueless, either. "That's for me to know and you to find out." They'd sat up half the night, shortly after Gonzo's little visit, puzzling out how they'd protect the kids from the gang leader and his self-appointed posse, only to turn in frazzled and frustrated by their lack of ideas. Later, when they were alone, he'd find out how long

Mitch had been working out the bugs on this little plot. Then he'd insist that the next time he cooked up some harebrained scheme, he'd let Dusty in on the planning. Especially if it involved his participation.

He'd save the thank-yous and pats on the back for last. *Wouldn't want his head to get* too *big,* he thought, grinning as the boys passed pancakes and syrup, eggs and toast up and down the table. *Like a real family,* he thought, smiling like a proud papa.

Dusty's smile faded, though, as he wondered if what they'd built here was enough to protect them from Gonzo's promises of gang solidarity. A cold chill snaked down his spine, because he'd learned the hard way how dangerous it could be, dwelling on thoughts like that.

Hopefully, he hadn't already jinxed the lot of them by entertaining doubt, even for a moment.

13

*A*fter spending half of her paycheck to rent the American Legion hall, it wasn't easy hiding her disappointment at the low turnout. Grace had bought enough food to feed a small army, too. What would she *do* with it all?

And then she remembered the way Dusty's boys hadn't left a crumb on their plates. On their serving bowls, either. True . . . it was last minute, but if they didn't already have plans, an invitation might solve her problem and give them something different to do, to boot.

Besides, she thought, dialing his number, *I'd never come up with a better—or more legitimate—excuse to shrink the gap between the last time I'd seen him and the Flag Day events at Fort McHenry.*

In the middle of the fourth ring, she told herself she'd give it one more before hanging up.

"Parker," he all but barked.

He sounded out of breath. Or agitated. Both, maybe. "Hi, Dusty?" she said, and could have kicked herself for the timidity in her voice. "It's me. Grace. Grace Sinclair?"

She heard muffled voices, paper rattling, a thump. "Hey," he said at last. "Good to hear from you."

Everybody said things like that, so why had hearing *him* say it made her heart skip a beat?

"What have you been up to?"

"Same ol', same ol'," he answered. "You?"

Instead of reciting everything she'd been up to since the funeral, she told him where she was right now, and admitted that of the long list of people she'd invited to the fundraiser, only a handful had shown up. "I hate to see all this good food go to waste. Or the DJ, for that matter. So I was wondering. . . . I just . . . I know how rude it seems, calling at the last minute this way, but I thought if you and the kids don't have other plans tonight, maybe—"

"Must pose a real challenge," he interrupted, "hiding your wings and a halo when you get dressed every morning."

Wings and halo? Grace might have said, "Who? *Me?*" if he hadn't added "I was just sitting here, trying to figure out how in the world I was going to feed this motley crew when the cupboard is as bare as Mother Hubbard's. Said to God, 'Pizza delivery angel would be nice, right about now.' And then the phone rang. And it was *you.* Offering a meal." He cut loose with a quiet, two-note whistle. "Now, either I'm fuzzy-headed from hunger, or you said something about your grandparents, naming their farm 'Angel Acres.' Right?"

"Right. They did. Because Angel is their last name. Was their last name, that is. . . ."

He laughed, and her heart did that crazy flip. Again. *Idiot,* she told herself, *don't read more into this than there is. . . .*

"If that isn't a prime example of irony, I don't know what is."

He asked for the address, and once she'd provided it, said, "It'll take half an hour or so to round 'em all up, check behind their ears, and load 'em into the van."

"It's only 8:30," she said, "and I have the hall until midnight. So don't rush them. It isn't like the food or the DJ is going anywhere." *And neither am I,* she thought, *now that I know I'll see you again. . . .*

She met them at the door, doling out hugs as each of the Last Chance boys passed her on their way into the banquet hall. Through it all, Kylie stood close beside her, doing her best not to participate in the welcome. The last one in had been the soft-spoken Axel, whose quiet West Virginia drawl broke through the girl's self-protective wall. Soon, she was clear across the room, laughing at the boys' antics while she stuffed her face with chocolate cake.

"I see what you mean about her," Dusty said, sliding onto the bench beside Grace. "If a couple hours with those mischief-makers doesn't make a difference, I'll eat my hat."

"You aren't wearing a hat." Grace smiled. "If you hadn't driven the van, I could suggest you eat your helmet, instead."

Chin touching his chest, he said, "O ye of little faith."

"You're right, of course," she admitted. "There's no reason to believe Kylie will crawl back into her lonely little cubby after the boys go home." Grace hadn't even realized that she'd rested her hand on his knee . . . until he gave it a gentle squeeze.

Then he picked it up, inspected the palm and every fingertip.

She answered his unasked question by saying, "I'll have you know I earned every cut and callus and blister."

"As a lumberjack?"

She explained the myriad chores that needed doing, every single day, over at Angel Acres. "Can't afford a foreman."

"So what . . . you mend fences and stretch barbed wire, all by yourself?"

"It's a *farm*," she said, laughing, "not a ranch. But there's plenty of shoveling and baling to do, not to mention the gardens and—"

"All by yourself?"

"All by myself."

"How many acres?"

"Only thirty."

"Only. . . ." He whistled. "All by yourself." Then he held up a hand. "I know, I know . . . it's a tough job, but somebody's gotta do it. . . ."

"It's cliché, but true."

"And you maintain the house all by yourself, too?"

"Yup."

"How many rooms?

She did a mental count, using the fingers of her free hand: Living room, dining room, kitchen, family room, sun porch, five bedrooms, two bathrooms and a powder room. . . . "Do bathrooms count?"

He smiled. "No. I don't think so."

"Ten, then."

"That's a lot of house for one tiny woman to take care of, all by herself." He eased a fingertip across the blisters. "Nobody should have to work that hard. Especially not a woman with a heart as big as yours."

She would have told him to stop, because it tickled . . . if he hadn't kissed the palm of her hand, then closed her fingers, as if to trap the kiss inside her fist.

Gently, he put her hand into her lap, and nodding at the kids, he said, "Think they'll get out there and dance?" he asked.

"Maybe." Her heart was beating so hard that Grace wondered why she didn't feel dizzy, what with all the blood it sent to her brain. "If the DJ plays something they know, they might." That inspired a little giggle. "You'd think somebody who spends hours and hours in the presence of teenagers would be more 'up' on the kind of music they like, wouldn't you? But you know what? I don't have a clue."

"That makes two of us." He waved to Mitch, who'd just dropped a golden drumstick onto his paper plate. "If he can't tell us, I guess we're doomed to a life of musical illiteracy."

"Oh, I don't know," she said as the younger man sat on her right. "Bet we could give them a run for their money . . . if the subject was hits of the 60s. Or the 70s or 80s, even."

"What's goin' down, dude," Mitch asked around a mouthful of chicken.

"*That,* for starters," Dusty said, pointing at the coleslaw dressing trail that marked Mitch's trip across the dance floor.

"Oh. Wow. Did I do that?" He put his plate on the bench beside him. "Better clean it up, before somebody slips and lands on their keister."

On his hands and knees, he used his napkin to sop up the mess as Molly Logan joined them. "What in the world . . . ?"

Grace leaped up and hugged her. "I'm so glad you decided to come!"

"I almost didn't," the woman admitted. "But after all you did for me, I just didn't have the heart to let you down." She pointed at the food table. "You weren't exaggerating, were you, when you said you'd ordered too much food!"

It seemed she'd only just noticed Dusty. If she recognized him, it didn't show on her face or in her voice. "Molly Logan," she said, extending a hand.

Even if she hadn't smelled alcohol on Molly's breath, Grace wouldn't have reminded her that it had been Dusty who'd found Missy, or that he'd waited in the hall at FBI headquarters, in case she might need him.

It seemed Dusty felt the same way, because when he got to his feet, all he said as he took her hand was "Name's Dusty. It's good to meet you."

Mitch joined them and introduced himself, then picked up his plate. "Name's Mitch," he said, touching a clear-plastic spoon to an imaginary hat brim, "but my friends call me Piglet." And as if to prove it, he filled his mouth with potato salad.

Laughing, Molly asked, "Is that as delicious as it looks?"

Nodding, something akin to "Yes, it is" passed Mitch's lips, eliciting a whole new round of laughter. "I haven't had a bite since breakfast," Molly admitted, "and watching you reminds me just how famished I am!"

"Let's fix you a plate," Grace said, taking her elbow. "What can I bring you when I come back?" she asked Dusty.

"I'll grab something in a minute," he said, winking, "after I have a word or two with Piglet, here."

"Hey," Mitch put in. "I said my *friends* could call me that. . . ."

"Aren't they a pair!" Molly said.

It was good to see her smile, and Grace hoped the booze hadn't been entirely responsible for her cheerfulness.

"Who's that?" Molly wanted to know.

Grace followed her line of vision to where Kylie still sat, giggling and talking with Axel and Toby. "That's Kylie. Kylie Houghton." Grace explained how the girl came by the surname, adding only a few peripheral details about her background.

"Oh, the poor little thing. No wonder she wears that strange hairdo and those ridiculous clothes; she's crying out for attention and affection. And I'm sure what you told me is only the tip of the iceberg. Why, it would probably reduce me to tears if I knew everything she's been through . . . things she probably hasn't told anyone. . . ."

It was quite an insightful observation, and Grace wondered if that, too, could be credited to liquor. The thought inspired concern, because what if Molly was using it to wash down the tranquilizers her doctor had prescribed? Even more worrisome, she'd driven all the way across town. Grace's own parents would likely still be here, if not for a drunk driver. She decided that minute to drive her home, even if it meant tackling her to get the car keys. Molly *might* make it all the way back to Ellicott City without incident, just as she'd managed to get here in one piece. But Grace wouldn't take the chance that Molly might lose control of her vehicle and cause that kind of heartache for another family.

She filled a plate, mostly to assure that Molly would, too, then introduced her to the DJ, who'd taken a break. "Mrs. Logan is quite the musician," Grace told him. "A little birdie told me that she used to play piano with the Baltimore Symphony Orchestra."

"Do tell," the bearded man said. "Name's Sean Thomas," he said. "I did a stint with the BSO, too. String section. . . ."

"Is that so? What years were you with the orchestra?"

"I'll be around, if you need anything," Grace interrupted. But if they heard her, they showed no sign of it. She knew little to nothing about Sean, but he looked like a man who could take care of himself. As for Molly, Grace had never seen her look more animated.

She headed back to where Dusty and Mitch had been sitting, but the bench was empty now, save an empty plastic cup and a paper napkin. She gathered both up and deposited them in the trash can, gaze scanning the room in search of them. Well, not *them*. Mitch seemed like a nice enough guy, but it wasn't him that she wanted to see. . . .

And then she spotted them, standing in the entrance hall, Dusty talking as Mitch nodded. *What on earth could they be talking about*, she wondered, *to paint those serious expressions on their faces?* Dusty looked up just then, and caught her staring. One side of his mouth lifted in a grin, while Mitch raised a hand in silent greeting. An invitation to join them? Grace couldn't be sure, so she looked for more trash to collect.

"You missed this," Dusty said, holding up a fork.

She met his smile with one of her own. "What *would* I do without you?" she said, reaching for it. But he didn't let go. Instead, he wrapped his fingers around hers, so that they were both holding the plastic utensil.

"If you have a minute," he whispered into her ear, "there's something I'd like to tell you. And ask you."

Grace's heart picked up pace, because she got the feeling that whatever it was that he wanted to discuss had something to do with the serious conversation between him and Mitch.

He relieved her of the fork and tossed it into the garbage. "Walk with me," he said, taking her hand. Then he led her out the side door and into the parking lot. He sat on the back bumper of his van, and patted the space beside him. "Plant your feet good and solid," he said as she sat. "It'll help with the balance. . . ."

"Says you," Grace shot back.

"I keep forgetting what short legs you have," he said, laughing. Then he slid open the side door and, without a word, placed a hand on either side of her waist and lifted her off her feet.

For a moment, as he held her at arm's length, eyes glittering in the moonlight like two bright blue diamonds, she thought he might kiss her. But all too soon, her rump made contact with the van's carpeted floor.

"There," he said, sitting beside her, "better?"

Well, she would have been . . . if he'd actually kissed her. "This is fine."

"You look nice tonight," he said. "Yellow is your color."

She'd chosen the sundress because it was one of the few things in her closet that didn't need ironing. The all-over print—white daisies with black centers—meant she could wear it with white shoes or black.

"Never would have pegged you for a red toenail kinda gal," he said, pointing at her strappy white sandals.

It was all she could do to keep from wiggling her toes. "So you wanted to tell me something?"

And there it was again . . . that adorable slanted half-grin. Now it took every bit of her remaining willpower to keep from putting her finger into the dimple it carved into his left cheek. Grace didn't want to rush him, but hostess duties waited for her inside. And if he kept looking at her that way, she wouldn't have to wait for him to kiss *her*. "And something to ask me?"

Nodding, Dusty exhaled a rough breath. "I could be wrong, but I get the feeling that you like my boys. . . ."

"Of course I like them." She pictured them, heard their raspy trying-to-become-men's voices. "What's not to like?"

"I think maybe I have an idea that would help you, and help me to help them."

"Sorry," she said, "but you're going to have to help me figure out that riddle."

Instead of the explanation she expected, Dusty said, "Did I tell you about the gang that's trying to take over our neighborhood?"

"Yes, yes you did. The night you told me about the dinner, where Mitch tried to talk the mayor into putting more patrol cars on your street." Grace frowned. "Wait. You don't mean to say that he decided not to help you out?"

"According to Mitch, she fell back on the old 'I would if I could, but I can't so I won't' excuse." He shrugged. "Budget cuts. Need I say more?"

Well, yeah, he needed to say more, Grace thought. *A whole lot more, since he seemed to think she was part of the solution to his problem.*

He took her hand again. "You shouldn't have to work so hard."

Much as she was enjoying this time alone with him—and the compliments, and the protectiveness that her unattractive hands had inspired—Grace was the hostess of that party going on in the hall. She didn't want to rush him, but what if Molly decided to drive home in her condition?

"What if the boys did the chores?"

"What if. . . . *What?*"

"Hear me out," he said, shushing her with a fingertip over her lips." They aren't safe at Last Chance. At least not now, with Gonzo and his goons running amok. But they'd be safe in Baltimore County. . . .

"In Baltimore. . . . Wait. You mean in my house? At Angel Acres?"

"You have what, four bedrooms?"

"Five."

"That's how many we have at Last Chance."

She held up a hand, hoping he'd read it as a signal to stop talking, to give her a chance to *think*. "Let me see if I understand this: You . . . you want to move the boys, all eleven of them, to *my* house."

"Just for the summer. As a test. Until I can figure out what to do about that stupid gang. They're big, healthy kids. Think of all they could do to help you out around the farm. And all you could teach them about the value of hard work. You have my word: It wouldn't cost you a dime. And if they caused any trouble, any trouble at all," he added, jerking a thumb over his shoulder, "out they'd go."

It made sense, in a convoluted kind of way. But she needed time. To work out the logistics. To pray for guidance, because her decision would affect eleven vulnerable boys. And Mitch. And Dusty.

Grace looked up in time to see Molly heading across the parking lot. "Oh, good grief," she said, hopping down from the van. "I have to stop her. She's in no condition to drive, half-lit like she is on . . . on only God knows what."

"Molly," she called, jogging toward the hall's entrance. "Molly, wait up!"

Thankfully, the woman stopped, which gave Grace time to run back to Dusty. "Look," she began, "I see the merits of your idea. Really, I do. But I need a little time to think about it, okay? How about if I call you, say, tomorrow . . . or the next day?" *Or never,* she tacked on silently.

He closed the van's side door. "Good idea," he said, nodding. "Not just the thinking about it bit, but making sure she doesn't get behind the wheel. I thought I smelled bourbon on her breath earlier."

"So I wasn't imagining things. . . ."

"Where does she live?"

"Be right there," she yelled to Molly. And to Dusty, "Ellicott City."

"What's that . . . a thirty-, forty-minute drive?"

"Each way." Grace groaned. "Say a prayer she'll hang around until everyone has left and I've written checks to the management."

"What time is it?"

"I know what to get *you* for your birthday," she teased, glancing at her wristwatch. "It's a quarter after ten."

"I've got a great idea. . . ."

"Uh-oh," she said, laughing. "I don't know if I can survive another one of your great ideas. At least, not so soon!"

"Hmpf," he said, sliding his wallet from his back pocket. "Good. I have enough cash to take a cab back here after I drive her home, if you're okay with hanging around with the boys until I get back, that is."

"I'm almost afraid to admit it," she said, elbowing his ribs, "but that really *is* a great idea."

"So maybe *you* can come up with an idea for a change . . . starting with how we'll talk Mrs. Logan into handing over her keys. . . ."

She pursed her lips. Frowned. Shook her head. "Sorry," she said, shrugging, "I got nothin'."

He pulled her into a hug. "Aw, Gracie," he growled, "that isn't how I see it."

Grace stood there in the comforting circle of his arms, blinking and staring and feeling like a simpleton. "Molly's gonna get in her car if I don't—"

"The way I see it," he continued, "you've got *every*thing." Then he pressed a sweet, too-brief kiss to her lips and spun her around. "If you ram her good and hard," he said, giving her a gentle nudge, "maybe you'll dislodge that suitcase she calls a purse, and when it hits the ground, you can grab her keys."

"And I thought *I* had nothin'," she said over her shoulder.

"Better watch where you're going. . . ."

His warning came a tick too late: Grace crashed headlong into Molly, and sent them both sprawling onto the blacktop. While Molly laughed and Grace apologized, Dusty chuckled. "You two okay?" he asked, giving them each a hand up.

And then he did the most amazing thing.

While Grace gathered up the contents of the woman's purse, he took her aside and, one arm around her waist, whispered, "I heard a little rumor that the cops have set up a couple dozen roadblocks between here and Ellicott City."

"Roadblocks? You mean—"

"Breathalyzer, walk the white line, touch your nose . . . the whole nine yards."

"Oh my. Oh no."

"Why don't you give me your keys," he said, "and I'll drive you home."

"Just so happens I have them right here," Grace said, handing Molly her purse.

"You're a lifesaver," she said, dropping the key ring into Dusty's upturned hand.

He opened the passenger door, and once Mrs. Logan had settled into the front seat, he made a phone of his hand. "Call you later," he mouthed.

And then they were gone, leaving Grace to wonder how in the world she'd say no to the tattooed, ponytailed preacher who'd stolen her heart.

14

*M*olly Logan had fallen asleep during the short drive from the banquet hall to her house in Oella, then staggered up the walk to unlock her front door . . . and dropped the enormous purse again. This time, the metal flask she'd tucked in an interior pocket clattered to the brick sidewalk, and when Dusty retrieved it for her, he gave it a little shake.

Empty.

Well, he thought as she fumbled with the key, *that explained why, after all that food and so many hours at the party, she hadn't sobered up.*

"You okay here by yourself?" he asked once she stumbled into the foyer.

"Yes, yes I'm fine."

But she wasn't. And to prove it, she walked into the front hall closet and collapsed on the floor, where she sat giggling like a child. He couldn't leave her this way. *What if she took a header down the stairs? Who'd find her, living alone as she did?*

Eyes closed, he tilted his head back and took a deep breath. "Is your bedroom upstairs?" he asked, helping her up.

"Yes, yes it is," she said, clinging to his arm. "Are you going to get me into my ch-ch-chammies?" she slurred. "Tuck me in an' read me a b—a bedtime story?"

The boys and the van were still at the hall. And so was Grace. But he'd be here all night at this rate. So he scooped her up, and carried her up the steps. Huffing and puffing when he reached the landing, he stood her on her feet. He'd forgotten that drunks were dead weight. Even petite, middle-aged drunks. "Which room is yours?" he asked.

She pointed, then wobbled through the first doorway and flopped face-first onto the bed. "I'll be jush-h-h fine," she said, voice muffled by the thick quilt. "You can go now."

Oh, he'd go, all right, as soon as he put her keys where she wouldn't find them until she'd sobered up. She was snoring by the time Dusty covered her with the blanket she'd draped over the arm of a flowery chair beside the bed. *One problem solved,* he thought, flipping on the master bathroom light. Just as he'd expected . . . a cut-glass tumbler, sparkling on the vanity. *Another catastrophe diverted,* he thought, picking it up, because she couldn't drop and break it if it was downstairs, in the kitchen.

While pulling into her driveway, he'd called a cab. With any luck, the driver would be out there waiting when he locked her front door behind him.

No such luck.

Then he remembered why he'd come here, and the fuss and bother he'd gone to on Mrs. Logan's behalf didn't bother him half as much. He sat on the top step of her stoop as thunder rolled overhead. "Oh, if you could see me now, Gracie," he said as a light rain began to fall.

He was soaked to the skin by the time the taxi rolled up. And how perfect was it that his driver believed in cranking the air conditioner to the max? Halfway between Oella and the hall, he dialed Grace's number, hoping her sweet voice would take his mind off his chattering teeth. Whether she hadn't heard the ring, or had been too busy to answer, Dusty couldn't say. But he felt like an idiot when disappointment swirled in his head. "You'll see her in fifteen minutes," he grumbled, snapping his phone shut.

The driver craned his neck. "What's that, sir?"

"Nothing. Just thinking out loud."

The man's grating laughter filled the cab. "It's been my experience that talkin' to yourself is a symptom of woman trouble. Also been my experience there ain't no solution. Come to terms with that, you'll be a far, far happier man. That's my opinion, anyhoo." He pulled up beside the curb and shifted into park, then turned off the meter and said, "That'll be twenty-three dollars, sir."

As he paid the man, Dusty thought he might call Derek, tell him he could earn thirty bucks in twenty minutes, by sitting on his butt. Then he remembered stories of cabbies who'd been killed for the few bucks in their cash box, and thought maybe Derek was better off at the Double T, where the worst that could happen was some cheapskate, stiffing him on the tip.

"'Bout time you got back," Axel said when Dusty walked into the hall.

"Yeah," Dom agreed. "We're the last ones here."

"Thought maybe we'd have to send a posse out to find you," Jack teased.

Posse—another way of saying "gang." The word alone was enough to make him clench his jaw. "Where's Mitch?"

Montel pointed. "Helping Miss Grace pack up the leftovers."

She couldn't possibly have heard her name from all the way over there. So what had made her look up just then? Man, but she was gorgeous, all flush-faced from her long night of seeing to others' needs. She was footloose and fancy-free, to quote Grace, herself, while he had more responsibilities than a Dalmatian had spots. If he had any decency at all, he'd load the kids into the van and take them back to Last Chance, not Angel Acres, and not even bother to look in the rearview mirror. Then she smiled, wiggled the fingers of one hand, telling him without words that she was happy to see him . . . and drove every 'decency' thought right out of his head.

"Look at him," Dom whispered. "The dude's got it *bad* for Miss Grace."

Was it so obvious, Dusty asked himself, *that the boys could see it? And if it was, could Grace see it, too?*

"Times like these," he said slowly, "I wish I was a cowboy."

"A cowboy," Axel echoed. "*Why?*"

"So I could saddle up the fastest horse and ride far, far from here, that's why."

"Yeah," Montel drawled, "and if you was a cowboy, you wouldn't get too far before you got to missin' your best girl."

He hated to admit it, but the boys were right. And before he knew what was happening, she was walking toward him, carrying bags stuffed with the zipper bags she'd filled with chicken and ham, potato salad and rolls.

"Will there be room in your van for these," she asked, "once all the boys are inside?"

"We'll make them fit," he heard himself say.

It never dawned on him to ask why she couldn't load them into her SUV, until she said, "I'd take them, but my car's filled to overflowing with paper products and condiments and decorations."

He relieved her of the bags, yet she walked beside him toward the van. "So how's Mrs. Logan?"

"She'll be fine, once her headache wears off in the morning."

"The poor thing," Grace said as he slid open the van's side door. "She's just so lost without Missy."

"I hate to be a killjoy, but she had problems before her husband and daughter died." He slid the bags under the nearest bench seat. "You know that, right?"

Her shoulders sagged and she nodded. "I suppose." She sighed. "It's just . . . I feel so helpless. If only there was something I could *do* for her."

"You're already doing it."

She made a face that he took to mean, "If you say so."

The boys started climbing into the van. "You two gonna stand there all night makin' googly eyes at each other," Trevor teased, "or can we maybe get home before the sun comes up?"

"Patience," Grace said, her forefinger wagging like a metronome, "is a virtue."

"Yeah, and the early bird gets the worm," said Billy, laughing.

Dusty tossed Montel the keys and told him to fire up the van. "Turn on the a/c," he said, "but keep it in park, okay?" Then he closed the door and led Grace to the back of the van, the only place on the vehicle that didn't have windows.

"So you'll think about my idea?" When she nodded, a curl fell over one eye, and he tucked it behind her ear.

"Drive safely," she said, and started to walk away.

But he grabbed her elbow, and drew her into a hug. "It's going to take some serious willpower," he said, "to keep from calling you every ten minutes, to see what you've decided."

"It's a big decision, but I promise not to keep you waiting too long."

Any other woman would see this as the perfect opportunity to take control of the situation, but Grace wasn't any other woman. If she had been, would he feel like a knobby-kneed boy, lost in the throes of a teenage crush?

"I hate to rush you," she said, "but with the price of gas where it is these days, shouldn't you hit the road?"

Grace didn't wait for an answer. Instead, she stood on tiptoe and pressed a light kiss to his cheek. "Drive safely," she said, knocking on the van's side door. "Precious cargo, y'know?" Then she turned on her heel and left him standing there, empty-armed and alone.

Dusty slept like a baby that night—and not the kind that was up every two hours, demanding a feeding, either. He'd almost forgotten what a full eight hours felt like, and after breakfast and church services, he had energy to burn. He spent it repairing the leaky faucet in the kitchen, and replacing loose tiles in the front hall. Then he oiled the back screen door and mowed the lawn, and fell into bed that night too exhausted to worry about Gonzo or wonder when he'd hear from Grace.

The phone woke him at eleven, and he remembered that the last time he got a call this late, it had been to inform him of the fire that killed Tucker and Keith. "Hello," he barked into the receiver.

"Dusty?"

Grace. He cleared his throat. "Hey. Hi."

"I woke you, didn't I."

"Don't worry about it. Everything okay over there?"

He heard the smile in her voice when she said, "I'm fine. Especially now that I've had some time to think. And pray. Do you have time to meet me for coffee in the morning?"

He sat on the edge of the mattress. "Why? So you can tell me to take a flying leap?"

She laughed, and the sound of it buzzed through him, reminding him of the time he'd gotten shocked, unscrewing an outlet cover.

"I'd never say a thing like that. I like your idea, Dusty."

Then she told him where the boys would sleep, that since the family room was pretty much wasted space, she could turn it into a bedroom for him and Mitch. "Unless you guys don't want to share the space, that is. . . ."

He hadn't planned on moving in, himself. Didn't think Mitch planned to, either. But she was on a roll, and he didn't have the heart to slow her momentum.

"I'm happy to tutor the kids—if they want me to—evenings, after supper. And I think they'll adjust faster if you and Mitch eat with us every night. What do you think?"

He wanted to tell her that he thought she was amazing. Beautiful, inside and out. The best thing to happen to him, ever. But, "You're right, of course," is what he said.

Grace went on to say that she'd never assign chores that were labor-intensive, and that on the days they manned the vegetable stand at the end of her road, she'd divvy the profits among them.

It made him feel like a sap, having thought she'd spent all this time asking if God thought the arrangement would work out for *her*. From everything she'd said, it was clear that Grace had dedicated every moment to plotting out what would be best for the *boys*. Other than Mitch, Dusty couldn't name a single person who'd ever put them first. Until Grace.

"It's the strangest thing," she said, her voice all dreamy and soft, "but last night, I was sitting there with the Bible in my lap, worrying about how I'd afford it all when—"

"When I promised it wouldn't cost you a dime," he interrupted, "I meant it."

"And I believe you. But there are bound to be expenses we can't anticipate, that we can't plan for. *That's* what I was thinking when the phone rang . . . and my neighbor asked if he could rent a couple dozen acres, to grow wheat and soy. I knew even before I hung up that moving the kids in here is the right thing to do. For all of us."

He heard the rain, pecking at the windows; except for the dim blue glow of the clock, the room was dark. Had he dreamed the whole thing?

"The only thing left to wonder about," Grace said, "is what will come of our . . . of our friendship."

Friendship. It was a decent word, one that ought to have filled him with a sense of pride, because Grace was some kind of woman. Instead, it left him feeling hurt. And hollow. Because he wanted to be more than her friend. A whole lot more.

But wait a minute, here. . . . Last time he'd checked, *he* was the one with the theology degree. So why had it been Grace whose talk had been thoughtful and spirit-filled? He slapped a hand to the back of his neck and prayed for a little divine intervention.

"What was that noise?" she asked.

Just me, he thought, *trying to smack some sense into myself.*

"So when will you guys move in? Tomorrow? Over the weekend?"

"Tell you what. How 'bout if I bring the kids over there tomorrow, and we'll work on putting your plan into action, together."

"Rearranging beds and dressers, and emptying closets and dresser drawers, you mean . . . ?"

"Yeah. Stuff like that. I've got a stack of plastic bins in the basement. We can—"

"Those things are already done."

"What do you mean, they're already done?"

"I finished tonight, right before I called you."

Dusty didn't know whether to admire her organizational skills and physical strength, or pity the fact that getting all that done—in less than twenty-four hours—meant she'd been lonely, living in that big, old house all by herself.

"I haven't told them any of this yet."

"Good grief. See . . . this is *just* the kind of thing that made the old 'cart before the horse' my grandmother's favorite adage."

He heard her groan. And sigh. And unless he was mistaken, slapped her*self* on the back of the neck.

"So it's entirely possible, then, that the kids might decide they don't *want* to live in the country, doing farm chores all day long. . . ."

"Anything's possible, but I'm fairly certain they'll jump at the chance to move."

"Tell you what," she said, quoting him, "how 'bout if you bring the kids over here tomorrow, and I'll give them a tour of the place. And then we'll sit them down and tell them, together, why this is the safest place for them. At least for the time being." And then, she hung up. Just like that.

This *had* to be a dream. What else explained the way things had gotten all twisted around . . . with her telling *him* why the move was a good idea?

What kind of woman turned her whole life upside down for a Harley-riding preacher and a band of misfit kids that nobody else wanted?

The kind for whom "grace" was far more than just a name.

If this is a dream, he thought, smiling into the now-buzzing phone, *I hope I never wake up.*

15

*T*he rain didn't let up for a week straight, postponing—then canceling—the Flag Day celebrations. It was disappointing, but only for a day or so, because moving the boys into the house had totally distracted everyone.

Those first few days had been the hardest—not for the boys, who'd changed addresses the way most folks change socks—but for Grace, whose experiences with "living together" were soft-spoken parents, everything-in-its-place grandparents, and the almost-tidy Leslie. Tripping over her college roommate's tiny slippers hadn't been anywhere near as traumatic as scaring the cat, who'd decided to take a nap in the toe of a size 13 sneaker.

Remove wet towels from their rooms enough times, she'd told herself, *and they'll learn by example that wet towels don't belong on the floor, or at the foot of their beds.* But on the morning she found *herself* questioning the theory, Grace decided to put "honesty is the best policy" to the test, and called a family meeting where she let them know exactly where she expected them to put dirty linens, soiled sweatshirts . . . and damp towels.

It hadn't been easy, hiding her amusement when the *boys* called a family meeting, and called her to task for removing and applying toenail polish while they were trying to relax in front of the TV. "The stink is enough to gag a maggot," Montel said, inspiring Grace's promise to perform all pedicures in her room from then on, with the door closed.

Grace never knew when one of them might wrap her in a big hug to tell her how much they appreciated the way she'd opened her home to them. They showered her with compliments about her cooking and housekeeping skills, and the way her laundry-sorting techniques put an end to drab grey undershirts. They appreciated the fact that she always knocked before entering a room, too, and never hogged the telephone.

They'd given her plenty of reasons to dole out praise in equal measure. The house had never looked better, thanks in part to Dusty and Mitch, who'd showed them the proper way to sand and scrape the clapboard siding in preparation for a fresh coat of pale yellow paint. They'd figured out—mostly on their own—which of the tools in her grandfather's shed would straighten lopsided shutters, and which silenced squeaky floorboards. Their fastidious care of the gardens must have terrified the weeds, because she hadn't seen so much as a sprig in weeks.

This morning, when a steady rain kept them indoors, Nick interrupted her bookkeeping to ask permission to explore the attic.

"No one has been up there in years," Grace admitted. "Only God knows what sort of mess you'll find."

Billy stepped up behind Nick. "Then we'll clean it up!"

Now Dom joined them. "We'll knock down the cobwebs and sweep. . . ."

". . . and when we're done," Jack added, "you can come up there, tell us what we can toss onto the burn pile, and what to save."

This might be fun, going through things her grandparents had thought important enough to pack away. "Well, okay, but before you get started, see if you can open the windows, because it's bound to be like an oven up there."

Tony joined the group, a coil of heavy-duty extension cord slung over one shoulder. "Cody's always showing off his muscles," he teased. "Maybe he can drag a couple of your box fans up there."

Hours later, as Grace stamped the envelope of the last bill she'd paid, their exuberant laughter filtered through the ceiling. "Why should they have all the fun?" she joked, shoving back from her desk. And after putting a dozen bottles of cold water into a bag, she made her way up the narrow staircase.

"Goodness gracious," she said when she reached the top, "I'm ashamed of myself!"

Eleven sweaty, smudged faces turned in her direction. "Why?" Cody asked, helping himself to a bottle.

"Because I thought you guys were up here, goofing off this whole time. But just look at this place!"

They'd swept every cobweb from the rafters, and the wood-planked floor was still damp from the scrubbing they'd given it. Round-topped trunks that had been covered with dust the last time she'd seen them now shone like quality furniture pieces. The mirror that had hung above her grandparents' mantel reflected the old metal headboards, castoff chairs, and a box marked "Christmas, 1972."

Nestor grabbed a water, too. "Who's that guy?" he asked, pointing to the oval frame, hanging beside the dormer window.

She eased it from the wall and blew the dust from its domed glass. "This is my great-grandfather, Thaddeus Angel," she told them, tracing the strong, square jaw, "in his doughboy uniform."

"Doughboy," Jack echoed, laughing. "Like in Pillsbury?"

Grace laughed, too. "No . . . that's what they called World War I soldiers. I'm embarrassed to admit this, being a teacher and all, but I have no idea why."

"Not your fault," Guillermo said. "You teach English, not history."

"And Art," Nestor added.

"When we're done here," Dom said, "I'll hop on the Internet and find out."

"By jove," she said, "I think you've just provided the topic for our evening lesson!"

At the conclusion of their good-natured groans, she looked at each boy in turn. "I'm going downstairs to fix lunch— something special, to show my appreciation for all you've done up here." She started down the stairs, and took the picture with her, knowing even before her feet hit the bottom step where she'd hang it.

Half an hour later, the portrait had a new home above the mantle. On its right, a photo of her parents; to the left, her grandparents. In both, the men stood straight and tall, one sleeve of their drab Army uniforms hidden behind their blushing brides. It seemed fitting that Grandpa Thaddeus, who'd bought the land that became Angel Acres, filled the space between.

Grace stood back to admire her handiwork, and the space she'd fill with a photo of her great-grandmother, just as soon as she found one. Pride and love . . . and a tinge of longing filled her heart. But she wasn't lonely, thanks to the boys who'd turned this house into a home again.

Knuckling at her traitorous tears, Grace took the stairs two at a time, and standing in the doorway that led to the attic, she called, "Lunch is ready; wash up, boys!"

Montel squeaked into the kitchen wearing brown-rubber hip waders, and Trevor strutted into the room in her grandfather's World War II uniform.

Axel drew her attention to the off-white gown he'd carefully draped over one forearm. "Whose was it, your mama's?"

"She wore it," Grace said, taking it from him, "but my grandmother wore it first."

"Well," he said as she held it against her, "looks like a perfect fit to me."

She'd prepared their favorite meal—burgers and fries—and all but Axel had filled their plates.

Jack squirted catsup over his fries. "You gonna wear it when you and Dusty get married?"

Grace swallowed. Were her feelings for Dusty so obvious that even the *boys* could see them? "We should say the blessing," she announced, more to change the subject than for spiritual reasons, "before everything gets cold."

"Maybe you oughta say it," Trevor suggested.

Grace wanted to put the dress away, so that later, when she was alone, she could inspect it for tears or moth holes before storing it in a safe place . . . just in case. . . . But she bowed her head and closed her eyes, and said, "Lord, we thank You for this food, and for every member of this family gathered here to share it. Protect us from all harm, Father, and keep us close to You, in everything we say, in everything we do."

She was about to say "Amen" when Axel said, "And God? We also ask that You give Dusty the courage to tell Miss Grace that he loves her."

Montel spoke next. "And to do it before they're both old and gray. Amen."

Quiet snickers and whispered "Amens" preceded, "Pass the mustard" and "Who's hoggin' the onions?"

"Don't wipe your hands on that jacket," Grace said, giving Trevor's shoulder a gentle squeeze.

He blanketed her hand with his own. "I won't. Promise."

Then the doorbell rang, and Grace left the room to see who'd come calling on this dark, drizzly day.

"Mrs. Logan," she said, opening the door wide. "Come in out of the rain."

She shook rain from her umbrella and stood it beside the front door. "What *will* it take to get you to call me Molly?" she said, wiping her feet on the foyer rug. "Makes me feel old and decrepit when you say that!"

"We're having lunch," Grace said. "Are you hungry?"

"No, but thanks." Frowning, she looked over Grace's shoulder. "So all of them are living here now, are they?"

"It's been quite an adventure for all of us, let me tell you!" she said, leading Molly into the living room. "Have a seat. Can I get you some lemonade? Iced tea?"

"No, no . . . ," she said, sitting on the sofa. "I know you must be busy, with all of them to take care of, but. . . ." She inhaled a shaky breath. ". . . but I was hoping you could help me with something."

"I'm happy to do anything I can," she said, meaning it.

She grabbed Grace's hands. "Am I imagining things, or did I hear Agent Spencer telling you that he had an 'in' of some sort with Taylor Manor?"

"Yes, as a matter of fact, he did." Though they hadn't said it in so many words, the agents knew Molly hadn't exactly been coherent that day, and who could blame her, having lost her daughter in such a violent way?

"You're a lovely young woman," Molly continued, "far too kind to admit what a mess you think I am. But I *am* a mess, and I need help, before I do something. . . ." She bit her lower lip, then gave Grace's hands a shake. "Will you call him for me? Get the name of his friend?"

"Of course." She said it without thinking. If she'd taken a moment before answering, Grace would have admitted she didn't know how to get ahold of Agent Spencer, because she couldn't remember where she'd put his card.

Molly reached into her pocket, withdrew a business card. "I've tried half a dozen times to dial that number," she said, pressing it into Grace's hand. "What stops me, every time, is that I have no idea what I'd say, knowing he'd seen me at my worst." Her eyes filled with tears, but she blinked them away. "But I remember how well you handled that greedy funeral director. Agent Spencer will listen to you, Grace."

She looked at the card. Ran her thumb over the raised FBI emblem. Nodding, Grace got to her feet. "Give me a minute to get the boys busy with . . . I don't know, a movie or something, so they won't hear anything when I call him."

Molly stood, too. "No. Please don't call him now. Give me time to get home, pack a bag, and get my head straight so that when he comes for me, I'll be ready."

"All right," she said, but her heart wasn't in it. Grace was afraid that if she told Molly the *only* thing the agent could do for her was provide the name of his friend, she'd change her mind. Getting to Taylor Manor, signing herself into the facility . . . that was up to Molly, and Molly alone.

They walked side by side to the door. "Will you call me," Molly asked, stepping onto the porch, "so I'll know what will happen next?"

"Will do," Grace said as the woman popped up her umbrella.

By the time she went back into the kitchen, the boys had finished lunch and had started clearing the table. "Who was that?" Jack wanted to know.

"Mrs. Logan."

"Fixed you a plate," he added, nodding toward the microwave.

Billy harrumphed. "She's not drunk again, is she?"

"No. She sounded sober."

"For a change," Nestor snorted. "Reminds me of my mom. Using drugs and booze because she's weak. And stupid." He tossed a handful of paper napkins into the trash can. "What did she want, anyway?"

Grace glanced at Agent Spencer's business card. "She asked me to help her get into Taylor Manor."

"She can't do that herself? Booze pickled her brain?"

"Aw, go a little easy on her," Cody said. "She just buried her daughter. Now she's got nobody."

The simple truth in his words rocked them, as evidenced by their sudden silence and distant expressions. It broke her heart to admit it, but they were probably thinking about circumstances that had made each of them Molly Logan's equals. "I rented that movie you guys wanted to see," she said. "It's in the living room. On top of the DVD player."

"Did it come with 3-D glasses?" Billy asked.

"It did."

"*Eleven pairs?*"

"Two were complimentary," she admitted, grinning. "It took a little finesse, but I talked the manager into throwing in the other nine."

The atmosphere had brightened, but only slightly. Hopefully, by the time the movie ended, they'd be back to their usual happy-go-lucky selves. If not, maybe homemade pizza would do the trick; she'd bought all the ingredients yesterday, thinking it would be fun to let them put on the toppings.

She waited until the movie's intro credits had scrolled by on the television screen, then went into the family room and

LOREE LOUGH

closed the door. With any luck, Agent Spencer would be at his desk, but in the event he was in the field, she said a little prayer that he'd return her call quickly, because it wouldn't surprise her to find out Molly Logan had already changed her mind about the rehab center.

Grace punched the digits and said another prayer: that Dusty would join her and the boys for supper, and take advantage of the room she'd rearranged and redecorated with him in mind.

16

When his wife left him, Eli Spencer swore off women. Well, not *women*, per se, so much as *relationships* with them. She'd taken everything. Every stick of furniture, every dollar he'd saved, even the house he'd gone into debt to buy because she'd fallen in love with it. It had taken five of the ten years since the divorce to dig himself out of the money hole she'd left him in. He felt entitled to his low opinion of women, would have bet his next promotion that divorce-induced bitterness would climb into the grave with him . . .

. . . until he met Grace Sinclair, who'd stuck by the Logan woman's side, delivering hot tea and warm hugs, aiming a cold glare Timmons's way when the agent's interrogation style got out of hand. Eli might have said *nosiness* explained it all . . . if not for the sadness glittering in her big dark eyes. Seeing the dead girl's body and witnessing the mother's grief hadn't put it there; if he had to guess, he'd say she'd been carrying it around for years.

He pegged her as the type who'd deny it if he asked her about it, and Eli knew *types,* thanks to the deceitful people he'd met and the ugly things he'd seen since finishing up at Quantico. He liked her, felt protective toward her—weird, considering he'd spent less than three hours in her presence. A dozen times since leaving the Logan house in Oella, he'd wracked his brain, hoping to come up with a legitimate excuse to call, so he could get to know her better, find out if he'd judged her accurately, or if he was all wet.

And then she'd called *him*, and he'd been so distracted by the music in her voice that he'd only heard every other word: Taylor Manor. Mrs. Logan. Rehab. Friend. He'd driven straight over there, and nodded politely when she introduced him to a guy with tattoos and long hair and a diamond stud earring—no doubt the owner of the shiny black Hog parked out front—and a dozen or so boys whose expressions told him they'd seen almost as much of life's ugliness as he had.

Then Grace had fixed him a sandwich—ham and cheese on toasted rye, with a slice of homegrown tomato and a side of chips—and while he wolfed it down, she repeated everything she'd said on the phone

Eli had given her his word: he'd call his pal at Taylor Manor to see if it was possible to skip the red tape and get Mrs. Logan into the facility's rehab unit, ASAP. For a minute, relief had replaced the sadness in her eyes, and he'd felt so good about putting it there that he'd asked about her plans for the Fourth.

"Something simple," she'd said. The parade in Dundalk for years, a backyard barbeque. The fireworks. Everything had been going great between them until he'd asked her to dinner, inspiring half a dozen excuses to bubble from her lips: Chores. Errands. Lesson plans for the boys. . . . "I homeschool them, you know?"

No. He hadn't known that, he'd said as she walked him to the door. Grace thanked him for coming over, for going above and beyond his original promise to help Mrs. Logan. And she'd waved as he got into the car. Asked him to let her know once things were set up, so she could drive Mrs. Logan to the facility. "Sure, of course," he'd said, half distracted by the beam of the porch light reflected in the Harley's shiny black motor casing . . . and the memory of the way her voice had gone all soft and sweet when she'd introduced him to its owner. Didn't seem right . . . gorgeous little gal like her, falling all over herself for a guy like that.

The thought had inspired an idea, and the idea had been responsible for the pages now tucked into the manila folder under his arm.

Eli rang the bell. The door swung open, and there she stood, looking even prettier than he remembered.

"Agent Spencer," she said, smiling.

"Please. Call me Eli. . . ."

"Good news about Mrs. Logan?"

"Too good to share over the phone," he explained as she closed the door. "It's awfully quiet around here. Where is everybody?"

She started down the hall, waved for him to follow. "Dusty's in New York," she said over one shoulder. "His aunt had a heart attack, so the doctor scheduled open heart surgery. She's more like a mother than an aunt, really, because she took him in after his parents were killed."

Grace pulled out the same kitchen chair he'd been in last time he was here. Eli slid the folder to the far end of the table and sat down.

"So to make a long story short. . . ." Laughing, she poured him a glass of lemonade. "I know, I know . . . too late for that, right?"

So far, she hadn't told him anything he didn't already know, thanks to his background check. Eli took a sip of the lemonade. "Fresh squeezed?"

"Well, yeah," she said. But her voice, her raised eyebrows, and her stance said, *"As if I'd serve anything but. . . ."*

"Did you skip supper again?"

"Matter of fact," he admitted, "I did." *Because I was hoping you'd ask. . . .*

She pulled sandwich fixings out of the fridge, assembled them on the counter. "So anyway, Dusty's in New York, with his cousins, who—"

"—are more like brothers than cousins," he teased, "seeing as they were raised in the same house."

"So, where are the kids?"

"Oh, they went with him, of course."

Of course? Nothing his research had turned up indicated that Parker had adopted the boys. . . .

"I have a theory," she said, using a butter knife as a pointer, "to explain that. I think he brought them along for two reasons. One," she said, slicing a tomato, "he's proud of how far they've come, considering their background." The toast popped up as she said, "And two, I think *he* thinks I needed a break from the bunch of them."

She slid the sandwich plate in front of him, then handed him a paper napkin.

"Well, do you?" he asked, draping it over one thigh. "Need a break from them, I mean."

She sat across from him and folded her hands on the table. "Actually, the exact opposite is true. The place feels so big and empty without them."

"Guess it's good practice, then."

"For when the state says they have to leave?"

Nodding, he bit off the corner of the sandwich.

"You're probably right. That won't be easy."

"I feel like a pig, sitting here stuffing my face, alone."

"I've already eaten." She sat back in her chair. "So . . . this good news about Mrs. Logan. . . ."

"Oh. Right." He took a swallow of the lemonade, then blotted his lips with the napkin. "Sorry. I was enjoying the sandwich so much, I plum forgot why I came here." *Liar,* he thought, glancing at the folder. Eli filled her in: the room is there for the taking . . . once Mrs. Logan submitted to a physical and psych exam. "Probably not a good idea for her to wait too long," he advised. "With everything that's going on in this crazy world, no telling how long the room will be available."

"I'll call her. Tonight."

As soon as she gets rid of me.

"Thanks," Eli said, shoving the plate aside. "That was fantastic."

"I have some pie in the fridge, if you have room for dessert."

"Sounds good."

She got up to cut him a slice, and her back was to him when she said, "So what's in the folder? Admission papers for Mrs. Logan?"

Moments ago, when she'd talked about Parker, had been one of the few times when the sadness left her eyes. Clearly, she cared about the good reverend. Maybe Eli had been wrong, and the man had turned over a new leaf. People changed, became better human beings, every day. *He'd* changed . . . after meeting Grace. . . .

If he was wrong about Parker, he'd erase her happiness in one swipe. But if he was right, he'd spare her another heartache.

Right?

"Hope you like apple," she said, putting the dish in front of him. "I can nuke it if you want, put a scoop of ice cream on top. . . ."

"Some other time, maybe," he said, spearing an apple. "Homemade?"

Again, with the "of course" posture.

Yeah, she was different, all right. Different enough to make him wolf down the pie, so he could open that folder, get the whole ugly business of Parker's past out of the way. He spelled it out slowly, starting with the not-so-honorable military discharge, ending with the troubles that nearly got him canned from the police department in New York. Then he sat back, wondering as she leafed through the pages, how she'd react once she read black and white proof that her Harley-riding hero had feet of clay

Grace closed the folder. "It doesn't matter what Dusty *was*," she said, sliding it closer to Eli. "The only thing I care about is who he *is*."

Now, why did that remind him of what his grandpa used to say? "Who you are is shouting at me so loudly that I can't hear what you're saying." Or something like that.

"Dusty is the most decent man I've ever known, with the possible exception of the grandfather who raised me."

Then she launched into a long list of the things he'd accomplished, starting with the boys who were his responsibility now and those who'd come and gone before them, and ending with everything he'd done at Angel Acres.

Eli picked up the file, thanked Grace for the sandwich and the pie, and made the most dignified exit possible under the circumstances. Mrs. Logan was her problem now, and so was her precious Dusty. Halfway home, he thumped the steering wheel in frustration. *You've got nobody but yourself to blame,* he told himself. He didn't live by many rules: tell the truth as completely and as often as possible; do your level best at everything you attempt; show up for work on time; don't let yourself be fooled by a pretty face.

The driver of the car ahead of him slammed on his brakes, forcing Eli to follow suit. And when he did, the folder slid from the passenger seat. It opened when it hit the floor, exposing the cover page he'd so carefully typed up and centered on the screen before sending it to the printer.

What galled him most was the possibility that Dusty Parker—long-haired, tattooed, Harley-riding preacher was a more honorable man than Eli Spencer, decorated FBI agent.

17

In the waiting room adjacent to the OR suites, Dusty's cousins paced.

"They're gonna wear out that rug," Jack whispered behind a cupped hand.

"You'd be right with them," Cody said, nodding toward the double doors, "if that was *your* mom in there."

Cody followed his line of vision and nodded. "Yeah. I guess you're right." Then he shrugged. "Guess when Dusty gets back with the coffee, they're really gonna give that rug a workout."

The middle-aged man flopped onto the nubby seat of the chair between them, and, leaning forward, grabbed a dog-eared magazine.

Tony put the rest of the periodicals back into a fan shape. "Who you waiting for, mister?"

He peered over gold-rimmed half glasses. "My wife." He ran a trembling hand through gray curls. "You?"

"Long story," Guillermo told him.

"I'm not going anywhere." He closed his magazine and propped an ankle on a knee.

"Well, the guy who takes care of us—"

"Our guardian," Trevor put in. "He's in the cafeteria. His turn to make the coffee run."

"—his aunt is in there."

"She raised him," Nick said. "Those are his cousins over there."

The man nodded. "What sort of operation is she having?"

"Not sure, to be honest. She had a heart attack, see, so—"

"Her doctor said a triple bypass," Jack said. "Maybe quadruple."

"Yeah," Nick agreed. "No way to know until he gets in there."

"That's pretty much what my wife's surgeon said. Except in her case, it's defective valves." He glanced at the Rolex on his wrist. "She's been in there four hours."

"Where you been all this time?" Billy asked.

"Got a call from her surgeon's secretary," he said, "in the middle of a meeting with the Japanese. Took a while to get hold of my pilot."

Billy's eyebrows disappeared behind shaggy brown bangs. "Japan?"

The man was nodding when the boy added, "Wait. Did you just say *your* pilot? Are you famous or something?"

"Only among computer geeks," he said, chuckling.

Montel picked up the magazine he'd just dropped. "Hey," he said, pointing at its cover, "is this *you?*"

"'Fraid so."

"So if you ain't famous," Montel said, "why's your pi'ture on the cover of *Time?*"

Jack peeked over Montel's shoulder and read the bold white sidebar. "Which name is yours, mister," he asked, "John Peterson or Pete Leonard?"

Dusty walked in just then, balancing a cardboard cup holder on each hand. It wasn't a good sign that the three of them were still walking circles outside the OR. "Give me a hand with this, Flynn."

His cousin stopped pacing long enough to take one of the cartons. "Which one's double cream, double sugar?" he asked, placing it on the table.

"It's all right there on the lids," Dusty said, grabbing the one with the big black B on top. "So, what's the word on—"

"Dusty?" The man from *Time* got to his feet. "Not Dusty *Parker. . . .*"

The boys looked from his face to Dusty's and back again.

"Well, if it isn't John Peterson," Dusty said, slapping the man's back. "Long time no see, you old codger." He could say things like that, now that John wasn't his boss.

"How long *has* it been?"

"A lifetime," he said. And it was true. He'd been a very different man, back when he'd worked security, keeping autograph hounds and panhandlers from pestering John. But at first glance, it seemed John hadn't changed a bit.

Of all the well-heeled executives he'd protected, John was at the top of Dusty's list. The media liked to paint him as a womanizing, gambling, party animal, and credited his father's wealth for John's gregarious, down-to-earth persona. He'd inherited millions, that much was true; but he'd grown his wealth, rather than squandering it on needy kin and dolled-up women who came out of the woodwork whenever he made a public appearance. He'd liked working for the man, mostly, because he respected him.

Dusty waved his cousins over. "Flynn, Connor, Blake . . . c'mere. I want to introduce you to an old friend of mine."

The men took a moment to trade names and handshakes before all three Parkers retired to a bank of chairs to sip coffee and stare at the OR doors.

"Dusty," Trevor said, "this dude's got his own *plane.*"

He knew, because he'd been in it, dozens of times. "Is that so?"

"And his picture on the cover of *Time*." Montel handed Dusty the magazine.

It wasn't the first time, Dusty thought, grinning. "What did you do to get there this time?"

This time, the boys' expressions said, *meaning . . . he'd been there* before?

John shrugged, as if it was no big deal, which told Dusty that whatever he was about to say would be a very *big* deal.

"Started a fund for the tsunami victims in Japan, and the donors insisted that I go over there to deliver it."

Made sense, since his wife had been born over there. "Everybody okay in Kim's village?" Her parents and siblings had been in America for generations, but she'd made a point of visiting extended family, every other year or so.

"She lost her grandmother. Two cousins."

Dusty nodded. "Sorry to hear it." Then, "So what are you doing here?"

Peterson told him about his wife's operation, then slid a leather checkbook from his pocket. "How much do you need?"

Hands up as if he'd pulled a gun, instead, Dusty frowned. "Put that thing away, John. We're doing fine."

"Some things never change," he said, twisting the cap of a sleek, silver pen. "Still a proud and stubborn idiot, I see." He used the pen to point at the boys. "You telling me they don't need shoes? Haircuts? Won't be summer forever, you know. What about winter coats? Boots and—"

"John. Seriously. We're holding our own." He nodded toward the OR doors. "Besides, we've got bigger things to worry about right now than stocking caps and mittens."

"You still riding a Harley?"

"Yeah. . . ."

"What do you do . . . take the kids to school, one at a time?"

Dusty laughed. "Have you grown so old and crotchety that you've forgotten a little thing called 'summer vacation'?" He elbowed John's ribs. "I'm kidding. They're homeschooled. And we have a van."

"Bet it's an old clunker." John waved the boys over. "What year is it, son?" he asked Montel.

"Eighty-eight. But she runs great, 'cause we take good care of her. Dusty taught us how to change the oil. Rotate tires. Replace hoses. That baby purrs like a kitten, don't she, Dusty?"

When she's in the mood to, he thought. Unfortunately, she wasn't in the mood to purr very often.

The OR doors hissed, and Aunt Anita's doctor appeared in the opening.

"He looked tired, but pleased," John said. "That's gotta be a good feeling."

After a brief consult with the Parker men, the surgeon ducked back into the surgical suite. "It is. And you'll feel it, too, just as soon as Kim's doctor comes out here." He turned to his boys. "You guys okay out here while I go in to see her?"

John answered in their stead. "All this talking and waiting has given me a powerful appetite. What-say you fellas keep an old man company while he gets something to eat?"

Within seconds, they'd formed a line behind him, reminding Dusty of ducklings, following behind their mama. Dusty pressed the big round button that opened the double doors, and caught up with his cousins. "Two at a time," a nurse whispered as they gathered outside Anita's cubicle in the recovery room.

Flynn and Connor went in first, and Blake headed for the men's room, leaving Dusty alone in the hall. With head down and thumbs hooked into his jeans pockets, he leaned against the wall. *You should be praying,* he told himself, to thank God for letting things go so well in the OR. Instead, the only thing he wanted to do was find a quiet place, where he could flip open his cell phone . . . and share the good news with Grace.

18

"Don't make no sense to me, either, Gonz."

"Shut up, Lenny. And quit callin' me Gonz." He scooted lower in the old barber chair turned tattoo-recliner, as the younger boy skulked off to a neutral corner and helped himself to a beer, then flopped onto a ratty, brown couch and flicked on the widescreen.

"I don't remember you askin' permission to look at my television."

Without looking up, Lenny said, "Okay if I watch me some tee-vee, boss?"

"You got half an hour. Then you get your butt out there and *do your job.*"

"But boss, you know what happened last time I—"

"Save it," Gonzo barked, levering himself up on an elbow. "You make 'em *understand*, you hear? They want protection, they gotta *pay* for it. Come back here without my money again, and I'll demonstrate how to make 'em listen . . . on *your* bony body."

Lenny turned off the TV and drained the beer bottle. It hit the trash can with a clatter as he stomped out the door.

Gonzo shook his fist. "That boy—he don't know how close he is to becoming a new statistic for the mayor's anti-gang campaign." Then he glared up at Rasheed. "And what *you* waitin' for, fool? Get that needle buzzin'!"

"Don't rush me, dude. Tattoos, they's *art,* man. Wouldn't want me to mess up your purty li'l teardrop, would ya?"

"Just get it done. You think I like sittin' here, inhaling your bad breath all this while?"

"Maybe if you paid me for inkin' up your greasy self, I could buy me some toof-paste."

Gonzo grabbed the bigger boy's wrist. "You don't get this done by the time Yesenia gets off work, I'll knock alla your teeth down your throat. What you gonna need a toothbrush for then, huh, smart guy?"

Rasheed clamped his teeth together so tightly that muscles bulged in his cheeks and lower jaw. But Gonzo pretended he hadn't noticed. Tomorrow, when everybody saw the second teardrop beside his right eye, he'd get a little *more* respect.

"You want I should color this one in, boss? You know, for bal-lance."

"You been sniffin' again, dude? Why would I want you to do that? Leave it open."

One teardrop, time served; closed up, no big deal. Open? Proof he'd earned his rank in *Los Toros de Lidia*. "Takes *machismo* to slit the throat of an enemy, and don't you forget it."

Rasheed muttered something that sounded an awful lot like "As if you'd ever *let* me forget it." But Gonzo let it pass. He wasn't in the mood for fighting today. At least, not with his fists. Soon, he'd see his precious Yesenia, and what would she think if he showed up, puffing and pawing like a *real* bull? *A good leader,* he told himself, *must choose his battles well.* He laughed to himself. *And they said you didn't learn anything in school. . . .*

Tomorrow. He'd save his rage for the full-of-himself preacher who'd put himself in charge of those losers who lived in the big, ugly house on the corner. But not to worry—to quote his sainted *abuela*. In time, they'd realize that he was doing them a favor, because when he got through with them, they'd be good soldiers . . . or dead . . . but at least they wouldn't be losers any more.

He'd begun to think maybe it would take another visit to get his message across, that he hadn't put the fear of God into the good pastor last time. But the house sat empty, day after day, no light glowing from every window after the sun went down. Either they were hiding in the basement, like rats in a hole, or they'd moved away.

So what if they had? They couldn't stay away forever. Tomorrow, he'd find out, one way or the other.

"All finished," Rasheed said, handing Gonzo a mirror.

He sat up, turned his face right and left. "Good job," he said, giving back the mirror. "You really are an artist."

"Remember the alcohol," the artist said, "so it won't get infected."

Gonzo got to his feet. "I think you're forgetting," he said, sneering, "that this isn't my first rodeo."

Then he threw a twenty-dollar bill at Rasheed's feet and headed into the storeroom. "Soon," he said to himself, nodding approvingly at his inventory of pipes and nails, gasoline and rags, "Last Chance will have a whole new meaning for Reverend Dusty Parker and his tribe . . . if they survive."

19

If Dusty's "attention to detail" skills were a pie, he'd slice it three ways, with the two biggest wedges going to the Marines and the police department, and a sliver to plain old nosiness. The talent is what made him notice and remember things, like how much sugar one person spooned into their coffee, or how close to E another might let the fuel needle get before driving to the gas station.

Grace, he'd observed, usually picked up the phone on the third ring.

Usually.

He'd called her twice since leaving the hospital this evening—ten rings the first time, fifteen the second—but not even the machine had picked up. With snoring boys in sleeping bags scattered all over the living room and his aunt still in intensive care, Dusty couldn't sleep, anyway, so he tried again. *Three's the charm* he told himself as he punched in the digits; if she read him the riot act for calling after midnight, well, at least he'd have her ire to prove she was all right. And if she didn't answer this time? He'd call Mitch, ask him to drive over to Angel Acres and check things out.

Most people set their answering machines to kick in on the fourth ring. Or the seventh. What number had *she* chosen, he wondered as the fourth ring jangled in his ear. "Pick up, Grace," he said through clenched teeth. "Pick *up*."

"Hello?"

"Well, it's about time," he said, breathing a sigh of relief. "I was about to call out the cavalry."

A nanosecond of silence ticked by, and then she said, "Dusty. . . ."

Man, it was good to hear her voice. "One and the same."

"Is your aunt all right?"

"She's doing great. Still in CICU, but unless she spikes a fever, her doctor says they'll move her to the sixth floor tomorrow."

"So what did they do, exactly? Double bypass?"

"Triple," he said, "using veins from her leg. Guy in the waiting room told me he'd had the same thing done a couple years back, and the incision on his calf gave him a whole lot more trouble than the one on his chest . . . even though they cracked him open like a walnut."

"Then we'll just have to pray that she doesn't have any trouble, won't we?"

Which reminded him: he still hadn't hit his knees to thank God for saving Anita. . . .

"How are the boys?"

"Good, good. Sleeping now, thank God."

"Are they enjoying the big city?"

"Well, they haven't seen much of it yet. I promised to do the whole tourist thing with them tomorrow."

"Ah, Central Park and the Statue of Liberty."

"Ellis Island."

"The Empire State Building." He couldn't put his finger on it, but she sounded . . . *off*. Was she annoyed that he'd called so late? Lonely for the boys? Missing *him*? "Hey, Gracie. You okay?"

"Of course I am. Why wouldn't I be?"

"No reason." *Except maybe Gonzo.* "You sound . . . I don't know . . . different."

"I don't usually admit things like this, but I guess I'm a little pooped. It's been a long, strange day."

He was about to ask what she meant by that when she added, "Nothing to worry about. Really."

But he was worried, because he'd heard her version of *tired*, and this wasn't it.

"How are *you* holding up?"

"Good, good," he said again. And then he remembered the check in his pocket. Dusty told her that he'd run into John, and how he'd worked for him, as a bodyguard of sorts, to pay his tuition. He told her about Kim's surgery, too, and that John had just come back from Japan, where he'd donated a ton of money to help rebuild.

"Because of the tsunami."

He told her Kim had been born in Japan, still had relatives over there. He'd never been a great conversationalist, especially on the phone. But once he started talking, Dusty couldn't stop himself. He knew why: if he stopped, she'd hang up, and he didn't want that.

"*Lord,* but I miss you," he wanted to say. "I'd drive to Angel Acres right now, if the kids weren't asleep. And my aunt wasn't intensive care. And getting from here to there didn't take four hours."

"More like five. Unless you're some kind of speed demon."

Dusty felt like a blithering idiot, because until she'd said that, he hadn't realized he'd blurted out his thoughts, aloud. Now that the words were out there, swirling someplace between his heart and her head, he couldn't take them back. But maybe he could hide them, under *more* words. And maybe, if he actually put some *thought* into it before he opened his big mouth, she wouldn't agree that he was a blithering idiot.

So he told her about the check John had insisted on giving him. More than enough to cross every item off the Last Chance "to do" list. "He wants to meet you," Dusty said, "so as soon as his wife can travel, he'll fly down there. Did I mention he has a private jet?"

"Well, despite that, he sounds like a very nice man. I'm looking forward to meeting him."

Then she yawned, and he took the hint. "Guess I'd better let you get to bed."

"You need a good night's sleep, too, if you're serious about doing the whole tourist thing tomorrow."

He told her goodnight and wished her sweet dreams, and stretched out on Anita's family room sofa and started making plans.

First thing in the morning, he'd pay a visit to the hospital, and if his aunt was holding her own, he'd chuck the boys and their sleeping bags into the van and aim for Baltimore. They hadn't seemed all that enthused about the tourist thing, anyway. And when he told them he was worried about Grace, they'd be in as big a hurry to get home as he was.

Almost.

Just as he'd expected, Grace was surprised when they arrived at suppertime, carrying a stack of pizza boxes. Not exactly the throw-herself-into-his-arms welcome Dusty had looked forward to, but at least now he could see with his own eyes that she was fine. Physically, anyway. It wasn't until the kids went to bed and Mitch headed to his apartment across town that he found out what had been bugging her, mentally.

It seemed that in addition to pulling a few strings to get Mrs. Logan into Taylor Manor, Agent Spencer had pulled a file on Dusty, as well. So now Grace knew about the going-crazy-after-9/11 routine that forced him to resign from the Marines. And the out-of-control behavior that preceded his resignation from the police department. His bout with alcoholism. Even the bankruptcy. "I'm surprised he didn't tell you that in third grade, I put worms in Mrs. Webster's desk."

At least *that* admission made her smile. A little. "Well, it's good to see that you have the decency to feel bad about it."

"Pains me to admit it, but I didn't at the time. Feel bad, I mean."

"How old were you?"

"Seven? Eight?"

"A little young to have developed a conscience," she said, and poured him more iced tea, then sat across from him again.

"This is my third glass. I'll be up all night."

"Good. You can use the time to read your Bible, as atonement for the worm incident."

Chuckling, he reached across the table and took her hands in his. "You're something else, Grace Sinclair. And I meant what I said on the phone last night. I missed you like crazy."

Dusty waited, to give her a chance to say she'd missed him, too. Instead, she patted his hand and told him that Honor had called around lunchtime. "It's a big secret, for now, but Matt asked her to marry him, and she said yes."

"High time, if you ask me." He told her the story of the stormy romance that stalled when Matt had to put all his SAR skills to use to find Honor when she got trapped in the mountains during a blizzard. "She'd been lugging around some serious baggage, so—"

"Well, no wonder she got stuck."

A joke? *And* a smile? It gave him a glimmer of hope that his past didn't matter to her. "Took a few years of counseling," he continued, "but from the sound of things, Honor got all that baggage unpacked."

"They'll make it public at T-Bonz next weekend."

"Must be something in the water over there. That makes twice that friends of mine have announced their engagement at T-Bonz." *Maybe you should take* Grace *there for a couple of meals,* he thought. Maybe all it would take to inspire a little "Missed you, too, Dusty" was a rack of baby back ribs. "Are you going to the party?"

"I don't know that it'll be a *party*. . . ."

"So . . . no cake, then. . . ."

She grinned. "Probably not."

"But you're going."

"Probably."

He'd pay a lot of money—every cent of the fat check John had written him—to know what was going on in that gorgeous head of hers. "Then maybe we could go together."

Grace focused on some unknown spot on the wall behind him. Then she cleared her throat and shrugged. "Sure," she said. "Why not?"

Had he been wrong to think his past hadn't changed her opinion of him? The possibility that it had stung like a hard slap to the face, but he shook it off. She was still holding his hand. Still looking into his eyes. That had to mean something good, right? So if he didn't do anything stupid. . . .

Dusty lifted her hand to his lips and kissed every chafed knuckle, every ragged cuticle, put there by the hours of hard work that went into keeping this place running, by all the loving things she did for the boys. For him, too, like turning a seldom used room into a place where he and Mitch could bunk down if they didn't feel like driving home at the end of a long day. Oh boy, what he'd give to show his appreciation by pulling her into a hug and kissing her cheeks. Her chin. The tip of her nose. Her *lips*. Crazy thoughts . . . for a guy who'd just warned himself not to do anything stupid.

So he shoved back from the table and got to his feet. Then he carried his empty iced tea glass to the sink and headed for the door. He was about to tell her goodnight when she said, "I made up the bed in the spare room. You're more than welcome to stay. I mean, in your shoes, *I* sure wouldn't want to go any-where at this hour. Especially after that long drive back from New York."

The way she stood there, looking all sweet and concerned and protective, he couldn't help himself. Stupid or not, he gath-ered her close and held on tight. So tight that he could feel her big, beautiful heart, thumping against his chest. He cupped her face in his hands, thinking to memorize every freckle, the arch of her brows, the curve of jaw, just in case the unthink-able happened, and—

She stood on tiptoe and pressed her lips to his. If his past *did* matter to her, it sure didn't show in that kiss!

He thought about it long into the night. By morning, he still hadn't figured out what he'd ever done in his whole miserable life to deserve a woman like Grace, but he knew this: If she'd have him, he'd spend the rest of his life earning her love.

20

"What's with the red-rimmed eyes?"

Startled, Grace missed the mouth of the pitcher and slopped tea onto the counter. "Gavin Martin, you scared me out of the last ten years of my life."

"You owe me one, then." Laughing through the back screen, he said, "I hear those are the worst ten, anyway."

She clucked her tongue. "Let me sop up this mess and I'll pour you some iced tea."

As he thumped into the kitchen, she said, "When did you trade the crutches for a cane?"

"Last week." He modeled the newer, shorter cast. "The old one got soaked at the parade." He hung the cane over the back of a chair and sat down. "Never would've been caught in that thunderstorm if I'd listened to my gut and stayed home."

"But then you'd have one less funny story to tell!" She handed him a glass of tea. "So how much longer before you're cast-less?"

"Four weeks. Five, max."

"Good grief, Gavin. Isn't the usual healing time eight weeks?"

"What can I say? Guess that's just one more way in which I'm unique." He took a sip of the tea. "M-m-m. Beats that instant stuff all to pieces." Then he put the glass down and folded his hands on the table. "But you never answered my question."

The red-rimmed eyes question, Grace knew. Hopefully, she could distract him with more small talk. Because she wasn't in a 'fess up' mood. "So who drove you to the parade?"

"Johnny Depp." He smirked. "Jealous?"

"Only if he was wearing his Jack Sparrow costume." Knowing Gavin, he'd hitched a ride with the divorcée who lived next door. He wasn't sensitive about much, but when it came to Lucille, he closed up tighter than Fort Knox. If he persisted with his "red eyes" line, she might just have to see about opening that subject.

"You're good," Gavin said, "but I'm better."

Grace sighed. She'd wave a white flag . . . if she had one. "Would you believe allergies?"

"Maybe. So what's the culprit . . . pollen? Dust mites? Dus-*tee?*"

He knew. She didn't know *how,* but Gavin *knew.*

He reached across the table and patted her hand. "Come on. Tell Uncle Gavin all about it."

She sighed again. "Honestly, I wouldn't know where to begin."

"You don't really want me to say it, do you?"

"At the beginning," they said together.

So she started with the way Dusty had cut his trip to New York short because he was worried about her, and showed up at suppertime bearing veggie pizzas . . . her favorite. "The kids aren't used to sitting in a car that long, so they turned in early." She told him about Agent Spencer's background check, and how instead of making her want to turn tail and run, the information had made her feel inadequate and shallow in comparison to Dusty.

"Whoa," Gavin interrupted. "Help me out here. You? Inadequate? I don't get it."

"It's just that he's been through so much . . . losing his parents at such a young age, moving in with relatives, fighting in wars, then finding out that his uncle died at the World Trade Center . . . yet he refuses to let it get him down. And me? Why I could put that pig in *Charlotte's Web* to shame, I'm so good at wallowing."

"Wilbur."

"Who?"

"The pig. In *Charlotte's Web*. His name is Wilbur."

Grace giggled. "Oh. Right." She thumped her forehead. "How silly of me."

"Yep, you sure are. Take 'war' off that list, and you might have been talking about yourself."

"No . . . I was older when—"

He patted her hand again. "Grace, give it up. You're not gonna win this one. If I wasn't old enough to be your dad, I'd give that empty-headed cousin of mine some competition."

Now how did he expect her to react to *that*?

"I'm told I have a knack for reading minds. But even if I didn't—have that talent, that is—I'd have no trouble reading yours, because you're as transparent as waxed paper."

"I am? Wow. Really?"

"Really."

"I don't suppose while people were praising your mind-reading skills they mentioned your knack for tact. . . ."

"Hey. I calls 'em as I sees 'em. And I'll prove it: You're thinking Dusty deserves a woman who's strong, thoughtful, capable . . . and you're not convinced you *are* that woman." He smirked. "Am I close?"

Grace nodded.

"And you're asking yourself how in the world you'll ever find out if you're 'that woman,' when, in your mind, God hasn't put you to the test. Yet."

"You're so close," she admitted, "it's downright scary."

He made his own list, starting with the way she'd been orphaned at sixteen, uprooted from New York and transplanted to Maryland before losing her best friend and her grandparents. "And you got through it all without a word of complaint, without a whimper. Your mom and dad—your grandparents, too—would be proud of the woman you've become."

It felt good hearing that. So good that tears filled her eyes and a sob ached in her throat. If she said one word, it would be equivalent to the Dutch boy pulling the cork out of the dike. She bought some "get hold of yourself" time by plucking a napkin from the basket on the table, and using it to dry her eyes. "You're a good friend, Gavin," she croaked out.

"And I'm picky, too. No way I'd buddy up to a wallower, if you get my drift."

She got it, all right, and it almost started the waterworks up again. "Did you hear that Matt and Honor are engaged?"

"No kidding? That's great! Have they set a date?"

"I doubt it. The engagement isn't even official yet; they're planning to make the big announcement at T-Bonz on Friday. I told Dusty about it, and he asked me to go to the party with him. I . . . I sort of hurt his feelings by not saying yes fast enough." *Sort of* didn't begin to describe the look that came over his face, but Grace pressed on. "It made me feel a little guilty, and I kind of threw myself at him."

Usually when she messed up, Grace faced things head on, without leaning on half-truths and qualifiers, so why had she used them just now? Was it proof that she *wasn't* the right woman for Dusty?

She remembered the tender look that gentled his face in those precious seconds before he gathered her close and held her as if he believed God shaped her from delicate porcelain. Remembered, too, the tenderness and yearning in his kiss.

He cared for her—probably more than was good for him, definitely more than she deserved. How else could she explain the way her moment of uncertainty had upset him?

It was reason enough to *become* the woman he deserved, starting now.

21

"Do we have great timing, or what?"

Grace jumped up from the table. "Matt! Honor! We were just having a little lunch. Come on in and help yourselves."

She gave them both a hug, then fetched plates and flatware while Dusty pulled two card table chairs from the pantry.

"If this is your idea of a little lunch," Matt said, helping himself to a square of lasagna, "I think we might just move in here."

"You might want to reconsider," Mitch said, passing him the basket of garlic bread, "since it means bunking in with Dusty and me."

"What . . . you guys are living here, too?"

"Don't look so shocked, Honor," Dusty said. "How else am I gonna keep an eye on these ruffians?" Laughing, he tousled Axel's hair.

"Hey, take it easy, dude," the boy said, leaning as far from Dusty as the crowded table would allow. "I spent ten minutes on those spikes."

"Spent a couple dollars' worth of gel, too, I see," Dusty teased, giving the reddish-blond spears another pat. "Nice change from the corn rows, by the way."

While Axel groaned, Dusty focused on his friends. "So what brings you two to Baltimore County?"

Matt leaned closer to Honor. "Think they'd buy it," he said from the corner of his mouth, "if I said we were just in the neighborhood?"

"Can't hurt to try," she said, mimicking his facial expression.

"Truth is, we made a special trip out here. Wanted you guys to be the first to know. . . ." Matt grabbed Honor's left hand, held it up so they could all see the diamond, winking on her ring finger. "This crazy broad has agreed to become my wife." He shrugged. "Go figger!"

Congratulations and high fives made their way around the table, and then Honor said, "The *real* truth is, we're here to ask you a favor, Dusty."

"Okay, but I have to warn you . . . there's no room for you in my will. . . ."

Matt snapped his fingers and started to get up. "C'mon, hon. No point wasting our time with *this* cheapskate." He sat back down and slid an arm across Honor's shoulders. "Is your preacher's license up to date?"

Dusty looked at Grace and made a *"What's he babbling about?"* face. "Yeah . . . why?"

"We haven't decided on a date yet," Honor said, "but when we do, we're hoping we can hold the ceremony in the Last Chance church. And we'd like you to marry us."

"If that isn't against the law," Montel said, grinning, "it oughta be." He shook his head. "Now I understand that old saying . . . 'Two's company, three's a crowd.' "

When the laughter waned, Dusty said, "I know the guy who owns the comedy club down on Water Street. Behave yourself, and I might be able to wrangle an audition for you, funny man."

"So what do you say, old buddy?"

"Haven't performed a marriage ceremony in . . . ever. I'll get the old wedding book out and polish up my 'Do you take this man' spiel." Then he looked at the bride to be. "It'll be an honor, Honor."

"Hmpf," Montel snorted. "Looks like maybe you'd better see if your friend's willing to listen to a double audition."

"Like Lewis and Martin," Mitch said.

Grace laughed. "Or the Smothers Brothers."

"Or those guys from *Laugh-In*," Dusty added.

"Rowan and Martin? They're hilarious!" Matt said.

"You mean 'were hilarious,' don't you?" Mitch shook his head. "Half of 'em are telling jokes to the angels these days."

"Aw, really? Even Tommy and Dickie? That's sad."

Matt patted his fiancée's hand. "There, there, dear. If they are up there," he said, aiming a thumb at the ceiling, "at least they could go directly to the source, to find out which one their mom liked best."

The boys exchanged puzzled glances. "You know what they're talking about?" Cody whispered.

Trevor sprinkled more Parmesan on his lasagna. "Not a clue. Pass the garlic bread, will ya?"

"So, Grace," Honor said, "have you seen Mrs. Logan lately?"

"Matter of fact, I have." She explained the whole Taylor Manor/rehab situation, providing only the necessary details. "It's only been a few weeks, but she seems to be doing really well."

"That's good to hear. Poor woman has been through a lot lately. If there's any way I can help. . . ."

Grace nodded, though she didn't see what any of them could do. Molly's success or failure depended entirely on the strength of her own will.

It dawned on her just then that everyone at this table had been through a lot. And they'd all come out the other side, happy and healthy and whole, thanks to a merciful God . . . and loving friends.

"How's that kid you were mentoring?" Matt asked. "You know, the girl with. . . ." He waved his hands beside his head. " . . . with the crazy hair?"

"You mean Kylie," Tony said. "She was over here day before yesterday. Her hair isn't crazy any more. It's plain old brown now, like Gracie's."

"Better hold back on the effusive compliments," Grace teased, "or I'll have to ask Dusty to fire up his chainsaw, so he can carve keyhole shapes into the doorways to keep me from bumping my plain, old, brown-haired head on the frames."

"I didn't mean it that way. Honest."

He looked so miserable that Grace got up and walked around to his side of the table. "I know that, you big nut," she said, hugging him from behind. "And just so you know . . . I love you, too." She looked at all the boys, at Mitch and Honor and Matt, saving Dusty for last. "I love *all* of you!"

"We love you, too, Gracie," Mitch said.

Honor and Matt chimed in, and one at a time, so did the boys. They all got back to eating and talking, so Grace doubted that any of them noticed the warm look that Dusty sent her way, a look almost identical to the one he'd given her the other night. The only thing missing, really, was the kiss that changed it from sweet and affectionate to—

"What're you staring at, Gracie?"

Blinking, she felt the heat of a blush creep into her cheeks. "Staring? *Moi?*"

Despite the chuckles that followed, not even Grace believed she'd fooled any of them. Least of all Dusty. Unless she was mistaken, *his* cheeks had reddened, too.

Did it mean he loved her? *A girl can hope,* she thought, returning to her chair.

22

She'd been crawling around in the rose garden when the big, old convertible rattled into the driveway. Tucking her hand spade into the bucket of tools, Grace got to her feet and peeled off her gloves, used them to whack mud from the knees of her jeans.

Two men, faces hidden by sun visors and identical aviator sunglasses, exchanged a few words. The one in the passenger seat whipped off his baseball cap and aimed the rearview mirror his way. He ran a hand through his hair and put the hat back on as the driver's door swung open. A second later, the passenger door opened, too. As they unfolded themselves from the front seat, she resisted the urge to holler out, "Whatever you're selling, we don't need any," because they didn't look like any salesmen she'd ever seen.

They weren't in any particular hurry to close the fifty-yard gap between her and the car. The tall one's gait put her in mind of John Wayne, enough that it wouldn't have surprised her if he threw his arm into the air and drawled a friendly, "Well, hello there, li' lady!"

There was something familiar about him, about his side-kick, too. The hairs on the back of her neck prickled, and her heart was pounding like a parade drum. *Never should have been so quick to suggest that the boys drive into town with Dusty and Mitch,* Grace thought. They could be looking for directions—though that seemed weird, given the length of her winding drive—or Jehovah's Witnesses. She'd never been one to jump to conclusions. Hadn't been much of a 'fraidy-cat, either. But unless she was mistaken, these two hadn't stopped by to ask directions or hand out pamphlets.

Grace glanced at her bucket of garden tools. She could probably get rid of them with a few terse words and a cross look. But just in case. . . .

She grabbed the three-pronged fork, a favorite for dislodging stubborn weeds, even from hard-packed soil. It looked imposing enough, she supposed, tightening her fingers around its wooden handle. Trouble was, the thing didn't measure a foot from end to end. That meant getting close, real close, if things got dicey. . . .

They were all of twenty feet away when the tall one shaded his eyes. "Gracie? Is that you?"

Oh good Lord, no . . . it can't be. . . . By the time she whispered "Uncle Mike?" he was close enough to cast a shadow. Is that what caused the shiver that slithered up her spine?

"How's my girl?" he said, arms open and waiting.

Arms tight at her sides, Grace endured the hug. It seemed to last forever, and when he let go, his son stepped up. She tightened her grip on the tool as her cousin Joe said, "My turn."

Mike pocketed his hands. "I can hardly believe what a beauty you turned out to be."

"Even dressed up like a scarecrow," Joe agreed.

Grace hadn't seen either of them since before her high school graduation. Hadn't heard from them, either. She'd tried to find them—Uncle Mike, in particular—when her grandfather died. Tried again when her grandmother was on her deathbed, and only then because the woman hoped to see her only son one last time before she joined her Maker. "I guess you heard that Gran and Gramps passed. . . ."

Mike nodded somberly. "Yeah. Yeah. Sad news, that." Then he shook his head. "How long has it been since—"

"Eleven years," she snapped.

His Adam's apple rose, then fell. *If you think I'm going to invite the pair of you inside for a spot of tea, you're sadly mistaken,* she thought.

"So why are you here after all this time?" As if she didn't know. Their reputation for gambling and carousing had been the family's shameful little secret for as long as she remembered. No doubt they'd run low on funds, and decided to hit her up for a loan.

Joe tugged at the bill of his cap. "Looks like you've been taking real good care of the place." He took a half-step closer to add, "You and your husband, that is." He nodded approvingly. "Fresh paint. Mowed lawn. Fields all plowed up and planted. . . . Guess we owe him and Grace, here, a big thank-you, don't we, Dad?"

"That we do," Mike said. "That we do."

"Got any kids, Gracie?"

What business was it of theirs whether she was married, or had kids . . . took care of Angel Acres or let it go fallow?

And then she understood: They hadn't come to borrow money. They were here to lay claim to the farm!

Mike slid a legal-sized envelope from his shirt pocket. Why hadn't she noticed it before, big as it was?

"What do you say about slapping a couple sandwiches together," Mike said. "We haven't eaten since breakfast. I figure you can have a look at that," he added, handing it to her, "while we eat."

"How far did you come to deliver this?" She couldn't read the numbers on their license from this distance, but the colors told her it wasn't a Maryland plate.

"Would you believe LA? I had a part in a movie."

"That's right. Joe, here, played the part of Anne Bancroft's son."

Did they think she was as stupid and uninformed as they were? The actress had died, *years* ago.

Grace folded the envelope in half—not an easy feat, thick as it was—tucked it into the back pocket of her jeans, then flipped open her cell phone. "I'm tired. And I'm out of patience. So do yourselves a favor, and *just leave* before I do something you'll regret."

Joe glanced at the garden fork, tapping against her side. "But—"

"I feel it only fair to warn you," she interrupted, "that my next-door neighbor is a retired judge, and his number is pro-grammed into my phone."

"I don't care if he's the president of the United States," Mike growled. "You need to read that document. It'll explain everything."

"You're trespassing on private property. The judge is very protective of me, since his daughter and I were in the same graduating class." Mike opened his mouth to add to his tirade, but she said, "Oh. And he's an avid hunter. You should see the stuffed trophies on his library walls . . . moose, elk, caribou, even a grizzly."

Joe started for the car. "All right. Have it your way. We'll leave."

"But we aren't going far," Mike said. "We'll be back . . . with the sheriff. Once he gets a gander at that document, we'll just see who's trespassing."

She stood her ground, even as an arc of gravel spewed out behind them when they peeled out of the driveway. When Grace was sure they couldn't see her, she dropped to her knees, praying that the envelope in her pocket was as useless as her Uncle Mike and her cousin Joe.

Because if it wasn't, Dusty and the boys would feel the impact, every bit as much as she would.

23

"Hey, what's that?"

Squinting, Dusty followed the line of Cody's arm. "Is that . . . is it *Gracie?*"

"What's she doing?" Dom wanted to know.

Axel poked his head between the front seats. "Looks like she's praying."

Mitch leaned forward, too. "In the middle of the lawn?"

"What's she praying *for*," Montel said, "rain for her roses?"

The boys chuckled, but only until the van drew close enough to see her face.

"Hey. She's crying," Billy said.

"Never saw her do *that* before. You s'ppose she hurt herself or something?"

Dusty didn't think so, but he didn't want to worry the kids. Or worse yet, scare them. He steered the van as close to the back porch as possible and turned off the ignition. "You guys help Mitch off-load the groceries and get them put away. I'm sure everything's fine, but give me a few minutes to see what's up with Grace, okay?"

Nodding, they filed out of the van and into the house, carrying bags and cartons and flats of bottled water.

When he reached Grace, Dusty knelt in front of her, and, lifting her chin with the tip of his forefinger, said, "Hey, what's wrong?"

She hid behind her hands.

"Not ready to talk about it yet, huh?"

Grace shook her head.

He sat cross-legged in the grass. "Well, then, I'll just wait right here until you are."

She handed him the envelope, and when he started to ask what it was, she choked out, "I haven't read it yet, but I know it's bad news."

He opened the flap. "Where'd it come from?"

She sat back on her heels and took a shaky breath. "My uncle and cousin stopped by today. Haven't seen them in . . . in *years*."

Unfolding the document, he read the first lines: Michael Angel and Joseph Angel were suing her for their share of the family farm. He deduced that since Michael's name was listed first, he was the uncle, meaning Joseph was her cousin.

Grace pulled a tissue from her pocket and blew her nose. "Sorry. Never did figure out how to do that without sounding like a Canada goose." Then she said. "Look at me. I'm a wreck. Grimy and sweaty and—"

"Oh, I don't know. I think you're kinda cute, all dirty and puffy-eyed."

His comment inspired a tiny smile, followed by a quiet giggle. But she sobered up when the breeze rustled the pages in his hands. "So does it look official? Or is it as phony as everything else about them?"

It looked pretty darned legit to him, but Dusty didn't see any point in adding to her worries. Especially considering her "loving" kinfolk had only given her two weeks to respond. "I know a guy whose son just graduated law school. Bet the kid would love a chance to sink his teeth into something like this." He stuffed the document back into the envelope. "I'll call him first thing in the morning."

"Thanks, Dusty. I don't know what I'd do without you."

He got up, pulled her up, too. "Let's hope you never have to find out."

"Think I'll wash up in the barn. I'd hate for the boys to see me this way."

Too late, he thought, falling into step beside her, because he could tell from the looks on their faces that they'd been nearly as worried about her as he was.

"Mitch sprung for a roasted chicken. We can open a couple cans of vegetables, throw some biscuits in the oven, and voilà. Supper."

"He's great. The boys are great. *You're* great."

"You're not gonna go all weepy on me again, are you?" he teased, drawing her near. " 'Cause if memory serves, that tissue has seen better days. And if you think I'm gonna let you borrow my sleeve. . . . Well, let's just say I'm crazy about you, but not *that* crazy."

"I'm okay. At least, I think I can control myself. Until later. When I'm alone in my room."

"Is that your tough girl way of saying you plan to cry yourself to sleep?"

"Maybe."

"Then I guess I'll just have to sit up with you. All night if I have to." He pressed a kiss to her forehead. "Can't have my best girl weeping into her pillow, now can I?"

She looked up, a crooked smile on her face, and sighed. "Your best girl, huh?"

He kissed her cheek this time. "Yup, and I know how to get your mind off that legal mumbo-jumbo."

"I hate to sound like a sissy, but I'm too pooped for a walk."

"For what I have in mind, you won't have to move a muscle." He lifted her chin on a bent forefinger. "Well, maybe one." He grazed her lips with his. "Two, if you count each lip separately."

She melted against him like honey on a hot-from-the-oven biscuit. If this was the end result of distracting her from bad news, well, it surely would take the sting out of the everyday cares and woes that were part of life.

24

$\mathcal{H}$e'd been looking forward to keeping her company until she fell asleep, but the phone call that interrupted supper put an end to that in a hurry.

"I always knew you were selfish. Now I have proof."

"And now *I* have proof that you're a spoiled brat," Gavin said. "All this whining because you didn't get to finish your chocolate pudding? Please."

"It was homemade. With whipped cream."

"Waa-waa-waa."

Dusty might have laughed, if he didn't know Gavin so well. The hard edge in his cousin's voice told Dusty that something was up. Something unpleasant that somehow, involved *him*. "So spit it out, why don't you, and maybe I can get back into the kitchen before one of the guys has stolen my pudding."

"Remember Frank Benedict?"

Retired Marine turned cop turned youth counselor. "Yeah, I remember him. How could I forget? The big lummox has been dogging my heels since boot camp."

"He called, not ten minutes ago. Seems *he* got a call from Social Services. Cops picked up a boy. Runaway. Fourteen, fifteen . . . no way to know for sure, because naturally, the kid ain't talkin'. He's been beaten. Badly. Fractured ribs, broken jaw, chipped teeth. . . ."

"Who did it?" Dusty made himself unclench his fists.

"Like I said, the kid ain't talkin'. Whoever it was, was bigger and stronger than the boy."

"Wouldn't you like to hunt down the creep, give him a dose of his own medicine?"

"Oh, yeah. It's right up there at the top of my bucket list. Right above 'remove cast.' "

Chuckling, Dusty said, "So what's this got to do with me?" As if he didn't know.

"It'll take days, weeks, even, to find a suitable foster home. So Frank and me, we were hoping you'd have room for one more over there at Angel Acres."

"Maybe. I'll have to run it by Grace."

"Well, if that's the only holdup, the kid's as good as there. That girl has a heart as big as her head. When she hears what this kid has been through? She'll probably give him *her* room."

"So where is this kid?"

"Jesse. His name's Jesse Vaughn. Or so he claims. And he's in police custody right now."

"What did he do?"

"Stole a bunch of Tasty Kakes from the 7-11 on Route 40."

"Whoa."

"Frank already got the paperwork started. Says they'll release him into your custody. But you really oughta get over there tonight."

Because if he didn't, the cops would have no choice but to throw him into general lockup, with men twice his age, who'd committed . . . who knew what types of crimes.

"Let me get the ball rolling over here. Unless you hear from me in the next, say, fifteen minutes or so, you can tell Frank I'll pick Jesse up by nine. Where are they holding him?"

"Eighth Precinct."

Good. That wasn't far. Meaning if he could talk Mitch and Grace—and the boys—into helping the kid out, Jesse could fall asleep in a clean bed tonight instead of a jail cell, and safe from the animal who'd beaten him bloody.

The minute he hung up, he waved Grace and Mitch into the bathroom and locked the door behind them.

"What's up?" Mitch asked.

Dusty repeated, almost verbatim, what Gavin had told him, then gave them a moment to mull it over.

"Well, what are you waiting for?" Grace said. "Go get him!"

"Need to talk to the guys, first. See how they feel about absorbing another kid at the last minute like this."

"Right. Of course."

Then she turned to Mitch, as if she already knew what the kids would say. "There's a roll-away cot in the basement. Would you mind bringing it upstairs? There's space for it in Dom and Nestor's room . . . if we slide Jack and Billy's beds closer to the window. . . ."

"Don't ya just love her?" Mitch said, giving her a sideways hug. "Always thinkin'."

Matter of fact, Dusty thought, *I do love her.*

Laughing, they shared a three-way hug, then split up . . . Dusty to bring the boys up to speed, Mitch and Grace to get things ready for Jesse.

The drive downtown took less time than normal, thanks to the late hour; and when Dusty arrived at the precinct, the cops greeted him by name. No surprise there, considering that he'd done this dozens of times with the kids who lived with him now and others who'd already passed through the system.

While they went to fetch Jesse, Dusty scanned the boy's file. Nothing in it surprised him, so he put it down and rehearsed the routine: Take the kid to the diner for some one-on-one over a burger and fries, so he'd know what to expect when they got back to Angel Acres, then stop at the twenty-four-hour Walmart to buy him socks and underwear, a couple of T-shirts and some jeans. Because experience had taught him that while these kids always clung to a sack full of clothes, the stuff rarely fit. Either that, or it was way beyond raggedy.

When the cops rounded the corner, one on either side of Jesse, Dusty didn't know what to think. He'd expected a black eye. Two, even. Cuts and scrapes. Maybe even a swollen lip. But this? The kid looked like he'd gone three rounds with Mike Tyson, with both hands tied behind his back.

He'd shake the boy's hand . . . if the fingers weren't puffed up the size of bratwurst. He'd pat him on the back, but hadn't Gavin said something about broken ribs? More than ever, he wanted to find the beast who'd done that to him, and mete out a little vigilante justice.

Fine way for a preacher to be thinking, he thought. *Where was all the peace and love and godly forgiveness he'd learned about in seminary?* He gave himself a little leeway, because even Jesus had lost his cool in the temple. . . .

Dusty needed to get word to Mitch, so he could warn Grace and the boys. No way to do it, though, without Jesse overhearing him. So he slid a business card across the counter to the cop behind the glass partition, waved him closer and whispered. "Do me a favor, and call ahead, so nobody faints when they get an eyeful of that."

Nodding, the cop picked up the handset. "Will do," he said, and started dialing.

Sweet Jesus, Dusty prayed, walking up to the boy, *tell me what this kid needs to hear. . . .*

"You can wipe that look off your face, preacher, 'cause I don't need or want your pity." His eyes and lips narrowed at the same time as he added, "I'll take your charity for a night or two, because *these* bozos don't leave me much choice. You can take this to the bank: soon as I can run, that's exactly what I'm gonna do."

Dusty relieved him of the frayed backpack and held open the door. "Van's out front," he said. "It's open."

Jesse bobbed his head. "If I wanted to get in, no lock woulda stopped me. . . ."

Something told him a one-on-one at the diner would be a waste of time and money, so he aimed the van toward Baltimore County, and prayed the whole way there that he wasn't making the biggest mistake of his career, bringing Jesse to Angel Acres, because if anything happened to Mitch or the boys, he'd walk away from pastoring and counseling, permanently.

And if his decision to help the vengeful, self-professed tough guy brought harm to his precious Grace, Dusty might as well saddle up his Harley and ride it into the ground . . . because he'd never be able to live with himself.

25

When Dusty arrived with Jesse, Mitch was watching *Jeopardy* in the living room with the boys, and Kylie was in the kitchen, baking cookies with Grace. He had a fifty-fifty shot at saying the wrong thing with this kid, so he didn't waste time searching his mind for the right words.

"Hey, you two," he began, hanging Jesse's backpack on the back of a kitchen chair, "meet Jesse Vaughn. The young one," he said, pointing, "is Kylie Houghton. And the other one is Grace Sinclair . . . and you're standing in her kitchen."

"Oh great," the boy muttered, "another bleeding heart."

Kylie had just popped a ball of cookie dough into her mouth, and his comment stopped her, mid-chew. "Who, me?" she said around it. "A bleeding heart?" She laughed. "He's funny, Dusty. Where did you find him?"

"At the police station," Jesse answered, crossing both arms over his chest, "where the cops were holding me for robbing a convenience store."

Kylie exhaled a bored sigh. "Oh, great," she said, "another tough guy."

On his way to the table, Dusty noticed Jesse's eyebrows slide together. "What're you girls making?" He made a move to scoop a fingerful of the dough when Grace smacked the back of his hand.

"Soap and water first, mister," she scolded.

"What a fussbudget," he said, winking at Kylie. "You'd think I just came from a dirty Baltimore City jail or something."

The girl grabbed a spoon from the drain board and filled it with dough. "We're making chocolate chip cookies," she told Dusty. But she held the spoon out to Jesse.

He lifted his chin. "Like I care."

Now she grabbed his hand, and put the spoon into it. "I don't know any kid who doesn't love the stuff. Just eat it and quit pretending you're all big and bad."

He looked at the spoon, at Dusty and Grace, then ate the dough. "Why do you think I'm pretending?" he asked Kylie.

"Because you have nice eyes," she said matter-of-factly.

Jesse shrugged and licked the back of the spoon. "Whatever."

"What part of the South are you from?"

He gave her a quick once-over. "How do you know I'm from the South?"

"Because I'm from Tennessee, and you sound like—"

She stopped talking and blushed, and Dusty sensed it was because she'd never revealed that particular piece of information about herself before. Grace knew the girl way better than he did; one look at her face confirmed it: it was news to her, too.

Kylie continued as if there hadn't been a momentary gap in her conversation. "You might as well deal with it, Jesse Vaughn: there are some things that I just *know*."

"Whatever," he repeated. But his hard expression softened slightly when he said it. "How long you been in Maryland?"

"Long enough that nobody knows I'm from Tennessee."

When Jesse mirrored her smile, Dusty could have hugged her. Instead, he said, "Let's get the rest of the introductions over with, so Grace can show you around."

"Whatever," he said. But he followed without complaint.

"He has a very limited vocabulary, doesn't he," Kylie said . . . loud enough for Jesse to hear.

No one was more surprised than Dusty when the boy chuckled quietly. "She's a piece of work, that Kylie."

Jesse's mouth started to form the W of *whatever*. But he grinned and said, "I like her."

Axel noticed them first, and he got up to offer Jesse his seat. "Hey you bunch of stupid-heads," he said, "the new kid is here."

In one moment, Jesse was surrounded by grinning, teasing boys of every size and age and ethnicity. In the next, he'd joined the rest of them, slouched on the sofa, feet propped on the coffee table.

"Yo. Fool. Get them shoes offa there," came Montel's whispered warning.

Cody agreed. "Yeah, dude. That table belonged to Grace's grandma."

"Oh. Sorry," Jesse said as both feet dropped to the floor.

"Don't worry about it," Jack said, snickering. "Took us all a while to learn all her rules."

Jesse grabbed a handful of popcorn. "How many are there?" he said around a kernel.

"Well," Nick started, "there's the no-shoes-on-the-furniture rule."

"And don't forget the shoes-ain't-allowed-on-tables rule," Tony added.

"The rule I hate most," Billy put in, "is furniture-is-no-place-for-shoes."

Laughing, Jesse toed off his sneakers. "What. You think I'm retarded or something? I get it, dudes. I get it."

"Good thing, too," Nestor said, "'cause I don't think we coulda come up with another rule."

It seemed safe to leave them, so Dusty headed back for the kitchen. He felt a little guilty, expecting the worst without having given Jesse a chance. First thing tomorrow, he'd figure out a way to move him into the room with Trevor and Cody. Tonight, maybe it was a good thing that he had a room all to himself.

"How's he doing in there?" Grace asked, sliding a tray of cookies from the oven.

She'd pulled her hair into a high ponytail; if Kylie hadn't been there, pressed up against her side, Dusty would have kissed the back of her neck.

"He had me worried for a minute there, but he's doing great."

Kylie harrumphed. "I told you he had nice eyes."

"Speaking of eyes, yours look mighty sleepy," Grace said. "Did you get any sleep at all last night?"

"Two or three hours."

"You're kidding, right?" Grace said.

And Dusty chimed in with, Girls your age need way more sleep than that."

Kylie frowned. "Why? So we can grow up big and strong to take care of our husbands and children?"

Grace sighed. "No. 'Course not. I didn't mean—"

"I'm just pullin' your chain," Kylie said, grinning. "Here. Have a cookie. It'll make you feel better."

Dusty did more than accept it. He took a big bite. "You know what? I *do* feel better," he said, grinning.

"I appreciate the fatherly concern, but I can make up the lost hours *after* I finish my essay."

"She'll start classes at the U of M in the fall."

"Fall, nothin'," Kylie said, snapping her fingers. "More like *Au-u-gust.* I can't believe how this summer has just gone by."

Dusty and Grace exchanged a knowing glance, and Kylie said, "What?"

"Oh, nothing," they said together. And when they laughed, Kylie said, "Oh, brother. I'm surrounded by mental illness."

"You know, the world *is* filled with crazy people," Grace said.

Dusty grabbed another cookie, and using it as a pointer, said, "Had a professor in college, and on the first day of class, do you know what he said?"

"Are you Goofball or Doofus?" Kylie guessed.

"No . . . but that's funny." He looked at Grace. "Who knew? The girl has a sense of humor!"

"It's the nice eyes," Grace said, grinning.

Kylie groaned. "So what did your professor say?"

"He said, 'Crazy people marry crazy people, and they have crazy kids, who grow up to marry crazy people, and they have—"

Grace said, "Wait just a minute, here. How could you and Gavin have been in the same Psych class? Isn't he, like, ten years older than you?"

"Nine." He frowned. "Why?"

"Because he told me the same story."

Jesse walked into the room and helped himself to a cookie. "So what's goin' on?"

"Nothing," Kylie said, grinning. Then she grabbed Jesse's hand. "Come on. I'll give you a tour of the place."

Backsides leaning against the sink, Dusty and Grace stood side by side, munching cookies. This felt good. Felt right. Uncle Brock and Aunt Anita had enjoyed a relationship like this . . . comfortable enough in one another's company that they didn't feel the need to fill every silence with banter. They'd had a lot in common, the way he and Grace shared a genuine concern for the boys, and their faith in God, and a love for chocolate chip cookies.

"So what do you think of Jesse?"

"Well," she said, "he has very nice eyes."

They were laughing uncontrollably when Mitch and the boys, and Kylie and Jesse joined them in the kitchen.

26

*I*n the days since Jesse's arrival, the hard edge of his personality had softened slightly, but there were still moments when he seemed wary and distant . . . except with Kylie. He got along well enough with the other boys that Dusty had Mitch help him move the boy's things into the brothers' room, just as Grace had suggested. A wise decision, as it turned out, since it didn't look nearly as obvious when he took the boys back to Last Chance to pick up the mail . . . and to make sure *Los Toros de Lidia* hadn't decided to use the siding as a canvas for gang graffiti.

Today, right after breakfast, while Mitch took the others for their regular dental checkup, he and Jesse would drive to the old neighborhood. If things went the way Dusty hoped they would, fixing leaky faucets and oiling squeaky doors would give them the one-on-one bond they'd missed out on the night Jesse moved in.

He'd balked when Dusty told him to strap on a helmet, and didn't think much of riding the back of the chopper, but his attitude changed once Dusty opened her up, full throttle. There were miles of winding, hilly country roads that cut straight through Maryland horse country. Lush fields, dotted with sleek thoroughbreds and Black Angus cattle, stretched as far as the eye could see. It surprised Dusty a little that the boy who claimed to hail from bluegrass country behaved like he'd never seen anything bigger than a pit bull in his life. When Dusty threw down the kickstand beside the Last Chance garage, Jesse all but exploded with questions about horse-power and handbrakes and the cost of a motorcycle license. Dusty answered him honestly . . . avoiding the fact that the Harley was a big, powerful piece of equipment that, under certain conditions, required upper body strength, leg muscles, and clear-headedness. Ten years and fifty pounds from now, Jesse might grow into a machine like this, but right now, he was just a scrawny kid with unearned confidence and a bad attitude.

If he showed some promise today, maybe he'd let him straddle the hog—while the engine idled—to get a feel for how much power he'd be expected to control. If he didn't? Maybe *wanting* to would give him the incentive to exercise some responsibility.

He put him to work in the upstairs hall, with instructions to take the tub faucet apart and replace the worn washers. It had only been a few weeks since his release from the hospital, so Dusty loosened things up to ensure Jesse wouldn't pull a muscle or shatter a healing bone. "When you're finished here," he said, "you'll find an oilcan under the kitchen sink. I'm hoping you'll have better luck getting rid of that squeak in the back door than I did."

"Gotcha."

"And if you finish before I get back, you can give the mail box hinge a few squirts."

"Where you goin'?"

"Out back, to mow the lawn," he said. "And out front, unless I run out of gas first."

"Oh."

Something—Dusty couldn't put his finger on it—didn't feel right, and he gave a thought to letting the lawn go for another week so that he could work inside with the kid. But how would that look, so soon after his arrival, especially when he'd made slow but steady progress?

"There's water in the fridge and chips in the pantry," he said from the doorway, "so make yourself at home."

"Right," he heard Jesse say as he started down the stairs.

What choice did he have but to trust him to the Lord?

It took longer than usual to get the old mower revved up, and it started with a pop and a puff of smoke. That money from John would buy a new one, but Dusty wasn't sure they'd be here next season.

He cut on an angle, because when the job was done, it looked like a ball field. Once he'd stowed the mower in the garage and swept grass clippings from the walk and driveway, he headed for the kitchen. The door didn't squeak when he opened it, Dusty noticed, smiling as he grabbed a soda from the fridge. He popped the tab and took a swig, then set it aside to splash water on his face and neck. The mailbox lid didn't squeak, either. "Hey Jesse," he called up the stairs. "Good job."

No answer.

"How you coming with that faucet?"

Nothing but the steady *tick, tick, tick* of the mantle clock.

Dusty took the stairs two at a time. What if Jesse had re-injured himself somehow, or tripped on a loose tile, and hit his head on the tub?

The tools were in there, right where he'd left them on the vanity beside the faucet washers, but Jesse wasn't. Dusty looked into every room, in the closets, out the windows. Then he raced downstairs and did the same thing in every room on the first floor. "Jesse," he hollered, "if you want to try your hand at driving the Harley, you'd better get in here. . . ."

Still nothing.

He ran next door, but old man Isaacs hadn't seen him. Neither had Miller or Shipley. That left one possibility, and the thought of it made him sick to his stomach. It was stupid, going there alone, but what choice did he have?

When he climbed the porch steps, Gonzo was rocking in a threadbare blue recliner, walking a toothpick from one side of his mouth to the other. Two of his soldiers were there, too, one straddling the railing, the other stretched out on the welcome mat, his face hidden under an iridescent baseball cap, matching high-tops crossed at the ankle.

"Lose something, preacher?"

"I brought a boy here. Fourteen, fifteen." He held his hand parallel to the floor and level with his chest. "About this tall," he said, "blond hair. He's new, so he doesn't know the area."

Gonzo removed the toothpick and inspected its pointy end. "If I see anybody looks like that, I'll let you know."

The guy on the floor crossed his feet the other way, the heel of his shoe landing with a sudden *thump* that it startled Dusty.

"A little jumpy today, are we?" Gonzo said, and flicked the toothpick so that it landed at Dusty's feet.

He knew something. For all he knew, Jesse was inside, playing cards with Lenny and Quinton.

"You got a cell phone, preacher?"

Dusty nodded . . . about all he *could* do, under the circumstances.

"You should report this new boy of yours as a runaway. Before he gets too far from home. You know?"

Oh, he'd report something, all right. And when he came back with the cops, they'd have a search warrant.

Fists clenching and unclenching, he turned to leave . . . and Gonzo got up, leaned casually on the post that supported the sagging porch roof. The guy who'd been sprawled across the welcome mat stood, too, and Dusty saw half a dozen faces lined up in the windows behind them.

"Maybe you should pay more attention to your special deliveries, preacher . . ." He laughed, and so did the others. ". . . because next time I send you a message, it won't be so subtle."

If he considered a brick through a window subtle, Dusty didn't want to know what his definition of *obvious* looked like. He knew this much: Jesse had been here, might still be here, and if Dusty did anything the *Los Toros de Lidia* saw as a threat, the boy would pay the price. Much as he wanted to wipe that self-satisfied smirk off Gonzo's face, he walked away.

Head down, he ground his molars together and prayed, because if anything happened to Jesse at the hands of these gangsters, it would be on his head.

27

*H*e'd been standing in that same spot for hours, staring silently out the window, as if he believed a miracle would happen, and Jesse would come walking up the drive. Grace pressed close to his side, rested her hand on his forearm. "Lunch is ready."

"Go ahead and eat without me. I'm not hungry."

"But the boys are waiting for you to say the blessing."

"I can't, Grace. They'd see right through me."

She was afraid to ask what that meant.

"I can't wrap my mind around it. 'Ask and you'll receive.' It's a promise as old as those hills out there. I've asked 'til I'm hoarse. So when does the receiving part kick in, huh?"

She'd never heard him talk this way—not when he spoke of losing loved ones, not even when he'd told her why he'd left the Marines and the police department—and Grace didn't mind admitting how much it scared her. She squeezed between him and the windowsill and forced him to meet her eyes. "You can't keep this up. It's been three days, by my count, since you've had anything to eat. And you can't tell me you've been sleeping, either, because those dark circles under your eyes keep getting darker."

Nodding, he looked over her shoulder. "Remember what Kylie said the night Jesse came to us, when I gave her a fit for staying up all night to work on her college essay?"

For a moment, she envied little girls, who could stamp their feet and cry when things didn't go right in their worlds. What in the world did something Kylie said a week ago have to do with Jesse, running away? "That she'd make up for lost time after she'd turned in her paperwork."

"Right." His voice was a soft monotone. "Well, I'll sleep when he comes home."

"Torturing yourself isn't good for you *or* the boys. They're worried sick about you. And scared, too." She crossed both arms over her chest and said, "We're *all* scared, and if you ask me, you're being selfish."

Every muscle tensed as she waited for him to say he *hadn't* asked her. Instead, he hung his head. "Don't mean to be," he ground out. "I'm sorry."

"You've done everything humanly possible to find that boy." She counted on her fingers. "Reported him missing, called the police morning and night to see if there were any updates, walked and drove through every neighborhood between here and the Inner Harbor, asking questions, showing his picture, hanging flyers. . . ." She squeezed his arm, then gave it a shake. "Do *you* remember his first night here, and how concerned you were that he wouldn't fit in . . . ?"

Dusty exhaled a sad sigh.

" . . . and how you kept saying, day after day that this kid was different, that something wasn't right, and you didn't know if you could reach this one?"

"Never should have said those things. Never should have *thought* them. He deserved better than that from me. From *us*. After all he'd been through, he had a right to expect we'd reach him, no matter what it took. But you're right . . . I had doubts, and Jesse wasn't a dumb kid. He knew I didn't have faith in him."

"Stop talking about him in the past tense. You don't know that he's dead!"

He nodded again, more slowly this time. Because he agreed, at least a little bit?

"I'm praying as hard as you are, just like those boys out there in the kitchen. We're all hoping that he comes back, safe and sound, and *soon*. But if he doesn't?" She gave his arm another shake. "If he doesn't, well, it won't be because you didn't look hard enough for him. It'll be because he *doesn't want* to be found."

His eyes shone with unshed tears, and she could see that he was struggling to keep from breaking down. Eyes closed, he tilted his head toward the ceiling. *Praying?* she wondered. *Or searching his mind for a gentle way to tell her to go away, butt out, leave him alone?*

"You're wrong, Grace. I wish to God you weren't, but you're dead wrong." Hands on her shoulders, he said, "If he doesn't come back, it's on me, because I *put* him out there, where . . . where. . . ." He bit off the rest of the sentence, as if unable to think the words, let alone say them.

"He was easy pickings for those gangsters . . . young and naïve, and looking for someplace where he could feel he belonged. And I took him over there, and left him alone. And Gonzalez knew that. And like the scavenger he is, he swooped in and took him."

Was he even aware that he kept referring to Jesse in the past tense? What made him so certain that Jesse was dead? "You don't know that. You *can't* know that. Only God can—"

"I know what I felt, standing in front of that maniac's house."

He began to tremble, like a man who'd been carrying a too-heavy burden for far too long.

She couldn't stand to watch him suffer this way, especially for something that wasn't his fault. "Come sit with me, okay?"

He started to object, but she silenced him with a finger, pressed to his lips. "I didn't ask for your sake," she fibbed. "I've been on my feet all day, and my legs are about to give out."

Just as she'd expected, he complied. Why hadn't she thought to bring a sandwich, a glass of water when she went looking for him, because maybe he'd eat something . . . if he believed it was for her benefit. *More than one way to skin a cat,* she thought.

Grace let him get settled, and, standing beside him, said, "Don't you dare move from there. I haven't had anything to eat all day, and I'm famished."

Then she darted into the kitchen, where the boys were eating and talking quietly. She knew them well enough to believe they'd handle the truth more easily than empty "everything will be fine" promises, and brought them up to speed on Dusty's state of mind. "I'm going to try and get some food into him," she said, grabbing a sandwich from the platter in the middle of the table. "So pray like crazy that he snaps out of this, fast."

She read the concern on their faces . . . and the hope in their eyes. "And while you're at it, pray for Jesse, too, okay?"

A chorus of "you got it" and "count on us" echoed around the room as she grabbed a bottle of water from the fridge, making her want to hug them all.

So she did. "You're the best," she said, kissing cheeks and mussing hair. "Lord in heaven knows how much I love the lot of you!"

Then she raced back to the living room. Thankfully, Dusty hadn't moved, save to lean back against the sofa cushions, eyes closed. When she put the sandwich plate and water on the table, he said, "No need to be so quiet. I'm not asleep."

Grinning slightly, Grace climbed into his lap. "*Now* let's see you go back to gawking out that window!"

One side of his mouth lifted, ever so briefly. He looked so lost, so miserable that she wanted to absorb his pain. When she wrapped her arms around him, Dusty burrowed his face into the crook of her neck . . .

. . . and quietly wept.

He'd always been the strong one, the guy who knew exactly what to say and do in every situation. Friends, neighbors, the boys, and, yes, even Grace turned to Dusty for advice, for comfort and reassurance. *Lord,* she prayed, *give me a glimpse into his heart, if only long enough to know what he needs to hear.* She refused to spout empty platitudes, like "Please don't worry" and "It'll be all right" or "Put your faith God." He deserved better than that. So much better than that!

Faith. . . .

Dusty had displayed more of it than anyone she'd ever known. He credited faith for getting him off the crooked path he'd once walked, and readily admitted faith was what kept him on the straight and narrow. If he stopped believing in that, what would become of him?

Eyes closed, she held her breath. Every muscle tensed and every nerve end jangled as she waited, waited for divine guidance.

But instead of the confidence-building Scriptures she'd expected God to whisper in her heart, Grace heard Dusty's tortured, ragged voice, admitting that he'd never felt more helpless. Not on 9/11 when his unit got word that America was under attack. Not days later, when he found out his beloved uncle died in the North Tower. Not even when he realized he was stuck in a war zone, fighting for people who might be blood kin to the terrorists who'd turned the whole world upside down.

"Don't you get it, Grace?" he ranted. "*If* Jesse's alive, he's out there somewhere, feeling *just like that*. I was a grown man, a seasoned soldier when it happened to me. But Jesse . . . Jesse's just a kid! A kid who believes he isn't lovable, because in his whole short life, nobody ever showed him any love."

The fear and fury and guilt he'd been holding onto for so long poured out in the form of tears that soaked her shirt and sobs that wracked his body. Maybe, upon hearing her prayer, God had decided *she* was the one in need of guidance. This was a divine reminder that while Dusty's heart had been true, right from the start, she'd judged him uncaring and cold, because he'd taught himself to cope with the ugliness of death and the pain of loss by hiding it, behind a rough exterior and gruff words.

You couldn't have been *more wrong!*

He'd taught her the meaning of *real* kindness and compassion—rare and beautiful gifts, possessed by only a handful of humans. She was fortunate to have them, and blessed to have *learned* them through Dusty's unwavering example.

The tenderness she felt toward him consumed her, and Grace held him tighter. He'd changed her attitude and outlook, her heart, her whole *world*. If she could, she'd gladly have traded places with him. Anything to give back a little of the joy he'd brought into her life. "Oh, you sweet, sweet man," she whispered into his ear, rocking him, stroking his hair, kissing his cheek, "do you at least feel a little guilty for stealing my heart?"

He sat up and sniffed, and hands bracketing her face, he said, "I didn't steal it, Grace. You gave it to me, with each big-eyed glance and silly smile . . ." he nodded toward the plate on the coffee table, "with every meal and perfectly brewed cup of coffee." He kissed her forehead, then reached past her and picked up the sandwich. "*How* it happened isn't near as important as *that* it happened." He took a bite, then washed it down with a gulp of water. "If it's any consolation," he said, taking another bite, "you've got mine, too."

Grace bowed her head to ask God's forgiveness for selfishly wanting Dusty to push through his sadness quickly, so he could go back to being the tough, honorable man she'd come to rely on.

"You're probably right," he said after a while, "and Jesse will come back, eventually. But until he does, I can't live another day without you. I know it's selfish, asking you to share all the craziness that is my life, but life is short, and good times too few. . . ."

If he's gearing up to pop the question, she thought, *Lord help me answer quickly.* Because in his state of mind, even the slightest hesitation would do far more than hurt his feelings. "If you ever decide to give up preaching, or counseling," she said, smiling, "you might want to consider poetry. . . ."

"See," he said, chuckling, "stuff like that makes me want to spend every waking minute with you." He put what was left of the sandwich back on the plate and folded his big hands, as if in prayer. "Will you marry me, Grace?"

28

$\mathcal{D}$usty hadn't been that low in a long, long time.

If Grace hadn't come into the room when she did, would he have given in to the temptation to fire up the Harley and ride until he ran out of gas . . . or skidded out? Hopefully not, but he thanked God for the diversion, all the same. Because going back to that life was as unthinkable as anything he could imagine. It would have started with him aiming the bike toward AJ's—one of a handful of Baltimore area bars that didn't mind bikers and boots, nor long hair and beards. He'd just as soon forget the way they'd tipped jigger after jigger of Jack Daniel's, talking about who they'd been and what their lives had been like before 9/11. . . .

He could hear her in the kitchen, cupboard doors banging and pot lids clanging as she prepared for spaghetti night, the boys' favorite meal of the week. She'd been so unbelievably happy—or was *relieved* the better word?—when she left him to start supper, because she hadn't understood that he'd only done what any honorable man would have done under the circumstances. Especially since it had been his self-centered behavior that—

Dusty cringed, remembering what he'd let her see. Ashamed that he'd lost control, that he'd opened his personal version of Pandora's box and started pitching the contents of it at her, had made him want to retch. So he'd dug deep, telling himself that he'd tried; that if Jesse had stayed, they could have shed some light into the dark murk that had been the boy's life. *But the kid had a death wish,* he told himself. Even Grace had pointed out that Jesse had run off because, having never experienced it before, he didn't know how to handle compassion. What she didn't understand was that Dusty had seen kids like Jesse before. Anybody with a lick of sense knew better than to leave one of them alone, even for a minute. Had Jesse gone back to sleeping on park benches, beside winos and bag ladies? Was he eating out of dumpsters again? Or was he riding high on life (and only God knows which drugs) and the promises Gonzo no doubt had made to lure him in?

Neither scenario had a fairy tale ending for Jesse. Dusty knew that. Grace did not. She hadn't lived an easy life—far from it!—but nothing in her background had prepared her for what to expect with a kid like Jesse.

She started whistling a tune he recognized, but couldn't name. In the moments it took to search for a title, Dusty admitted that even if Grace *had* been exposed to the aching disappointment that came with admitting you'd lost another one, she would have leaned on her faith, and let it lead her to the bright side. What kind of preacher was he, that he'd completely skipped over that step?

Now Grace was humming. Probably making mental lists, things like who she'd share her good news with first, which friends would stand as witnesses at the ceremony, whether they'd marry soon, or wait until spring. It might have made him laugh . . . if it wasn't so blasted *sad.* He didn't know if she dreamed of a storybook wedding or what her favorite color was. Had no idea if she preferred Dickens to Shakespeare, or Pepsi to Coke. Did she have a collection of Teddy bears in her room, a bunch of Eagles CDs on her nightstand? He'd learned other things in the four months since they'd met . . . that she had the biggest heart God ever put into a human, which went a long way in explaining why every one of those rough, tough street kids behaved like little Lord What's His Name in her presence. She'd had a civilizing effect on them—on him, too, if he was honest. Being completely without family—those two losers who'd filed the lawsuit didn't count—she'd counted the lot of them as her own. And he felt the same way. *Family.* It had been a large part of the reason he'd come up with his whole "move to Angel Acres" idea.

That day when Jesse disappeared, Gonzo had made it clear: he aimed to take over the neighborhood, house by house, boy by boy, by any means necessary. By bringing the kids here under the guise of "helping her out," he'd bought a little time to prevent it, that much was true. But in so doing, he'd put Grace in Gonzo's sights, too.

And now, because in a weak-willed moment he'd blurted out the secret he'd been holding in his heart, she believed they had a future. Like Austin and Mercy, or Matt and Honor, who'd overcome all manner of craziness to be together.

At least you had the good sense to tell it like it is, Dusty thought, remembering his "I know it's selfish to ask this" line. If she knew *how* selfish, she would have run screaming from the room as if her hair had been on fire.

And he probably *would* have jumped on the bike to drown his sorrows in jigger after jigger of Jack Daniels. It's what he did in the old days when things seemed out of control . . . before Griff got hold of Dusty's old drinking buddy and scared him straight with Scripture and good old-fashioned fire and brimstone. He'd never know the details of the night when Griff had found Austin, passed out cold in AJ's parking lot, because Austin wasn't talking. He knew all he needed to know: Austin quit drinking. Quit going to AJ's. Quit cussing and smoking and chasing skirts *and joined the church!* In the privacy of his own head, Dusty had given it a month. Two, tops before his drinking, carousing, brawling buddy was back on track. But he'd been dead wrong. Months passed, then a year, yet Austin stayed on track. And two months after earning his one-year sober coin, it was Austin who found *Dusty* in the parking lot at AJ's. The morning after, he didn't know if the hammering headache would kill him, if his parched throat would just decide to close up and choke him . . .

. . . or if Austin would nag him to death.

The memory made him smile.

But it didn't last.

Because he kept picturing himself, curled into a ball like a spoiled boy, blubbering into Grace's shoulder. By the grace of God—and Grace Sinclair—the boys had been spared the pathetic sight. But he would have bet the Last Chance house and everything in it that they knew what was going on in her living room. And if he'd given in to the urge to head for AJ's, well, they would have figured that out, too, and he didn't know how he would have faced them if that had happened.

So as Dusty saw it, he had two problems. Big ones. And both needed to be dealt with, quickly.

He had to find Jesse.

And he had to make sure Grace understood what kind of man she'd hitched her wagon to.

※

Dusty had joined her and the boys for spaghetti night, and all through the meal, it was obvious how hard he was trying to behave as though Jesse wasn't missing, and Gonzo wasn't a threat, and he hadn't proposed marriage to a woman he'd known a mere four months, one week, and three days. He'd turn forty on his next birthday, and had managed to live every year of his life unencumbered by relationship-type commitments. What did he want with an almost-thirty-something woman with more emotional baggage than a luggage carousel at BWI?

One of the lessons life had taught her was to thank God for all blessings—big and small, deserved or not. She'd have to watch him closely, very closely from now on. He was a man of honor, and now that he'd committed himself, Dusty would not go back on his word. So if she saw even a glimmer of regret or indecision in him, she'd find a graceful way to let him go, even though it would be the greatest regret of *her* life. But if a wedding actually took place at some point down the road, she'd put everything she had into making sure Dusty never regretted his decision, and she'd start by showing him how grateful she was for what he'd done to ease her mind about the lawsuit.

It hadn't taken long for his friend's son to find out that her uncle's document was a forgery. If she wanted to, the fresh-out-of-law school attorney had said, he'd file a lawsuit on her behalf . . . right after turning her uncle and cousin over to the cops. "They could serve two to nine years," the young man had said, "for illegal use of a notary seal."

"No, let's not file a report," she'd told him. "I'll handle them, myself."

They no doubt remembered how she'd panicked at the prospect of standing before a judge when her parents' wills had been read, and how terrified she'd been when her grandparents had filed for legal custody of her. Two years ago, they would have been correct in assuming she'd hand over the ten acres that their phony pleading demanded. To be honest, she might have caved *one* year ago.

But that was pre-Dusty. Pre-Montel and pre-Axel and pre-all of the boys. She was a stronger woman now, and thanks to them, Grace had good, solid reasons to fight hard for the humble little farm that her grandparents had built from nothing. And fight she would . . . just as soon as her so-called relatives showed up to hear what she'd decided.

"I was *hoping* we could settle this without lawyers and judges," Uncle Mike had said.

"Yeah," Joe had added, "why should the shysters get paid to do what we can do ourselves? We're family, after all!"

Family, indeed. If they had any idea what that meant, they wouldn't have disappeared when Gramps fell ill. And after he passed, they'd have helped Grams, left alone to do a man's job in the twilight of her own life. They hadn't shown up for either funeral, and Grace would have *bet* the ten acres they'd been drooling over that they wouldn't have shown up now, if Uncle Mike hadn't reached retirement age.

Well, Mikey, *you won't be rockin' on* this *porch in your golden years,* she thought, staring across the lawn.

Thanks to Dusty and the boys, she'd been able to bring all twelve cows back from her neighbor's farm. It had galled her to move them over there, but teaching from September until June, then working all summer as a waitress at the Double-T left no time to care for them. Their feed and vet bills, added to the cost of keeping the lights on and food in the fridge, didn't leave much for her savings account, but Grace held fast to the belief that one day, God would reward her for her faithfulness—to Him, to her grandparents' dream, and to this place that had been home for fifteen years.

The wheat her neighbor planted was tall enough now to sway with every puff of wind, and the soy plants sat squat and lush in their tidy, green rows. Beyond that were fields of ryegrass and fescue, and she could hear the occasional lowing of the cows as they ambled from the sunny fields to the shade of sugar maples, white ash, and honey-locusts planted by her grandfather. "Silly bovines," he liked to say, "think I put 'em out there for *their* pleasure." Mostly, the trees prevented erosion, but it was still a sight to behold when the cows flopped down for a cool nap, side by side by side.

She thanked God yet again for Dusty's intervention, for without it, Mike and Joe would have put into practice the "give 'em an inch, they'll take a mile" rule. It was unfair on so many levels that Grace could barely contain her anger.

Then came the familiar sound of a car's tires, grinding up the long gravel drive. Too soon to be Dusty and the boys, returning from another attempt to find Jesse. A chill snaked up her spine, and Grace wished she hadn't insisted that Mitch go with them, because it would have been comforting to have his bulky presence standing nearby when Mike and Joe stepped out of the car. "Well, Uncle Mike," she muttered as the big, old boat rolled up to the porch, "you weren't here for Gramps or Grams's funerals, but you'll get your chance to say a final goodbye . . . today. . . ."

"Hey, there, Gracie girl," Joe said.

Feeling mighty sure of yourself, aren't you, cousin. . . . To this point, she'd conducted herself like a proper Christian, and she'd rather have them go right on thinking that's exactly what she was. But with these two? No telling what threats might spill from her mouth before she sent them packing, once and for all.

"Don't suppose you have anything cold to drink," Mike said, drawing the back of his hand across his brow.

"What's the matter? No air conditioning in your Caddy?"

"Well, of course there is," Joe answered, "but the a/c uses more gas. And with the price of—"

"Stay put," she interrupted, "and I'll get you both a bottle of water." She'd already set up the rockers so that two sat side by side, with a third, facing them. She handed them each a bottle of water, then sat in the one by itself and uncapped her own. "Have a seat," she said, smiling.

"Good to see you're willing to be civilized about this, Grace."

"Yeah," Joe agreed. "I would've sworn we were gonna have a big fight on our hands."

"Oh?" Grace took a sip. "Why would you think that?"

"Well, you've been here all these years, and then we show up." Mike shrugged. "Naturally, we figured you'd decide the place was more yours than ours." He uncapped his bottle. "Even though I'm the rightful heir." He grinned. "As Mom and Dad's only son."

Funny, she thought, *that Joe was the one who seemed nervous. Had he been the one who'd drawn up the official-looking pleadings? Maybe he was wondering if he'd forgotten to dot an 'I' or cross a 'T.'* She slid the envelope from her back pocket, separated it into three stacks on the table.

"I took the liberty of making duplicates," she said, watching as they each grabbed a copy. Mike seemed calm and sure of himself, but Joe's hands were trembling. *Patience,* she told herself; in a moment, Mike would be shaking, too. "So I take it you're aware what the penalties are for forging court documents?"

Mike scowled and Joe blanched.

"Forging? That's crazy! This," Mike said, shaking his copy, "is as real as the nose on your face."

"I should be insulted that you think I'm so gullible that I'd sign this without having it validated."

Joe swallowed. Hard. "Validated? How? By who?"

"*Whom*, you idiot," Mike said. Then he zeroed in on Grace. "I don't know what you think you're trying to pull, Gracie, but—"

"You have five minutes," she said, standing. "That's plenty of time to finish your water."

Mike stood, too, and took a step forward. "But Gracie girl," he said, flipping to the last page, "this isn't signed. 'Fraid you'll just have to put up with us until you write your name, and the date, right *here*."

She looked at the smudge on the signature line. "Gee, Mike, thanks."

"Thanks?" He tucked his chin into his collar. "For what?"

"For leaving forensic evidence on your phony paperwork. When I call the cops in . . ." She checked her watch, "three minutes, I'll have your fingerprints as proof that you were here, making threats and trying to pass off a forgery as a legitimate document."

Eyes narrowed, he ground his teeth together. *Keep that up,* she thought, *and you'll pulverize your molars.*

She tapped her watch. "Tick, tick, tick. . . ."

"This isn't over," Mike said, heading for the steps. "Come on, Joe. Let's go back to the courthouse and file a complaint."

At least Joe had the decency to look guilty. "I'm a little surprised how you turned out," she told her cousin. "Grams always told me you had more sense than . . ." Using her chin, she indicated Mike. ". . . than him. She knew he'd never amount to anything, but she had high hopes for you."

His cheeks darkened with a guilty blush.

"Much as I miss her, it's a blessing to know she isn't here to see how wrong she was."

When Joe joined his father on the bottom step, Mike said, "Don't pay her any mind. She's as crazy as that no-good father of hers was."

Grace only shook her head. "Oh. I almost forgot. I have something for you." She fished a twenty-dollar bill out of her pocket and handed it to Joe.

And he took it. "What's this for?"

"Gas. For your clunker over there. So you can crank up the a/c on your way back to whatever rock you drove out from under."

Mike stomped toward the Cadillac. Then, leaning out of the passenger window as Joe backed away from the porch, he snarled, "This isn't over."

She met his defiant glare with one of her own and repeated, more slowly this time, "Tick. Tick. Tick."

Relief washed over her as the car made its way down the ribboning drive. When the last of the dust settled, she took a deep breath. They wouldn't be back. She knew it like she knew Angel Acres was hers: cows, guest cottage, and fences.

She could hardly wait for Dusty to get back. If this trip to the city didn't roust out Jesse, he'd be even more despondent than he'd been yesterday; maybe knowing that he was largely responsible for the good news she'd share would lighten his load, a little bit, at least.

After putting the rocking chairs back where they belonged, Grace picked up the water bottles and headed for the kitchen. Tonight, they'd have pot roast with all the fixin's. If Dusty didn't find Jesse—and it would be a miracle if he did—he'd need a good, hearty meal in his belly. He and Mitch and the boys didn't need to know it would be a celebration of sorts for *her.*

The roast was on the stove and the cake in the oven when she called Molly Logan's room at Taylor Manor. Her mood brightened considerably when a nurse said, "She's out on the tennis court, laughing like a teenager."

Next, she called Gavin. Last time they'd talked, he told her the cast was coming off this week. If he could drive, she'd invite him to supper . . . one more pleasant distraction in case Dusty came home with bad news.

Half an hour later, his mood was hardly jubilant when he told her they'd hit a dead end in the search for Jesse, again. Then his cousin arrived and the boys started milling around the kitchen, setting the table, pouring milk, adding chairs for Mitch and Gavin.

Watching the roast, potatoes, and carrots disappear as they chatted amiably reminded her of the nature documentary she'd watched on Animal Planet one night. A parade of giant ants in a Brazilian rain forest devoured leaves and twigs and grass, leaving nothing but dry dirt in its path.

Dusty's cell phone rang as she put the pot in the sink to soak. Hopefully, the caller wouldn't keep him long; she wanted to get his reaction to her grandmother's recipe for chocolate fudge cake. When Grace walked back into the kitchen, the boys and Mitch and Gavin were oohing and ahhing over the treat. "Coffee's hot. Or I can pour you a glass of milk," she said, pointing to his plate.

"No time for dessert," he said, grabbing his keys. "That was the hospital. Jesse's on his way to the OR."

29

*T*he waiting room was crowded with pacing boys and a limping Gavin. Nothing Grace said seemed to calm them as they waited for Dusty and Mitch to come back with a report on Jesse's condition.

Until she suggested that they pray together.

It was Montel who agreed first. "Can I say the prayer?" he asked.

"Of course you can," Grace said.

The boys gathered round, and, without being asked to, bowed their heads. Grace found herself fighting tears, because not long ago, not one of them knew the Lord. *But look at them now,* she thought as, eyes closed, they folded their hands.

"Sweet Jesus," Montel said, "watch over Jesse. He ain't nothin' but a skinny white boy, Lord, and needs all the help he can get, pullin' through this. When them doctors get done with him," he continued, "he'p us to know how we can get him better, fast. . . ." He paused, and in the silence, the boys looked up. He was smiling when he finished with " . . . 'cause it's about time he learned to pull his weight around Angel Acres."

Like a Gregorian chant, their soft amens filled the waiting room.

And then Dusty joined them. He looked tired, so very tired, that Grace just wanted to gather him up and rock him to sleep. "Where's Mitch?" she asked instead.

"Getting coffee and sodas," he grated. "You guys okay to hang with us here for an hour or two, 'til Mitch can take you and Grace home?"

Home. He'd called Angel Acres home!

Axel piped up with, "We can stay as long as you do." He looked at Grace and wiggled his eyebrows. "Ain't like the teacher is gonna write us up for bein' late for class."

"No," she countered, matching his grin, "but I could put you to work, doing chores around the schoolhouse. . . ."

"Well," he drawled, "we done stacked the firewood for the woodstove, Miz Sinclair, an' swabbed the outhouse, too."

"So good to know you were paying attention to my mini-lecture about the settlers," she said.

Montel seemed restless and edgy. "So what happened to Jesse?" he wanted to know. "Did he run out in front of a car or somethin'?"

Dusty looked at Grace and shrugged. He had hoped to avoid that question, his posture and facial expression said.

"The *Los Toros de Lidia* got hold of him," Dusty said. "Near as I can figure, pride is as much to blame for what landed him here as that bunch; if he'd told them he was still healing from that beating he took before he came to us, they might have delayed the 'beat in.'"

"What a blockhead," Nick said. "He was actually gonna go through with a gang initiation?" He shook his head. "I know he's just a dumb kid, but *that* dumb?"

The rest of the boys grumbled their agreement as a nurse stepped into the waiting room. "He's asking to see you," she said.

Dusty nodded. "On my way."

"Not you, sir . . . the young lady."

"Me?" Grace didn't understand. She probably hadn't exchanged two dozen words with the boy since he moved in. Why would he—

"I believe he said your name is Grace?"

She looked at Grace. "If you'll just follow me. . . ."

"Tell him we're pulling for him," Guillermo said.

"And praying," Nestor added.

Dom crossed both arms over his chest. "And that if he talks to any of those Bulls again, I'll kick his butt, myself."

"You okay, going in alone?" Dusty wanted to know.

Smiling, Grace shook her head. "Going in alone," she quoted. "You make it sound like I'm with the S.W.A.T. team, on my way to talk a hostage-taker into surrendering."

Dusty bobbed his head. "All right. Okay. But I'll be right outside. In the hall. If you raise your voice, for any reason, I'm in there. Got it?"

"Got it." She looked up into his handsome face, hoping that things would work out so that she could keep *on* looking into it, every day, for the rest of her life. Then she followed the nurse into the ICU.

"Two minutes," the woman said, "and not a second longer. He isn't even fully conscious yet."

"Do you mind telling me what the doctors had to do? So I'm sure not to say anything I shouldn't, I mean. . . ."

"Epidural and subdural hematomas," she said.

"Blood clots? Where?"

"There were blood clots in his abdomen, stomach, and brain. And a rib punctured his left lung. The team also had to insert steel pins in his femur and humerus."

"The team? How many doctors were involved?"

"Wow," the nurse said, "let me see." She began counting on her fingers. "Miller's with orthopedics, Harrison is a neuro-surgeon, I think Mendell is a vascular surgeon, and—"

"Sorry I asked," Grace said. "Guess he looks pretty bad, huh?"

"Yeah, that's a pretty good guess."

"So what's the prognosis?"

She shrugged. "They've done all they can for him, surgi-cally. Now we wait. And hope."

"And pray."

Another shrug. "If that works for you. . . . Long as he doesn't develop an infection, or pneumonia, or pick up MRSA, he should be out of here in a week. Two at most."

"Guess I'll get in there." Two weeks in the hospital. Grace had no idea how Dusty would pay for that. But knowing him, he had a reserve set aside, just for such emergencies.

The nurse sat at her tiny desk, with a clear view of Jesse on the other side of the glass wall, and began pecking at her com-puter keyboard. "Two minutes," she said without looking up.

"'Zat you, Grace?" Jesse whispered.

With tubes and cords running every which way, he looked like the creation of some mad scientist. "Well, look at you, Skippy." Thankfully, the steady *beep-beep-beep* of the monitor told her some things were functioning normally. "Wide awake and free of the ventilator already. That's a good sign. A very good sign!"

The corner of his mouth lifted in the slightest hint of a smile. "Skippy?"

She patted his hand, but didn't let go. "Don't ask me why, because I don't have a reason!"

"Closer . . . ," he rasped.

"What can I do for you? Big Mac? Starbuck's frappuccino? Remote control for the TV?"

Another tiny smile again, and then, "I want you to know, in case something goes wrong, that—"

"Jesse Vaughn, let's have no more of that kind of talk, do you hear? You're going to be just fine. The boys asked me to tell you they're praying for you. If you take your time and do what the doctors and nurses tell you to, you'll be home again in no time."

His eyebrows lifted slightly. "They hardly know me. Why do they care?"

"Because they see what I see: A sweet, warm human being, hiding behind an angry tough-guy façade."

Eyes closed, he nodded. "Anywa-a-ay," he slurred, "you need to know I didn't tell them anything."

Who? she wondered. *And what hadn't Jesse told them?*

And then she knew: *Los Toros de Lidia.*

His breathing calmed, and she thought he might have fallen asleep. "May the angels watch over you, sweet boy," she whispered, pressing a soft kiss to his forehead.

He spoke so suddenly that it startled her, and Grace straightened.

"They don't know where you are," he said on a sigh. "They asked, over and over, but I swear to you, Grace, I didn't tell them."

"Jesse," she blurted. "You mean to say . . . you let them do this to you . . . to protect *us?*"

"Partly. It was s'posed to happen. 'Beat-in,' y'know? But then. . . ."

His voice trailed off as a furrow formed on his brow. "Are you in pain, Jess? Let me call the nurse."

"Give it a minute," he ground out. "If it doesn't pass, you can get her."

The nurse looked up just then and held two fingers in the air. Then she mouthed, "Time's up" and used her thumb to motion "Out."

"I have to go now, Jess, so you can get some rest. But before I do, I have to tell you . . . I think you're the most heroic boy I've ever met. Why, I don't know many *men* who would do what you did."

The minuscule grin again. "Dusty would."

"Yes, I believe you're right. But he didn't get his start at being a superhero as early as you did. Just imagine what you'll be like when you're his age!"

A serene expression relaxed his features, and he nodded slowly. "Will you come back, Grace?"

"Only if you promise to work hard to get better."

The only sound in the room was the high-pitched bleep of the monitor. Until the nurse said, "Miss . . . you'll have to leave now. . . ."

"All right," she told her. Then she leaned close to Jesse and added "Well, what do you say?"

"Promise."

She kissed his cheek again. "I'm gonna hold you to that."

Jesse nodded once, then drifted off to sleep.

Please God, she prayed, *heal him, inside and out . . . and make sure you don't forget his big, protective heart that was broken by his parents—the two people in the world he* should *have been able to trust above all others.*

30

$\mathcal{H}$e left the boys alone in the barn to practice the CPR tactics he'd taught them, and headed for Bayview to visit Jesse. After what had happened to the kid—and hearing the EMTs and doctors talk about how close he'd come to dying out there in the street that night, Dusty decided his boys would learn as much as their punkin' heads could hold.

Using the manuals he'd studied to earn his SAR certification, he badgered them like a drill sergeant. Over and over, they practiced stitching cuts (using scraps from his old leather jackets). Again and again, they splinted one another's arms and legs, fashioned makeshift crutches from boards and branches, memorized how to take a person's blood pressure using an old-fashioned tube-and-bladder cuff, and did the math to determine pulse and heart rate.

They took to it like squirrels to sunflower seeds . . . once he got them started, they couldn't get enough. If—God forbid—an urgent situation cropped up at Angel Acres, they'd be more than equipped to handle themselves. Would they get nervous those first couple of times? No question about it. But practice makes perfect, he'd told them; the more often they play-acted emergencies, the more prepared they'd be for the real thing.

Dusty shook his head as he walked into Jesse's room. Grace, God love her, had insisted that the boys bring cards every time they stopped by, so many that the entire wall beneath his TV looked like a collage. She'd picked flowers from her gardens, and, using empty butter tubs and milk jugs, spaghetti sauce jars and soup cans for vases, covered every flat surface with blooms. Mylar balloons floated here, stuffed animals sat there, and books and magazines were scattered across his tray table.

"I don't mean to sound ungrateful," the boy said, grinning, "but it'll be good to get out of here, just so I can get rid of all this *stuff.*"

"It is a little excessive," he agreed. "Want me to tell her to back off a little? Maybe take some of it out of here next time she—"

"No way! That would only hurt her feelings. She's only doing it to make me feel special, and, well. . . ."

"Loved?"

Jesse blushed. "Yeah." He shrugged his good shoulder. "I know she means well. And I appreciate it. Honest. It's just. . . ."

"Good incentive to do your part during physical therapy, so things will get back to normal?"

"Yeah," he said again. "So what're the guys doing?"

Dusty told them how he'd been teaching them CPR and all that went with it. "Mitch is going to bring some of them this afternoon, and the rest will come with Grace, tonight."

"Well, that isn't very smart."

Dusty chuckled. "What isn't?"

"Letting her take the night shift. Wouldn't it be better if she came in the daylight, instead of Mitch?"

"You know, that's an excellent point. And I'm going to see about making that switch, just as soon as I get home."

"So you rode the Harley over here?"

"Yep."

"Can't wait 'til I'm well enough to take another spin on that thing. Didn't think I'd like it, but hoo-boy, was I wrong."

Dusty understood, perfectly. "It's addictive, I've gotta warn you. . . ."

"One habit I wouldn't mind having. Once I'm better. And old enough for a license. And have a job to pay insurance. And buy my own hog."

He said he wanted a red one, not black like Dusty's. But the helmet would have to be black. "One of those sit-on-top-of-the-head kinds, because they look *cool*."

"True enough."

"If you think so, why don't *you* have one?"

"Because an older, wiser friend pointed out that if I ever got in an accident, I'd better hope I land on the top of my head. That's the only place you get any real protection with one of those."

"True enough," Jesse quoted, nodding. "Never really thought about that before."

"So how's it going with your exercises?"

"Miserable. I hurt everywhere."

Dusty wasn't surprised; there weren't many places on the kid that the Bulls hadn't banged up. "Mind if I ask you a question?"

"Not if you don't mind me sayin' 'none of your business' if it's none of your business."

He returned the boy's smile and sat on the pink plastic chair beside the bed. "Who do you suppose chooses the color schemes for hospitals?" he wondered out loud.

"I hear ya," Jesse said. "Puke green walls, pink chairs, black and yellow tiles on the floor. Somebody color blind, I'd bet."

Laughing, Dusty sat back in the chair, rested an ankle on his knee.

"So what's this burning question?"

"How did you end up all the way down the block at Gonzo's place that day?"

"Saw those guys out there, lyin' around like they didn't have a care in the world. Lookin' cool and tough and in charge, y'know? I saw a news thing about gangs, heard some of 'em say they're like family. That they have each other's backs. And I thought to myself, maybe that's what I needed. To belong someplace. To be a part of something."

Dusty nodded. He'd heard it all before—from cop friends who specialized in gang violence. He wondered if Jesse understood that once you're in, there are only two ways out . . . head first, or feet first. "Feel the same way now?"

Eyes wide, Jesse shook his head, then winced. "Ow," he said. "I keep forgetting they messed up my neck." Then he looked at Dusty. "They said the beat-in was a test. To see if I deserved to be with them. 'Gotta know you have what it takes to stand up to the enemy.' That's what Gonzo said."

"Why didn't you tell them you'd just gotten out of the hospital?"

"They didn't ask."

Dusty read the look on his face: *I was afraid to tell them.* He understood that; from everything his cop pals had told him, they delighted in torturing the weak. It explained why, during other initiation methods, new recruits were required to rob a store at gunpoint. Beat an innocent civilian senseless. Rape a woman. Kill somebody. Senseless violence that had one purpose: prove your *machismo.* Cross the leader or one of his favorites, they'd all find out sooner or later, and be victim to the same cruelty.

"So what's on the menu for lunch?"

"I picked grilled cheese, mac and cheese, and tomato soup. And hopefully, the Jell-o won't be *green* for a change."

Dusty laughed. "Hopefully."

"So you need anything, kiddo? Magazines? Puzzle books? A squirt gun to torment the nurses with?"

When Jesse giggled, it reminded Dusty just how young he really was. He'd escaped the Grim Reaper this time; if it came calling again, he wouldn't be as lucky. Not that enduring a pounding that crushed bones and shredded tissue was luck. But maybe this had taught Jesse that he could enjoy the benefits of a family atmosphere without getting his head bashed in.

"Can I ask you another question?"

He smoothed his covers. "Shoot."

"What happens if Gonzo comes back?"

"He won't."

"You sound awfully sure of yourself."

"I am."

"Mind if I ask why?"

"What are you, a lawyer in disguise or somethin'?" Jesse snickered. "You sure are fulla questions today."

Dusty pocketed his hands. "Sorry. Don't mean to be nosy."

"Aw, I was just kidding. I really don't mind answering." He took a pull from the straw poking out of the green plastic cup on his tray. "I know he won't be back 'cause I heard him telling the others that I was weak. 'Put him someplace the cops will find him,' he said. 'I ain't gonna face no murder rap 'cause this skinny, li'l white boy can't cut the mustard.'"

Ah, Dusty thought; *Jesse had failed the "are you tough" test. Ironic—that pack of two-legged wild dogs felt superior enough to reject "a skinny white boy" because he couldn't handle a beat-in.*

"You ask me," Dusty said, "this was a blessing in disguise."

"Didn't ask." He laughed again. "Kidding. Just kidding." But he grew completely serious when he said, "I know I'm lucky. You don't have to worry . . . I'm not retarded. No way I wanna go through this again."

"That's good to hear. Real good," Dusty admitted. Then, "Well, better get back. Make sure those guys didn't get too serious about those rough and ready splints."

He turned to leave when Jesse said, "Can I ask *you* a question?"

"Sure. Long as you don't mind me sayin' 'none of your business' if it's none of your business."

"You gonna teach me that CPR stuff when I get back to Angel Acres?"

"Yep."

"So I *am* going back there, then?"

"You bet." Dusty winked, snapped off a small salute and said, "Catch you later, kiddo."

He was in the doorway when Jesse called his name. "Can I ask you one last question?"

"Shoot."

"You gonna marry Grace?"

The mention of her name sent his heart into overdrive. "That's the plan."

"What happens to us, afterward?"

"Nothing changes for you guys. *Nothing.*"

"So, is the reason I'm going back to Angel Acres because there are no foster homes available?"

Translation: *when a space opens up, will you kick me to the curb?*

"To tell you the truth, I never looked into it." He winked. "And that was three questions, not one."

Jesse shrugged. "So . . . are you going to?"

"Wasn't planning on it. I like things just the way they are. Besides, with you in the house, we have an even dozen kids."

Grinning, he said, "That's good to hear. Real good."

They shared a laugh over the one-liners they'd repeated. Then, on a hunch, Dusty walked to the bed and gave Jesse a hug. "See you tomorrow, kiddo."

He'd carry the memory of the look his hug had induced for a long, long time.

31

$y$ou know what I wish?"

"What?"

"That one of these old rocking chairs was a two-seater."

He'd been sitting there in the dark, eyes closed as the summer breeze riffled through the porch, enjoying the rhythmic sound of tree toads and crickets, and the occasional katydid. "You know what my uncle used to say?"

"Hmm . . . ?"

"That when you hear the katydids, it's only eight weeks until winter begins."

"Weird."

"No it isn't. It might be off by a couple days, but I kid you not, it's not just an old wives' tale."

"No . . . I said 'weird' because my grandfather used to say the same thing. And follow it up with stuff about the width of wooly worms' stripes and how lots of acorns on the ground are signs of how severe the winter will be."

He reached for her hand. "I wish one of these squeaky old things was a two-seater, too."

Somewhere in the far distance, a siren wailed. A dog barked. A truck horn blared. But here, at Angel Acres, it was quiet enough to hear the wind rustling the tree leaves. He liked it here. Once the back-and-forth shuffle of visiting Jesse in the hospital was over, he'd see what she thought about selling the old, drafty house in the city, and living here.

"So how was Jesse when you saw him earlier?"

"Looking better every day. And what's this he tells me . . . you think I'm incapable of holding my own in the dark?"

Her voice was stern, but that shaft of moonlight, falling across her face, told him otherwise. "Only if you stepped into a bear trap. Or drove the wrong way over those "don't go here" spikes in a parking lot."

"Hmpf."

"Well, can you blame me? You're barely bigger than a minute. What do you weigh . . . a hundred pounds soaking wet?"

"Never got on the scale soaking wet. I have no idea."

He liked this . . . the quiet easy way they were together. Even with a houseful of boys of all shapes and sizes, colors and ages, the place pulsed with peace. "So have you thought about a date yet?"

"A date. . . ."

"Don't gimme that. You know exactly what I'm talking about."

She laughed, and oh, how he loved the sound of it. A strange little prayer popped into his head, and made him laugh, too: *Please Lord, don't ever let her get laryngitis; I'd miss that voice and that giggle like crazy!*

"I was thinking maybe December. You know, so I could wear satin and you could wear velvet."

That sat him up straight. "Velvet? You're kidding, right?"

"One of those fancy tuxedos with tails, and a ruffled shirt. A black satin bow tie. And oh! A top hat!"

He leaned forward, to get a better look at her face. *Thank the good Lord,* he thought, *she* was *joking.* "And here I was going to suggest a drive to the Inner Harbor tomorrow. Just the two of us. An early dinner in Little Italy. A walk around the promenade. Maybe stop in a jewelry store so you can pick out your engagement ring. . . ."

Now she was leaning forward, too, and smiling, the moonlight flashing like white lights in her dark eyes. "*Was*?"

"I just recited half a novel, and you focus on *was*?" He laughed. "Life with you will be a lot of things, Grace soon-to-be-Parker, but boring sure ain't one of 'em."

"You're going to think I'm crazy. . . ."

"Ha. What's this 'going to' stuff? I *already* think you're crazy."

Her eyes widened as her brows disappeared under dark, curly bangs.

"Well," he said, getting onto his knees in front of her chair, "you said yes to a future with the likes of me. How sane could you be?"

She pressed a palm to each of his cheeks. "You know, when you're right, you're right." Then she kissed him, long and slow and sweet, leaving him too breathless to respond when she said, "I'm crazy about *you*, that's for sure."

Dusty would have kissed her again . . .

. . . if his cell phone hadn't buzzed in his pocket. Grumbling under his breath, he flipped it open. *Nah, can't be,* he thought, reading the caller ID line. But how many Randi Fletchers could there be in the world, with a New York area code?

He couldn't imagine why she'd be calling after all these years, but as usual, her timing stunk. "I'd better take this," he told Grace.

She didn't ask who it was. Didn't tell him it was too late for phone calls. Didn't ask him to hurry inside. Not Grace. She stood, and pressing a loving kiss on his chin, went inside without a word. A moment after he said "Hello" into the phone, she whispered through the screen door, "When you're done there, we need to pick up where we left off. Which, if memory serves, had something to do with engagement rings?"

She disappeared down the hall as Randi said into his ear, "I know it's been a long time, and I wouldn't have bothered you now, but. . . ."

Why the slight hitch in her husky voice? Maybe she'd run out of friends who'd cough up bail money, and thought maybe he'd come through for her in a pinch . . . for old time's sake.

"I'd really rather not do this over the phone," she said. "Is there any way you can meet me tomorrow?"

"Randi, you're in New York. I'm in Baltimore. How's that possible?"

"No need to speak to me as if I'm a three-year-old," she snapped, reminding him of the arguments that far outnumbered the good times they'd shared. She'd been a darned capable partner . . . until she got into the bad habit of snorting cocaine.

"I'm in town," she said, "staying at the Sheraton downtown."

Keep your big yap shut, he told himself. *The less you say, the sooner she'll hang up and get out of your life. Hopefully this time, for good.*

But he'd said that the last time they were together, and here they were, embroiled in the beginnings of a bickerfest.

"Same old Dusty, I see. . . ."

He didn't have to ask what *that* meant. Wait long enough, experience had taught him, and she'll tell you. A couple dozen times, if memory served.

"Don't you care why I'm here?"

On the heels of a heavy sigh, he asked, "Why are you here, Randi?"

"Because I have cancer. And I'm dying. And with no family to turn to, there's no one I trust to take care of Ethan."

Dusty's heart skipped a beat, remembering the night they'd gotten plastered, when she asked him what he'd want to name his son, if ever he had one. He'd said Ethan. And if he had a daughter? "Brigid," he'd said without thinking, "because it means *strong*." And Randi had said, "Done!" It had been good for a laugh at the time. But now? "What are you trying to pull?" he demanded.

"Look. I know this is a shock, and out of the blue and all that. But I swear on my mother's grave, everything I've said is the gospel truth. If you'll just meet with me tomorrow, I can prove it."

Half of him believed her; her voice *had* sounded a bit hoarse. The other half remembered all too well lies upon lies that she'd told while they were together. Lies that not only ended her police career, but ended them, as well. "Did you fly into town?" he asked

"No. I drove. And Ethan is here with me."

Ethan again, he thought. It was tempting to say . . . *is Ethan my son?* Instead he said, "I'll meet you in the hotel restaurant. Say, ten o'clock, to beat the lunch rush." He wondered, if the boy was with her, what she planned to do with him while this *get-together* took place.

She didn't answer right away, and that worried him. "I'm hoping your cell provider didn't drop the call. . . ."

"No. I'm here," she said. "Ten is fine. But in the lobby, not the restaurant."

"Fine." He didn't ask why, because he didn't care. If she had some convoluted need to be in control, so be it. She'd called the meeting, after all.

Ethan, he thought, listening to the silence. Was it possible that he had a son?

She'd always been easily distracted, especially with a nose full of coke. Was she high, now? "Here's a question for you," he said. "How'd you get this number?"

Randi snickered, but he didn't hear any humor in it.

"I was a cop, which, as my partner, you know better than just about anybody."

Former partner, he wanted to say. But he didn't.

"You really aren't a hard man to track down. I Googled you, and something like ten thousand links popped up . . . one, an article about you in the *Baltimore Sun,* where the reporter quoted you as saying the city needs more places like the Last Chance." She paused. "What kind of name is that, anyway? Sends a pretty bleak message to those kids you say you're trying to help, don't you think?"

He and Mitch had had the same argument no fewer than a dozen times over the years, and he'd won them all with pure, simple logic: "The church I bought the house from is called Last Chance for God. Made sense to hold on to the connection."

More silence. This time he filled it with unasked questions: If Ethan was his son, how old would he be? Dusty thought back, trying to remember the last time he and Randi had been together. Sometime after Christmas, six—no, seven years ago— near as he could recall. A party at their sergeant's house; he'd brought enough beer for everyone, Randi . . . enough cocaine to get her through the night. If he allowed nine months for nature to take its course, that would make the boy nearly six years old, come September.

Enough of this hanging on to dead silence, he thought. "See you at ten, then, in the lobby."

He was about to hang up when she said, "He's yours, Dusty, and I can prove it."

And then she hung up.

32

*H*e hadn't even stepped out of the revolving doors before a kid said, "Hey. Mom. Look over there. Is that him? Is that my dad?"

Several hotel guests frowned. One woman clucked her tongue. Even the concierge looked a bit put off by the question. He did his best to ignore the judgmental stares, and resisted the urge to say, *I only just heard about this yesterday. Give me a break, folks!*

He crossed the room to where Randi and a small boy sat side by side on one of the lobby's brown leather sofas, staring at him as if he'd grown a second, head. Dusty couldn't think of a situation when two heads were better than one. "No," he said, hand up to stop her when she started to stand. He sat in the chair across from them, looking from her haggard face to the boy's. What was he supposed to say now? "It's good to see you"? "You're looking great"? Neither was true, so he said, "So. This is Ethan."

He leaned close to his mom and whispered in a voice loud enough for the desk clerk to hear. She shot Dusty a dirty look when Ethan said, "He really *does* look like me, doesn't he, Mom!"

Her expression said *told you so*. But her mouth said, "He saw a picture of you, years ago. Hasn't cut his hair since."

He wanted to deny it, but the boy was right. He looked exactly like Dusty had at that age, right down to the gap between his two front teeth and the big dimple in his right cheek. He even covered his top teeth with his bottom lip when he grinned. If Dusty had a dollar for every time someone said, "Nice Stan Laurel impression," he'd have enough money to buy DVDs of the 1930s and 1940s movie comics, Laurel and Hardy.

"Mom is sick," Ethan said. "She's trying to make an appointment with some big-shot cancer doctor at Hopkins." He shrugged. "So far, no luck."

Well, *there* was a character trait that had changed in the years since he'd been with Randi: back then, she'd been the most guarded woman he'd ever met. More than once, he'd compared getting anything out of her to trying to break into the Pentagon's innermost ring. The fact that she'd been that honest with him about her condition? A surprise. A big one.

"You feeling up to a walk?" he asked her.

"I suppose. Where to?"

He heard the more important, unasked question: *Why?*

"Thought maybe we could browse the shops. Let Ethan, here, play some games in the arcade while we, ah, have coffee and, um, catch up."

Half an hour later, Randi was using a French fry to draw squiggles and curlicues in the puddle of catsup on her plate, while Ethan pounded the controls of an ancient Miss Pac-Man machine. Already, Dusty had grown tired of waiting for the proof she'd promised to deliver.

Look," he said quietly, "I'll grant you he looks a lot like me." The truth was, they shared a dozen mannerisms, too, but he couldn't admit it. Yet. "But short of a DNA test, I don't know how you hope to prove he's mine."

"I'm okay with that . . . if you are."

Her directness unnerved him, but he couldn't admit that, either.

"So tell me about your, ah, illness."

"Cancer," she said. "It's okay to say it. Nothing politically incorrect about calling a spade a spade." Then she shrugged, and with a nod toward Ethan, said, "He knows the obvious stuff, but all the gory details? I've turned myself inside out, trying to spare him that."

It started with the smoking, she told him—cigarettes, pot, half a dozen other recreational inhalants that kicked off a host of benign symptoms. Coughing and wheezing, shortness of breath, a raspy voice. "If I didn't have bronchitis, it was pneumonia," she said, "and after a couple years of that, my oh-so-alert GP ordered a battery of tests. Sputum screening—I know, gross—X-rays, CT scans, MRIs. Finally, I ended up in Sloan-Kettering, where they lopped off some of my left lung. And then the *real* fun began. . . ."

Chemotherapy, radiotherapy, heated cisplatin, she added, none of which put a dent in it, because the cancer had spread to her liver and diaphragm, lymph nodes, and chest wall. "Nothing to do now but wait for that bright white light every-body says they see when it's 'time.'" She drew quote marks in the air.

"I'm sorry, Randi." And he meant it. Sorry that she'd suf-fered. Sorry that she'd gone through all that—pretty much alone. Yeah, she'd caused him tremendous heartache and more misery than anyone he'd ever known, but he still had a soft spot in his heart for her.

"Knock it off, Parker," she said, frowning.

"What?"

"Looking at me as if I'll fall over dead, right here."

"I'm not. Am I?"

"Have you ever known me to beat around the bush?"

It's your M.O., he thought. But what good could come from admitting that now?

"I don't need your pity. I need you to step up. Do the right thing. Get to know your son before I croak. Because he's going to need you once they plant me, and—"

"For all that is good, Randi," he said, wincing, "there's a difference between beating around the bush and . . . and *graphic*."

"What? You want me to cry? Wring my hands? Stamp my feet and demand to know why God let this happen to *me*?" She dropped the French fry and sat back, arms crossed over her chest. "Been there, done that, sweetheart . . . got the T-shirt and outgrew it, long, *long* time ago. This is all brand-spankin' new to you, but I've been dealing with it since Ethan was five."

"Why didn't you call me *then*?" *Why didn't you call me when you knew you were pregnant?* Had she spent a little time after the breakup, looking for comfort in all the wrong places? Places that made her think that maybe somebody else was Ethan's father?

She leaned both elbows on the table. "Look, I hate to be blunt, by I'm sure you understand why I've taught myself not to waste time in silly pleasantries. I didn't call you because I didn't have time for dilly-dallying. And that was your M.O., remember?"

Dusty frowned. "Big difference in that and not wanting to decide which movie to see or whether we should eat Italian or Mexican."

Randi harrumphed. "That isn't what I'm talking about, and I think in your heart of hearts, you know it."

"No," he said, not caring any more if impatience was evident in his voice. "I really am that thickheaded. So why don't you spell it out in easy-for-idiots-to-understand language?"

"Okay. Fair enough. How's *this*?" She leaned closer, lowered her voice, flattened her hands on the tabletop. "I figured you were the same old hard-drinking, skirt-chasing, bar-brawling *boy* you'd been when we were together. *That's* why I didn't tell you." One glance at Ethan was enough to soften the hard edge of her ire. "But then I got sick, really sick, and it scared me to death, because . . . what would become of Ethan? Then I remembered how having him changed me. I thought maybe, just maybe, there was the ghost of a chance that something, some*one* had changed you, too. So I Googled you." Randi laughed quietly. "And whoa. Was I one surprised skeptic! When you change, you go all-out, don't you?"

Ethan ran up to the table. "Need more quarters, Mom. That machine is gobbling them up like candy!"

She dug around in her purse. "Sorry, sweet boy," she said, grinning, "I'm tapped out."

Dusty took two dollars' worth of quarters from his pocket. And after handing them over, he tousled Ethan's hair.

He could see the wheels spinning in the boy's head as he tried to decide whether to call Dusty by his first or last name . . . or *Dad*.

"Better get over there," he said, sparing him the decision. "Looks like somebody's eyeballin' your machine."

"Reminds me of a cartoon character when he does that," Randi said when he darted off. "He's, like, *poof*, gone in a blur."

"So how are you set for money?"

"Well *that* was out of the blue!" She laughed. "Money isn't a problem. Never has been. But now that I've stopped treatments—

unless you count aromatherapy and acupuncture—I'm even more okay, financially."

Dusty had a hard time believing that, so he only shrugged.

"Seriously, I'm fine. Thanks for asking. I have all that moolah from my grandparents' and parents' estates, remember? Lucky for me, I had the good sense to put it in the hands of an investment counselor. Scary dude with Albert Einstein hair and Andy Rooney eyebrows." She shuddered. "Never spent a dime because I was always too afraid to explain what I needed the money *for!*"

He'd almost forgotten how funny she could be, how much fun they'd had together. Which reminded him of Grace . . . ten times the woman Randi had ever been, with a sweet sense of humor and a heart as big as her head.

"So who's the lucky lady?"

He looked up so fast, he nearly upended his coffee mug.

"Oh, come on. You can tell me. We're old pals, right? Besides, it isn't like you're doing a very good job of hiding it. Let me tell you this, *pal,* if you'd ever looked at *me* that way," she teased, "I might not have kicked you to the curb."

"Hmpf. The way I remember it, I left *you.*"

"Revisionist history."

He chuckled as she coughed into a paper napkin. She'd tried to be discreet, but he'd seen the bright splotch on the napkin.

"So what's the prognosis?"

"No need to pussyfoot. This is *me* you're talking to. Tough. Hard as nails. Able to leap tall buildings in a single bound. . . ."

"Okay. Have it your way. How long do you have?"

That sobered her up, fast. "Six months. Eight. A year at best."

"Sheesh. . . ."

"Yeah. Tell me about it." She took a sip of water. "Now you see why I'm kinda desperate, here. Can't leave Ethan with my friend. She already has four kids, which was great for Ethan when he had to stay with her, but she's pregnant. *Again*." Randi rolled her eyes. "I swear, the girl must have rabbit somewhere in her ancestry. But I digress. Not only is she adding another bunny to her herd . . . her oldest son was just diagnosed with leukemia." She sighed. "Adds a lot more brine to the pickle water I'm in: she can't handle the extra stress, and it isn't fair to let Ethan get lost in the shuffle."

Randi hadn't been exaggerating, Dusty thought, *when she'd said "desperate."* "So what's this about you seeing a Hopkins specialist?"

She waved the question away. "Oh. That. I had to tell him something. He's every bit as smart and astute as his dad. I needed *some* valid excuse to come all the way down here."

Smart and astute as his dad. . . . It would sound good. Real good. If it wasn't so scary.

"Look, there's no reason to break a sweat, here. Ethan's a good kid. Easy going. Honest. Works hard in school. Empathetic . . . way, *way* easier to deal with, I'd guess, than those hoodlums you've been working with for years."

"They aren't anything of the kind. Abandoned, neglected, abused. . . . Do they come to Last Chance with problems? Are they furious? You bet. And they have every right to be. But it doesn't take long, in most cases, before they figure out they weren't responsible for the crazy things their parents did. I could list dozens of success stories."

"I'm not worried about those," she said quietly. "It's the failures that terrify me. Because if Ethan moves in with you, he'll move in with them, too."

If? Better question was, why had her "if" stirred so much disappointment in him? She still hadn't shown him any real proof that Ethan was his. . . .

Randi exhaled a hoarse sigh. "So I guess there's only one way to ease your mind. We'll go to a clinic. Tomorrow. For a blood test. DNA comparisons. I'll tell Ethan it has something to do with one of my treatments. He won't give it another thought."

"It takes weeks to run tests like that."

She stared him down. "And your point is?"

The point, he thought, *was that every day spent waiting for some fool test results to come back was a day wasted.* And she didn't have a day to waste. Neither did Ethan. He'd need every moment between now and the ugly end to adjust to life without his mom. And Randi had been right about something else, too: Ethan needed to get to know Dusty, now, so that when that awful day came, he'd have a loving father to lean on.

"Look. This is a lot to absorb. I realize that," she said. "I know you're a Christian now. A *preacher* of all things . . . never would have predicted *that!* Believe it or not, so am I. Came to a whole new way of thinking and living the minute I found out I was pregnant. And I've been straight ever since."

Seemed more than unfair, Dusty thought, *that after everything she'd done to upright her upside-down life, she faced a death sentence.*

"What I'm trying to say—and not doing a very good job of it—is that I figure you need time to sort things out. To think and pray. Decide how you're going to break the news to your sweetie pie."

Grace. Dusty took a huge breath. He'd have to tell her. Everything. The sooner, the better. But first, Randi had been right: if he hoped to make the right decision, here, the one *God* wanted him to make, he'd better hit his knees, first chance he got, and stay there until things made sense. Or as much sense as they *could* make, considering. . . .

Ethan ran back to the table, put his hands on the arm of Dusty's chair and smiled up at him. The nanosecond passed with the lightning speed of flashback scenes used by movie directors:

The dimple. The gap in his teeth. The lone freckle in the middle of his left cheek. Eyes that sparked blue, lavender, even gray, depending on the light . . . colors he'd seen only in the mirror . . . until now. Those lashes? Randi hadn't been the only woman to wonder why she needed mascara to get the look Dusty was born with. And what about Ethan's tendency to nod while talking, as if to underscore certain words, and the way his left brow rose when someone *else* was talking. . . . Coincidence? Dusty didn't think so. A strange, sweet warmth churned in his heart, and made him believe—

"Hate to be a pest, Dad, but. . . ."

Dad. . . .

The warmth swirled in his head now, too . . . with a bit of regret mixed in. Dusty had known the boy less than an hour, and already, he'd let him down. Then he was keenly aware of all the years that had passed, and wondered what Randi had told Ethan, to explain why he didn't have a father.

". . . but did you get those quarters?"

Dusty took a deep breath and fished around in his other pocket, came up with three quarters, and, holding the small hand in his own, pressed the coins into Ethan's palm. "Will that do for now?"

Ethan looked at the money, at Dusty, at Randi. "You're right, Mom," he said, grinning. "He really *is* a decent guy!" Then he patted Dusty's forearm. "I hope you're keeping track of what I owe you. Mom says only losers and deadbeats borrow money and don't pay it back."

"It's good advice, and if you take it, I guess we can be pretty sure *you* won't grow up to be a deadbeat or a loser." Dusty put an arm across Ethan's shoulders. It seemed such a normal, natural thing that he wondered why he'd waited so long to do it. "But how about if we call it a gift. Then neither one of us has to keep track."

"Whoa. Cool. Thanks, Dad!" And then he ran off to drop the quarters into the nearest coin slot.

"He's a great kid. You deserve a lot of credit, doing that all by yourself."

"Well, he gets most of the credit, for being a 'do the right kind of thing' kid." She paused long enough to take another sip of water. "You get some of the credit, too, y'know."

"*Me?* No way! I didn't even know about him, so—"

"A lot of who he is was built in, thanks to DNA."

Dusty didn't know what to say to that, so he shook his head. It was a lot to wrap his mind around: Deception. Lies. Secrets. *Fatherhood.*

But he'd sort through all of that later. Right now, he heard a giant imaginary clock, ticking off the moments left in her life. "If it's okay with you, maybe I can take him for a spin on the Harley tomorrow, buy him a hot dog someplace, give you a chance to take a nap or something."

Her eyes widened and she smiled, *really* smiled, for the first time since they'd reconnected. Because she believed he'd do the right thing.

And why wouldn't he?

Ethan was his son.

His *son!*

33

I don't mind admitting . . . never thought I'd see the day when *you'd* be a dad."

Dusty frowned. "Okay. That settles it. *You're* buying the coffee today."

"No. Wait," Austin said. "That didn't come out right. I didn't mean it that way. Exactly. But seriously?" He shook his head. "Pretty amazing, is all I'm sayin'."

Dusty more or less understood why Randi had made the decision to keep her pregnancy a secret. He hadn't exactly walked the straight and narrow during the many months they were together. But *Austin?* Best buddy and long-time confidant, who'd questioned his sanity when he made the decision to trade temptation of every shape and size to work with a bunch of troubled boys? Dusty flattened a palm against his chest. "I'm hurt. Deeply."

Austin laughed. "Save it for some guy gullible enough to buy the Brooklyn Bridge. This is *me* you're talking to."

Randi had said something similar, when he'd tried to avoid providing details about Grace.

"So what does Grace have to say about all this?"

He grimaced. "Haven't told her yet."

"Mistake. Big mistake. Women have been known to be understanding—it's rare, I know," he said, laughing—"but only if you can convince them they were in on things from the ground floor."

"Hasn't even been twenty-four hours yet since I found out."

"Then you should've told her twenty-three and one-half hours ago." Austin whistled. "I'd love to be a fly on the wall when you spring this on her." He bobbed his head and tried his best to impersonate Grace. "You've known all this time," he said, his voice a reedy falsetto, "and you're just now getting around to telling me? I'm hurt, Dusty. Hurt!"

"She isn't like that," Dusty said, laughing.

"You believe that?"

"Sure."

Austin shook his head. "Okay. Whatever. But like I said . . . fly on the wall, brother. Fly on the wall. . . ."

"I'm going to tell her. Today. Just wanted to take a breath. Make some sense of it. I mean, how does a guy tell the woman he's gonna marry that he fathered a kid, way back in—"

"Whoa. What's this? You popped the question, and she said yes?"

"Thanks for the vote of confidence, friend. Remind me why you're my friend?"

"Don't get me wrong. I thought she was great from the minute you introduced us at Tuck's funeral. But you've got yourself all wrapped up with those kids. And she's. . . ." He made a rolling motion with his hand, as if that would stir up the word he was looking for.

"Footloose and fancy-free?" Remembering the day Grace had said those very words to him, Dusty smiled.

"Give me a little credit," Austin said, feigning shock. "Given time, I could have come up with something a whole lot less . . .

sissified." And then he laughed. Loud enough to draw the attention of the two elderly women at the next table.

"Keep it down, goofball, before one of 'em pulls out a ruler and smacks the back of our hands."

Austin tipped an imaginary hat at them. "Sorry, ladies. Got a little carried away when my buddy, here, told me that he asked his best girl to marry him."

Amid the gushing congratulations, Dusty felt the heat of a blush creeping up the back of his neck. When it ended, he zeroed in on Austin. "I was about to ask you to be my best man. But now I'm thinking . . . maybe not."

"You can't kid a kidder." Then, "So have you two set a date yet?"

"Haven't even bought her a *ring* yet. She said something about December." The comment reminded him of the way Grace had teased him, about wearing a velvet tux with tails. At least, he hoped she'd been teasing. . . .

"Speaking of dates and rings and such," Austin said, "did you hear about Matt and Honor?"

"I did." He nodded approvingly. "'Bout time, I'd say."

Austin nodded, too. "Here's an idea . . . if you talk Grace into saying the I Do's sooner, maybe I can get double duty out of my rented monkey suit."

"Nice to know who's first in your book."

"Hey. A hundred bucks is a hundred bucks! I'm a married man now, with a gorgeous little mouth to feed."

"How *is* Katie?"

"Terrific. Perfect. Best thing ever happened to me, if you want to know the truth."

Dusty wondered if the day would come when he felt that way about Ethan.

Austin got to his feet. "Well, better get to work," he said. "Call me after you've spilled the beans, *Humpty*. I'm told I'm pretty good at putting the pieces back together again."

"You're all heart, you know that?"

Austin tapped his temple. "Heart, and brains . . . smart enough to know you'd better hotfoot it over to Angel Acres and bring Grace up to speed."

He tossed a fiver on the table and headed for the door. "Seriously. Call me."

The next thing he heard was the tiny bell above the café door, signaling Austin's exit. *Funny,* he thought, climbing onto the Harley, *that bells alerted people to telephone calls, visitors at the door, the last line typed on an old-fashioned typewriter.* They even got special mention in that old movie: "Teacher says every time a bell rings, an angel gets his wings." But they indicated the start and end of every boxing round, too.

He buckled his helmet's chinstrap, frowning at that analogy: would hearing his news hit Grace like a TKO?

Turned out it was *Dusty* who felt as if he'd been sucker punched. If he'd known that, maybe he would have had the good sense to feed it to her a little at a time, over the course of a few days, instead of spitting it all out at once that way.

She hadn't said a word, not even to ask questions as he spelled it out, detail by detail. And when it was all out there in the open, he waited. *Say something,* he thought. Even a cold slap would be easier to take than her stoic silence. Finally, *blessedly,* she took a deep breath, and on the exhale, said, "I hate to ask this, because I'm sure hearing from Randi has been really hard on you, but would you mind very much going back to Last Chance, just for a little while? Mitch and the boys can stay—no need to disrupt their lives while I sort through this—but I need. . . ."

He watched as her brow furrowed, as she bit her lower lip, swallowed and shook her head. Clearly, Grace was having a tough time with this. And who could blame her?

" . . . I just need a little time."

It surprised him a little . . . the lump that formed in his throat, blocking words. So he nodded. Blanketed her hand with his. Because he'd have given anything to spare her this. Since he couldn't, he'd do whatever it took to make it easier for her. Especially if it meant she'd come around, in time.

She walked with him to the porch, took his hand. "Do you need to get anything? Socks and T-shirts? Jeans? From your room, I mean."

God love her, thinking of his best interests, even now. "No. I have duplicates over there." *Besides*, he thought, *I'll be back in a day. Two, at most.* He hoped.

Dusty wanted to hold her. Kiss her goodbye. But . . . what was the protocol in a situation like this?

She answered the question by sliding her arms around him and snuggling close. "Maybe on second thought. . . ."

His heart beat harder, hoping to hear her say she didn't need time.

" . . . maybe Mitch should go with you." Grace looked up, her brow furrowed with concern. "You know, with that gang so close by. . . ."

Disappointment battled with the relief of knowing she cared enough to be concerned. In the end, love won out. "I'll be fine," he said, kissing her forehead. *Lord, help me win this one. . . .*

Because if he had to choose between this loving, capable, remarkable woman and the boy who'd grown up without a father, who'd soon lose his mother . . . ?

He climbed onto the Harley, fighting tears as it rumbled down the drive, praying that God would move this mountain-sized problem aside and make a way for them to be together. Because without her, life with Ethan wouldn't be nearly as sweet.

34

She hadn't slept a wink since waving goodbye from the porch two days earlier. Hadn't thought about much of anything except how she'd deal with "The Truth According to Dusty Parker."

Of course, he'd had romantic entanglements. What man his age—and with his personality and good looks—didn't? That, she could handle. That Randi had no confidence in him as husband or father material? Not nearly as easy to handle.

Grace had two choices, as she saw it: Figure out how to live with the news, or become another episode from his past. She loved him. Just as important as that, she believed Dusty loved *her*. Did anything else really matter?

In a word, *no*.

And so she'd made the scariest phone call of her life. "What would you say to dinner out tonight? Just the two of us."

"I'd say I can be there in half an hour. Wear something pretty. I know just the place."

That was twenty minutes ago.

He didn't walk right in, the way he used to before she'd sent him packing. Instead, Dusty rang the bell, and when she opened the door, he stood smiling, a bouquet of roses in one hand, a heart-shaped box of candy in the other. "You're gorgeous," he said.

She hadn't seen him in a jacket and tie since Keith's and Tucker's funerals. He'd looked handsome that day. Today, *striking* was the only word that came to mind. Grace stepped aside. "Come in," she said, wondering why she felt giddy and twittery, like a shy young girl on her first date.

"After you put these in water," he said, handing her the flowers, "we can leave. I made reservations. For seven. At Ciaparelli's."

Her favorite Italian restaurant. She remembered having told him during one of their first conversations, that it was the only place that served gnocchi, rivaled only by her grandmother's recipe. "The boys and Mitch are in the living room," she said, heading for the kitchen. "In case you want to poke your head in and say hi, that is."

He took the cue, and Grace smiled when she heard the immediate welcome they gave him. It made her feel guilty, for having sent him away; they hadn't said it in so many words, but they'd missed him. She'd missed him, too, and if she hadn't insisted on putting some time and space between her and Dusty, she may never have realized how different her world looked and felt without him in it.

He walked into the kitchen as she was placing the vase in the center of the table. "They're beautiful. You didn't have to, but thank you." She glanced at the chocolates, sitting on the counter near the microwave. "Wherever did you find a heart-shaped box at this time of year?"

"Same place I found the roses," he said, bending to sniff one. "Hopefully, they're not left over from last Valentine's Day."

"It wouldn't matter if they were."

"It's the thought that counts?"

"Something like that." Small talk. Grace knew how much he hated it, and searched her mind for something meaningful to say. She stepped into the hall, and grabbed her purse and sweater from the foyer table. "Did you see Jesse today?"

"I did. He looks great. Did he tell you . . . they might let him come home in a day or two."

"That's the best news I've heard in a long time."

Dusty flinched at that, and a ripple of guilt coursed through her. She hadn't meant to remind him of the whole Randi-and-Ethan saga. At least, not consciously. "I'll fix up the room you and Mitch are using, so he won't have to maneuver the stairs. At least at first. You guys will have to grab whatever beds are empty, I guess." She shrugged and opened the door. "Sorry."

"Don't be. I'm just grateful to *have* a bed."

Outside, she saw the Harley, leaning on its kickstand behind the van, which Mitch had nosed up to the rear bumper of her SUV. "Seems a terrible waste of gasoline," she said, pointing to the van, "driving that."

"Want me to drive your car? I could top off the tank on the way back."

Grace hoped he knew her well enough to believe she didn't have a problem riding in the big, old thing. She glanced at the cloud-streaked sky, alight with strands of orange, red, and pink, painted by the setting sun. "It's a beautiful night. How would you feel about taking the bike?"

His eyebrows shot up. "But . . . you're wearing a dress. And what about your hair? Won't it get all mussed and mashed under the helmet?"

She shrugged into her sweater. "I'll tuck the skirt under my thighs. And this?" She fluffed her curls. "A little flattening won't hurt it."

Grace looked up at him while he buckled her helmet and imagined waking up to that beautiful face, every day of her life.

"What?" he said, tucking her clutch into the chopper's saddlebag.

"Oh, nothing."

Dusty threw his leg over the bike, and when she climbed on behind him, he said, "Hold on tight."

Gladly, she thought, pressing herself into his strong back, *literally and figuratively.*

He didn't know it, but she'd never been on a motorcycle before. She'd never understood why anyone would want to get from place to place this way, exposed as drivers were to traffic, the weather, bugs. . . . She'd never be able to say that again! The ride was exhilarating, and as the wind and the city lights zipped by, Grace wondered how it might feel to be *in control* of the vehicle.

As the hostess seated them in a remote corner of the restaurant, Grace was still smiling about how he might react when "Motorcycle!" would be her answer to his, "What would you like for your first anniversary?" question.

If he noticed, Dusty didn't show it. Because of the candlelight, ancient brick walls, and the soft tones of an Italian tenor adding to the ambiance? She didn't think so. And it wasn't the sounds of laughter from other diners, the quiet *clink* of fork against plate that kept him quiet, either. *She* was the reason he seemed so edgy and out of sorts. Would what she had to say help bring back his calm, easy smile?

"So," she began, scooting her chair closer to his, "I've been thinking. . . ."

He cringed, adding to her guilt. *Only one way to smother it,* she thought, and pressed on. "The guest house is nearly finished. All it needs, really, is a good dusting and it'll be move-in ready."

Dusty steepled his fingers under his chin and nodded, confusion raising his left eyebrow.

"We can ask the boys to whack down the cobwebs in the walkway. That way, when they go back and forth—or we do—no one will get all spider-webby."

"Spider-webby, eh?"

She couldn't allow his tantalizing smile to distract her. At least, not yet. "And I think the ceremony should be small, because I'd hate to steal Honor's thunder." Grace remembered all he'd told her about Matt and Honor, who had nearly allowed misunderstanding and stubborn pride to keep them apart. Nothing like that would come between her and Dusty! "After all they went through to get to this point," she continued, "they deserve their moment in the sun."

Grace watched his expression change, from uncertainty to hope. "And speaking of the ceremony, this seems as good a time as any to admit that I've never been one of those girls who dreamt of a big, storybook wedding. Which is what I was about to tell you the other night when. . . ." *When Randi's call interrupted us.*

In the time it took to entertain that thought, Dusty's optimism faded just enough that she felt compelled to blurt out "And sweet as it was of you to offer to take me shopping, so I could choose the perfect diamond engagement ring, there's no such thing, in my opinion." She splayed her hands on the tabletop, and laughing, said, "Look at these babies! I'm way too clumsy and spend way too much time digging in dirt, painting, and shoveling manure for delicate jewelry. And even if I wasn't?" She shrugged. "While other girls were paging through *Modern Bride*, looking for the perfect ring, I pictured a plain gold band on the third finger of *my* hand."

He lifted her chin on a bent forefinger. "You're something else, you know that?"

The warmth of his touch and the genuine affection emanating from his gray-blue eyes almost diverted her attention.

Almost.

Grace wanted—no, *needed*—to make him see how much he'd come to mean to her, that he'd changed her in ways it would take a lifetime to explain. The stuff Agent Spencer had dug up about his past had only made her love Dusty more, because if he could overcome all that, it proved not only the strength of his character, but the strength of his *heart*.

"So anyway, I want to meet Randi. And Ethan, of *course*. The sooner the better."

"Okay. . . ."

She heard the suspicion in his voice, and while Grace didn't blame him for doubting her sincerity, it hurt. During those first few lonely hours after she'd sent him away, Grace had considered all the facts as she knew them: he'd left nothing to her imagination where his child was concerned; when cancer took Ethan's mother, Dusty would pick up where she'd left off. And in the meantime, he aimed to get close to the boy—not only to make up for time lost because of Randi's deception, but to give Ethan time to adjust to *having* a full-time father. He'd left nothing to the imagination about how much he cared for Grace, either. The fact that Dusty was willing to sacrifice this chance at a happy marriage to do right by his son only made her love him more. Her "find peace in the Word" moments led her to 1 Corinthians 13:7, and she believed every comforting word: "Love bears all things and believes all things, hopes all things." In the tranquil moments that followed, a plan took shape, and she knew without a doubt who its architect was. . . .

"From everything you told me about Randi's illness, it's clear that time is of the essence. So I've been praying that she'll agree to move in with us. There's plenty of room for all of us in the guest house. I'll fix up that little bedroom on the first floor so she won't have to maneuver the stairs. Ethan can have the front bedroom upstairs, and we'll take the back bedroom. And with all of us there, it frees up my old room at the main house for two or three more boys."

Dusty scooted his chair closer, too, putting him a mere breath away.

"Not *right* away, mind you," she rambled on, "because the most important thing is that, while I'm taking care of Randi, Ethan will have time to get to know you. And me, too. And get used to us as a couple, so that when—"

He silenced her with a kiss. Not a long, passionate kiss, but one that felt like "Thank you" and "I think you're terrific" all rolled into one. When it ended, he said, "Guess I'd better get used to this. . . ."

To shushing me with sweet kisses? She wouldn't mind that, at all.

"When you get on a roll," he finished, "there's just no stopping you, is there?"

A busboy stepped up, shook open the legs of a tray table, then disappeared while the waitress delivered their orders. When she was gone, Grace said, "Maybe I should have taken a job here, instead of the Double-T."

He flapped a big red napkin, then draped it over one knee. "Why's that?"

She answered by flexing her right bicep. "I didn't get these guns by letting busboys heft *my* trays."

Dusty sat back and laughed. And as she sipped her water, he said, "I thought you wanted a December wedding."

"Haven't you heard? There's an ancient saying that goes something like, 'It's a woman's prerogative to change her mind.'"

He twirled pasta around the tines of his fork. "Yeah. I've heard. But I never would have guessed that old saw applied to you."

"Why not?"

"Because," he said matter-of-factly, "I've never lumped you in with ordinary women."

"You give me way too much credit, Parker."

The truth was, she *had* wanted a winter wedding. But then the whole "surprise baby" thing cropped up, and Grace knew that putting things off for four long months wouldn't be good for any of them, least of all, Randi and Ethan. But how could she admit that without admitting she *was* like other women? "Truth is," she fibbed, "the more I thought about you in a red velvet tux, the less appealing the whole scene looked."

"Red?" He groaned. "Good thing you didn't tell me *that*."

"Because . . . ?"

"Because I'd do anything to make you happy. Even. . . ." He grimaced, held his stomach. "Even that." Then he shuddered. "Doesn't mean it would have roused happy memories, twenty-five, fifty years from now when we flipped through our wedding album. . . ."

Twenty-five or fifty years from now. . . . It told her everything she needed to hear. "Here's the *real* reason," she said, hoping God would forgive back-to-back fibs, told to spare Dusty's feelings. "If we get married now, while the weather's still balmy, I can wear the dress my mother and grandmother wore and not have to cover it up with a jacket or a shawl."

"When you say 'now,' what exactly do you have in mind?"

She speared a gnocchi. "Saturday."

He chuckled. "*This* Saturday?"

"Well, sure." She winked. "Are you forgetting that you said yes when I offered to keep your calendar? I happen to know you don't have other plans that day."

"No, I'm not forgetting, and yes, I know I don't have other plans. But . . . it's Tuesday already!"

"O ye of little faith," she teased, popping the mini-dumpling into her mouth. "If you think I can't pull this off in four days, think again. I happen to know there's plenty of time to get a license, and that Pastor Jackson from the Last Chance church is free that day." She giggled. "Well, not *free*. I'm sure he'll expect the usual 'offering.' And there are more than enough burgers and dogs and rolls in the freezer for a simple backyard barbecue afterward. Just you, and me, and Austin and Mercy—who said they'd love to be our witnesses, by the way—and the boys. Kylie and Gavin. Molly Logan. Agent Spencer." She put a hand beside her mouth to add, "I get the feeling he's a little sweet on her."

He was laughing when he said, "And here I thought you'd arranged this dinner to give me the heave-ho in a public place, to spare yourself a repeat of that waa-waa-poor-me scene from your living room."

"I'll say this for you . . . when you're wrong, you're wrong." During those lonely hours without him, she'd thought of the hundred or so times she'd watched as he built his boys' confidence. He made them feel valued and protected, until they believed it when he promised they were good and decent, and strong enough to survive whatever life decided to throw at them. Because he'd given her the same gifts, Grace vowed to be a life partner who'd go far beyond telling him that she believed he'd hung the moon . . . at least in her world; she'd make sure he knew that he could turn to her, always, when life made him doubt himself.

"So are you okay with the plan?"

"I'm so okay with it, I'm afraid my heart might explode."

If that wasn't an answer to her prayer, Grace didn't know what was. *Thank You, thank You, thank You, Lord!* Unfortunately, her plan involved more than just Dusty and herself. "You think Randi will be okay with it, too?"

"If she isn't, she's crazier than I remember." Dusty relieved her of her fork, then put his down and linked his fingers with hers. "Tomorrow, first thing, we'll go shopping for a gold band," he said, kissing her naked ring finger. "And then the two of us will sit Randi down and—"

"I could be wrong, here, but I think she'll be more receptive to the idea if I present it, alone. You know, considering your, ah, history with her and all."

"What's that got to do with anything?"

"If I loved you enough to have your baby—and didn't trust you enough to tell you about it—I don't know that I'd be 100 percent confident in your choice of women."

"I don't like the sound of that."

Grace shrugged. "I didn't say it to hurt your feelings. You know that, right?"

"'Course I do." He kissed her knuckles. "I was referring to your use of the word 'if' just now."

She replayed the sentence in her mind. *If I loved you enough to have your baby. . . .*

"Now *I'm* the one who's worried her heart will explode!" Few things could have made her happier than knowing he wanted children . . . with *her.* "*If* God sees fit to bless us with a baby," she said softly, "I pray it'll be just like you."

"Weird. 'Cause I was just sitting here, hoping He'd give us the gift of a little girl who's every bit as sweet and big-hearted as her beautiful mother."

Tears of joy filled her eyes, and he kissed them away. Kissed her lips, too, and this time, Grace read "I love you" in it.

So she put everything she had into sending him the same message.

35

She hadn't known what to expect. Certainly not a tall, willowy redhead who reminded her of the gorgeous TV actress from that hit hospital show. Certainly not a loving mother, or a woman who exuded genuine warmth, either.

But there she sat, looking tired and pale, yet surprisingly serene as she smiled and complimented the curtains and the buttery yellow of the walls. If a stranger had walked into the kitchen just then, they would have thought Randi and Grace had been friends for years, instead of two women who'd only met an hour ago . . . under less than normal circumstances.

"I'm so glad you agreed to meet with me," Grace said, refilling her teacup.

"Yeah. Our boys needed some one-on-one time."

True, but not nearly as much as Randi needed to say yes to Grace's proposal. She'd given it a lot of careful thought and prayer; last thing she wanted was to sound phony and shallow, and leave Randi with the impression that the offer was tantamount to calling her a charity case, even though that's exactly what she was. Not financially, according to Dusty, but in just about every other way Grace could name.

"So I guess it was a shock, hearing Dusty has a kid. . . ."

Not nearly as big a shock to me as it was to Dusty, she thought. But if the admission sounded self-righteous and judgmental to her, how much more so would it sound to Randi? "I'd be lying if I said it wasn't. But seeing Dusty so happy made it a whole lot easier to wrap my mind around it."

Randi dumped a spoonful of sugar into her cup. "Did he tell you why we ended things?"

"Yeah. He did. I'm sorry he put you through all that."

"Oh, I gave every bit as good as I got," she said, grinning. "Bad timing, mostly. We were both so stupid and selfish back then. It never would have worked out."

"Still . . . it had to be tough, thinking you couldn't turn to him for help with the pregnancy, with Ethan, once he was born. . . ."

She dunked a biscotti into her tea. "Trust me, I called him just about everything *but* 'father material,' for years."

Randi bit off the point of the cookie. Took her time, chewing and swallowing, as if buying time to figure out whether or not to say more.

"Then Ethan started developing a personality. Displaying character traits that reminded me of all the good things about Dusty. The older he got, the less angry I was. And pretty soon, all I felt was gratitude, because if it hadn't been for Dusty, I wouldn't be able to say I'm the mother of the most terrific kid in the whole world."

Tears misted in her eyes, telling Grace that Randi had meant every word.

"To be fair, I wasn't exactly 'mother material' back then, either. Wasn't easy, admitting how far out of control I'd let my life get. But every time I looked into those baby blues, I knew that if I didn't get *back* in control, he'd pay the price."

Grace only nodded; God would show her the best time to spell out her plan.

"My grandmother used to have this saying: 'Life and all its glories.' She said it whether the sun was shining or lightning and thunder were crashing outside her window. I didn't get it . . . until the diagnosis."

Her lower lip quivered as she ran trembling hands through sparse auburn strands.

"Got my act cleaned up. Set up a college fund for Ethan. Bought a nice house in the suburbs, where he'd be safe. Went back to church, to set a good example for him. But before I knew it, I'd turned myself over to God. *Man*, I thought, *could life get any better?*" A shaky sigh passed her lips. "And then . . . and then. . . ."

Then the doctors diagnosed cancer, Grace finished mentally, *and began a series of painful treatments and operations that only weakened her further.* If she knew her better, Grace would walk around the table and hug her.

But why did she have to know her better?

At first, Randi stiffened, but in seconds, she'd slumped against Grace like a frail child, and wept.

Finally, she sniffed and sat up a bit straighter, plucking a napkin from the basket on the table, "I'm really sorry about that. If you knew me better, you'd know I'm not usually such a crybaby."

"I don't need to know you better to see how strong you are. How strong you've always been."

Randi blew her nose . . . a loud honk got them both to giggling. "Well, nobody will ever accuse *me* of being a prissy finger-in-the-air lady, now will they?"

They shared a good laugh over that, and the fact that people had often compared Grace to a Canada goose when she blew *her* nose.

"I should probably find Ethan," Randi said on a sigh. "Much as I hate to leave, it doesn't take much to wear me out these days. Guess I should get back to the hotel."

Grace's heartbeat quickened. She couldn't have asked for a better opening. "You know those big signs apartment complexes hang on the sides of their buildings: 'If you lived here, you'd already be home'?"

"Yeah. My question has always been, what poor fool has to climb up there and hang them?"

Smiling, Grace said, "If you lived here, *you'd* already be home."

Randi laughed, which provoked a coughing fit.

When Grace saw the blood on the napkin Randi had used to blot her eyes, she ran to the sink and ripped a paper towel from the holder. After dampening it, she bent at the waist and gently dabbed the corners of Randi's mouth.

"I-I can't apologize enough. Sorry you had to see that, Grace."

She pulled the nearest chair closer to Randi's, and, facing her, said, "I'll tell you how you can make it up to me. You can promise not to say a word until I tell you what I have in mind. And why."

Grace didn't give her a chance to agree. Instead, she plunged right in, and described the many positives of having Randi and Ethan here at Angel Acres. When she finished, Randi said, "I saw the way you looked at Dusty."

Grace failed to see what that had to do with her proposal.

"And I thought to myself, 'Wow. This girl is crazy about him.' I see I was only half right." She grinned. "You're just plain *crazy!*"

"Can't argue with that." Grace grinned, too. "So, is that your roundabout way of saying you agree? Moving in here makes sense? That it's best for everyone concerned?"

Randi harrumphed. "For everyone but *you*, maybe."

"Why don't you let me be the judge of that?"

"You have no idea what you're letting yourself in for, Grace. Things are going to get real messy. . . ."

"I know *exactly* what I'm getting in to. My grandmother died of cancer, and spent her last days, right here with me."

A deep furrow formed on Randi's pale brow as she studied Grace's face. "If I wasn't such a selfish broad, I'd walk out that door, right now."

"I know it won't be easy, watching Ethan grow closer to Dusty, and to me, too. Not to mention being under the same roof, day in and day out, with the guy who let you down, who hurt you. The fact that you're seriously considering the move is all the proof I need that you're anything *but* selfish."

Randi sat quietly, studying her hands for a long, silent moment. "Before I give you my answer," she said without looking up, "you need to hear a few things."

Grace held her breath, bracing herself for the confession. *Dear Lord, give me the strength not to behave like a jealous shrew when she admits that she still loves Dusty. . . .*

"First of all, I came to the reckoning years ago that love wasn't the glue that kept Dusty and me together all those months. If anything, it was neurosis. We'd been rookie cops, sharing a squad car, saw some pretty grisly things on the streets. Saw even more horrible stuff on 9/11, and for months—years, even—afterward. It made sense, in a twisted sort of way, to try and block all that out by denying it happened. And with risky behavior. Substance abuse. The ugly truth is, the only thing Dusty and I share are bad memories. And Ethan." A slow smile brightened her face. "Although I have a strong suspicion that in very short order, we'll share admiration for *you*, too."

Grace wanted to hug her. Instead, she said, "So you'll stay?"

"Ethan deserves to belong to a real family, where he'll feel safe and loved. I don't know why, but God help me, I believe that's exactly what he'll get with you and Dusty. I'd be crazy to deny him that." She snickered. "And let's not forget that—by your own admission—*you're* the crazy lady in the room."

Laughing and crying at the same time, the women hugged . . . while Grace prayed for the strength to deliver everything she'd promised.

36

When she'd gone back to the hotel to pack up for the move to Angel Acres, Randi had started the legal ball rolling. It hadn't been easy, keeping Dusty and Grace from seeing any of the paperwork, but she'd managed. She'd known about the inheritance Dusty had invested; money would never be a problem for him. But that didn't stop her from resting easier, knowing that everything she'd owned was now in Grace and Dusty's names.

The most important document: The Certificate of Adoption that ensured no one would ever question Dusty's rights to his son. She'd spent years, justifying the bitterness that had inspired her spiteful response when the nurse asked how to fill in that blank line on the birth certificate. "I have no idea who the baby's father is!" Back then, she'd rather have people see her as a woman of low character than admit she'd been stupid enough to get pregnant by a man like that.

A man like that. Randi looked around the space that Dusty had helped turned into a homey hospital room, flinging dressers and chairs and the weighty hospital bed under Grace's direction. Remembered, too, the many times over the past week he'd gently helped her hobble to the big comfy recliner in the family room, so she could spend time with Ethan and the boys who'd come to view her son as a little brother. It had been Dusty who'd made countless trips into town for prescription refills and air cushions to ease the pressure on her skin-over-bone behind, who'd uncomplainingly dispensed of bloody tissues in the trash can beside her bed. *Could have done worse, way worse,* she'd thought no fewer than a hundred times, *than to give Ethan a father like that.*

As for her part, Grace—that sweetheart—got up hours earlier than usual to make healthy, easy-to-digest soups, then bustled through her daily chores to ensure she'd have time to put clean linens on the bed, help Randi bathe, gently rub lotion into her sheet-parched skin.

And those boys she'd called hoodlums? Dusty had been right: they were anything but. They played cribbage with her, entertained her with silly songs, made up on the spot, dragged a small color TV from Grace's room into Randi's, then sprawled on the floor to keep her company while she watched the news, sappy, old movies, and *Wheel of Fortune,* always doing their best to hide their boredom.

They spent hours and hours with Ethan, too, teaching him to field grounders and catch pop-up flies, to put *just* the right spin on the old pigskin, and pitch it in a high, distant arc. They showed him how to make a fishing rod, then taught him how to use it. Snuck him cookies before dinner and cupcakes at bedtime, and patiently listened as he recited the seemingly endless list of people he wanted God to watch over. Quite the gesture of love on the boys' part, considering that since moving to Angel Acres, Ethan's list had more than doubled.

Randi loved them all. Dusty and Grace, Mitch and the boys, even the goofy cousin, Gavin, who'd stopped by daily to deliver tabloids and crossword puzzles and groan-inducing one-liners.

How odd that a woman like her, who'd spent a lifetime boasting that she didn't need anybody, was surrounded by friends. People she'd miss, and who would miss her.

It made the pain more bearable—and it was excruciating and almost constant now. To hide it from them—from Ethan in particular—Randi had been spending more and more time in her room. She needed to rest up and dig deep, so that on Saturday she'd be well enough to sit front and center at their wedding. How ironic that they'd moved the date *up* for her benefit . . . and that because of two trips to the hospital in the back of an ambulance . . . they'd postponed it, twice. That last time, she'd forced the ER doc to admit she was living on borrowed time. "I hope your affairs are in order," he'd said, slapping a Fentanyl patch onto her arm.

The drug took the edge off the pain, enough so that when Randi got home, she was able to sit up and make plans, then place the phone calls that would put things in motion. And tonight, after Ethan was fast asleep, she'd call Dusty and Grace into her room and give them their wedding gift. As the hours ground slowly by, Randi hadn't known which caused more discomfort: Her pain, or her impatience. And now that they were here, she wished for more time. Because how did one begin a speech like this?

"So what's up?" Dusty asked.

"The sky? The price of gasoline?" Randi joked.

"Ha ha," he said, sitting on the corner of her bed. "Quit stalling. I've got cows to feed."

She took a rattling breath and slid the envelope from where she'd hidden it under the covers.

"What's this?" Grace asked, peeking inside. "Legal documents?"

Randi nodded. "I've had a lot of time to think. And pray. You're holding the results of all my brain strain."

Dusty and Grace put their heads together, reading.

"I hope you two won't mind driving into town tomorrow, to have everything notarized." She twirled a pen like a tiny baton. "But you'll have to sign them first, of course."

Dusty looked up from the adoption papers. "You're kidding, right?"

He looked insulted that she'd taken legal steps to name him Ethan's father . . . and make Grace his official mother. "Oh, get over yourself," she snapped. "Surely you didn't expect me to leave without ensuring Ethan's future." She looked from Dusty to Grace and back again. "You had to know for that to happen, *this* had to be the first step."

There were tears in Grace's eyes when she said, "But Randi, this is . . . so. . . ."

"Final. Right." She shrugged. "I know this makes you uncomfortable. If you want the truth, it isn't exactly easy as pie for me, either." She smoothed the top sheet and lifted her chin. "But we've *all* got to stop feeling sorry for ourselves and do what needs to be done."

She waved them away. "I'm pooped. I need a nap. Turn off the light and close the door on your way out, will you, please?"

Randi watched them walk woodenly toward the hall, exchanging worried glances.

The light clicked off, and as the swath of light spilling in from the hall narrowed with the closing door, she said, "Oh, there's one more thing. . . ."

"Anything," Grace said.

And Dusty followed up with, "Name it."

Good thing it's dark in here, she thought as tears puddle in her eyes. "Don't come back here until those papers are signed and notarized."

Silence, save the quiet dialog of whatever show the boys were watching in the living room across the way, then the quiet click of the closing door.

It would be tough, she knew, saying a final farewell to these two who'd come to mean so much to her.

But not nearly as tough as the final speech she'd be required to make . . . to say goodbye to Ethan.

37

$\mathcal{L}$ook at you!" Randi said when she rolled her wheelchair into the living room. "You're . . . you're positively *gorgeous!*"

Grace looked into the foyer mirror, hands clasped under her chin. "You think so?"

"Dusty's gonna think he's died and gone to heaven." She reached out and touched the filmy lace overlay of the dress. "Your grandma had good taste, I'll say that much. What's even more amazing is that the material and seams held up all these years."

"We have careful packaging to thank for that. Tissue paper, sealed box, steamer trunk. . . . Believe me, I paid attention as I unwrapped it."

"So that when your little girl gets married, she can wear it, too."

Grace nodded. Down on one knee, she wrapped Randi in a gentle hug. "It's the answer to a prayer that you feel well enough to sit up today."

"Hush. You'll wear yourself out. Can't have that this early in the day. You've got a lot on your plate!" Randi counted on her fingers: "Get married, hostess the reception, leave for Fells Point. . . ."

"Fells Point?"

Randi laughed into her hand. "Oops. Did I say that out loud? Sorry. Blame the drugs. Sometimes, I talk out of my head."

Grace would have pressed for more information, but Randi said, "Roll me over to the French doors, will you, so I can look outside?"

Grace had taught the boys how to make huge white satin bows, and they'd helped her wire them to the fence posts and deck rails. Two dozen white folding chairs sat in tidy rows along the back walk, and potted ferns flanked the arbor, where she and Dusty would exchange vows. "Looks lovely," Randi said, squeezing Grace's hand. "You and those boys do excellent work."

"I'm just praying the rain holds off until after the reception."

"Yeah, the minute I saw those dark clouds rolling in, I said the same thing." Then she winked. "But what's the worst that can happen? We all get a little wet. Isn't like any of us are made of sugar—though we're sure sweet enough to be."

Grace only nodded.

"Scared?"

"A little."

"Don't be. I have it on good authority you're gonna be a great wife. And a super mom."

"From your lips to God's ear."

Randi aimed a thumb at the ceiling, then pressed her palm to her chest. "I'm more sure of that than I've ever been about anything."

Then she struck a pose. "So," she said, fluffing her sparse curls, "what do you think?"

She'd spent considerable time applying false eyelashes and drawn-on eyebrows. But at least the pink scarf she'd draped around her neck put a bit of color into her cheeks.

"I'm going for the gaunt look. Did I hit the mark?"

Grace winced.

"Aw, sweetie. I'm sorry. My sense of humor tends to be maudlin these days. Didn't mean to rain on your parade. No pun intended." Then, "Come here. Give your bony old pal a hug. It's the last time I can do this while you're a single woman."

Grace obliged her, taking care not to squeeze too hard.

"Roll me outside, why don't you, so I can enjoy some of that sweet breeze before the ceremony starts."

Grace looked out the window, saw Dusty standing under the arbor, facing Pastor Nolt. On his left, Austin. And on his right, Ethan. "I can't," she said. "He's out there already."

"Well, *there's* one groom who doesn't have cold feet," Randi said, laughing.

"Too hot out there for cold feet," Mercy said, joining them. "Oh my goodness, Grace, you're a vision. If the heat doesn't bowl Dusty over, you in that dress is sure to do it."

She'd never been a vain woman, so the thoughts running through her head made her frown. "You really think I look all right?"

"Honey, you put those roses in your garden to shame."

Mercy glanced at the clock. "Tell you what, I'll take Randi outside, then cue the boys to start the music." She giggled. "Have you seen them out there, all dolled up in their suits?"

"I doubt any of them has ever *worn* a tie before," Grace said. "If it's as hot out there as you say, they'll hate me before the day is over."

"Not a chance," Randi said over her shoulder. "Don't forget your flowers . . . they're in the fridge."

Minutes later, Grace found herself under the arbor, standing side by side with the man of her dreams. Only the quaking of roses in her bouquet made her certain this was anything but a dream. That, and the pastor's droning voice, reciting Bible verses, spouting a brief sermon. And then. . . .

"Dusty Parker, do you take this woman, Grace Sinclair, to be your lawfully wedded wife?"

Ethan tugged his sleeve. "Say yes, Dad!"

Chuckling, Dusty winked at the boy, then took her hands in his and said, "I do."

"And do you, Grace Sinclair, take this man, Dusty Parker, to be your lawfully wedded husband?"

She glanced at Ethan, nodding excitedly. Smiling, she said, "I do."

"Then I now pronounce you man and wife."

Ethan did a little dance while Dusty lifted the filmy fabric that veiled her face and gently arranged it around her head. Then gently, he cupped her face in his hands and tilted her face up, to receive his kiss. A line from the age-old hymn, *Amazing Grace,* sang in her head as he pressed his lips to hers. *"I once was lost, but now I'm found. . . ."*

She hadn't realized how long they'd stood there, locked in one another's arms, until Gavin's gruff voice rang out with "Atta boy, Dusty!"

Laughter floated around the yard as Ethan clapped a hand over his face. "Shoo-eee," he said, "is *this* what I have to look forward to for the rest of my life . . . *mush?*"

" 'Fraid so, son."

And it did Grace's heart good to know that Dusty and Randi had said the words, together.

Hours later, as the stereo thumped with the soft guitar strains of Piazolla's *Estancia,* Dusty and Grace stood mesmerized by the harbor view from their suite at the Inn at Henderson's Wharf. "Can't believe I lucked into this room," Dusty said, drawing her into a hug. "It's usually just for people who pay the big bucks to get married here at the hotel."

"It's stunning," she admitted, gesturing to the brick walls and floor-to-ceiling windows. "Who wouldn't love being surrounded by the luxurious, nautical décor of this historic building?"

"You sound like a talking travel brochure."

Grace pointed at the antique desk, where a full-color pamphlet lay open on the blotter. "Caught me," she said, laughing. "But honestly, you didn't have to go to all this bother and expense. I would have been just as happy, staying home."

"I know you would, Miss Plain and Simple." He kissed her gold band. "Make that *Mrs.* Plain and Simple." Then he kissed the tip of her nose. "But I would *not* have been just as happy, staying home. Not tonight."

She read the flicker of desire in his eyes, felt his big loving heart, pounding under the palm of her hand.

"We need to make the most of this night, because for the rest of our lives, it'll be boys and noise."

Grace nodded. "As long as I'm with you, I don't care where we are."

Now, Rossini's *Sinfonia* floated from the speakers as Dusty scooped her up and gently deposited her on the bed. "Guess that's one more example," he whispered, "of the differences between men and women."

Then he kissed her, and the low notes of ships in the harbor and the enthralling guitar serenade faded away.

38

When Grace and Dusty returned from their one-night honeymoon, their joy turned to immediate sorrow when they saw Randi. "Hardly seems possible," Mitch said, "that she could go downhill that far, that fast."

Gavin agreed. "It's like she was just holding on, until you guys were married."

"She's been asking for you, Dad."

He took one look at the boy's worried, heartbroken face and nearly wept, himself. Because he'd been slightly older than Ethan when his parents were killed, Dusty knew that nothing he said now would comfort the boy. So he swept Ethan up and held him close, walking and rocking, rocking and walking until the sobs subsided.

"You okay for a few minutes, kiddo, so I can go to her?"

Ethan knuckled his eyes and nodded. "How come you never married her?"

It hurt like a hard right to the gut, coming from out of the blue that way. "Because it wasn't in God's design," Dusty said. It was a stupid thing to say to a kid his age, and he regretted it instantly.

"That's what she said, too." Ethan heaved a shaking breath. "Better get in there," he said. "I'll be okay." He looked up at Grace. "She wants to see you, too."

Blinking, Grace led the way to Randi's room. "Oh, good," she said once inside. "She's sleeping."

"Just resting my eyes." Her voice, muffled by the breathing mask, sounded far, far away. She lifted both hands, patted the mattress. "Sit down. I have something to say to the two of you."

Grace balanced on Randi's right, Dusty on her left.

"I should never have let you go without your oxygen yesterday," Grace said, adjusting the clear-plastic tubing. "It was too much, especially in all that humidity."

"Tell her, Dusty, that nobody tells Randi Fletcher what to do."

Dusty only shook his head. "She's right, and you know it. You should be in a hospital."

"Why? So they can load me up with drugs? I never needed to be wide awake and alert more than right now."

"Shh, Randi. You should rest. All this talking is wearing you out."

"Gimme a break, Grace. I'll be resting for all eternity."

The strength of her voice belied her condition. Randi looked so tiny, so frail lying there in the hospital bed that it looked king-sized, and it was hard to tell where the linens ended and she began. But she found the strength to grab his hand. "You have a birthday coming up. Sorry I'm gonna miss it."

"I'm too old to celebrate birthdays," he said, forcing a grin.

"That's crazy. I think having Ethan around will be good for you. Keep you from talking like an old man."

She took Grace's hand, too. "Is Ethan asleep yet?"

"No. Not yet."

An almost indiscernible sigh escaped her ravaged lungs. "Amazing, isn't it?"

"What is?" Grace wanted to know.

"The way God brings people together, exactly when and where they need each other most." Her green eyes bored hotly into Grace's, into Dusty's. "You'll be good for each other. And good for Ethan. I can't tell you what peace it gives me, knowing he'll grow up in a house that's filled with love. And laughter."

Dusty didn't think there would be much laughing around here for a long, long time. Randi hadn't been with them long, but her presence had had a huge impact on everyone at Angel Acres.

For a moment, the only sound in the room was the hiss of Randi's oxygen machine, puffing a steady supply of air into her mask.

"You think maybe you could bring Ethan in here?"

He hated the thought of the poor kid, seeing his mom this way. But he remembered how powerless he'd felt when they told him his own mom and dad were gone, and how fuming mad he'd been that they'd died without a last "I love you" or a final goodbye.

Ethan went quietly to her, climbed into the bed and snuggled close. "I know you're sleepy, sweet boy. So when we're through here, I want you to go straight to bed, okay?"

The boy nodded as one silvery tear tracked down his cheek.

"Remember what we talked about. . . ."

Another nod, another tear.

"It's going to be all right. I promise. And you know I've never *ever* broken a promise to you."

"I know you'll be in heaven," he croaked out, "where you won't hurt any more. I'm glad about that, but Mom . . . I'm really, really gonna miss you."

Dusty could see Grace over there, struggling not to burst into tears. He held his breath, to keep from blubbering like a boy, himself. But Randi, remarkably, continued stroking Ethan's hair. "But you know I won't be *all* the way gone, right?"

"You'll live in my heart and in my dreams," he whispered softly.

And Dusty wondered how many times she'd made him rehearse *that*.

"Okay, time for bed, sweet boy. Give your ugly ol' mama a goodnight kiss."

"You aren't old, and you aren't ugly. You're the most beautiful mom a boy ever had."

She mussed his hair. "Aw, you're good for a gal's ego." Randi held out her arms, and he nestled closer. "Now, off to bed. See you in your dreams."

Ethan knew as well as Dusty and Grace what she was saying: *by the time you wake up, I'll be gone.* Nodding solemnly, he kissed her cheek and walked silently from the room.

"I'll be right up to tuck you in and hear your prayers," Dusty called after him.

But he only nodded as he rounded the corner.

"Give me your hands," she said squeezing her eyes shut.

Grace and Dusty obliged her. "I know you'll take good care of him. But I want you to promise me . . . you'll always take good care of each other, too."

They nodded, but that didn't satisfy her. "Say it," she demanded.

"We'll take care of each other," they said together.

"Promise?"

"Promise."

When the furrows on her brow smoothed and she sighed, Grace hugged her. "Aw, Randi, I love you like a sister. I'm going to miss you so much!"

"Ditto," Dusty said.

And Randi chuckled. "The man of many words." Then, "I love you, too, you big idiot." Then she looked at each of them in turn, and smiled serenely . . . one pinky in the air.

Dusty looked at Grace. *"What's that all about?"*

"She told me once that nobody could call her a sissy pinkie-in-the-air woman." Grace squeezed Randi's hand. "You're a nut, you know that?"

"Anything but a sissy. . . ."

Then she fell silent and closed her eyes.

"'And lo, I will tell you a mystery . . . ,'" Dusty recited.

"' . . . in the twinkling of an eye,'" Grace picked up, "'the trumpet will sound. . . .'"

"' . . . and the dead will be raised, imperishable,'" Randi finished. Nodding slowly, tears trickled from the corners of her eyes. "It's been . . . swell," she said. "A real pleasure."

And then her grip on their hands relaxed, and they knew she had left them.

"The pleasure was all ours," Grace said, reaching for Dusty's hand.

Taking it, he nodded. "All ours."

39

Two weeks before Thanksgiving . . .

*D*usty was mucking out stalls, pretending not to notice the fog from his breath floating on the crisp, cold air. Next spring, he'd figure out some way to heat the barn. His cell phone chirped, "Grab that for me, will you, Montel?"

"Sure thing." He flipped it open and struck a 'Dusty' pose: One hand on the back of his neck, feet planted shoulder width apart. "Y'ello," he said into the mouthpiece.

Chuckling, Dusty shook his head. It was good to see the kids goofing around again. They'd all been pretty subdued since Randi's funeral back in August. All but Ethan, that is. At eight, he still believed in Santa Claus and the Easter Bunny; when Randi told him she'd live forever in his heart and dreams, he'd swallowed it, hook, line, and sinker. *Oh, to be eight again,* he thought.

"It's Mr. Miller," Montel said, handing Dusty the phone. "Something about graffiti and trash at Last Chance."

"Aw, man," he complained, "you'd think those thugs would have better things to do than vandalize property, big and tough as they claim to be."

"You think it's the Bulls?"

"Who else?" If it wasn't *Los Toros de Lidia,* Dusty would eat his work-grimy gloves. He took the phone and listened as Miller lectured him about how the neighborhood was going to hell in a hand basket, how it didn't help when homeowners let their houses stand empty, and how between the economy and people like Dusty, property values had plummeted.

He couldn't very well disagree, so Dusty apologized and promised to clean up the Bulls' mess. "Guess I'd better get over there," he grumbled.

"Not by yourself, you ain't."

"Well, I suppose the cleanup will go faster if you and a couple of the guys come along. See what Nestor and Trevor are up to," Dusty said, "while I grab some cleaning supplies and trash bags."

Half an hour later, Dusty and the oldest Last Chance boys piled into the van. "Wish you had more faith in guns," Montel said.

"It's because I have *too* much faith in them that I won't have one in the house."

Nestor said, "But you were a soldier. And a cop. I don't get it."

He didn't know how to explain the philosophy of war to boys this age. Maybe in a year or so, or when he had enough time to do the job right. For now, he said, "When I was a cop, I saw way too many instances when some regular joe thought he'd be safer, brandishing a firearm. Trouble is, regular joes don't realize how tough it is, standing eye to eye with somebody who's willing to kill him. In the fraction of a second it takes him to decide whether to shoot or be shot, the bad guy has already pulled the trigger. And doesn't give a fig that he just ended a human life."

"You ever shoot anybody, Dusty?"

"Once," he told Trevor.

"Did you kill the man?"

"Wasn't a man," he growled. "Just a big, stupid boy who didn't *know* he was stupid." Jaw clenched, Dusty shook his head and harrumphed.

"Why'd you shoot him?"

"'Cause he decided to pay for his 7-Eleven Twinkies with the shells from his sawed-off shotgun."

"So . . . so he shot the cashier? For *Twinkies?*"

"Yep." Dusty didn't tell them that by the time he and Randi rolled up in their squad car, the man behind the counter had bled out, thanks to a point-blank blast to his chest. Didn't tell them it had been Randi's first armed robbery, or that the sight made her upchuck the cheeseburger and fries she'd had for supper.

"What about the robber? How'd you find him?"

Frowning, Dusty told that part exactly as it happened: "He was sitting on the counter, shotgun across his lap and washing down the Twinkies with a Mountain Dew when we got there."

"That's cold," Trevor said. "So I guess he aimed the gun at you?"

"At my partner, actually," Dusty said. "A green recruit named Randi Fletcher."

"*Our* Randi?"

"Yep."

They'd grown to think of her as an older sister, and she'd come to like them, too, in the little time they shared before she died.

"So you *had* to shoot him," Nestor said, "to save her."

Dusty nodded, remembering how Randi's eyes had grown big and round as she stood stock-still and stared into the hollow end of the weapon.

"Man. That's wicked."

He heard the crack in Montel's voice. As the oldest—and the kid who'd lived at Last Chance longest—it must have shocked him to find out his hero had feet of clay . . . clear up to his hips.

The sun loved to beat on the front of the Last Chance house from dawn until noon. Then it slipped around the side. And that's precisely where the Bulls had decided to paint the weird gangland scribbles that told other gangland scribblers, *"Hands off. This place is ours."*

He'd seen landfills that didn't look as junky. Empty beer cans and half-full bottles of rotgut whiskey and gin littered the grass; and newspapers blown against Miller's chain-link fence fluttered like those first unfortunate ducks shot down on opening day. A discarded cardboard box that had once transported a dozen four-packs of Charmin pressed up against the porch, and a grimy, holey sneaker, big enough to have belonged to Sasquatch, sat in the middle of the walk. And the plywood Dusty had used to repair the broken front window was missing, and the rectangular opening taunted them, like a dark, unblinking eye.

Trevor slapped his thigh. "How we gonna get paint off the siding? Looks like enamel!"

Unfortunately, the kid was right. Fortunately, Dusty had thought to slide a knee-high stack of old towels, a box of rubber gloves, and a gallon jug of mineral spirits into the back of the van. "Nothing a little elbow grease won't take care of."

The kids and Dusty hadn't been at it more than ten minutes before Miller hung over the side rail of his front porch. " 'Bout time you got over here and took some responsibility for that pig sty," he hollered. " 'Fore you know it, we'll have rats nesting in that mess you call a yard."

Dusty waved. "I told you we'd get it cleaned up, and we will."

"Yeah. Well. What about next time? And the time after that? Those lousy goons spend as much time smokin' dope on your porch as they do on their own. Maybe we'll all get lucky, and they'll burn the eyesore down. Pile of ashes would be an improvement, you ask me."

"Nobody asked you, old man," Nestor muttered. He'd volunteered to stuff trash into a big, black bag while Trevor and Montel grabbed scrub brushes and rags to erase the strange, black scrawl that zigzagged across the house. "That dude's gonna pop an artery, he keeps bellowin' that way."

"He's meaner than a grizzly," Montel said. "Can't do or say nothin' to please him, so don't even try. Just keep your back to him," he added, grinning. "He's like a rabid dog . . . you make eye contact, he might bite you!"

Grace had packed them one cooler full of sandwiches, chips, and sliced apples. In a second, she'd iced down a dozen water bottles. Dusty carried both around to the back porch, and after a short lunch break at the leaf-strewn plastic table, he and the boys got busy inside the house.

"Looks like a snow sky," Dusty observed.

Moments later, Trevor spun a slow circle, taking in the mess in the living room. "Looks like it snowed in *here*."

Droppings told them birds and squirrels had seen the missing window as an open invitation to set up house. Here, shredded magazines were scattered on the floor; there, frayed electrical—evidence of serious gnawing—hung limp from table lamps. Dusty unplugged the fire hazards, then kicked his way through white tufts that had once been inside the sofa cushions.

"Well," Montel called from the kitchen, "now I know why some dude said not to cry over spilt milk." Trevor and Nestor's expressions told Dusty they had no desire to go in there and find out what he was talking about, either.

An hour later, Dusty leaned the broom against the living room wall. "Well, that's the worst of it. I think we can head back now."

"Yeah, but like ol' man Miller said . . . how long 'til next time?"

Good point, Montel, he thought. For all he knew, Gonzo and his soldiers were out there, lurking in the shadows and waiting for them to leave, so they could re-do what Dusty and the boys had just undone.

It was full dark when they made a last check of the window and door locks, grumbling the whole time about it being an exercise in futility. Then they stepped outside, stretching and yawning, muttering about paint fumes and people who had no respect for others, and when the city would replace those broken bulbs in the streetlights.

Dusty unlocked the van's back doors and chucked the cleaning materials inside while the boys laughed and tussled in the frost-covered grass. They'd put in a long, hard day— and did it without a word of complaint—so he figured they'd earned the right to blow off some steam. Leaning his backside against the van's grill, an all too familiar *something's wrong* sensation crept up his spine. He'd felt it during night maneuvers in Iraq, on stakeouts in Hell's Kitchen. But this time, he knew, the enemy wasn't the Taliban or some street punk, trying to sell a couple grams of crack to a spoiled rich kid from the suburbs. It was Gonzo, come to make good on his promise: get out, or give in.

"Okay, guys, let's make tracks. It's getting late, and you all need showers before you hit the hay."

The playful pushing and shoving continued as they got up, dusting dried grass and brown leaves from their jeans, just as a sleek, white low-rider coasted slowly up the street . . . no headlamps, no radio. Marine and cop training kicked in the instant he saw the flash of metal rising slowly in the open passenger window.

"Get down!" he bellowed, diving toward the boys like a deranged Olympian on his way into the pool. He was mid-air, arms outstretched, when the unmistakable blue-white discharge of a handgun flashed in the car's interior. Three, four, maybe half a dozen times.

He landed hard, so hard that air whooshed from his lungs as he sandwiched the kids between himself and the winter-brown lawn. He rolled off, gasping for breath, struggling to get up onto his knees, so he could check them out, make sure he hadn't hurt them. He hurled himself through the air like a human cannonball that way.

Dusty's head lolled left, and he nearly lost it when he saw bright red on Montel's shirt, on Nestor's jeans, and on Trevor's white high-tops. Frantic, furious, afraid, he reached out, intent on pawing through their clothes in search of the bullets' entry points. He'd only seen one pistol, but there must have been more than one, all firing at the same time, because . . . because there was *so much blood.*

He willed himself to relax. *Can't help them if* you're *a jumpy mess.* . . . Gaze fixed on the black sky above, he frowned. Must be some kind of atmospheric phenomenon, like the green flash at sunset, because he'd never seen bigger, brighter, or more colorful stars.

Montel's worried face hovered above him, blocking his view. "Nestor . . . Trevor. . . . Get them towels outta the van," he whispered through clenched teeth. "It's bad. Real bad."

Trevor's voice wavered. "But the towels are filthy."

Take it easy, Trevor. Remember what I told you: things are never as bad as they seem at first glance.

"They can fix an infection in the ER," Montel all but growled, "but he'll never make it to the hospital, bleeding this much."

Must have been Nestor they were talking about, because his was the only voice Dusty hadn't heard.

Then an angry shout from somewhere to the left. "What's going on over there? You'd better skedaddle, you useless punks."

Miller. The man really needs to get himself a wife. Or a job. Something to focus on besides what goes on beyond his front door.

"Hear that?" Miller said. "The cops will be here any minute to cart the bunch of you off to the hoosegow!"

As if on cue, Dusty heard sirens getting louder, closer. It reminded him of the steamy morning last May, when he joined the search party at Gunpowder State Park. The strobes of police cars and ambulances had sliced through the dark sky that day, too. He remembered getting sick to his stomach after finding the poor kid, mangled and bloody and left in the weeds like yesterday's garbage. Remembered Grace, sinking to her knees at the sight. The thunderstorm that had followed him around the Beltway. Yellow police tape. Agents and cops, interviewing bystanders. That guy and his dog. . . . What was wrong with him, that he couldn't remember if they'd caught the killer?

"What happened here?" asked a voice he didn't recognize.

"Drive-by," said another.

And a third said, "Got a couple handfuls of brass from the middle of the street."

"Automatic?"

"Semi; .44 casings."

"A miracle you kids weren't hit."

"We woulda been. . . ."

Montel, and he's crying. . . .

" . . . 'cept Dusty jumped . . . and knocked us down. Took the hit instead of us."

"We tried CPR, pressure on the wounds, but there were too many. We didn't know which ones to—"

Dusty tried to lift his head, reassure the boys that he was okay. That they'd be home any minute . . . *and don't think for a minute that just 'cause it's late, you can skip those showers. . . .*

But he couldn't move. Couldn't speak. And he was cold. So very cold. . . .

"Any of you boys have a license?"

A cop?

"Nosir."

Nestor. . . .

Car doors slamming. Footsteps . . . a parade of them, from the sound of things. Rustling paper. The distinctive *snap* of surgical gloves, popping into place. Hands, inspecting every inch of him. Then a blanket to warm him, finally.

"Bateman, over here!" he heard. Then, "Take these kids home, will ya?"

And Montel's firm refusal: "We won't leave him. Take us to the hospital, instead. If you get us his cell phone—he keeps it in his shirt pocket—we'll call his wife, have her meet us over there."

No one spoke for a second.

"Get into that bus, Bateman; see if one of the EMTs found this guy's cell."

No, Montel. It's not in the shirt. The lawn. Dusty remembered seeing it from the corner of his eye, when he looked toward the sound of Miller's voice. *It's somewhere in the grass. . . .*

"Nothin' in his pockets, Sarge."

Could've told you that. . . .

Next, a sound like none other: The legs of a gurney being lowered, then slid into the ambulance. It didn't dawn on him until now that *he* was the patient.

Inside the ambo, the lights were bright. He could tell that much, even with his eyes closed. So why couldn't he *see?*

Someone grabbed his hand, squeezed hard. "Don't die, Dusty. *Please* don't die."

Not to worry, Montel. There was too much to do. He had to keep being a good dad to Ethan, a good husband to Grace.

"Stand back, kids."

A door slammed, and the bus lurched forward. Dizziness washed over him, and he felt disoriented. He blamed his position—head to the driver's seat—and the motion of the speeding vehicle. Who knew the siren would sound as loud inside the ambo as it did outside?

"My name's Amanda," said a soft voice near his ear. "I'll be right here with you, all the way to Hopkins."

Dusty was thirsty, so thirsty, and did what he could to let the EMT know it.

"Sorry, pal. Gotta get a doctor's okay to give you anything by mouth."

How many times had he said the same thing, after finding a lost hiker? He tried to nod, so the guy would know that he understood, but he failed at that, too.

"10-45C!" the woman shouted. "Vitamin D, stat!"

He understood the code: *Condition, critical; step on it.* Seeing that low-rider had terrified him, but right now, he was more scared than he'd ever been. He'd taken a direct hit in the Persian Gulf, but it hadn't been anything like this.

How long since he spotted the car? Five minutes? Ten? No more than that, by his estimate. So unless they'd used high-velocity ammo, or nicked a major artery, he should be okay.

Not *should*, he told himself, *will*. He had to make it, get home to Grace and Ethan. And the boys. Jesse had really turned a corner here lately; would he backslide if . . . ?

He couldn't let himself think that way. Dusty pictured Grace's loving face and his son's big trusting eyes, and he heard Montel's last words: "please don't die. . . ."

And though he tried not to, Dusty slipped into unconsciousness.

40

"I know it's scary," his lead surgeon said.

Scary didn't begin to describe what Grace felt.

"Nine bullet wounds perforated his spleen, pancreas, and colon," Dr. Applegate said, "and the drain removed most of the blood from his abdominal cavity." Shaking his head, he added, "He lost more than three liters of blood at the scene, and while his body is working hard to replace it, he's weak."

Matt and Austin had donated blood. So had Gavin and Montel, Nestor and Trevor. Much as she appreciated their contributions, it was frustrating, knowing that thanks to an Rh factor flowing in *her* veins, she couldn't add to the life-saving supply of O+.

To add to her fears, she'd been in the wrong place at the right time as the ER staff hustled Dusty off to the OR. "And so begins the golden hour," one nurse said to another. If Grace could have found her voice, she might have asked what that meant. Minutes later, in the elevator on the way to the chapel, she vowed not to let another opportunity to slip by, and put the question to an orderly, transporting an elderly patient to Radiology. "I was a medic over in Afghanistan," he told her. "For us, the golden hour referred to blocks of time lost . . . at the scene, transporting the patient to the field hospital, in surgery and recovery . . . and the hours after, while we watched for infection."

Four operations and six days later, Dusty survived the golden hour. Still listed in critical condition, he lay still and pale, attached to monitors and a ventilator, unable to do much more than blink while feeding tubes provided nutrients and kept him hydrated.

Grace split her time at the hospital between the chapel and Dusty's room, and divided her time in ICU holding his hand and chattering nonstop about the weather, what the boys were up to, or the latest cute thing Ethan had said. At Gavin's advice, she'd brought the boy to see Dusty twice, and she'd kept the visits short. Today would mark his third trip to the hospital, and Grace dreaded watching him stare, lower lip trembling, at his father's unmoving face.

Last time, she'd distracted him by describing the purpose of each tube and wire, and defining the meaning of each glowing, green symbol on the monitor. Each number and jagged line showed proof that Dusty was working hard to come back to them, healthy and whole.

For a boy who'd just lost his mother three short months before, Ethan was doing better than could be expected. According to Gavin, the fact that the child wasn't afraid to ask questions and make comments was proof that he trusted Grace to deliver the truth.

It hadn't been easy, doling out information in dribs and drabs—and in language Ethan could understand—but Grace managed, thanks to the boy's stout spirit and her own multiple visits to the chapel. Maybe this would be the day that hearing his little boy's voice would rouse Dusty to consciousness. And if it didn't?

The mere thought sent a wave of dizziness and nausea coursing through her. *Your own stupid fault,* Grace told herself. The only sleep she'd gotten in days had come in fits and starts, sitting mostly upright in the uncomfortable chair beside Dusty's bed. She hadn't eaten anything, either, save stale chips from the vending machine and the occasional dry sandwich, she'd wolfed down in the cafeteria. Cup after cup of bitter coffee kept her awake and upright . . . and wreaked havoc with her stomach. When switching to Coke didn't temper the queasiness, Grace decided to make an appointment with her GP, this morning, when she went home to shower and change into fresh clothes.

The plan was to take Ethan out for lunch before taking him up to see Dusty, and afterward, she'd take the patient advocate up on her offer to introduce the boy to kids his own age whose parents were also Hopkins' patients. She was hopeful the action would give Dusty's boys a break. From the oldest to the youngest—and even Jesse—had lavished Ethan with "big brother" affection. But hard as they tried, not a one of them could turn back the clock and become eight years old again.

She'd just left Dusty's room and was on her way back to the chapel for a moment of quiet prayer when her cell phone rang.

"Hey Grace, how's that ornery cousin of mine?"

If only she could tell Gavin that he'd come out of the coma. That his vital signs were stronger. That he no longer needed the breathing machine. "Holding his own, I suppose," she said, trying not to sound as down in the dumps as she felt.

"How long, do you think, before the docs let me come see him?"

"You're the closest thing to a brother he has in Maryland, so I don't see why it should be a problem if you stopped by today."

"Speaking of brothers, I got a call from Flynn last evening. He's driving down today, bringing Anita. Connor and Blake are coming, too."

"The poor things," Grace said. "They were just here a few days ago. It has to be hard on them, driving all that distance here and back, when they can't really even visit with him. . . ."

"They're managing."

I wish I was. She remembered how hurt Dusty had been when, after finding out they'd gotten married without saying a word to anyone in New York, his cousin Flynn had cold-shouldered his phone calls. "Everybody up there says they can't wait to meet you," he'd told her after his trip north to see his mom.

"How's Anita, by the way?"

"From what I hear, she's better now than she was in her forties. She's already training for the Boston Marathon next April." He harrumphed. "Hope I'm half that industrious when *I'm* sixty-five."

"That's wonderful." And Dusty would agree . . . if only she could share the good news with him. Grace shrugged it off and told Gavin about her plan to put Ethan together with other kids like himself, and Gavin supported the idea. "It means a lot, hearing you say that," she admitted. "I'm just a lowly teacher. What do I know about a little boy's psychological health and well-being?"

"You don't give yourself enough credit, Grace. Never have. I know firsthand what it's like, working with high school kids. Especially ones in poverty-stricken neighborhoods."

There was some truth to that. But what did it matter now? Her principal had been more than accommodating when she'd handed him her resignation letter. Between caring for Randi and helping Ethan adjust to life without her, Grace hadn't given her career more than a passing thought, except for the evening hours she'd spent, homeschooling the boys and Kylie, who'd become a fixture at Angel Acres, thanks to her decision to help Jesse with his at-home physical therapy. And now, with Dusty at death's door, teaching was the last thing on her mind. But it wasn't fair to dump her fears and apprehensions in Garvin's lap, so she took a deep breath and started over. "So what time do you think you'll be here?"

"This evening, after school. I have a meeting with a couple of seniors, and then I'll be right over."

By that time, Ethan would be sound asleep in his own bed. "Sounds good. I'm looking forward to seeing you."

"What are your dinner plans?"

"I'll probably grab something quick in the cafeteria after I drive Ethan home. I haven't had much of an appetite lately."

"*Still?* Good gravy, Grace, how long has this been going on?"

Pretty much since they brought Dusty to Hopkins, she thought. "Oh, just a few days. I'm sure it's just nerves. And that nasty potion they call coffee down in the cafeteria."

"Did you make that appointment with your doctor, like you promised?"

"It's on today's To Do list. Literally."

"Ah-ha . . . and what's your GP's name again?"

Grace laughed quietly. "Oh, no you don't, friend. I might be sleep-deprived, but not so much that I don't know where *that's* leading."

"Okay. All right. But just so's you know: if you don't have an appointment when I get there tonight? I'll call the guy and make one *for* you."

"I don't know how you expect to do that, when I have no intention of telling you his name."

"Wow, you can be a brat," he teased. "But you're forgetting how resourceful I can be. . . ."

Grace didn't have the time or patience to puzzle out his riddle. "Better go," she said, punching the elevator's down button. "Promised Ethan that I'd be home by nine. And it's almost that, now."

"Tell him I said hey. And you drive safely, hear? All those busy highways on the couple hours' sleep you've had since this craziness started?" He whistled. "You're an accident waiting to happen."

"Listen. Gavin. As long as I have you on the phone, can I ask your professional advice about something?"

"Sure. Anything."

"About Ethan. . . . How much truth can a boy his age handle? Especially considering all he's been through these past few years."

"You're handling things the way any loving mother would . . . dispensing only the pertinent facts, and only when he asks for them."

"But . . . what if he has questions, but he's afraid to ask them? Or doesn't know *how* to ask them?"

"You're watching his facial expressions carefully, I'm sure."

Like a hawk, she thought.

"And keeping an eye on his body language."

"Yes, and I've noticed that he's been biting his fingernails. You should see his cuticles. They're a swollen, bloody mess."

"All of a sudden?"

"Only these past few days."

"I'd have to talk with him to know for sure, but I'd wager he's using it as a comfort mechanism. Like a baby, sucking his thumb to help him get to sleep. I wouldn't worry about it. Except for the germs he's ingesting, it's relatively harmless. He could be doing scarier things."

"Such as?"

Gavin told her how some kids, when under emotional stress, resorted to cutting themselves with razors and ordinary knives found in their mothers' kitchen drawers. "I've seen a few decorate themselves with safety pins, jabbed into the skin . . . and worn in place of typical piercings."

Grace gasped. "Compared to that, nail biting seems all kinds of tame!"

She thanked him for the advice, and for caring enough to tell her to drive safely, then hung up. When the elevator doors opened, she was still wincing at the nail biting versus cutting images in her head.

A man in a three-piece suit raced across the lobby. "Mrs. Parker . . . Mrs. Dusty Parker?"

He had the look of a reporter. For his sake, she hoped he was selling insurance. Or magazine subscriptions. Tupperware. Because he did *not* want to hear what she thought of smarmy newsmen who saw lead articles and breaking news stories in every tragedy.

"Adam Miller," he said. "My dad lives next door to Last Chance."

She took his extended hand as he added, "He feels awful about what happened the other night."

"Why? From what I hear, if he hadn't called 9-1-1, Dusty probably would have died that night."

"Well, still. His conscience has been eating at him. He knows he's been pretty unfair about those kids."

"And now?"

"And now he wants you to know if there's anything he can do over there . . . until your husband is on his feet again . . . you only need to call." He handed her a business card. ADAM MILLER, it read, CHARM CITY REALTY. "And when Dusty's ready to put the Last Chance up for sale, I can hook him up with some interested buyers."

Thankfully, he'd said *when,* not *if.* She accepted the card. "Thanks, and be sure to thank your dad for me."

"Dad would have come, himself, but my mom has Alzheimer's and can't be left alone."

"Oh, my. I'm so sorry."

"Don't be. We're more or less used to it by now. So tell me, how *is* Dusty?"

"Critical," she said, "but stable. So his doctors tell me, though I fail to see how a patient can be both."

"Sorry to hear that." He took her hand again. "He's in our prayers." Then, "Well, I hate to run, but I'm late for a meeting. Glad I caught you before you left."

And then he was gone, leaving Grace to gawk at the business card in her hand. She tucked it into the outside pocket of her purse and stepped into the enormous revolving door, wondering about the ominous and chilling feeling that went with her.

41

No less than twice a day, Dusty wished he could remind the staff that not every comatose patient was incapable of processing conversation. Not even the "look what I memorized last night" speeches of interns and residents who gathered around his bed to absorb some learn-by-osmosis medical lesson—by reading his chart, by poking and prodding and shining lights in his eyes.

What they'd been saying, day after day, hadn't changed much. Oh, they expressed their deep concern in different voices, with differing accents, but the message was the same: does anybody know if he's an organ donor?

He'd lost track of time, lying here, listening to the inane banter of nurses as they flirted with surgeons. More annoying than that was the way their syrupy repartee turned gossipy and mocking the minute those self-important quacks were out of earshot.

Once, Dusty had held nothing but the utmost respect for the men and women of the medical field. But if they couldn't see that he was *fine* under all these bandages, behind the snarl of tubes and wires, then they weren't worth the outrageous salaries that put Porsches in their garages and imported Italian marble on their bathroom floors.

Today, he got an entirely different message from the group gathered around his bed. They spoke in specifics, about the damage to his pancreas, about the blood that, despite their best efforts, continued to leak into his abdominal cavity. About low blood pressure and a thread pulse, and infection that had set in when the bullet that nicked his colon sent waste throughout his system.

Dusty had studied *just* enough medicine to know things weren't improving.

And it scared him.

He'd be an idiot if he *wasn't* scared.

Right?

He heard Grace's sweet voice, ringing out with its customary greeting as she passed doctors and nurses, aides and lab techs on the way to his room. They knew her by name, and she knew them. And if asked, Dusty wouldn't have been able to say who liked whom more. He knew one thing: not one of the Hopkins employees could hold a candle to his wife.

She breezed into the room and sang a cheerful, "Good morning, Dusty m'dear!"

He wondered how much of what was going on inside his head was visible on his face. None of it, he hoped, because he'd hate for her to read the stark, cold fear beating in what was left of his pitiful, gunshot heart. If it was God's will to take him, well, there wasn't a blessed thing he could do about it. But maybe a heartfelt prayer would at least convince the Big Guy to give him thirty minutes, an hour, even, so he could tell Grace the things she so deserved to hear.

Tonight, when she went down to the chapel (she wasn't fooling *him* with that "I'm going to the cafeteria for a bite to eat" nonsense), he'd lay it all out for the Almighty. He hadn't exactly lived a saintly life, but then, neither had David. Or Paul. If God could find it in His merciful heart to answer a few of their prayers, why not *his?*

Grace adjusted his covers and his pillow, just like she did a dozen times an hour. He knew she wasn't doing it because the stuff had shifted; how *could* it when the only thing moving on him was his chest, as it rose and fell with every puff of the ventilator? No, his loving wife needed to *do* for him, and since she couldn't fix him a meal or rub his shoulders, she rearranged magazines on his tray table and tidied his nightstand, talking a blue streak the entire time.

"Oh, look," she said, patting his shoulder. "Flynn is here to see you."

He heard her walk toward the door. Heard every third word of their whispered discussion: *No change* and *surgery* and *a week from now.* But for the life of him, Dusty had no idea how to put it together and make a lick of sense out of it.

You're lucky I can't talk, he grumped. *Or I'd remind you both how rude it is to talk about a guy behind his back.*

"As long as you're here . . . ," he heard Grace say. To Flynn? Or to him? Dusty would have shrugged—if he could—because what difference did it make? Gone is gone. " . . . I have a few errands to run. You'll be here when I get back, right?"

"Sure. Of course. Good chance for goofball here and me to spend some one-on-one time."

Very funny, Dusty thought.

And now—O joy!—it's Flynn's turn to spew a steady stream of jibber-jabber.

The weather. The traffic on the drive down from New York. The construction all the way around Baltimore's Beltway. "And guess what? Connor's wife is pregnant. Again."

But didn't she just deliver twins, like, six months ago?

"Back in a few," Flynn said, giving Dusty's hand a squeeze. "Gonna get some coffee."

Good. Get me a cup while you're at it. Black, with a double shot of espresso.

And when his cousin was gone, Dusty prayed:

Father, I haven't asked for much. I don't use Your name in vain. Never lie—unless it's to spare someone's feelings—and I don't cheat on my taxes. Just this one thing, Lord, okay? It's asking a lot, but it's more for Grace's sake than mine . . . just an hour without this machine pumping air down my throat.

Next thing he knew, a nurse's agitated voice echoed down the hall. "His eyes are open!" she all but yelled. "He looked right *at* me!"

Then, a crowd of white coats stood gawking at him. "You're right," one whispered. "He's making eye contact."

"Can you hear us, Mr. Parker?" asked another.

Dusty nodded. Not much, but enough so they could see he'd heard them, that he'd understood and reacted appropriately.

A third one said, "Get Peterson down here, stat. He's starting to gag on the ventilator tube. Maybe he can breathe on his own. . . ."

An hour later when Grace and Flynn came back, a few of the gizmos that had kept him among the living were shoved to the side of the room.

"I didn't believe them when they said they'd removed the tubes," Grace said, kissing his forehead. "This is the best thing, ever. The answer to my prayers. To *all* of our prayers!"

She was crying, hard, and a hot tear plopped onto his upper lip. He caught it with the tip of his tongue. "Salty," he rasped, startled by the sound of his own voice.

"Flynn, can you believe this?"

"Nothing short of a miracle," his cousin said.

And he was crying, too.

"Couple of sissies," Dusty grated, grinning.

"Are you thirsty, hon?"

Dusty nodded and licked his lips.

"Let me find out if it's okay to give you something."

And she darted out of the room in a blink.

"Good to have you back, bro," Flynn said, dragging a knuckle across his damp cheeks.

Don't get too used to it, he thought, *'cause I'd hate to get your hopes up only to. . . .*

"You need anything? Pain meds? Pretty nurse to give you a foot massage?" Flynn laughed. "No. Wait. You're a married man now. Not that I know from personal experience, mind you, having been excluded from the wedding guest list and all."

"Randi," he managed to scrape out, "dying. Needed to. . . ."

"Yeah, yeah. Grace filled me in. What happened? Did getting all shot up kill your sense of humor? I was kidding, you big goof."

"I do need something."

"What. Anything. Name it. It's yours."

"Tape recorder."

Flynn chuckled. "Tape recorder? For what?"

"Handheld. Battery-operated. Small. Y'know?"

"Wait. So you're serious?"

Dusty nodded again. "Dead serious."

"Exercise a little tact, will ya?" And then he laughed again. "Soon as Grace gets back, I'll see if I can scrounge one up."

"Nurse's station," Dusty croaked. "But Grace can't know."

Flynn's eyebrows rose, and then he shrugged. "Okay. She's your wife. But I gotta tell you, pal, keeping secrets from your wife can be expensive. Last secret I kept cost me dinner out . . . followed by a chick flick. Trust me. You don't want to do a lot of secret-keeping."

Smiling, Dusty said, "After this, no more." He raised his hand, formed the Boy Scout salute. "Honest."

❧

"This truly is a miracle," Grace said. She'd scooted the hideous pink-plastic recliner close to his bed, leaned her cheek on the back of his hand. "I don't mind admitting it, now that you've taken a turn for the better, but you had me scared there. Really scared."

"Sorry," he said, meaning it. "Tell me about the kids. How's Ethan?"

"Oh, you'd be so proud of him, Dusty. He's taking this like a champ. I can't wait to bring him here, so he can see for himself that you're back."

Good idea to bring him; might not be so smart to tell him I'm back, though.

She started tidying his night table, and Dusty thanked God he'd had the good sense to tell Flynn to hold on to the tape recorder. "You look kinda peaked," he said.

"Sitting vigil at your husband's bedside after he was mowed down by a volley of machine gun fire will do that to a girl."

"Pistol," he corrected. Dusty hated to admit it, but every breath was a chore and it hurt to talk. "Machine gun . . . you'd be talking to a headstone."

She cringed, reminding him of what Flynn had said. Dusty made a mental note to exercise more tact, a lot more, especially when Grace was around.

"I don't know what I would have done if . . . if . . . you know."

He nodded. Yes. He knew better than she realized. "You'll be fine."

"No. You loved telling me that I was tough and capable, but I'm not. It's *you* who's the strong one. Any strength I have, I draw from you."

"Silly goose."

"I'm serious! The boys, and Ethan . . . how would I take care of them without you? *You're* the one with the fancy degrees and political clout and—"

"Mitch is devoted to those kids. To the program."

"But no one could ever replace *you*."

"Nut. . . ."

"I saw Dr. Peterson today."

"Good. Like I said. Peaked."

She giggled, and it did his heart good to hear it. "I'm pregnant, Dusty."

Oh, God . . . what glorious news! But what was he thinking? If he didn't pull through this, that would mean he was leaving her with *two* kids to take care of. Alone.

"You sure?"

"Positive."

Dusty closed his eyes, mostly to keep her from seeing how scared the news had made him. His heart ached, and not in an "oh wow, I'm disappointed" way. He prayed the pain wasn't a signal of cardiac arrest. And then he relaxed. Because if it was, the monitor would have started singing like a canary. Flynn had been right: keeping secrets from your wife could be costly.

Dusty patted the mattress. "C'mere, gorgeous."

She dropped the side rail and snuggled up beside him. Oh, how wonderful it felt, being this close to her again! *Hate to appear greedy, Lord, but . . . if You can see fit to let this go on, indefinitely. . . .*

"So how you feelin'?"

"A little tired, but that's normal. Other than that, never better. Especially *now*." She kissed his cheek, as if to punctuate the sentence.

"Any morning sickness?"

"Oh *yeah*," she said. "Big time. But it'll pass. Besides, I can get through anything, now that I know you're okay."

From your lips to God's ear. . . .

She yawned. There wasn't much he could do for her in his present state, but he could help her rest. Just for a few minutes, at least. "What-say we catch a few Z's?"

In place of an answer, Grace pressed another kiss to his cheek, then closed her eyes and exhaled a long, restful sigh. A minute later, maybe less, he felt her soft breaths, puffing into the crook of his neck. Greedy or not, he didn't want this to end. Ever.

His own eyelids grew drowsy, so he let them drift closed, and joined her in easy, peaceful slumber.

❧

Harsh, high-pitched beeping startled her awake.

Levering herself up on one elbow, she saw Dusty, wide-eyed and gap-mouthed, gasping for breath. "Nurse!" she hollered, pressing every button on the bed, on the hand remote. Where was the fool woman? Wasn't there supposed to be someone, right outside the ceiling-to-floor window at all times, watching, listening, monitoring every little change in ICU patients' rooms?

Much as she hated to leave him, Grace ran into the hall and yelled it again. "Something's wrong! You've got to hurry!"

It took all of a minute for his room to fill with blue-garbed staff, snapping off orders and carrying them out, quickly and efficiently. She recognized most of them: Murphy and Boyd,

Chase and Mariani. They knew what they were doing. She'd seen them go into action before, with others in the ICU.

Then why was she so terrified?

When they rolled the ventilator against his bed, she turned her back to them, because she just couldn't watch them put that awful tube down his throat again.

"Book an OR," Chase shouted. "And get Peterson!"

Mariani guided her into the hall. "Sorry, Mrs. Parker, but we're going to have to ask you to leave."

"But why? He was fine just a few minutes ago. Breathing on his own, talking, sleeping peacefully." She felt like a scared little girl, blubbering nonsensically, as if she believed that would change anything. "What happened?" she demanded.

"It's too soon to know for sure," she said.

"Then *guess*. I give you my word, I won't repeat it."

"He's been fighting an infection for the past day or so. . . ."

Grace knew that. She'd been *right there* when the lab results came back.

" . . . and unless I'm mistaken. . . . See the way his stomach is all distended?"

Grace nodded while the team continued to prep Dusty for surgery. *Another* surgery!

"It means there's probably blood in the abdominal cavity. Only way to know what's leaking is to go in and patch it."

She could barely see through her tears, and Grace wondered if the nurse was making sense of anything she'd said in between the sobs. "But he's already so weak. How can he survive another operation?"

"We've got the best here. You know we'll do everything we can for him." She hugged Grace. "We like Dusty, too, y'know."

Pull yourself together, Grace. If Dusty was aware of his surroundings, she certainly didn't want him further stressed by seeing her go bonkers.

"You can walk with us as far as the surgical suite. Then maybe. . . ." Mariani shrugged.

"Then you can find me in the chapel."

"That's what I figured."

Grace walked alongside the bed, holding Dusty's hand. When they paused outside to wait for the big double doors to open, she leaned in close and kissed the corner of his mouth. "You'd better come through this," she said. "I mean it. Because if you don't—"

Mariani's gentle voice reached her. "It's time, Mrs. Parker."

"—because I love you, Dusty Parker. You got that?"

❧

The chapel all but bulged with people who, like Grace, loved Dusty Parker. Someone had alerted Pastor Nolt, who stood up front, clutching a worn Bible to his chest. "Would you like me to pray, Grace?"

"Yes," she whispered, "would you please?"

There in the front pew, with Ethan clinging to her right side and Montel holding up the left, Grace bowed her head as the preacher's deep baritone reached every corner of the tiny church:

"Dear heavenly Father, it is with heavy hearts that we come to You. You are the Almighty Creator God, holy and full of grace and love. Yes, our hearts are heavy because of a dear one who is trying to leave us, Lord, and fear is just waiting to take us down. We thank You, Father, that because of Your Son, Jesus, You know our pain and sorrow, intimately. We thank You, too, for showing us that *Jesus* is the way through this dark shadow. When the time is right, Lord, take the hand of our beloved brother Dusty and make Yourself known to him. Keep that which is Your own, and take it to eternity to be with You; in Jesus, death is but a shadow, but keep that shadow far from Dusty, Lord, unless it is Your will to take him home. Take our hands, too, Father, as we lay our fears at Your feet. Send Your peace on the wings of the Holy Spirit and fill us with faith that will not let us waiver and doubt. In the name of Christ Jesus we pray."

Whispered "Amens" encircled Grace.

Flynn drew her into a hug. "He wanted me to give this to you."

She looked at the small recorder, balanced on his big, broad palm.

"Said there are things on the tape that you need to know. That we all need to hear."

Now she met his red-eyed gaze. "You haven't listened to it yet?"

"He asked me to wait. So I did."

She took a deep breath and let it out slowly. "Well, then. I guess we'd better hear it."

The family pressed near, and when Flynn hit the play button, quiet sighs whispered all around them at the sound of Dusty's exhausted, raspy voice:

"First, I gotta say I never thought I'd see the bunch of *you* in a church, together. Guess miracles happen after all, don't they."

Grace heard the smile in his voice; she smiled, too.

He recited a list of the documents Grace would need in the days and weeks ahead. "Don't know what possessed me to do it," he said, "but a couple of days after the wedding, I figured I'd better get my act together." She was now sole beneficiary of everything that was his, and with nothing more than a notarized signature, she'd become Ethan's mother, too. The boy clung tight to her side, hearing that, and Grace pulled him tighter still.

Next, he named everyone in the room, one at a time. Montel, who'd been as much a friend as a foster son; Nestor, whose quirky sense of humor could turn even the most dour mood bright. Axel and Tony and Trevor were given explicit instructions to keep up with their schoolwork and graduate on time. On down the list he went, telling each boy why he'd been proud to know them . . . and what he expected them to accomplish with their lives. He had a little something for each of them to remember him by . . . a guitar, a CD collection, favorite books . . . things he'd shared with the boys to ensure a bond that was strong and lifelong.

"On the day you accept your high school diplomas," he continued, "Mitch will give you the check I've written out in your name. It'll be more than enough to buy a fast car and snappy clothes . . . but don't be idiots. Invest in your future, instead, by enrolling in college.

"And when you're holding your university degree in your hand, you'll get another check. That one," he said, laughing, "you can use to buy a car; you're gonna need it to get back and forth to work."

Dusty thanked Matt and Austin for their steadfast friendship, thanked their wives for turning them into better men. His aunt received effusive praise—for loving him as if he'd been her own, for teaching him to wipe his feet and brush his teeth, and the importance of opening doors for the ladies, for pulling out their chairs and helping them into their coats . . . "but it would have been helpful to know how to tell a lady from an imbecilic fog-for-brains feminist, 'cause it sure would have spared me a lot of 'I can do it myself' snarls and dirty looks."

When it came time to say something to Flynn and Connor, to Blake and Gavin, Dusty choked up. "If I have to tell *you* guys how I feel about you," he said, "then, well, I guess you're even dumber than I am."

There was a considerable pause, making them wonder if the tape had run out . . . or he'd run out of things to say. But he cleared his throat and picked up again with "Ethan. Son. God knows how much I love you, kiddo. If I'd known. . . . Well, we've been over all *that* before, haven't we?"

Grace felt the boy nod, saw him smile—if only a little—at the memory.

"I was blessed, truly blessed, to have known you."

A long, shuddering sigh, and then he said, "Gracie. . . ."

She clamped her teeth together so hard that her jaw ached. But she couldn't cry. *Wouldn't* cry. Not yet. Not now.

"You're the one God chose for me. There's a country song out there that explains it. Almost. Something about how all the other stuff on life's broken road led me straight to you.

"I love you more than anything, but I can be selfish—as anyone in that room can tell you—so you've got to know that if I could beat this. . . ."

A long ragged sigh issued from the recorder's tiny speaker, followed by, "You're strong and tough, with a heart as big as your head and a soul to match. I'm proud of you. Proud to have known and—

"You *do* know, don't you, that you turned an ordinary guy into a man of honor? Don't know many women who could have accomplished that. I love you, Grace, more than—"

The tape began to fizz and hiss.

It had come to the end.

Or so they thought.

"Just one more thing," Dusty said. "If I pull through, and even one of you so much as *mentions* this meandering bunch of mush and goo, I'll personally kick your bee-hinds clear around the block . . . just as soon as this bum leg of mine heals enough to get it up that far."

The audible click told them that this time, Dusty was finished.

A long, palpable silence followed. It was Gavin who broke it with, "I don't care what he says. When he pulls through this, I'll never let him live it down!"

And the chapel pulsed with laughter, and tears, and love.

∼✺∼

The doctor left nothing to the imagination. Left nothing to hope for, either.

"I've run every test at least three times," he said, slow and soft, "but the results are always the same. Dusty's brain dead, Grace. There's nothing more we can do for him."

"Short of a miracle, you mean."

He only sighed. "The ventilator and feeding tubes are keeping his organs from shutting down. But. . . ." He shrugged. "You want my advice?"

Grace wasn't at all sure that she did. Yet she felt herself nod.

"Pull that big loving family of yours together and let them help you with this. It's the toughest decision, by far, anyone ever has to make. You're blessed that you don't have to do it alone."

She nodded again, unable to speak.

"Something else?"

What could be left to say, now that he'd dashed every hope she had of Dusty pulling through this.

"If God wants him, Dusty's as good as in heaven, already." He pointed. "Those machines, all the tubes and wires and whatnot? Smoke and mirrors. A pretty 'aren't *we* doing a great job' show for potential donors to the hospital. And if God *doesn't* want to take him home yet? We can disconnect all that stuff, and. . . ." He shrugged again. "I'm just sayin'."

Grace had taken the good doctor's advice, and pulled the family together. In the chapel. One last time.

In the end, it was wisecracking Gavin who turned the tide.

"Dusty has always been the type of guy who got deep into your soul. He knew every last one of us better than we know ourselves. If that was me in that bed? He'd know exactly what I'd want him to do."

"Which is?" Flynn asked.

In place of a straight answer, Gavin said, "What Dusty is doing up there in the ICU? That ain't living. It's existing. And, much as it pains me to say it, he's brain dead. After you've said that, what more is there to say?"

Grace shared with them what the doctor had said, about how the machines couldn't keep him alive against God's will . . . and disconnecting them wouldn't kill Dusty, either, if it wasn't what the Lord wanted.

She got to her feet and headed for the door. "You don't have to be there if you don't want to. I know it won't be easy. . . ."

But they followed her to Dusty's room and lined up against the glass wall, nodding their approval as she walked up to his bed. "I love you," she whispered, looking at the face that had brought her so much joy. "Otherwise, I would never do this. I'd keep you with me, forever."

Sniffing, she wiped her eyes.

"You sure you wouldn't rather let me do this?" Mariani asked.

Grace shook her head no. "He'd do it for me," she said, because she knew that he *would*.

The nurse helped Grace disconnect the feeding tubes from the clear-plastic bags that had delivered life-sustaining liquids into Dusty's veins, one drop at a time. That done, she pointed at the ventilator, and the big, square light that outlined the off button.

Hand trembling as she reached for it, Grace hesitated.

He'd do it for me, Gavin had said.

The click echoed in the quiet space. The only sound in the room now was the tinny *beep* of the heart monitor. Mariani made quick work of removing the tube, and while she rolled the machine to the other side of the room, Grace climbed onto the bed and stretched out beside Dusty, snuggled close and buried her face into the crook of his neck.

No need to hold back the tears now. Could he feel them, puddling into the hollow of his collarbone? Did every bone-jarring sob shake him, too?

Grace held her breath, and, with every beat of her heart she prayed, *Save him, Lord. Save him, Lord. Save him, Lord.*

Nothing, save the last gurgling, rattling breaths that squeaked from his exhausted lungs.

She saw one, lone tear slide down his haggard cheek. Hers? Or one of his own?

And then the heartbreaking, steady, one long note of the monitor.

And Mariani, crying hard herself, calling time of death.

Grace slogged into the hall. Into the waiting arms of his family—now *her* family, too—remembering the last thing Dusty had said to her, before she'd drifted off to sleep.

"You can do it. God built you strong. You'll do it for *me*."

And she had.

Epilogue

Five Years Later

The sunny, yellow kitchen was jam packed with family and friends, and Grace smiled as they chattered and laughed.

Angel Acres was a thoroughly happy place again. Self-supporting, too, thanks to the boys' ingenuity and hard work. They'd redesigned the chicken coop and vegetable stand, and after studying up on hens and roosters and produce, built a thriving business that supplied area restaurants, grocery stores, and the local farmer's market.

And it had all taken place under the watchful eye of Mitch Carlisle, who'd finally got his way when he hung a shiny new sign from the porch:

ISAIAH HOUSE

Eye has not seen, ear has not heard
What God had prepared for those who love Him.
Isaiah 64:4

All of the Last Chance boys had come home for the weekend . . . though it was hardly fair to call them boys after all they'd accomplished and become. . . .

Inspired by the newsmaking murder trials of Hector Gonzalez and his gang, Montel was now a full-time student at the University of Maryland's School of Law, and Nestor would soon begin training to become an EMT.

Trevor, Tony, and Cody had just graduated high school; in a few months, Trevor would enroll in the police academy, while Tony had his eye on med school. Cody, frustrated that Melissa's killer had never been caught and brought to justice, set his sights on becoming an FBI agent. Jesse planned to enlist with the Marines just as soon as he was old enough, like his beloved mentor, and the youngest boys were doing their best to follow in the older boys' footsteps.

Mrs. Logan had changed her name to Molly Spencer, and after formally adopting Kylie, she and her FBI agent husband helped the girl get into Johns Hopkins School of Nursing, where Kylie hoped to specialize in pediatrics.

Austin and Mercy had two kids now—both girls, every bit as pretty as their dark-haired mother; and Gavin . . . was still Gavin, almost as dedicated to maintaining his bachelorhood as Matt and Honor were to adding to their family.

"Is it time yet, Mommy?"

Grace scooped up the dark-haired girl and gave her a fierce hug. "Sweetheart," she said, "I think it is." And after gently depositing her in the chair at the head of the table, she clapped her hands. "Everybody," she called. "Everybody. . . ."

Anita cut loose with a shrill, ear-piercing whistle that inspired Flynn, Connor, and Blake to wince while their wives and kids covered their ears. When it was quiet at last, she laughed and said, "It's time!"

While the family joined in an off-key rendition of "Happy Birthday," Grace thought of the day so many years ago, when she spoon-fed broth to Randi—too weak to feed herself, but not so weak that she couldn't laugh at a fond memory. "I asked

Dusty once what he'd name his son," she'd told Grace, "if ever he had one, and he said Ethan, because it means *enduring*. And if he was blessed with a daughter," Randi continued, "he'd call her Brigid, because it means *strong*."

Today, at 5:04 p.m., little Brigid Randi Parker would turn four years old.

Ethan stepped up beside her and whispered, "Can I light the candles, Mom?"

"I don't see why not."

Oh, how she loved the boy who was a smaller, younger version of her precious Dusty! He never reminded Grace more of her husband than when he smiled, and his black-lashed eyes glimmered with mischievous joy. He'd inherited his father's sense of humor—dry and droll—and wasn't the least bit shy about dispensing compliments to anyone and everyone, every chance he got.

He stood six inches taller than Grace and outweighed her by fifty pounds, and yet, he was every bit a thirteen-year-old *boy*. When he finished lighting the candles, he proved it by singing out "Ta-da!" Then he stood behind Brigid's chair and planted a hand on each of her shoulders. "So what're you gonna wish for, little sister? Think hard, now, and don't waste it, 'cause you only get one. . . ."

Brigid, small for her age, favored Grace in every way . . . except for her extraordinary ever-changing blue eyes. Squinting, she doubled up her fists and held her breath, putting her all into a really good wish. "I wish . . . I wish that I could see Daddy, looking at us from heaven."

Then she puckered up, and blew for all she was worth. "Can I have the big, purple frosting flower?"

"I think that's only fair," Grace said, "seeing as you're the birthday girl."

"And purple is my favorite color?"

Laughing, Grace sliced cake while Anita dropped a scoop of ice cream onto each plate. Soon, the people who had known and loved Dusty Parker were happily devouring sweet ice cream and chocolate cake . . . his favorite, passed on to his little girl.

Grace took a big breath, and blinking back joyful tears, looked up at the ceiling. Somewhere up there, beyond the ceiling and the roof tiles, above the clouds of God's heaven, he *was* watching. Her Dusty. The father of her children. Who'd given his life to save others. Whose lungs and heart would save still more.

Dusty, her man of honor.

You can do it, he'd said. *God built you strong; you'll do it for me.*

And she had.

Discussion Questions

1. Think back to what you were doing on 9/11; can you imagine yourself going through what Dusty and Grace went through?

2. What, in your opinion, is Dusty's most commendable character trait? If you feel he had a *least* admirable trait, what would it be—and why?

3. Now let's consider Grace. What would you say is the best element of her character? And what's her biggest weakness?

4. Who is your favorite secondary character . . . and why?

5. Do you have a least favorite secondary character? Who is it, and why?

6. Do either of these individuals remind you of people in your own life? Who . . . and why?

7. Which life experience is most responsible for any change you detected in Dusty's personality?

8. What event influenced Grace's character growth?

9. Which of the following would you say plays the most important role in this story: Faith, acceptance, or forgiveness?

10. Were you happy to see that Honor and Matt finally got together?

11. What spiritual lesson(s) did you learn from the story's ending?

12. Which of the secondary characters would make the most interesting main characters in the next First Responders story?

Want to learn more about author
Loree Lough and check out other great
fiction from Abingdon Press?

Sign up for our fiction newsletter at
www.AbingdonPress.com/fiction
to read interviews with your favorite authors, find tips
for starting a reading group, and stay posted on what
new titles are on the horizon. It's a place to connect
with other fiction readers or post a
comment about this book.

Be sure to visit Loree online!

www.theloughdown.blogspot.com
www.loreelough.com

FBM112220001   PACP01002597-01

What They're Saying About...

The Glory of Green, by Judy Christie
"Once again, Christie draws her readers into the town, the life, the humor and the drama in Green. *The Glory of Green* is a wonderful narrative of small-town America, pulling together in tragedy. A great read!"
—Ane Mulligan, editor of *Novel Journey*

Always the Baker, Never the Bride, by Sandra Bricker
"[It] had just the right touch of humor, and I loved the characters. Emma Rae is a character who will stay with me. Highly recommended!"
—Colleen Coble, author of *The Lightkeeper's Daughter* and the *Rock Harbor* series

Diagnosis Death, by Richard Mabry
"Realistic medical flavor graces a story rich with characters I loved and with enough twists and turns to keep the sleuth in me off-center. Keep 'em coming!"—Dr. Harry Krauss, author of *Salty Like Blood* and *The Six-Liter Club*

Sweet Baklava, by Debby Mayne
"A sweet romance, a feel-good ending, and a surprise cache of yummy Greek recipes at the book's end? I'm sold!"—**Trish Perry, author of** *Unforgettable* and *Tea for Two*

The Dead Saint, by Marilyn Brown Oden
"An intriguing story of international espionage with just the right amount of inspirational seasoning."—*Fresh Fiction*

Shrouded in Silence, by Robert L. Wise
"It's a story fraught with death, danger, and deception—of never knowing whom to trust, and with a twist of an ending I didn't see coming. Great read!"—Sharon Sala, author of *The Searcher's Trilogy: Blood Stains, Blood Ties,* and *Blood Trails.*

Delivered with Love, by Sherry Kyle
"Sherry Kyle has created an engaging story of forgiveness, sweet romance, and faith reawakened—and I looked forward to every page. A fun and charming debut!"—Julie Carobini, author of *A Shore Thing* and *Fade to Blue.*

Abingdon Press fiction
a novel approach to faith

AbingdonPress.com | 800.251.3320